GOOD LUCK CHARLIE

DICKY PALMER

REDFISH PRESS

Good Luck Charlie

Copyright © 2024 by Dicky Palmer

Cover design by Hayden Palmer

Brazilian Portuguese Translation by Sofia L. Jacalone

Italian Translation by Francesca Petroni

Chapter 1

Charlie Herlong had had enough. If his Daddy needed a wife bad enough to marry a pretend socialite from Worthington Springs, that was his choice. Charlie didn't need to hang around and watch her ridiculous attempt to replace his late mother. Evelyn Herlong could make David Herlong, Sr wear a necktie on Sunday then work the saw on Monday morning. Evelyn was the driving force behind the mill, the freight company, the turpentine distillery, and David Herlong. If you asked anyone about her husband, they'd tell you he was tough as whit leather but easy to work with. As for his wife, Evelyn, she was tough as a pine knot, hard and burned hot. But Yellow Fever doesn't care how tough you are, and she was gone. Anne Mary McQuagge couldn't sit comfortably in his mother's rocker, let alone replace her.

Charlie held a bag stitched from scraps of leather and saddle hardware by Timothy Alpata, an afro-indigenous saddler for Welford Echols, the blacksmith in Lake City, Florida. Timothy had always liked Charlie, maybe because he was the son of the only white man in Columbia County who seemed to trust him. Trust was a big commodity to Timothy, and he would return it to David Herlong whenever he could. Timothy was a Seminole, owned by no man and loyal to few.

Charlie's bag had a hidden space in the bottom, Timothy told him to use it for his most important possessions, so if he met up with thieves or highwaymen in his travels, they might let him keep an old valise reworked from chaps and a saddlebag. Charlie had his cash, all 17 paper dollars in his pocket. The Remington Model 1858 Army revolver, which Charlie had found in the bunkhouse, was wrapped in a cotton Terrebonne Sugar Mills sack.

"Put your pistol in there," Timothy said, "and put padding around in there to keep it from banging around. No, take it out of the sack. If you need it quick-like, you don't want to be foolin' with the sack. Here, let me show you." Timothy's hand dropped a bit from the weight of the huge handgun as he pulled it out of the sack. He looked hard at the ancient Cap and Ball pistol and opened the cylinder. "You know how to operate this thing, Charlie?"

"I reckon I do. I'm carryin' it, ain't I?" Charlie scoffed.

"Ok, where's your shells?"

"I'll get shells tomorrow."

"Yeah? Where at, Charlie? From the man that sold it to you? Where'd you get this Hog Leg from, anyway?" Timothy demanded.

"The man I got it from ain't gonna be needin' it anymore," Charlie said, "I'll buy shells from the Futch brothers tomorrow."

"They ain't going to have anything to fit that, Charlie. That's a Cap and Ball pistol. They ain't made fixins for that gun in 20 years. Why don't you borrow a gun from your Daddy? Why are you going way up yonder to the Futches, for anyway? You ain't give this much thought, have you? Hold on, here. You ain't taking the train, you're hopping a train, ain't you? Like a tramp!"

Charlie started grabbing his gear and stuffing it into his bag. "You sure do ask a lot of questions, all of a sudden. You sound like that bunch at the house. Why are y'all so nosy about my business?"

"It's because we've all known you longer than you've known anything, Charlie! Are you talking about Miss Darla and Miss Sassie up there? Ain't we been taking care of you for your whole life? And not 'cause we had to, either, but 'cause we owed it to your Mama and Daddy. They been mighty good to everybody round here. Sit down, Charlie. Why are you sneaking off, like this?"

Charlie sat down on a saddle form and said, "Cause it's time for me to go, Timty. I know how to do every job here, just like every foreman Daddy has. And tellin' them what to do is kinda disrespectful, ain't it? Least that's what Daddy says. And Lord knows, I can't say anything to Daddy. If I do, he'll do the opposite. Won't he?"

Timothy laughed, "Well, he ain't got Miz Evelyn to help him no more..."

"Yeah, now he's got Miz Aggie McQuagge," he answered, "and she don't know turpentine from teatime to her own behind."

"Well, that's Mr. David's wife, you need to show some respect."

"Daddy ort to show some respect, she ain't that much older than me," Charlie answered.

Timothy changed the subject, feeling uncomfortable speaking of Mr. David like that, knowing that wasn't the first time it had been said. "Well, where are you going, and why ain't you taking your horse or riding the train like decent folks?"

"Number 1, it ain't my horse, or tack and saddle either. Besides, I ain't gon' have money to board him when I get over there. And as far as 'decent folks' go, they make me itch."

"Well, you need to take a bath, then," Timothy teased, "and I got some tack you can borrow till you get back. That is if you make it back. Tramping the train is a dangerous thing to do these days, son. How far are you going?"

"Jacksonville's the biggest and the closest. They're building ships over there, and lots of freight goes in and out. I figure a fella can find ways to make a buck," Charlie said, his feelings picking up a bit.

"But hopping a train, Charlie, they don't just kick you off. They lockin' folks up and make 'em work turpentine for free; you know that." Charlie thought about that and how his father had refused to use prisoners at their place even if it cut into an already thin margin of profit. "Maybe you should talk to your father and see how he feels about letting you go."

"I already have," Charlie replied. He laughed and said that's throwing good money after poor planning. He already had one son off spending his money in Atlanta, at school, and he wasn't going to send another to the school of hard knocks. He said to wait until Davy got back."

Charlie was on a roll, "And who knows how long that's going to be, and if he'll even want to come back to this mudhole in the middle of the woods? I ain't waiting around to die of Yellow Fever or get my hand cut off and bleed out like Judee did. They got a hospital over in Jacksonville and real equipment to work with, not homemade slapped-together junk waiting to kill somebody."

Charlie got to thinking about Judee Coupee, his friend and mentor, the hardest-working man Charlie had ever known. Judee was born into slavery in Pointe Coupee, Louisiana. He came from a huge sugar and cotton plantation, in an area packed with plantations and thousands of people set free by the results of the civil war. Whenever the subject of emancipation came up, Judee was quick to point out that "Freedom just means having choices and the wrong choice leads to the worst whipping."

In 1866, Judee joined the 9th Cavalry in New Orleans, thrilled at the prospect of having a job and being clothed and fed. He soon realized that following orders and being proficient led to better things. He was proud and happy to be a Trooper. Judee spent the next 15 years fighting members of the Comanche, Ute, and Apache tribes, keeping order between groups of all races fighting over land and power.

He fought in the El Paso Salt War: "Yeah, we had to ride down there and save the Texas Rangers when they got their asses handed to 'em. Texas Rangers always acted like folks ort to pack up and leave if they told 'em to. Them Tay-Hawnoes, had a different idea. They'd been gettin' that salt free for they whole lives. They was ready to kill erry white man out there. But the Texas Rangers are tough, boy. Just goes to show how important salt is, I reckon. I'm glad we brought enough people to run 'em off back into Mexico."

Charlie would ask him about the Indian Wars and what they were like. Judee was happy to shoot the breeze if the work was finished. His battle tales were very entertaining and invariably ended with a certain kind of respect for those he engaged in battle, saying, "Most of the time, people are trying to kill you because somebody told 'em to. Well, that and I was doing my damndest to kill his ass, too!"

Judee taught himself to read and write to reach what he thought was the highest rank a black man could reach: First sergeant. In 1882, his regiment was sent to Oklahoma to prevent whites from settling on Indian land. There, he met his new unit commander, a second lieutenant, one of the first black graduates of West Point. Judee resigned soon after learning he would need to go to West Point to rise in rank.

"I done been as far west as I want to go," he said.

Judee arrived in Lake City and met David Herlong, who was struggling with a team of mules when delivering lumber. David offered to pay Judee for his help and Judee countered with a request for dinner and a place to sleep for the night, as the hotel in Lake City didn't allow colored guests who had fought countless US Army battles. David accepted and Judee went to work for him from that point on.

Timothy interrupted, "Is that why you're running off? Charlie, Judee was drunk that day, running a saw that he should not have been running because somebody else accused him of being old and lazy. You know how Judee was, he thought he ran the whole show when Mr. David wasn't there."

Charlie was shocked that Timothy would say that, not knowing that other folks didn't hold Judee in the same regard that Charlie did. It made him angry.

"You want to know where Mr. David was? He was inside, wasting daylight tending to his new wife. He was inside changing my Mama's house to her style of decorating. He had no problem throwing money to New Orleans to make her happy. He should have been out there running the crew and making sure the still was turning out. Timothy, my Mama would be turning over in her grave if she knew how fast my Daddy was letting that place go to seed."

Timothy knew Charlie was too much like Miss Evelyn to talk him out of his current state of mind. It was curious to Timothy that Charlie was so much like both of his parents. Whip-smart and likable, able to relate to people like his father, and able to see the potential in most things. He walked over to the tack room and pulled out a bit and bridle, a leather latigo, some steel rings of different sizes, along with some braided leather rope. He pulled a wool blanket out and rolled it up, tying it with the leather straps and then to the top of the bag.

"This'll help you when you get a ride," he said, holding up his hand to quiet Charlie's protestations. You can pay me back next time I see you."

"Thanks," Charlie said, his voice quieter now.

"Charlie, you know you ain't going to find any shells for that pistol, don't you?"

"Well, it was Judee's. I'm going to hang on to it. Those thieves in the bunkhouse took everything else of any value. They even took his Cavalry hardware. Jackasses."

"Well, who knows? Maybe you'll use it to hammer a nail or something. The only way you're going to hurt somebody is to hit them in the head with it."

"That'll work," Charlie laughed as he walked out the door of the shop.

Chapter 2

Charlie rode through the gate and heard the last dinner bell, a notice to anyone still hungry to hurry before the dogs were fed. Charlie didn't want cornbread and pot liquor, he went straight to the cookhouse.

Miss Darla came out yelling, "Charlie Herlong, I done told you not to bring that horse around this cookhouse! You know you got to take care of yo' tack fo you can eat! Where you been? Junior said he ain't seen you since they watered the mules. They fittin' to start cuttin' that new load ...."

Charlie tied the mare to a post and trotted to the cookhouse. He stuck his head in and exclaimed, "Where's my future bride?"

"It's me, today, Chippy, and I ain't never blushed once. Darla saved you some chicken. Yo Daddy wants to know where you been."

"You tell Darla she's the purtiest one on this place."

"You'll lie when the wind blow," Miss Sassy said, "I am."

Charlie said, "I tell her that so she won't feel bad about how purty you are. I'll always be your Chippy."

Miss Sassy gave him extra cornbread, "You best get, it's almost two. And you better not leave that plate out there! Send it back with one of the little boys."

Charlie spooned beans and chicken as he ran. He was glad Miss Darla saved him a piece; the chicken was reserved for meals inside. Charlie wished he could sit down and enjoy his lunch. He wouldn't be doing so much longer. People wanted to work for David Herlong because he treated his people well. Many said it was dinner every day, beans and cornbread mostly.

David and Evelyn Herlong believed that workers were best when well-fed. Many of them lived in the bunkhouse, and a list wanted to. During busy times, temporary workers camped near the spring that fed the creek down into Alligator Lake.

Charlie got to the mill and gave his plate to the smallest helper, who gobbled down the leftovers and ran to the cookhouse. Charlie hopped into the captain's seat to run the saw, exclaiming, "If you're waiting on me, you're backing up!" Junior Duncan whistled and waved a timber dolly to the saw, where men used timber jacks to roll the huge pine onto the saw platform. He was checking the boiler when David

Herlong called, "Mr. Junior, take over," and moved to the captain's seat. David walked past Charlie and motioned for him to follow.

Junior pulled out his watch, an annoying habit to make a point, "You heard Mr. David." Junior grabbed the brake handle and yelled, "Breaktime's OVER!" He released the brake and the roar of the saw commanded everyone's attention.

Charlie sighed and followed his father across the yard. David turned and reminded him, "Put that mare up and take care of your tack. I need to ask you some questions."

Charlie called, "Can't I answer them out here?"

David continued his long steps toward the big house.

Charlie saw this might be more than missing dinner, so he unsaddled the mare but left the bridle on. He walked without hurry or concern, till he noticed his bag was missing. He then saw his father on the porch holding the bag.

Charlie thought of a saying his father often used, "Better to play dumb and listen to the stupid."

"Well, hey, Charlie, we missed you at dinner, have you eaten?" Anne Mary asked. "I'll have Sassy make you something."

Charlie cut her off as he walked by, "No thank ya, I ate in the yard with the rest of the help."

Anne Mary McQuagge Herlong had hoped he'd notice her new sporty outfit, so her feelings were hurt. She turned, walked through the kitchen door, and in a high-pitched yodel, "Darla! We need you!"

As Charlie's eyes adjusted, all he could see was his father's silhouette in the window. Without turning around, David said, "Have a seat, son. Whose portmanteau is that? I was worried we had a Carpetbagger come to visit."

"A portman-what?" Charlie asked, committed to acting dumbfounded.

"That good-looking leather suitcase over there. Is that yours?"

"Yes, sir."

"That's nice, you're going somewhere?"

He had watched his father play this cat-and-mouse game his whole life. He knew his father would eventually get to the point. "Not right now, I ain't," Charlie replied, "I should be making that load of lumber out yonder."

"They'll manage. Where did you get that Portmanteau? Travel bag. Gladstone bag. I bet that cost you some money."

"No sir, it was a gift." Charlie wanted to say it didn't cost anything near that ridiculous outfit his new wife was wearing but fought the urge. "Timothy gave it to me."

"That sure is nice, he always makes me pay for the work he does for me."

"Don't Mr. Echols make you pay him? I think Timothy gives that money to him."

Charlie felt good in this verbal joust, hoping he could make his father commit to the real point before he was ready.

"That's an excellent point, Charlie. Maybe I'll get him to make me a nice bag." David was still pleasant and conversational.

"Oh Daddy, that bag was made from scraps lying around the shop, I'm sure you would want a matching set. Maybe you and Miz Aggie can get some made next time y'all go to New Orleans." Charlie said.

Charlie decided to press the issue and get things moving along. He stood up, giving a little grunt-sigh as his father did just before ending a conversation. "Well, this has been nice, Daddy. I learned a lot about luggage. I think I'll get back to work."

"Sit down," David said, hard and aggravated. Charlie felt like he was winning.

Charlie sat again. Anne Mary walked in carrying a tray with lemonade and buttermilk pie. "I told Darla to make y'all a little snack. I made this pie this morning."

"We just had dinner, Anne. Put it over there. We're not through, yet."

Charlie perked up, "Miss Anne, I'll take some lemonade. Hey, is that one of those bicycle dresses? It looks sporty, y'all getting bicycles?"

Anne Mary arched her back a little and twirled. Charlie had to admit, she was about the best-looking thing that ever walked through the gate. "I've been trying to talk your Daddy into getting a Safety Bicycle, one with aired-up tires that can ride on sandy roads."

"I think y'all ort to get two! That way y'all can both have bicyclin' outfits!" Charlie pulled her along, knowing his father was about to snap into a cursing fit.

David stood up, walked over to his young, beautiful wife, and eased her toward the door. "Anne, Sweety, please, give us a minute. We'll have some pie later." He closed the door, walked to his desk, and drew a bottle of whiskey from a drawer. Charlie knew he was angry because he took a swallow from the bottle, chased it with some lemonade, and then poured another shot into the lemonade glass.

"I asked you where you were going, Charlie. Are you going to keep playing like a Jackass?" Mr. David asked.

"Jacksonville."

"That ain't what I hear," Mr. David snorted, "I hear you're on a red ball to liberate the Cubans!"

"In Jacksonville?" Charlie asked, "They make good money rolling cigars. They don't need my help."

"No. In Cuba. They've been having a war for ten years. They sunk the Maine," David explained.

"The main what?" Charlie asked.

"What?" David paused, then realized what Charlie was asking. "A Battleship, the USS Maine. Part of the US Navy? For Christ's sake, Charlie, read a newspaper."

"Oh. What were they doing there? Just hanging around, cleaning their cannons? What were the Spanish supposed to do? Sit around and wait for them to start something? What's that got to do with me? The Cubans will have to liberate themselves."

David laughed, relaxing after the whiskey and learning that Charlie wasn't running off to join the Army. David was too young to have fought during the Civil War, but he knew a good number of men whose lives were ended or ruined because of it. It still bothered him to see a blue army uniform.

"Well, why Jacksonville?" David inquired. He still felt that he hadn't gotten the whole story.

"Well, go over there and see about making my mark."

David snorted. "Your mark? What can you do?"

This got the hair on Charlie's neck up. "I can run a sawmill. Break it down and set it back up. Anything that can be done hauling freight or trees, I can do that too. I can handle a horse and mules. I know enough about stills to make turpentine, liquor, and chemicals, too."

"You already do all that here, Charlie!" David exclaimed, "Why do you have to go to Jacksonville? Is this about money? How much do you need? I'm paying you $4.00 a day, that's double what the crew makes, plus, I give you room and board."

"That's part of the reason why I have to go. It doesn't make good sense to pay me what you pay Junior or Wad." Charlie said.

David responded, "Well, son, there ain't no other job around here other than mine, and I ain't going to give mine up just yet. Just wait a few more years, I'll turn it over to you and Davy."

"I don't think I can wait on that, Daddy, there might not be much left. The way y'all are spending it..." Charlie regretted saying it, thinking his father would be defensive.

David wasn't defensive. He chuckled and responded, "You may be right! It sure is fun, though. Your mama could squeeze a nickel till Liberty shed a tear. I like spending money. That's all right with you, ain't it? That I spend my money like I want to? That I go where I want, buy what I want, run my business, pack my clothes in the portmanteau that I choose?"

"Marry who you want to marry." Charlie sullenly added, a little shocked that it didn't bother him as much as it had.

"You damn right, Chippy. Want to know why? Because I earned it. I'll let you in on a little secret, Charlie. Working for your mother was hard. That's right. I worked for her just like everyone else. I never understood why we would break our backs and never take a chance to enjoy it. Like it was a sin to enjoy yourself."

Charlie looked at his father with dead eyes, "I wonder what she would say about how things have turned out."

"She worked herself to death, Charlie," David said, "Yellow fever just finished the job. I loved your mother and respected her. What would she say if she heard you talking to me this way?"

"She'd probably do what she always threatened, 'Slap the taste out of my mouth!' right after she tossed Miz Fancy Pantalettes out into the yard and burned all that furniture."

David leaned forward in his chair, "You keep running your mouth about my new wife and I might make you whip my ass over it. As for Anne Mary Herlong, refer to her by her name. Who would you have chosen? No one would have lived up to your specifications, anyhow."

"But, dang, Daddy, she's so young, she ain't that much older than me."

"And high-spirited, too. Don't forget easy on the eyes and lots of energy." David was beaming. "Don't worry about that one, she knows how to enjoy life and me."

"I'm more worried about you," Charlie stood to leave.

"Well, know that I'll go doing what I love." David reached into a drawer and walked over to Charlie, "Here, take these and go buy a horse and a saddle from Echols. He's got a bay over there that looks pretty solid." He handed Charlie ten gold Spanish Doubloons and hugged him tight. "There's no use in talking you out of it; you need to go over to that Big River and see for yourself. You can come back over here when you get homesick. Don't take too long, though, Anne Mary is wearing me out!"Charlie opened the door, and looked back at his father, as Anne Mary swept in, saying, "Y'all done with all that man talk?"David said, "Yes we are, sweet thing. Charlie is just leaving. Come on over here and let's sample some of that pie you're so proud of. Close the door on your way out, Charlie. Good luck!"

Chapter 3

Charlie walked north toward the Springs camp. Earlier, he had gone to Mr. Echols to buy a horse and saddle, only to find scant mounts anywhere in town. Timothy said most had been sold to speculators to be moved south. Those left were old, long in tooth nags with racehorse prices.

Charlie wished he had gone with his original plan. He could have been to Baldwin by now, halfway to Jacksonville. As he neared the camp, he heard many more voices than he expected. Eight or nine men were around a smoky fire, arguing what sounded like politics, something you would hear in a barbershop, not a hobo camp. It was odd; they were drinking and should have been moving down the line.

Charlie had always heard that hopping trains was relatively easy if you kept quiet and respectful. You jumped off the train before junctions and hustled to catch it again several hundred yards further down the line after the switch.

He saw three younger men sitting off to the side. He decided to sit near them and play dumb for a bit.

There were two whites and one black, about Charlie's age, 20 or 22 years old. The whites were dressed like dudes, Charlie thought. Blue flannel shirts, khaki pants with legs tucked into their high boots, and slouch hats pinned up on one side. Like their first day on the job, brand-new clothes that would be in tatters after a week. The black man was tall and lean, not dressed like the colored folks Charlie knew. He was dressed in work clothes, heavy jeans, a hickory stripe shirt, boots with pointed toes, and a felt hat with a high crown, all high quality but not fancy. He was working on a piece of leather, stretching it, sewing a thin cord into it. The two dudes looked up, faces bright, like they were thrilled to see a new face. The other man cut his eyes toward Charlie and continued working on what Charlie could now see, which was a calfskin glove.

"Howdy!" one of the dudes popped up and stepped toward Charlie with his hand out. "I'm Walter King. That there is Raymond Denton. We're from Mobile, part of the Lomax Rifles, 2nd Alabama Volunteer Infantry. I'm not sure what that feller's name is; he don't talk much."

"Well, dang, Walter, that's a mouthful. What are y'all doing out here in the woods?" Charlie replied, avoiding the handshake and giving Walter a little wave as he sat on a cabbage palm trunk.

"We were hitching a freight when it stopped up there, and they shooed us all out. We just kind of followed the rest of the men down here. I reckon we're waiting on the next one that comes along." Walter seemed happy to talk, a real Carolina Parakeet, Charlie thought.

Walter continued, "Me and Ray are trying to get to Miami. Do you know where that is? That's where our brigade is shipping out. We were going to Tampa, but that place can't handle the size of our Army, so a bunch of units are leaving through Miami."

"And they're making y'all hoof it to the boat? How come y'all ain't wearing uniforms?" Charlie asked, immediately wishing he hadn't because he was already getting tired of Walter's voice.

"Well, we got separated from our company, and we're trying to catch up," Walter said, slowing his pace as his face started to flush with embarrassment.

Charlie noticed his change in demeanor, not interested enough to sort out the details of why they were hoboing it and dressed like rough riders.

"Separated, huh? Walter, I'm more interested in how y'all decided to take a rest break waiting on the train. You say they shooshed y'all out of the train? What'd they tell y'all to do? Come to this depot over in the woods and wait for them to come to get you?"

At this point, Raymond spoke up: "Well, they did tell us there was a camp down here and fresh water. After they told us there weren't no more free rides and get the hell out of the train. It was just two fellers. Some of the others started giving them some back sass, and one of the train men said that the train wasn't moving until they all got out."

"How many of y'all were in there?" Charlie asked.

Walter cut in, "Hell, it was crowded. There were about a dozen in our car and at least that many in the one behind ours."

"I only see about ten. Where are the rest?" Charlie was very interested now and leaned forward.

"I don't know where they went, but I'm glad they left. They were a rough lot and stunk like they'd been butchering hogs. I was glad to see 'em leave." Walter swatted at a mosquito on his neck, "And these damn skeeters can go with 'em."

Charlie figured the group that left were veteran rail tramps, and they knew something wasn't right. Charlie knew it, too, and stood up. "I ain't staying here. Trains don't stop for no reason, and telling y'all there was a camp down here ain't right either. They're eventually going to start that train up and move on to the next junction, which is Baldwin. If you've filled up your canteens, there ain't no reason to stay here."

Charlie figured he had about a mile and a half to get down the tracks past the junction, enough to catch the train heading east. The black man was already up and moving before Charlie had turned to leave. Walter and Raymond hustled their gear together and trotted after them into a path worn through years of travelers moving to the other side of the junction.

About a mile down the trail, the four came to the junction that allowed trains moving south through Lake City to turn off. Trains that took this spur were mostly for passengers and small freight that would pick up in Lake City and join a more extensive line leading to Gainesville. The Florida Central and Peninsular Railroad was a patchwork system of tracks through North Florida that connected to Plant and Flagler routes into Florida.

Two men ran out of the brush on the other side, "Bulls! On horses!"

Charlie knew of a clearing on the north side of the tracks. The Herlong Company once had a sawmill there. He started running north across the tracks to the woods, hoping to get there before the raiders could see him. The others followed Charlie as he seemed to know what he was doing. When they reached the woods, they crouched in the bushes and saw two men on horseback ride from the east across the tracks and toward the spring camp. As one of the riders passed a running tramp, he clubbed the man across the head and shoulders, driving him to the ground.

The four young men kneeled in the brush, occasionally seeing a running man get knocked down and trampled by a horse. "Low down motherfuckers," Walter growled. "What did they do to deserve that? They caught a ride on a train."

The black man uttered, "They rode the man's train, that's what."

Charlie had never heard the term Walter used, but he knew it wasn't a compliment. He guessed Walter had learned it in the Army. "What's your name?" He asked the black man.

"P. Henry Whitfield," he replied. "I swear, I ain't never seen white men treat other white men like that."

They heard gunfire, and all three of Charlie's new acquaintances pulled pistols from their bags. Charlie didn't bother to pull his out. He had forgotten it until the others showed theirs. Charlie made a mental note to be more aware next time and to buy a gun that would fire.

Men wearing bowler hats and suit jackets bound the travelers and tied them to a long rope. Eventually, a group of 14 men, bound at their hands, were being led down the tracks toward Lake City. Charlie recognized two deputies of Sheriff Archie Dasey, who took the prisoners from the railroad detectives. The deputies led them down the spur toward Lake City. He wondered what they would be charged with. Vagrancy? Trespassing? Bad luck?

"By the way, you ain't told us your name yet. That would be us right there if it weren't for you," Walter said. "Or worse, yet, dead."

"Not me," Raymond said, "I believe I would have shot it out."

Charlie sat quietly, grateful he didn't have to make a decision more pressing than running. He remembered Raymond wasn't grabbing his pistol as they were running. P. Henry Whitfield slid his Colt Peacemaker back into a black holster that looked like a military issue. P. Henry noticed Charlie watching and said, "So, what about it? You gon' tell us your name or what?"

"Charlie Herlong, pleased to meet y'all."

They stayed hidden and saw eight riders come from down the tracks, followed by the train heading toward Jacksonville.

"Wonder when the next train comes by," Raymond said, "Any idea, Charlie?"

"Yeah, that same one will be coming back tomorrow, heading back to Tallahassee, then up to Chattahoochee," Charlie replied. "That was my ride to Jacksonville. The day after tomorrow, there'll be one that will turn here and head south through Lake City. It might be better to catch a Plant train on the other side of Lake City if they're putting folks in jail for trampin'. I believe that's what I'll do and then ride from Gainesville back up to Jacksonville."

"Dang, Charlie, how do you know so much about it? Have you been working for the railroad?" Walter asked.

"I been watching folks leave this town all my life," Charlie said.

"You live here? Hell, let's go to your house. Can your Mama cook?" Walter went on, "I'm bout tired of eating dreams."

"No, my mama don't cook anymore," Charlie said, "Besides, I've already said my goodbyes. I'll camp tonight back at the spring and walk the creek into town tomorrow. Y'all can get a meal in town if you want, but I'm going to head south and pick up a freight heading to Gainesville."

"We might find some grub back there at the spring," P. Henry said. I don't reckon the boys had much time to pack before they went to the hotel down there in Charlietown."

Charlie gave a little laugh and thought, "I like this P. Henry Whitfield."

Chapter 4

Henry Whitfield was trying to ignore Walter King's constant chatter. He figured he already had a nine-foot cotton sack full of information about Walter, his family, their friends, their home, Mobile, Teddy Roosevelt, Cubans, Spain, bicycles, and Cock-a- damn-doodle what else. Whitfield thought he was one boll of cotton, white, new, full of seed, and needed a lot of work to be helpful.

He thought of his Uncle Eddie Lee Baker, a Master Sergeant in the 10th Cavalry Regiment of the United States Army, and why he was on this trip. Eddy Lee had written his sister that the 10th was being moved to Florida to prepare for the invasion of Cuba.

P. Henry's mother was disappointed when she learned the army coming to San Antonio didn't include her brother. San Antonio was a training site for the 1st United States Volunteer Cavalry. The Rough Riders were training and carousing on the Westside of San Antonio.

The Whitfields were on the east side, where P. Henry's father owned a general merchandise store and a church. Well, a congregation they usually met outdoors under a tree. P. Henry's mother ran a small school for those folks of color with the desire to pursue reading and arithmetic. Most folks on San Antonio's Eastside spent most of their time trying to eke out a living and feed others in their family. San Antonio was a bustling metropolis of 30,000, with many opportunities for the east side to serve the west side. P. Henry's parents had assumed he would follow his father into the ministry and were shocked when he announced he was going to Florida to join his uncle. They pleaded with him to find another way to help that traveling through the South was a dangerous and challenging task. P. Henry thought it was easy up until this point, but now, he was seeing an ugly part of the world.

Walter kept a running commentary about how lucky they were despite the circumstances. "Them fellers that got tied up and led down the tracks, where was they going? What'd you call it, ... how far is the town, uh, what's your name again?"

Charlie wasn't sure who he was talking to, so he kept walking.

"Hey, stranger, what's your name again?" Walter repeated.

"Charlie Long," Raymond said, "Remembering is something you need to work on, Walter."

"Well, that's what I got you for, Raymond. Mr. Long, where were they taking them boys, tied up like pack mules?"

Charlie figured correcting this boy would take more effort than it was worth. "Lake City jailhouse, I 'magine."

"I wonder if they'll get supper. I'm getting kinda hungry, myself. Jail seems a might strict for camping out," Walter rambled on, "Oh shit, look, there's a dead guy."

An older man with long grey hair and a beard, dirty clothes in tatters, had been living outdoors for a long time. There were two giant bruises on his chest, and his arm was twisted awkwardly behind him. His face was swollen and discolored. Charlie saw three more bodies with bullet wounds, and he waded into the spring pool a bit to pull out a corpse.

"I don't believe I'd a touched that bum; he seemed kinda sick before," Walter piped.

P. Henry said, "That's somebody's drinking water, Walter. That creek probably runs into town."

This got to Raymond a little bit, "I don't believe you need to be talking to a white man in that kind of tone."

P. Henry stopped, turned toward Raymond, and squared up. "I do believe if you think I'm like those Alabama niggers, you might need to tote that fancy little Colt in your bag."

"Hey, hold on, fellers, no need for all that, dang. I think enough people have died here today for no reason. He was just trying to help, Ray. You know, lots of times, ni... um, colored folks have great ideas. Like that year we won the national, everybody was all womsquoggly over them colored units joining the drill competition ..."

Charlie shot a look at Raymond and asked, "Womsquoggly?"

Raymond said, under his breath, "Discombobulated."

Walter continued without missing a beat, "We learned a bunch of stuff from them, boys; they could snap it, son. The fact that they were in the thing made it better; I mean, that's why we were there, right? To drill like soldiers?"

Charlie couldn't stand it anymore, "Walter, what are you talking about?" keeping an eye on Raymond.

"Our unit, the Lomax Rifles, Company B 2nd Alabama Volunteer Infantry. We compete in the National Army Drilling competition, against other units from all around the country. One year, they started letting colored companies compete. I know, it makes a lot of people mad ..."

"Drill competition? What'd they ... ?" Charlie felt like he was dreaming.

"Yes, they let nigger companies compete against white companies. No offense," Walter looked at P. Henry.

P. Henry chuckled, "I don't have much opinion about marching."

"No, I mean, can you call colored folks niggers in New Orleans?" Walter clarified.

"I can, you can't, or you shouldn't. It's rude. 'Colored people' is better. But I'm not from New Orleans; I don't know how they are." He looked at Raymond and showed his palm, "Just trying to help."

Walter said, "Didn't you tell us you were from New Orleans? Ain't that what he said, Ray?"

"You asked me where I got on this train, and I said, 'New Orleans.' They made colored folks get off the train I was on. Then they filled that car up with whites. I guess nigger money isn't as good as white folks' money. At least they gave me part of my money back."

"And you snuck onto that train, just like we did." Walter nodded.

"What were y'all drilling!" Charlie exclaimed, not believing how hard this conversation was to follow. For all the talk running out of Walter, he sure was leaving a lot of stuff out.

"Marching, Long. You know. What soldiers do? All in step, turning, backing up, marking time. The ones that do it the best win." Raymond added.

"THAT'S why y'all are trampin' to Miami? To march?" Charlie laughed, "Y'all fittin' teach them Spanish a thing or three, ain't you?"

"We're going to fight!" Walter was a little offended, "We're an infantry unit, and we ain't going to be shooting bottles, either. We have just as much right to kill Spaniards as anybody."

P. Henry realized these boys weren't trained and they weren't going to Cuba. He sat down on a palm trunk and watched them rummage through the gear strewn around. He wondered what kind of home training they had received in Mobile.

Charlie was bothered, too. Charlie remembered that Judee wanted to know particular facts about someone who claimed to be ex-military. Judee would run them off if their story didn't add up; he wouldn't have "cowards or deserters" around. Charlie attributed it to Judee's peculiar ways, but it was on his mind.

Walter rekindled the fire, and Raymond held a frying pan. Charlie mentioned how cheerful they looked, walking around dead bodies and abandoned chattel like they were in a general store.

"They act like a couple of buzzards, don't they?" Charlie asked.

"What were you poking around, looking for?" P Henry replied.

"Life," Charlie said, "It's a shame. Those men look like they were on their last miles anyway; they have folks somewhere."

"That's possible," P. Henry said. "What would you have done?"

"I don't know," Charlie sighed, "Try to help them, somehow. But that don't matter now. They just killed the pitiful ones. Your buddies over there are fittin' to have Sunday dinner."

P. Henry said, "They aren't my buddies. They're a couple of horseflies buzzing around, making noise, and threatening to bite. They're glad to find something to eat; I haven't seen them eat since Mobile."

"I hope they enjoy it; I ain't so hungry right now," Charlie murmured.

"I'm not hungry, either. But that doesn't matter; those boys won't break bread with me. Besides, I don't want to get too close to them; hanging around dumbasses is dangerous, too," P. Henry declared. "Is there a café in town? With colored folks working in the kitchen?"

"Sure," Charlie replied, "they usually have cake."

"If you'll point me toward the back door, I'd appreciate it," P Henry added.

"Easy, we'll get by there in the morning," Charlie said as he stood to walk toward the dudes. "What'd you hunters and gatherers find?"

Raymond said, "We found our dinner; what'd you find?"

Charlie replied, "I found four dead men. I didn't go through their pockets; it seemed like they would have had holes, too."

"Them bums were only interested in whisky. They gathered firewood to get a handout," Raymond added, "I reckon if you were hungry, you could just go home, couldn't you?"

"That's a good point, Ray, but I've got supplies."

"Don't be rude, Ray," Walter said, almost pleading, weary of trying to keep Raymond from fighting everyone. "Why don't you have a drink of that whisky you found."

"Whisky is what got us into this mess, Walter. You talk too damn much, you know it?" Raymond snapped and sat down, then rose and went to a pack and pulled out a bottle of whisky, taking a drink anyway.

"No, fadoodlin' got us into this, although whisky helped convince Clara Stubbs and her cousin from Daphne that a slice of that pie would not only be fun but good for America!" Walter laughed loudly, stopped, and turned his attention back to the pan.

Charlie eased back over to the log, where P. Henry was snacking on smoked beef and soda crackers.

Walter took a swig from the bottle, said something to Raymond, and then called out to the others. "Hey, boys, y'all mad? Come on over and join us, have a drink, tell a joke or something."

"Now's your chance, Charlie. Those birds are fixing to start singing," P Henry said. "I'll just stay over here with the colored folks."

"No, sir, I'd rather you come along if you don't mind; it'll keep things more polite," Charlie muttered.

"Ok, but I ain't drinkin'; I'll leave that to y'all; I feel the same way about drunks as I do dumbasses."

Raymond laid a piece of dog fennel over the fire, hoping it would drive off some of the mosquitoes. Charlie had heard about using dog fennel for insects, including fleas and ticks, and knew of people rubbing it on their skin when going into the swamp.

"What are you doing with that weed, Ray? That's smoky, ain't it?" Charlie inquired, feigning ignorance.

"I ain't used to these mosquitoes. I'm hoping this dog fennel will drive some of them off," Raymond gruffly answered.

"Man, I hope it will, too," Charlie said. What'd you call it, dog what?"

"Dog Fennel, Long," Raymond corrected, "Fennel with an F."

Walter, feeling good on a full belly and several hits of whisky, says, "That's right, and Dog, with a D-O-G. Hell, Ray, you'd make Miz Hanratty proud. She was our schoolteacher. Hanratty, Hanratty, she's kinda homely, but she shore dress natty! HaHAH! Ain't that what we used to say, Ray?"

Charlie and P. Henry shared a bemused glance, almost laughing at this traveling comedy show.

"She didn't like me worth a damn, I know that," added Raymond.

"That's cause you had them wandering eyes," Walter said, turning to Charlie, "Looking at my paper, hell, I ain't know either!"

"That mule face, old maid, give me the rod over it," Raymond laughed, "and give you a dose, too! That made it worth it."

"Purty teachers get married up, quick," Charlie said to keep it going. "How about you boys, y'all leave any girlfriends back in Mobile?" Charlie asked, fishing.

"Every damn one of them, Charlie!" Walter hollered, "Since the Maine got sunk, anybody in our troop has been a hero, served pie from every gal in Mobile County!"

"That's enough, Walter!" Raymond demanded, finishing the bottle.

"I don't know why you're so embarrassed. We missed the fuckin' train. It's not like we had to go; we're volunteers!" Walter said.

With that, Raymond lunged at Walter, both fighting hard like only brothers or lifelong friends can. Raymond grabbed Walter's stampede string and landed solid rights to his face. Walter kicked Raymond in the groin and then brought his knee up into Raymond's face, knocking him upright and falling where the back of his head hit an oak stump. It was quiet except for the buzz of cicadas. Walter cried out, "Ray!"

He dropped to his knees and shook him, crying, "Oh Ray, I'm sorry, oh Jesus, what have I done? Ray! Ray!" Walter exclaimed, slapping his best friend's face.

Raymond took a massive gulp of air and slapped Walter so hard he fell. Raymond was on him, punching Walter's face. Walter was laughing, hugging Raymond, and thanking God.

"Ray, you're alive! Thank you, Jesus! Stop hitting me, God Damnit! We thought you were dead! Ray!" Walter shook Raymond, and he stopped hitting him.

Raymond looked at Walter, confused, and looked at Charlie and P. Henry.

Raymond dropped his head and vomited, which caused Walter to do the same, which prompted Charlie and P. Henry to rise and walk off. Raymond and Walter stayed there, arm in arm, heaving together like the lifelong friends and brothers that they were.

Chapter 5

Charlie awoke when a grasshopper landed on his neck. Panicked, he got up and clawed at it. He flung it away and looked around for a witness to his dance of fear. He heard the drone of cicadas and smelled coffee but saw no other person. He checked his bag. The area around the fire had been picked up, and the items were in two piles.

P. Henry walked out of the woods near the spring, carrying a washcloth, a bar of soap, and his backpack. "Man, you sleep hard. Those boys moved out of here before daylight, tryin' to be quiet. They sure are a peculiar lot—saying one thing, doing another, and always arguing, like old folks."

"I figured you had gone, too. All your stuff gone. Who cleaned up? Yesterday, it looked like a hurricane. Did you make that coffee?" Charlie answered.

"Yeah, Raymond gathered up so much gear, he could barely lift it. He then started dropping stuff on the ground to lighten his load. Took coffee cups but left the pot and the coffee. He kept that heavy behind frying pan and then made Walter carry it. Have some coffee; we need to get moving before the sun gets too high." This was more than Charlie had heard P. Henry say since he met him yesterday, and Charlie wondered if it was the coffee talking or if P. Henry started to trust him.

Charlie blew out a cup and poured the last of the pot.

"That coffee may be burnt up by now," P. Henry said. It was really good this morning. I know how to make coffee, no brag." P. Henry poured the grounds into the firepit and banged the pot on a rock. He pulled a piece of cloth from one of the piles and wiped out the pot. He put a half bag of coffee into the pot and placed it on the other pile.

It was good coffee, Charlie thought. Better than camp coffee but not nearly as good as Darla's. He was already a little homesick, wishing he had some grits. P. Henry was looking at him, not staring, more like expecting something.

"It's good," Charlie nodded, tipping his cup. "What made you come back?"

"Just now? 'Cause I was finished, I guess. I was just dropping some wolf bait," P. Henry chuckled. Are you still plannin' on taking me to the café?"

"Yeah, I reckon. That's what I said. I just thought you were gone; there wasn't a trace of y'all left." Charlie answered.

"Well, I wasn't going with those birds. For a fact, they were shuffling around, trying to be quiet, making more racket than a chuck wagon; I pretended to be asleep. But I kept an eye on them. Once they left, I got up." P. Henry said. "Oh, I carried my pack 'cause I don't know you yet, pardon me for sayin'. Just like you checked your bag when you thought we were gone. You never know about folks."

"I've heard that. Folks are sweet till they ain't!' and 'God knows how people really can be, and only He knows it.'" Charlie laughed, hearing Sassy's voice in his head.

"My mama used to say that all the time," P. Henry said.

Charlie finished up his coffee, getting grounds in his mouth, and spitting them out as he stood to walk toward the spring, spitting, bothered by the grounds.

P. Henry chuckled, "Last one up gets black grits," referring to the last of the coffee.

P. Henry grabbed a canteen from the pile and followed. When he got to the spring, he asked, "Do you have a canteen? I reckon you can borrow this one till you see the man it belongs to."

Charlie filled the steel vessel loosely wrapped in leather and said, "Ain't nobody coming back for this. All those men are going to be charged with something and sent to a turpentine camp unless they're able to pay the fine or have money wired to them."

"Dang," P. Henry said, a little disheartened at how close he had come to becoming a slave. "I had heard of that over in Texas and Louisiana. That's just wrong."

"You're right," Charlie said.

As Charlie walked along the creek trail, he could feel P. Henry's presence at his back, as if Charlie wasn't walking fast enough. Charlie stepped to the side and said, "You want to take the lead?"

"I'm sorry, was I crowding you? I don't know where we're going, for one thing, but I want to get there," P. Henry said, "if we're going to be walking, I might need to find a horse."

"Ain't no horses worth a damn in town, I already checked. Everything broke and not broke down has been sent to Tampa, for the Army. The man at the livery, Echols, tried to sell me a crock with teeth so long he could pick a nickel off the ground. Like I ain't never rode a horse before." Charlie ranted.

"How much he wanted for it?" P Henry asked, evidently serious about getting a ride.

"I didn't even ask. Wouldn't 'a spent confederate money for it." Charlie scoffed.

"Well, I need to get to Tampa," P. Henry iterated.

"I'm thinking I need a horse, too," Charlie added, "but there ain't none here for a reasonable price. There might be better options in Gainesville. Let's get something to eat, some coconut cake at the cafe, that'll make it all better."

"Only if that cake comes with a saddle," P. Henry said, and they both laughed a bit, realizing they enjoyed talking to one another.

Walking along the creek trail, Charlie would occasionally direct P. Henry to take the fork leading away from the creek to avoid low swampy areas. At one such fork in the path, P. Henry asked what Charlie was avoiding, to which Charlie responded, " Gators and suck mud."

P. Henry didn't know what suck mud was but felt the mention of 'gators was enough for him to avoid it. "They have that over in Mobile?" he asked.

"I reckon so; I ain't never been over there. What's it look like? You ort to know better than me." Charlie answered.

"To tell you the truth, the country all looks the same since over near Houston. A couple of times, the train had to stop, and men would check the tracks. They were slap underwater! When they did stop, the bugs were awful. I mean terrible. Women fussin' and babies cryin' in the car. But that wasn't as bad as when they closed the windows; then it was so hot we liked to be suffocated. The skeeters aren't so bad here as they were there. That's why I'm asking. Walter and Raymond moaned about the skeeters like it was a plague on Moses." P. Henry said, more accessible to speak now, realizing he was a little more worldly than Charlie. However, two weeks ago, he hadn't been further from San Antonio than Charlie had traveled from Lake City.

Charlie noticed that he hadn't seen any fresh tracks since they started and asked, "P. Henry, which way did Walt and Ray go, I don't believe they went this away."

"They walked up the tracks toward the junction. Do you think they might have kept on going to Jacksonville?" P. Henry asked.

"I wouldn't venture a guess where they would decide to go, but if I had to bet, I'd say they followed the tracks into Lake City," Charlie said, "It's 40 miles to Baldwin, not that they know that. Not impossible to walk, but them boys ain't marched that far ever, for fun or prizes. No, they followed that track into Lake City, and it's going to be a punishment they likely deserve. Hot, no shade. No water. Hell, we'll probably beat them there."

"But no 'Gators, though," P. Henry said, sounding a bit leery. "I ain't never seen one and don't need to, either. I'm surprised to say it, but I wish they were with us, walking the point, stepping into that suck mud before I do."

"Awe, they'd a never made it this away. Them songbirds would have been bit at least. If not somebody's breakfast," Charlie said.

"This away. Sometimes you talk real country, Charlie, if you don't mind my sayin', and other times you speak like you been educated. How far did you go in school?"

"We have a good school here in Lake City, Columbia High School. I finished up there in 12th grade. But that's it, no more school for me. I figure if there's anything else for me to learn, I'll just have to ask someone who knows. But, I IS C- C- COUNTRY, Mister Whitfield, suh! I ain't had no shoes till I was nine! Let me carry something for you." Charlie clowned.

"But that's not country; that sounds like colored folk," P. Henry said.

Charlie said flatly, "Mister, I just talk the way I talk."

"Like that, Charlie. I've never had a white man call me mister. I've never heard a white man talk like colored folks talk. I mean naturally, not in a mocking way. I'm not saying there's anything wrong with it; I've just never heard it. You've been around lots of colored folks, Charlie?"

"Looks like I am, today, don't it?" Charlie said, not sure how to take the conversation. He'd never given any thought to how he spoke other than trying to be clever or restrained if it suited his objective. He had been corrected to use proper grammar or "speak like a white man." That was always peculiar to Charlie, considering he was white, but when talking to old, bilious white men, it was good to be restrained. But he had never heard a colored man speak the way P. Henry did. It occurred to Charlie that those men would have preferred him to talk like P. Henry. The irony tickled Charlie, even if he didn't know what irony was.

They continued to walk in silence. Charlie took the lead in longer, more determined steps. After a half mile, the path widened alongside a road leading to town.

As they neared Lake City, the landscape changed from heavy forest to farmland. Small homesteads were carved into the pines and oaks, many of which the Herlong family business had cleared and cut the lumber for. Occasionally, wagons would pass, and the people riding would wave and call out Charlie's name. It was becoming evident that Charlie was a famous young man in Lake City.

"Dang, Charlie, do you know everybody?" P. Henry finally said, after a carriage with two women and their teenage daughters waved, the young women giggled as they passed.

Charlie said, "No, not yet."

"They sure know you, though," P. Henry responded. "Those two girls nearly fell out of the carriage waving. I bet you danced with both at the last social, didn't you? And their mamas weren't shooing flies; they were waving as hard as the girls."

Charlie kept walking, "Yeah, it's a curse. Tell you what, how 'bout we talk about you for a while? Like where you learned to talk like a Tallahassee lawyer and how crowded your dance card was?"

They were walking on the left side of the road, and P. Henry pulled Charlie toward the shoulder.

A freight wagon, fully loaded with lumber, was barreling toward them, four mules at full gallop. Just as they turned, the teamster stood and pulled up the reins, bringing the team to a violent stop that raised a cloud of dust, sand, and debris that surrounded Charlie and P. Henry. The driver, a tall, wiry, muscled-up black man not much older than Charlie, turned and called out, "Mister Charlie! Where you gwine?"

"I done been where I was gwine! Hey, Jasper!" Charlie called back, laughing.

"No, you ain't, I just left yo house!" still laughing, "Mister Charlie, I thought you was gone to Jacksonville?"

"I was, but now, I'm fittin' to go down to Gainesville."

"No foolin? Shoot, I'm going down there tomorrow. You ain't walkin', are you? Why don't you wait till tomorrow, and you can ride with me, keep me company? I'm taking a load of meal down there."

"Corn meal? To Gainesville? What in the world for? They ain't got any in the mills down there?" Charlie asked, puzzled.

"Shoot, Charlie, I don't know. I just drive these mules where they tell me." Jasper said, "Like this lumber. Hop on, I'll take you where you going."

Charlie said, "Thanks, Jasper!" Turning to P. Henry, "Hop in the back."

Jasper cocked his head at Charlie and said, "Uh, Mister Charlie, you know Bob Wadby say nobody outside the company on company stock."

"Mister Wad also say don't run the mules, don't he?" Charlie snapped a thumb at P. Henry. "P. Henry works for me, and if he does, then he's working for the company, ain't he?"

Jasper looked at P. Henry, and his smile came back. "That'll work! Boy, get Mr. Charlie's gear and hop on them 2x10s. We got to go."

P. Henry picked up Charlie's bag and repeated Charlie's earlier clowning, "Yes, Suh, Mr. Charlie, dey anything else I can carry for you?"

Jasper laughed, "Yes, SIR, in a little bit, you can carry some pine for me!"

P. Henry shot a look at Charlie, and he gave a little shake of his head as if to say, "No, not really."

Jasper drove almost as hard as before, and soon they came upon Echols Iron Works and Livery.

Charlie asked, "Can you hold up here? I gotta see a man about a horse."

"He ain't got none. They ain't none in town nowhere." Jasper said, slowing, "I got to get this load into town, Charlie."

"Yeah, I know, but we're getting out," and Charlie hopped out of the wagon as it was rolling.

"I thought y'all was going to help me unload this lumber! At least let your boy help me." Jasper pleaded, the wagon still slightly rolling.

P. Henry jumped out with both bags and rolled into the ragweed on the side of the road.

Jasper yelled, "Ha, Nigga, that's what you get!" and roared with laughter as he snapped the reins and pushed the mules into a trot.

P. Henry followed Charlie, muttering, "You better come get this shit, I don't work for you!"

Chapter 6

Timothy Alpata walked out of the shop and announced, "We ain't got no stock. Mr. Echols sold the last animal we had yesterday. The train station is down yonder," pointing.

"I'm looking for the café," P. Henry said.

Timothy motioned toward town and said, "Take that alley, and you'll smell the café. There's a bell out there for colored folks. Go on, now."

Timothy craned his neck to get a better perspective. "Where'd you get that leather bag?" He stepped toward P. Henry, placing his hand on his knife.

"Timty! Geeeeeeee, Alpata! You 'round? Haw!" Charlie was in the shop.

Timothy called back, "I'm out here, Charlie! Talking to your boy."

P. Henry dropped Charlie's bag, and as he passed, he said, "I am Cyrus and Ruth's boy, no one else."

Timothy grabbed Charlie's portmanteau and followed P. Henry to the cool shadows of the shop.

Timothy was agitated, "Charlie! Is this how you treat the bag I made? Leaving it outside for anyone to steal? Have you seen the tramps coming through town?"

"Yeah, I saw a few get killed at the spring camp. You might let Dempsey know before a gator drags the bodies into the spring." Charlie shared, adding, "This here's P. Henry Whitfield, from Texas. We need horses."

"Was he there when they raided the camp?" Timothy wondered, "I tried to tell you the other day. How'd he get to town?"

"I'm right here. In a freight car from New Orleans." P. Henry broke in.

Timothy continued, "Well, y'all are in a fix. Ain't no horses. Or trains, neither. I ain't never seen such a thing. Y'all might be stuck here till things get straightened out."

"I ain't going home; I'd never hear the end of it. We need to get in touch with your cousin. Tiger, what his name? He got those little horses, don't he? The Army won't buy them."

"He's on the other side of Hog Town," Timothy said, "I'd like to see big ol' Tex here riding a Marsh Tackie."

"P. Henry Whitfield, if you don't mind."

"P. Henry Whitfield!" Timothy sang out, "That's a mouthful, ain't it? I bet Mr. Cyrus and Miss Ruth don't call you that. Why don't we keep it friendly since you runnin' with Chippy? Let's see, Hank? Pee? Naw."

"Well, what's YOUR NAME, then?" P. Henry countered. "Timty?"

"No, Charlie's started that since he couldn't say Timothy. That ain't my name, either. Crackers ain't comfortable with Indian names, so they change it. My Creek name is Tomitkee. It means Thunder."

"Thunder? I thought it meant 'Gator?" Charlie exclaimed.

"Alpata means alligator. That's a white thing, too. Last name after your people. And it was just the name of this place before Lake City," Timothy explained.

"Mexicans keep both their parents' names," P. Henry mentioned.

Timothy continued, "I got Cubans in my family, like my cousin. His name ain't Tiger, and it ain't Driggers, either. It's Tsitaga, which means Rooster, and Rodriguez, which is his mama's name, which is Cuban. My uncle and my Daddy, we're black Seminole, ran cattle to Punta Rassa with the Rodriguezes. You ort to know this, Charlie."

"I just heard it, and I still don't know. But what's Punta Rassa?" Charlie repeated, "Is it in Florida?"

"Way down south," Timothy said, "So far, it was too much trouble for white folks. My grandfather took his whole family down there rather than go to Oklahoma. All kinda bands of Indians and colored folks alike. It's hard living, but better than Oklahoma. My uncle went to Oklahoma, and we never heard from him again."

"Is it near Tampa?" P. Henry hinted, "This is a great story, but I need to get to Tampa."

"We're working on it, Pee," Charlie said, glancing over to Timothy, "You're right, Pee don't work, sounds like Piss," laughing.

"It's just too long," Timothy concluded, "What's your Mama call you?"

"My Mama's my business. Call me Henry," he said.

"Henry, it is," Timothy said, "we're almost on friendly terms. Do you have any tack? Hold on," Timothy went into the tack room.

Henry asked, "Is everybody over here so peculiar? What does he care what my name is?"

Charlie smiled and said, "That's the way he trades. If you're just some stranger off the road, you're a customer of Echols. I trust him."

Timothy returned with tack like he had given Charlie earlier. "Henry, do you have a saddle blanket?"

Henry responded, "No, sir, just a regular blanket."

"That'll work if you do find a mount. Can you ride bareback?" Timothy asked.

"I'll ride a goat if it'll get me to Tampa," Henry insisted. "How much is all this going to cost?"

"That depends," Timothy grinned. "What does your Mama call you? Not when she's mad, but when she's saying what's for dinner?"

This made Charlie laugh, and Timothy shushed him. "I know you said to call you Henry, but that ain't what you go by. What's the P. for?"

Henry stood, watching Timothy, waiting him out.

"That'll be two dollars. Two and a quarter if you want the saddle blanket," Timothy sighed. He pulled a blanket out and folded it, placing the other items on it and handing it to Henry.

Henry reached into his pocket for five half dollars. He handed them over, and Timothy walked toward the tack room. "I'll be right back with your change," he said.

When he returned, Henry said, "Pinkton."

Neither of the other men answered. Henry said again, louder, "Pinkton. That's what P. stands for."

Charlie had a puzzled look on his face, "That's what you been holding against your chest? Pinkton? Pinkton Henry, you can't call us peculiar anymore." Charlie laughed.

"No, that ain't why and his Mama don't call him Pinkton. His name is Pinky! But, Henry, I won't call you Pinky. Hold on, let me get a little pouch so you won't have hardware rattling when you walk."

Henry was placing items into his pack as Timothy quietly slipped the rings and the $2.50 into the pouch and then handed it to Henry, his new friend.

Timothy turned to Charlie and said, y'all need to get moving if you're going to catch a freight.

"We need to get down to the café first," Charlie added. Timothy and Henry shook hands on their deal.

Charlie walked toward the back door, pausing with a sweep of his hand, "After you, Pinkton!" He pointed a finger and said, "I'll see you next time it rains, Thunder!"

They headed up the wide alley behind the businesses of Lake City.

"How do you figure Alpata knew my people call me Pinky?"

"I don't know, guessing?" Charlie replied, "I know he was trying hard to be friendly, but you weren't. You don't like Indians?"

Henry answered quickly, "I have nothing against anyone till they give me a reason to. 'God knows how people can be..."

"and only God knows it." They finished the sentence together and gave a little chuckle.

Henry continued, "But he kept at it. Why do you think it mattered so much to him?"

"Well, he can tell how people are. It ain't like he loves everybody. Some he won't tolerate. He must have noticed something he liked. Like I said, I trust him. Whoo! Smell that chicken? That's the Tasty Plate!"

The café building had a 10'x20' cook shed and a shaded dishwashing area behind it. Cooks and helpers moved back and forth from the cook shed into the indoor kitchen, carrying pots and dishes to be served or cooked. A bay laurel tree shaded a series of empty benches lined up in a V pattern.

Charlie lamented, "Dang it, we're late; we might have to wait. Lord have mercy; they look busy." They continued to the shade and sat on a bench.

Henry said, "He was right, though."

"Who's that?" Charlie asked.

"Alpata. Everybody in San Antonio called me Pinky. It was a joke, knowing a colored man named Pinky."

"Hell, it could be worse, I guess. Henry's good. That ok, P, P, Partner?" Charlie teased.

"You ought to be in some kind of traveling show," Henry answered.

Beverly Briley, head cook at The Tasty Plate Cafe, saw them at the bell post and waved, "Charlie Herlong, y'all too late for breakfast! Come over here! And bring that tall man I KNOW ain't from 'round here!"

They stood and walked to the washing tent. "Hey, Miz Beverly, why y'all so busy?" Charlie said, with a little wave.

"Lord, Charlie, I don't know, something's wrong with the train in Fort White. They keep bringing them up here on the little train, 'cause they ain't got no way to feed 'em. It's a mess, and they're mad as itchy-nose mules! Shoot, we ran out of biscuits and sold 5 pounds of pone. I'm fittin' to run out of meal." She turned and yelled, "Check them biscuits before they get burned!"

The teenage girl washing dishes had stopped. Beverly scolded her, "Melly Duncan! You need to finish them plates and heat some rench water! And don't spill none on that fire; I just put new wood in!"

Melly stammered, "I'm sorry, Miss Bev, I ain't NEVER seen such a purty man."

Charlie said, "Aw, Melly, you know me, I work with your Daddy."

Beverly murmured, "She ain't talking about you, Chip." She giggled a bit, turned, and yelled again, "If you all burn them biscuits, I swear, I'm going to beat somebody with a switch. Get 'em out!"

Charlie said, "If they burn 'em, we'll eat 'em."

"What I need is firewood, Charlie. We fittin' to fire up the pit. I bet you we sell the whole hog, too. If you cut firewood for me, I'll keep you in biscuits. Who's your handsome friend, the one's got Melly all swimmy-headed?"

"Oh, pardon my manners. This is P. Henry Whitfield from San Antonio, Texas. He's headed to Tampa, going to fight the Spanish in Cuba," Charlie answered.

"He don't need a pardon, does he? He took his hat off." Beverly turned her attention to Henry. "Can you split wood, young man?"

Henry assured her, "If you have a sharp ax, ma'am, I cut pretty well. How much do you need?"

"I reckon till you get tired, son," she said.

"If you don't mind my asking, are we talking about food or money?" Henry continued.

"What'd he say your name was? Henry, if you cut me enough wood to cook that hog, you'll eat till you can't, and I'll get Mr. Leamon to pay you what's reasonable. Charlie, you with him?" She said, turning to Charlie, bareheaded.

"Not right now; I need to figure out a way to get to Gainesville," he replied, "but I sure could use a biscuit or something; we ain't eat yet."

Beverly turned to Melly and said, "Melly, go get Mr. Whitfield a plate of lunch and bring Charlie a biscuit so he can avoid chopping wood."

"Aw, Miz Beverly, it ain't like that!" Charlie pleaded.

Beverly turned on her heel, threw up her left hand, and said, "Charlie, I ain't got time for horse-trading. I got chicken to fry. Come back once you get your affairs in order. Willis! The beans are boiling over. Move them off the fire!"

Charlie turned to Henry and said, "I'm going to find us a way to Gainesville. We may have to get Jasper to give us a ride tomorrow."

Melly returned with a plate of chicken, rice, beans, and squash piled so high that it was oozing off the edge with pone and a biscuit on top. She gave Henry a spoon and handed Charlie a bindle, "Charlie, there's a biscuit and a thigh in there, too. I snuck it out in my apron, so it might be a little wet."

"Melly, you're the sweetest Duncan in the whole bunch."

Charlie walked south, Henry started eating, and Melly watched him chew. Beverly's voice roared, "Melly! Get your behind on them pots and pans!"

Chapter 7

Charlie made his way further up the alley and over to G.W. Watts' store. Watts was the go-to lumber source in the region, so his supply was consistent due to his relationship with the Herlong company. He did a lot of business with Herlong using their freight capability.

Jasper was almost finished unloading the lumber as Charlie was hustling into the lot. "Charlie Herlong, where you gwine?"

"Well, Jasper, to help you unload this pine, but now you gon whine 'cause I'm all out of time," Charlie sang.

"Oh no, you can finish this load, and that'll be fine," Jasper finished the song as he sat on a rusty piece of farm equipment, then said, "Yes, that will be fine. Ha!"

Charlie smiled, moving the lumber to the stack, and asked, "Hey Jas, how would you like to earn an extra couple of dollars today?"

"How?" Jasper said, sounding doubtful. "I ain't fittin' to do nothin' slick. I like this job just fine."

Charlie looked surprised, and said, "Jasper...you know better. I mean by taking a load of meal to Gainesville, today. I'll get Mr. Hart to pay extra; Henry and I will help you load and unload it."

"Well, that does sound fine, Charlie, only Mr. Hart ain't going to do that," Jasper said.

Charlie boasted, "Yes, he is, 'cause I'm going to talk him into it. You know I can."

"I know you cain't, and I bet you he ain't." Jasper sang.

"You think you so hot? How much you got?" Charlie was challenged.

Jasper sang louder, "You said two buck, quack, quack like a duck."

Charlie hesitated; he knew Jasper wasn't going to bet a full day's pay unless he was sure, but he was a little angry that Jasper was challenging him.

Jasper had him on the run, and he knew it, "How much YOU GOT? What rhymes with chicken? Haaaawwwww!"

"Calm down, son, I'm still kickin', and what I got is some delicious fried chicken. I'll buy you lunch at the Tasty Plate, fried chicken against your two-dollar rate." Charlie crossed his arms.

"Today? Bet!" Jasper laughed and moved to step up into the driver's seat.

G.W. Watts was walking across the lot from the back of the store and called out, "Charlie, I'm surprised to see you. I heard you were off to fight the Cubans! Are you back already?"

Now Charlie was aggravated. "Do what? I mean, excuse me, Mr. Watts?"

"I heard you were on your way to Tampa to fight alongside Teddy Roosevelt, be a Rough Rider!" Watts said, "I guess you haven't left yet."

It rankled Charlie when he was the subject of unfounded gossip. To him, it was an invasion of his privacy. Some would see it as flattering, but Charlie, not knowing any better, let it bother him.

"No, sir, I don't know any Roosevelts. I'm trying to go to Jacksonville, but today, I'm trying to find a way to Gainesville."

"Well, why don't you just ride one of your father's horses, Charlie?" Watts continued.

Charlie replied, "No, sir, there isn't any stock in town to replace it, and the stock we have all have a particular job."

"Well, I'm sending a load of corn meal down there tomorrow. Maybe you can drive that down. Jasper is taking a load of lumber down there, too. Junior and them are supposed to be cutting it right now, didn't Jasper tell you?" Mr. Watts asked.

"No, sir. He must have forgotten. And someone else will have to drive that load of meal; I won't be coming back." Charlie was staring a hole in Jasper, and Jasper was staring a hole in the back of a mule, trying not to laugh out loud.

"You ain't coming back? Charlie, this is your home." Mr. Watts said with genuine concern.

Charlie half rolled his eyes as he climbed into the seat alongside Jasper and said, "No sir, I don't mean never; I just meant tomorrow."

"Well, that's good, son, 'cause we're going to miss you something fierce. Don't be a stranger. Jasper? You'd better get this wagon on out there so they can load it up. See y'all in the morning!" Watts waved and walked back toward the store.

Jasper called out to Watts again in a singing voice, "No, sir, Mr. Watts, I sure don't want to miss my lunch, do I, Charlie?" Laughing, he turned the wagon around and headed to the street.

"You a sorry sod," Charlie said, and Jasper shot back, "And you a sorry gambler!"

They both laughed, and Charlie said, "Go on up to the mill; I still have to talk to Mr. Hart."

He snapped the mules into a pace, and they proceeded up Marion Street toward Escambia.

"Do it seem like they's lots of strangers in town, Charlie?" Jasper wondered.

"Yessir, and they are. There's a train full of folks stopped down in Fort White, and they're bringing them up here to be fed and watered. Miz Bev said they were about to eat her out of food, and the hotel was full. As a matter of fact, take me down there. You can water the team at the station while I talk to Mr. Caldwell," Charlie said.

"Now, Charlie, you need to get me my fried chicken and let me get on back to the saw so they can load me up. If I ain't there by the end of dinner, Mr. Wad is gon have my foot in a trap," Jasper pleaded.

"I'll be back out by the time you get the team watered," Charlie assured him.

Jasper drove the four-mule team, pulling the heavy freight wagon to the depot, and turned them in a massive J-turn in the middle of the street. Jasper was an outstanding teamster, and the maneuver was tricky at any speed, but he executed it quickly and precisely, scaring the bejesus out of visiting jaywalkers and horses.

Charlie hopped off the moving wagon, and Jasper continued toward the freight area of the station, waving to the pejorative shouts of those disturbed by the commotion. Charlie headed for the Station Master's office, and Ulysses Caldwell met him on the porch, reacting to the screams and shouting, "What in the world is going on out here?"

"Oh, just visitors to town, not used to big city hustle and bustle, I suppose," Charlie answered, extending a hand to shake Mr. Caldwell's.

"Oh, I see, that Gallum nigger, driving like a madman again. He's gon' get shot one day if he runs over somebody. I hope your Daddy ain't looking to send any freight, cause we're in a Mell of a Hess right now," Caldwell said, wiping sweat from his brow and bald head. "There ain't no freight or passengers can be moved from Ocala down to Tampa 'cause there ain't no room on the tracks. All these folks are waiting to get to Gainesville, and there's already a huge freight loaded with Army supplies and livestock stalled in Gainesville. They're having to offload the livestock 'cause it's too hot in the cars, and they ain't got enough help to handle the critters when they get out."

Charlie turned and looked at the people on the streets and said, 'Well, I don't see any soldiers; all I see is a boodle of rich folks."

"Yeah, ridiculous, ain't it? They're going to Tampa to see the soldiers off and stay at Henry Plant's big hotel. I don't know what they think they're going to see. Tampa ain't that much bigger than Lake City, and all these folks are mad cause we can't just fire up the engine and run over the trains already there. I don't know when they can reboard and move on to Gainesville. Our hotel ain't big enough for all these folks. What's your business today, Charlie? You trying to get to Tampa, too?" Caldwell asked.

"No, sir, Jacksonville, and I don't want to wait till later this week. I figured I could get down to Gainesville and ride something up there," Charlie replied, "You think they might have some horses down there?"

Caldwell shrugged and said, "Charlie, I wouldn't bet a nickel or a biscuit on anything after what I've seen today. Tell you what, sometime after two, we're going to send the little train back to Fort White, and there shouldn't be many folks on it. If you want to ride that far, it'll be okay. I'll tell the porter you're running an errand for me."

"Oh, that'd fix my flint for today, at least! I've got a man traveling with me. Can he go, too?" Charlie asked, hoping Caldwell wouldn't ask too much about P. Henry.

Caldwell turned and was besieged by passengers, needing information he didn't have, "Yeah, I guess if there's room, Charlie, just don't cause me any more headaches... Yessir, of course, we have a hotel..."

Charlie glanced at the station clock, which read 10:50, and hustled toward the watering trough.

"Man, I can taste that chicken already, Charlie; let's get down to Miz Bev so you can sweet talk her into my lunch," Jasper said as he tossed the water bag toward the hook next to the trough and hung it with a perfect shot. "Damn, I'm good, ain't I?"

"I'd rather be lucky than good, but first, pull over to the mill, and maybe I can get you breakfast tomorrow, too," Charlie quickly replied, hopping up into the seat. What are you waitin' on, Jas? Let's go!"

"If you waitin' on me, you're backing up!" Jasper said as he grabbed the reins and smacked the backs of the mules with them. The front mule turned and looked over his shoulder, and Jasper muttered, "What the hell you looking at, Sampson? I just gave you a drink," which seemed to satisfy Sampson, and they moved down the block toward the mill.

Charlie was off the wagon and trotted into the mill again before the wagon stopped. Again, Sampson turned and looked over his shoulder at Jasper, to which Jasper said, "I don't know, ask Charlie."

Charlie moved into the mill and saw J.B. Hart, "Hey, Charlie, I hope you ain't here to load your wagon; I'm pretty backed up here at the moment," Hart waved.

"Oh, I see. Well, if it will help you out, I can have Jasper or somebody come back in the morning. Will that help?" Charlie cheerfully answered, "They'll have to be here real early, though."

Hart looked relieved. "Oh yeah, that'll be fine, Charlie, and it's a big favor to me; I appreciate it."

"Well, maybe you can help me out a little bit. Miz Bev, up at the Tasty Plate, has run out of corn meal and is really low on flour due to all the travelers in town. I told her I would get her some cornmeal. Can I take a bag to her? I owe her a favor," Charlie inquired.

"I bet she is turning some out today; where're all these people coming from? They swarming like bees! Hell, yeah, Charlie, you can have a bag, and I got some flour in the back, which I'll give you, too. I'm happy to give it to you, and I'm real proud of you going off to help Teddy Roosevelt, you be safe, now," Hart turned and called to a worker, "James! Go in the back and get Charlie a bag of that double xx flour we have back there! Just grab a sack of meal, Charlie; I'll see you in the morning."

Charlie didn't bother correcting Mr. Hart about Teddy Roosevelt. He then walked over to a stack of full bags and hoisted one to his shoulder. James hustled past him with a bag of flour and disappeared outside. As Charlie was getting to the wagon, he could hear Jasper: "James, I'd like to help you, but I don't do any hiring out there. Shoot, ask Charlie; he's closer to Mr. Herlong than I am."

"Not much closer, I ain't," Charlie protested. Besides, my Daddy will have to ask Mr. Wad first and tell the truth, James. I don't believe Wad likes anybody!"

"Ain't that the damn truth," Jasper roared, laughing, "And I better get out there before I'm asking you for work, James! Heeeaaaah! Let's go, Sampson!"

Soon, they were near the alley, and Charlie said, "Jas, I KNOW you ain't fittin' to take this big ol' wagon up the alley."

"Why not? They's room, and the wagon is empty. I need to be getting along. If I can get some chicken here and get out there, I can have two lunches! And then my luck come in bunches!" Jasper rhymed.

"Yeah, but if these animals drop brown apples in the alley, you'll be gone, and I'll get cussed out," Charlie scolded.

"Man, hush. These mules shit when I tell them to, ain't that right, Sampson?" Sampson reared his head a bit and raised his bobbed tail, "Samp, you better not, or you can eat grass today instead of corn!" Sampson lowered his tail and headed up the alley, bobbing his head like he was laughing.

CHAPTER 8

Henry chopped wood at a steady pace and had a massive pile of split wood. He felt good getting in some work rather than traveling.

Melly was dawdling, trying to make conversation. Beverly's voice made her jump and nearly trip. Backpedaling, "Yessum. I was waiting for Mr. Henry to finish his water!"

"I'm a finish you if you don't get them snap beans ready!" Beverly snapped as she walked up, drying her hands on a small towel. "Lawd have mercy, son; I reckon that ax is sharp enough!"

Henry walked over, handed her the cup, and said, "I'm about out of logs, ma'am. Do you think this is enough to cook that hog? I want to try your barbecue and see how this oak cooks. It splits easily, has a real straight grain, and is a little green. We use mesquite or cottonwood at home; it's harder to split."

"Well, son, you ain't having no problem splitting ours; that's the truth. I expected this pile of logs to take you till about three o'clock. Whereabouts in Texas you from and how you know so much about splitting wood and cookin' with it?"

"We cook a lot of food in our church and sometimes for other folks in San Antonio. If they have a big crowd, they know my father can get the people to do that sort of thing," Henry said with pride.

"Oh, you go to church, too? P. Henry, you might be somethin'. A tall, handsome man who knows how to work and go to church?" Beverly exclaimed, "You're some catch, son."

"I don't know about all that, ma'am. In a way, my parents ARE the church. We don't have a building yet, but folks gather behind our store for service, and my father is the preacher. We're working on building a sanctuary, one day, God willing," Henry said.

"Hold still. Do you all have a store, too? What kind of store?" Beverly was incredulous.

Henry was startled that she seemed not to believe him. "Yes, Ma'am, it's a General Store, selling dry goods, some hardware, notions, and catalog goods..."

"For colored folks..." Beverly asked.

"Well, for anybody, really, colored, Mexicans, Indians. Sometimes white folks, but they mostly shop on the other side of town," P. Henry added, beginning to sense that maybe Beverly hadn't been to a large city before, where segregated communities offered goods and services for non-whites as well. He tried to change the subject. "I'm almost through with these logs. Do you have any more?"

"No, sweety, just finish what we got; we'll have to get someone from Herlong's to bring us some more, I reckon," she responded, glad that P. Henry eased them out of an embarrassing situation. Beverly thought to herself that she liked that P. Henry Whitfield.

When Beverly saw Jasper and Charlie turn onto the lot, she started, "Jasper Gallum, get them damn mules out of this yard and down that damn alley; we got enough flies around without mule shit all over the place," turning to glance at P. Henry, a little ashamed of her language, but not enough to stop, "Turn that rig right around or I'ma bust yo ass with them reins!"

Jasper was off the wagon and had the bag of flour in his arms before she could finish, "I'm fittin' to move it, Miz Bev, but you gon' stop cussin' when you see what I brought you!"

Charlie had the sack of corn meal and shook his head at how fast Jasper was trying to take credit for the flour. Jasper placed the flour on the ground and turned to Charlie, "I'm taking the wagon down to Echols. Now, don't forget our deal, Charlie; I'll be right back."

Beverly looked at Charlie with one eye squinting into the almost noon sun and said, "What deal? Charlie, I ain't in the 'feedin' Charlie's men business; somebody's got to pay for all the food that comes out of here, just like Mr. Joe Hart is going to be paid for those sacks of meal, even though lawd knows I need it."

"No, ma'am, Mr. Hart said it was no charge for either sack for something I'm doing for him, but he would appreciate a piece of coconut cake if you had a slice to spare some afternoon. And Jasper is part of the deal to get to the mill so early in the morning." Charlie was trying to talk fast and make sense to Beverly, but she knew something wasn't adding up.

"Charlie, what else? A biscuit and a slice of cake? For Mr. Hart, who would charge a skeeter for blood if he could find a piece of paper that small to put the bill on? What else?"

"Well," Charlie dragged, then quickly, "Jasper needs a fried chicken lunch to make the deal square."

"Like now? During the rush? Charlie." Beverly sighed and said, "OK, because we're still going to run out of chicken anyway, but that still don't equal two sacks of mill goods. What do you have to get, Charlie?"

"A kiss on the jaw, Miz Bev, 'cause I love you like the day is long," Charlie crooned. With that, Beverly grabbed him, kissed him on the cheek, and squeezed him so hard it took Charlie's breath. "Oh," Charlie added, "I'm taking your wood splitter. We have to be somewhere."

Beverly turned to the cook shed, hand raised, "I knew he was too good to be true," and started barking orders to her people.

Charlie sat on the bench to rethink his options for getting to Jacksonville. Tramp the next train? Nope. Wait until someone decides to move these folks to Jacksonville. Wait till tomorrow, ride with Jasper? Charlie was tired of waiting. Head toward Gainesville, maybe catch a train headed north. What about P. Henry? He's going to need a horse; taking the train south won't happen for a while. Of course, he might have ideas of his own. Simple. Keep moving.

Jasper came up the alley, rubbing his belly.

"She's working it up right now, making sure she has enough chicken for the lunch rush. Calm down," Charlie cautioned, thinking no one ever calmed down hearing that.

"Break time's over, Charlie; I could have been there by now," Jasper exclaimed, sitting hard on the bench. "Waiting ain't good."

"She knows that, and guess what? There's a little something for you in the morning, too." Charlie hoped that would calm him down a bit.

"Why she gon' do that? She already giving me lunch." Jasper was suspicious, knowing Charlie was hard at work today.

"Well, Mr. Hart needs to load the meal in the morning, and that was why he gave us the flour," Charlie explained.

"She don't know that, and Wad don't care. Even more reason. I need to catch that young nigga they gon' send to drive the meal wagon," Jasper reasoned.

Charlie continued, "That's right. You can catch lunch at the yard, too. Just remember to tell Wad."

"I ain't got to remember shit, so I need to git! How come you don't just tell 'em? That way, you can ride with us, sit up front out of the dust?" Jasper did have a way with words.

"No, sir, I won't be with you. Please do what I need you to. I'm taking the little train to Fort White to find a horse. If I don't, I'll catch you on the road to Hog Town," Charlie explained.

"How come you so perturbed about Jacksonville, anyway? Ain't nothing over there you can't get here," Jasper asked.

"What you don't know would fill a barn," Charlie said, "I'll get there and find me a charm."

Henry had finished the splitting and walked up to the benches. "What's the story, Mr. Herlong? I'm about done teaching Florida how to split wood. Are we walking to Greensville?"

"Gainesville," Charlie corrected, "And maybe walking, but we won't be waiting. We're on a train for about 20 miles then, worst case, Jasper's going to give us a ride the rest of the way."

"South? On the way to Tampa?" Henry asked.

"It's on the way, but you ain't the only one going." Charlie said, "The track's backed up to Ocala. Finding a horse might be the only way. And it ain't no easy ride, about 150 miles."

"Then let's get to Gainesville, and I'll figure it out then," Henry said.

"Well, where am I supposed to find you?" Jasper asked. We'll be in Fort White by ten at the latest."

"On the road, I reckon, but don't wait on us. If I find something that moves, I'm taking it," Charlie told him.

Jasper jumped and said excitedly, "Here come Miz Bev, totin' your debt! Some of her good fried chicken, I bet. This is just how I come to get 'cause Charlie ain't know the deal been set."

"Jasper, there's two legs and a wing in here with some potato salad," she extended the bundle, then pulled it back, "Did you clean up after them mules?"

"My mules have manners, ma'am, that's the troof, they only drop apples where there ain't proof!" Jasper said, taking the food and his leave.

Beverly handed Henry a silver dollar. "Mr. Leamon is tight as a box cooter, so a dollar it is, Mr. P. Henry Whitfield. Thank you so much. We'll have to serve you some barbecue next time."

"That's fine, Ma'am. That lunch was worth all the chopping. I do hope to see you again. Please tell Miz Mellie thank you for me," Henry gave a slight bow.

"I ain't sayin' nothing to her till you're good and gone, or she'll be chasing after you. God bless you, son," Beverly said, placing her hand on his shoulder.

Charlie and Henry picked up their bags and headed toward the station.

"Wait! Wait! Mr. Whitfield! You forgot your cake!" Melly covered the 25 yards from the wash pot to the alley in seconds.

"Damn, that girl can run!" Charley said, "You've made some impression, Henry."

Melly handed Henry the package and breathlessly said, "You ort to come back tomorrow; we'll probably have smoke stew!"

Charlie started to correct her, but Henry stopped him. "If not then, Miss Melly, then sooner rather than later."

"I don't know what that means, but I hope sooner! And you can call me Melly! Bye now!" and turned to run back, yelling, "Seeya, Charlie!"

"Damn, and cake was all I wanted," Charlie said.

"I'll share," Henry replied, "so what's the story on this Little Train? And what are they going to say about colored people?"

"The station master will say I'm working for him, and you work for me. Just don't bow up on nobody," Charlie explained.

"Anyone," Henry corrected.

"Anyone what?"

"Just don't bow up on anyone. Nobody is a double negative, which means bow up on every person, actually," Henry explained.

"Ok, professor," Charlie mumbled.

"Dang, this cake is good," Henry exclaimed.

"That's what I said. Little Miss Melly is trying to get you to stay around," Charlie said.

"Charlie, I didn't leave Texas to light here," Henry said, chewing. But this cake will make you think. Here, take the rest before I get distracted."

"Happy to help," Charlie chuckled.

"And where is this train taking us?" Henry asked.

"Fort White. The Plant System line takes you to Tampa. Who knows how long they'll be backed up? Waiting here ain't, uh, isn't going to get us anywhere," Charlie caught himself, "so we'll figure something else when we get there."

"How is going south going to get you to Jacksonville? It's east of here," Henry asked.

"More options. I know I'm not fooling with FC&P after seeing that business yesterday. To hell with the Florida, the Central, and the Peninsular or whatever they call it next month," Charlie was getting fired up. Timothy was right; the railroads are dangerous."

Henry was weighing his options and felt moving south was the best thing. Doing so with Charlie was probably a good way, at least until the road led him to Jacksonville.

"You say Tampa is a hundred miles from Gainesville?" Henry asked.

"It's way over a hundred miles," Charlie replied, "lots of it rough country. I guess the best way would be to ride and follow the railroad."

Charlie continued, "Or maybe you could make it over to Palatka. There might be Plant trains running to Tampa. I would think they would make allowances for colored folks on those trains. I guess we'll see."

For the first time since he left Texas, Henry felt that his parents might have been right; this trip was filled with trials of biblical order.

CHAPTER 9

Charlie and Henry spent the next hour avoiding the heat. Henry used a well behind the laundry to freshen up a bit after his hard morning. At the station, they sat in the freight area, taking advantage of the breeze.

The conductor made his way back to Charlie and Henry. "You still want to go to Fort White, Charlie? There's no telling when the tracks in Gainesville are going to be clear enough to move south, so that train in Fort White may be there for several days," he said.

Charlie stood and said, "Yes, sir, we're going to keep moving. If there are any horses, we might try to buy one. If we get stuck, can we get a ride back here?"

"Well, yeah, but as soon as we get the word, we're going to move these folks to Gainesville as fast as we can." Caldwell turned and moved on to other passengers.

Soon, they were on the train headed to Fort White, which had become little more than a junction for the Plant System. Five years before, it had been bustling; tons of fruit were loaded to begin their trip north, and the Florida economy was thriving. Peeling paint and neglected siding gave the station a rough appearance.

"Well, I suppose that's the train with no destination," Henry said as the little train slowed, "I can see why people were leaving; ain't much here."

"It used to be real busy before the orange groves froze two years in a row," Charlie said. It looks like times are hard."

The Florida Southern train, with mail, freight, passenger, and baggage cars, sat cold and still. "Dang, they're not even keeping the fire going on the boiler, Charlie," Henry continued, "That train won't be leaving any time soon."

"I'm more disappointed that there's no stock car," Charlie said, "Let's see if a coach or something is moving towards Gainesville. If not, we'll head down the road. There'll be a spring where we can camp with good water."

They disembarked and followed the other passengers into the depot, hoping to get more information. There were trains at every stop in the same situation as Fort White.

The station manager, Calvin Mulberry, was having a heated discussion with a portly passenger who wanted answers immediately.

"Mister, I imagine they do conduct business differently in St. Louis. And Memphis and Birmingham and any other track that's EMPTY! But right here, in FORT WHITE, FLORIDA, there ain't nowhere to go. Unless you'd like to sit on the hot track between here and High Springs, sweating through that fancy-assed suit you're wearing and then feeding most of the mosquitoes in Alachua County." Mulberry wasn't used to dealing with passengers, and it showed, "So, Mr., uh, what was your name again, sir? Waddler?"

"It's WATTLER. James Wattler. I don't believe I appreciate your manner, sir, I was only..." Wattler indignantly replied.

Mulberry's face was red, and he was rolling, "Like I said, WADDLER, you were ONLY coming back down here to give SOMEONE a piece of your mind. Well, you need to keep as much of it as you can because you don't seem to understand our situation here! There ain't nowhere to go until they clear up track space, starting with the next station, High Springs. The people on that train, they ain't got nowhere to go. I bet they would love to spend a few hours in Lake City, and that's where I suggest you get to because that little train you just rode here on will be leaving at 3:30! As soon as we can, we'll send word for you and everyone else to continue to Gainesville. You better hurry, go over to the Tasty Plate, and have a little supper. They got the best Coconut Cake you'll ever put in your mouth, better than St. Louis, even, I'd wager."

With that, Wattler waddled back over to the little train and looked down the tracks toward High Springs.

Mulberry turned and asked the half dozen standing there, stunned, "Will there be anything else?" All except Charlie and Henry turned and walked toward James Wattler.

Mulberry's eyes got a little bigger, and Charlie quickly noted, "I believe you're right about that cake; we had some today." Both men eased away from Mulberry toward the opposite end of the platform.

"That cake is dang famous," Henry noted, "I guess you figured this wasn't a good time to ask about a stagecoach?"

They checked in with the local blacksmith, who had no mounts or saddles, but learned there was a spring four miles down the road.

Walking. Charlie thought of Judee, who often said that a long walk would "Sweep the corners of your attic." Now, it just made him appreciate having a horse. Or a mule, for that matter. He regretted not trying to get something from his father's company, not even asking, now, when his pride didn't seem as important.

"MAN, I should have filled my canteen back there," Henry exclaimed, "The further I get from Texas, the closer we get to hell, I believe."

"It don't get hot in Texas?" Charlie asked, glad to get his thoughts away from not having a ride.

"Doesn't," Henry corrected, "yeah, it gets real hot, but this seems hotter, makes it hard to breathe, and sweating like a well pump. I can't get enough water."

"Man, it ain't got hot yet," Charlie replied, "We'll get to that spring before you get leaned on," Charlie said.

"Leaned on by whom?" Henry asked.

"The bear," Charlie replied.

A short while later, Charlie saw two men come out of the woods on the right side and continue up the road. Henry instinctively moved to the edge of the road, and Charlie said, "Looks like that might be our spring. Let's see if those boys can tell us something."

"No, let's not," Henry cautioned, "They didn't even look this way when they came out. Don't forget, all the folks on the railroad are out here just like we are. So, the countryside can be dangerous, too."

"Don't be scared," Charlie teased.

"I'm not scared, Charlie." Henry's tone turned serious, "I saw men get killed for no good reason yesterday, and I'd rather not see any killing today." Henry then opened one of the straps on his pack and stuck his hand in, checking his pistol. Charlie didn't notice but became more aware.

They walked the sandy path further into the woods, shady and cooler than the road. Henry could hear voices, but Charlie could not; he was speaking loudly about being thirsty until Henry shushed him. Men were arguing, and as they got closer, Charlie could hear them.

From the clearing at the spring, Charlie heard a familiar voice, "Hey, mister, we found all this gear, and you weren't around. What were we supposed to do, leave it for the next fellers to come along?"

The other voice was loud and angry, "You flat-footed mudsill, you saw what them bulls did to everyone there, and somehow you were lucky just like we were, and you stole it just the same, like a damn graverobber."

When they got to the clearing, they noticed that one of the voices was Walter King from Mobile. He was standing next to Raymond, who was wearing a gun belt, standing behind his pack, which was on the ground. They were squared off with three men, all wearing pistols. An older one was doing the talking, flanked by two younger ones. All were wearing pistols except Walter.

Walter was trying to diffuse the situation, "Hey, Mister, if any of this stuff is yours, then we'll give it back to you, but, honest, we figured y'all were either dead or gone to jail. You ought to thank us for saving your stuff."

Then Raymond spoke up, "Nope. I ain't giving you a God Damn thing. If this shit used to be yours, then you should have taken better care of it. Now, back up."

"Hold on, now Ray, ain't a thing here worth fighting over ..." Walter said again, trying to be the voice of reason.

"Listen to your buddy, boy. You can't outdraw all of us," the older man said, "If you draw that pistol, you're going to die."

The sound of Raymond's pistol was the last sound the older man heard. His chest splashed with blood, and he fell to the ground. Raymond turned the smoking pistol to the man on his left, and they shot simultaneously, killing each other.

The third man yelled, "Daddy!" and half turned, half kneeling to aid the older man. Walter turned and started running. The third man stood calmly, drew his pistol, cocked the hammer, and shot Walter in the back as he was running. Walter fell on his face in the sand.

Charlie exclaimed, "Well, for the love of …" which caused the last man to turn and cock the hammer on his pistol again.

Henry shot the third man before Charlie could finish his sentence.

Charlie yelled, "What the hell did he want to kill us for? We just got here!"

Henry said nothing and quickly walked toward the bodies, gun drawn, only to find what he had hoped to avoid: four bloody corpses. He reached down and moved their pistols away from their bodies, just in case one wasn't dead yet.

"I still can't believe what just happened," Charlie was stunned. "Did you see how fast Raymond shot that man? And then, what? Did he and the other guy shoot each other? And then, what was that bell ringing? Thank God you were ready for that guy …"

"Please be quiet, Charlie," Henry said, "We still don't know who is around."

"Well, pardon the hell out of me," Charlie whispered excitedly, "I ain't never been in a gunfight before. But you sure have, ain't you? You dropped that sumbitch like this was a dime novel!"

"I've never killed anyone before, Charlie. I hope God will forgive me for doing so today." Henry took his hat off.

"Well, I'm damn sure glad you did, that rascal was pointing that gun at us!" Charlie continued in a low tone, "You don't think those other guys will come back, do you?"

"I don't know what to think right now. Just hush, please. Gather up these guns and put them under something. I'm going to pray over these men." Henry walked over to the man he shot and knelt.

With that, Charlie gathered the guns strewn around and sat on a downed log, placing the weapons, still hot from firing, under a blanket he found next to Raymond's pack.

Henry placed hats on each of the men's faces after straightening their bodies and praying over them. Charlie noticed tears on Henry's cheeks, and it puzzled him. Henry didn't know these men anymore than Charlie did and had only met Raymond recently. Even then, Raymond had shown nothing but contempt when

Charlie met him yesterday. Regardless, Charlie was sure he had never met anyone quite like P. Henry Whitfield, and Charlie was glad that he had.

When Henry had finished praying over Raymond, he turned and silently walked where Charlie sat. They quietly sat for several minutes.

"Thank you for saving our lives, Henry," Charlie finally said, "Surely there's something in the bible about stopping evil. It was self-defense."

Henry said nothing.

"Weren't you going to Cuba to kill Spaniards? What did you think was going to happen down there?" Charlie asked.

"Charlie, I don't know what to think. All those things you just said, I've already asked and answered that. But this is for real, today. I guess I'll get over it, but right now, I'm not sure how I feel." Henry sighed and took his canteen out.

Charlie took it from him and said, "Let me fill that for you. When you get settled, I have some questions about what exactly happened here." He took the canteen and walked the 10 yards toward the spring.

Henry recalled, "They were fussing about being thieves and what happened yesterday. I think Walter was trying to calm everything down, and then Raymond shot the old man and the skinny one. Skinny must have gotten off a shot, and it killed Raymond. Walter took off, and the third one shot him in the back. Oh, I forgot to say a prayer over Walter.."

Charlie returned with the canteen, and Henry took a long pull of fresh spring water, "Aah, man, that is good," then stood.

"Wait a second, he ain't going nowhere, right now," Charlie said, "I want to know how Raymond killed two of them before he got killed. He sure didn't seem like no desperado gun hand, did he?"

"Shoot, I don't know, Charlie. Let's take a look at those guns. Hand me that short one there; that's Raymond's." Henry looked it over and removed the shells. "This might explain it; this is a double-action .38." Henry pulled the trigger several times quickly.

"You might as well be speaking Spanish. I don't know what any of that means," Charlie said.

"You don't speak Spanish, either." Henry pointed to the other pistols, "Those other guns are single-action; you have to cock it back to shoot it. Raymond's is double action; you can fire it from the trigger, like this," and snapped off three more dry fires.

"So why would anyone want those big, heavy ones?" Charlie asked.

"Cheaper, and those single action guns right there are .44s, which means the slug is bigger, does more damage, and travels farther than a smaller one. Haven't you ever shot a pistol?" Henry asked.

"Of course," Charlie lied.

Henry asked, "Do you have a gun now?"

Charlie said, "Yeah, but I ain't got any shells for it."

"Well, they're no good empty," Henry said, "Let's see it."

"Well, ok, don't laugh," Charlie said, opening the secret bottom compartment of his portmanteau.

"Dang, Charlie, a secret stash, fancy. I've never seen that." Henry noted.

"What are y'all doing here?" Walter was standing behind Charlie, and it scared Charlie so that he backhanded the heavy, ancient pistol and struck Walter, knocking him unconscious.

Henry had his pistol out and cocked, but as Walter fell backward into the sand, he exclaimed, "Charlie, you killed him … again, … I think."

CHAPTER 10

About an hour later, Walter regained consciousness. He had a big, black bruise on his jaw, where Charlie whacked him, and a huge bruise and cut on his forehead. The .44 slug had struck the skillet in his pack, causing Walter to fall on limestone, and it knocked him unconscious the first time.

Walter's first words were, "Is Raymond dead?"

Henry said, "Yes, Walter, I'm sorry, the skinny one shot him at the same time Raymond killed him."

"Where is the one that shot me?"

"Right over there, dead," Henry said.

Walter stammered a bit, "So, ... why am I alive?"

Charlie spoke up, "Walter, you're alive because the frying pan in your pack deflected the shot intended to kill you."

"Where is the one that shot me?"

"P. Henry Whitfield shot him dead when he tried to kill us for no good reason," Charlie said.

Walter looked at Raymond, dead and bloodied, "He's been my best friend since we were minnows. What am I going to tell his Mama?"

The rain started as sporadic, heavy drops, prompting Charlie to gather dry palm fronds to use as cover. Previous visitors had built a lean-to shelter between small pines, and Charlie filled gaps in the roof. Henry produced a large Bowie knife from his pack and chopped a few green fronds.

Walter remained seated on a log but turned to face Raymond's body several feet away. Henry hustled back to the fire area and gathered all their bags. As he returned to the lean-to, Charlie was taking a knee under the shelter. The rainfall was increasing. Walter remained seated in the rain, crying and staring at Raymond.

"I got the guns," Henry said, "they're in Raymond's pack, that oiled canvas job there. I didn't see your ball-bat, though. Did you get it?"

This confused Charlie, "Ball bat?"

"Yeah, that big ol' smoke pole you tried to kill Walter with," Henry was looking around. "You were about to show it to me."

"I put it up after I accidentally hit Walter with it," Charlie answered, "His resurrection was a shock now. How long do you figure he's going to stay out there in the rain?"

Charlie reached into the lower compartment and brought out the pistol, which had snagged the sugar sack, and he wiped it off and handed it to Henry.

"Yes, I know it's old, and you can't get shells for it," Charlie said.

"I know, my Father has one just like it. Remington 1858. Cap and ball, my uncle gave it to him. He said it suited him since he wouldn't shoot anyone anyway. Where'd you get an Army-issue pistol, Charlie?" Henry asked without criticism.

"A friend of mine worked with us and ran crews until he got too old. He died on the job not too long ago. That man taught me just about everything I know about working."

"Charlie, this is a Buffalo Soldier pistol," Henry exclaimed, "here, someone scratched, 9th Cav."

"Right. The 9th Cavalry fought Indians and Mexicans, but according to him, they mostly built barracks and Post Offices. He wouldn't let anyone call him a Buffalo Soldier, though. He hated that and let people know it," Charlie replied.

"Charlie, I think your friend was being modest. They did a lot more than being carpenters. My uncle said they were and still are the toughest group in the Army," Henry said.

"Maybe so," Charlie said, "He did say they had to do things no one else could stomach. He also said he killed lots of folks just because someone else told him to. It wasn't anything he was proud of."

While they were looking at the Remington, Walter appeared, dragging Raymond. They gave room, and Walter propped Raymond up against a corner pole. The rain continued falling heavily for almost ten minutes and then quickly slacked to a sprinkle, then stopped. Walter reached into Raymond's bag and tossed the four pistols out into the wet sand, then retrieved small articles of clothing from the bag. He unbuckled Raymond's gun belt and threw it with the pistols. Charlie and Henry stepped out of the dripping shelter, collected the pistols, and walked toward the fire area.

Walter removed Raymond's bloody shirt and used rainwater to clean his friend's body carefully. He put a cloth in the wound to stem any further bleeding. He put a clean shirt on Raymond, buttoned it, unsnapped his slouch hat, and placed it on his head to cover his face. Raymond looked as if he were dozing, leaning up against the pine. Walter slid down to a lying position on the palm log and closed his eyes.

Henry walked over to the other corpses, "This looks like a man and his sons. Look, both the young ones have shirts cut from the same cloth, and don't they look alike?"

"Yeah, they're bloody and not breathing," Charlie snapped, "I ain't never seen so many dead folks in my life. That's another thing Judee said, my friend Judee Coupee, the former soldier. He said, 'The more guns around, the more folks get shot.' He wouldn't allow them around him, even when we were cutting timber."

"You were glad a few minutes ago," Henry added.

"I'm still glad," Charlie said, "we're taking these and the holsters and shells. And you're going to teach me how to use them. Being ignorant is worse than being hungry. That's another Judee saying."

"Well, they're worth money. We might be able to trade them for a ride."

Charlie took a kerchief from one of the bodies and wiped blood and sand from Raymond's gun and holster. Henry collected the other firearms, wiped and holstered them.

"The decent thing would be to bury them, I guess," Henry said.

"With what? You got a shovel in your pocket?" Charlie wanted nothing to do with digging four holes. "Besides, it'll be dark soon. When we get to High Springs, we'll tell someone there, and they'll wire the Sheriff in Lake City. This is Columbia County business."

Walter was up and standing next to them. "We ain't burying Raymond out here, and the Keyes can be buzzard shit in a few days; they were jackasses, the lot of them."

"The Keyes? Who is that? I don't want to know about these people, Walter," Charlie pleaded.

"Well, you're bound to know all about that family, now," Henry mumbled, "the whole dang chapter."

"Assholes, the lot of them," Walter sneered, "Fake aristocrats from Jackson. Raymond knew they were liars and probably thieves..."

Walter's easygoing, happy manner was gone. Charlie sensed that he would never be the same after today.

"They didn't even know who Johnny Witner was!" Walter spat.

He dumped the Keyes' belongings on the ground. A carpet bag contained clothing, underwear, socks, personal items, soap, and a razor. A saddle bag held two boxes of .44 cartridges, chewing tobacco, a wallet, and a leather pouch. Walter shook the pouch; it clinked, and he opened the wallet.

"Just because you got banknotes from Jackson don't mean you belong there," Walter said to no one in particular. He put the cartridges, wallet, and other items back in the saddle bag. Walter put a handful of coins in his pocket and the pouch with the rest of the gold in his shirt, saying, "This ought to be enough to get us back to Mobile, Ray. I'm going to give these boys your pistol; I'm sure your Mama don't want it; she said it would be the death of you."

He then handed the saddlebag to Charlie, "Raymond's got three boxes of .38s over there; I'll get them and his belt for you."

Walter walked to the lean-to, and Charlie turned to Henry. "Looks like two headshots have spilled his cider. He ain't right."

"Charlie, he just gave you everything that can be connected to these men," Henry deadpanned, "three guns, four guns, personal property, and banknotes from the dead guy's bank."

Charlie took the cartridge boxes out of the saddle bag and laid the bag next to one of the Keyes. He walked over to the lean-to, where Walter had retrieved the shells, and stared blankly at Raymond's comb and brush set.

"I'm buying these shells and guns from YOU for $17 in bank notes from Lake City. These men were dead when we got here. Henry works for me, and he didn't even fire his pistol."

"I'm proud to lie and say I killed that bastard," Walter said, chest out, "and we're going back to Mobile. Florida's cured my taste for killing." Walter stood and reached into his pocket and gave Charlie and Henry 5 gold pieces, shaking their hands.

As he shook Henry's hand, he said, "I ain't never shook a colored man's hand, and I'm sorry it took a killing for it to happen. Thank you for saving my life, and I hope to make it up to you one day."

"I'm sorry for your loss, Walter King," Henry said. "And if you think about it, Raymond saved your life by making you carry that heavy-behind frying pan."

"Ray brought it on himself, I guess. He's wanted to shoot something with that fancy pistol since he bought it, and he got what he wanted," Walter answered, "and please, call me Walt." Walter then walked over to the Keyes, selected the wallet and a few items from the pile, spoke to Raymond, and walked into the scrub behind the lean-to.

"Yeah, I believe you're right about him being off-kilter," Henry said when Walter was out of earshot.

"But he was kind of a tart orange, to begin with, wasn't he?" Charlie replied.

"How am I going to carry all this iron?" Charlie was attempting to jam the Keyes' holstered pistols into his bag.

Henry quietly said, "Carrying guns is heavier than you think," the earlier shooting was still heavy on his mind.

Timothy had sewn leather straps into the middle, where Charlie tied Raymond's holstered gun and then struggled to close the two sides. Now, the bag looked overstuffed and was almost too heavy to lift.

"That looks like two pounds of grits in a one-pound bag!" Walter called out, pulling two small trees and more green palm fronds out of the scrub. He produced a small hand ax and began removing small branches from the trees to fashion two poles 1 or 2 inches in diameter. He then removed the fan end of the fronds and tossed them over near the lean-to.

Henry glanced at Charlie, who shrugged and asked quietly, "Where'd that ax come from?"

Walter answered, "Old man Keyes loaned this to me. You can have it when I'm done, but you're going to need a mule pretty soon."

Charlie thought to himself, 'If I had a mule, I'd a never met you,' ruing past decisions. He then asked, "What are you making there, Walter?" He again made eye contact with Henry, who cocked his head and bugged his eyes as if to say, 'Hush!'

"I seen a guy yesterday carrying his gear on a kind of table that he dragged behind him. If we're going to get back to Mobile, Raymond is going to have to keep up. Charley Long, you ought to consider making one, too. Carry that arsenal you're going to be totin' around. If I have to drag his ass to Pensacola, I guess this is the way to do it, and I want to get him stretched out on this thing before he stiffens up. I wonder if there's an undertaker back there in that little town. There's bound to be a train running west eventually, but we can't stay here. I just seen a buzzard looking at us like he was at a barn dance..." Walter continued, using a ball of jute twine he had also borrowed from Mr. Keyes. He tied the palm stems from each pole to the other, creating a travois.

Charlie was unable to control himself, "I see what you're doing there, Walter; I believe you call that a Travis."

Henry had heard enough, slapped a mosquito, rose, and muttered, "Trav-wah," and left to find material dry enough to burn for fire as the day ended and Walter's next speech was starting.

Charlie asked, "You hungry?"

Henry said, "My gut is telling me I am. I must be stretched out after all that food this morning. It's starting to stink around here. We're about to call every fly in the area. What was that green stuff that smoked so much? Does it work?"

"Dog fennel—some folks swear by it. We probably need to drag these bodies near the woods to keep the flies off us. Will you help me?" Charlie replied.

"Yeah, I'm about sick of this place and most of the people in it, especially the dead ones." Henry rose and dragged the skinny Keyes to the other side of the stream opposite where the lean-to was. "How far is the next town, Charlie? Do you think we can make it before dark?"

"Jasper will be along in the morning. It ain't a good idea to be two strangers walking around town after dark; there's too much to get blamed for," Charlie grunted, pulling the older Keyes along. Are you going to get that one?"

"No, I'll go find more firewood and that smoky stuff." Henry walked toward the path coming in, avoiding any more thought of the man he just killed.

When he returned, Charlie had brought their packs over near the fire, and Walter was still under the lean-to. Raymond had been placed on the travois, his head propped up on the log. Walter laid down next to him on the sand, propped his head on the log, and pulled his hat down, ready to sleep.

Henry brought back a double arm's load of dog fennel dropped in a pile, placed a few pieces on the fire, producing a cloud of smoke, and asked Charlie sarcastically, "Don't you want to tell Walter good night?"

"How about I just say it to you?"

CHAPTER 11

Charlie awoke to a blowfly on his lip. He swatted at it and rose quickly. His bags were beside him, and Henry was at the spring. He saw no sign of Walter. The Keyes were hosting a thousand flies. Charlie stretched and yawned as the breeze shifted, inhaling a lung full of fennel smoke. He was gagging and coughing as Henry returned.

"When did Walter leave?" Charlie asked, spitting into the sand.

"Gone when I woke, with nothing to argue about, they got it together and left. It's almost eight; we need to go, too." Henry said. "Walter must have thought you needed that pack more than Raymond. He took the saddle bag, which makes me more comfortable."

Henry was wearing his gun belt, so Charlie opened his bag and untied Raymond's rig. On the third try swinging it around his waist, the pistol fell and landed in the sand.

"Isaiah's blistered feet! Here's your canteen. You need water, don't you? I'll put these other rigs in Raymond's bag," Henry said, wiping sand off the Colt.

Charlie returned and asked, "Where's that short gun? Show me how to load and fire it. Three minutes won't get us much further down the road."

"It makes sense," Henry said. This door opens, and you can slide a shell into the chamber. Every time you pull the trigger, the cylinder spins and puts the next round in the barrel. This paddle moves a rod that pushes empty shells out. Put one shell in, skip one, and put four more in."

"That's only five," Charlie said.

"Yeah, leave the top cylinder empty. That way, when you drop it again, it won't land on the hammer and shoot someone in the foot."

"Funny you should mention that," Charlie said.

"We need to go." Henry turned and walked toward the road; school was over.

Charlie held the holster, swung the belt around, and fastened it. He drew the pistol and cocked the hammer. A buzzard joined four others on the top rail of the lean-to. Charlie thought of Walter's joke about the barn dance and aimed.

Henry was almost out of the clearing and turned to see what was keeping Charlie. He was startled by the roar of Charlie's new pistol. A buzzard dropped to the ground as a second shot hit another, taking flight. Charlie holstered his smoking pistol, collected the two heavy bags, and struggled toward Henry.

"The hell you can't shoot! You must be the desperado gun hand!" Henry shouted.

Charlie grinned and awkwardly passed him, "Don't we need to get gone?"

He was sweating as he turned on the road to High Springs, hoping that Jasper was coming soon. Henry caught up and said, "That might be some of the best shooting I've seen. You dropped the one on the right and the second on the wing! Why act like you've never shot before?"

"That was the second and third shots I've ever taken," Charlie puffed. "I was aiming at the one on the left. I got shook and hit the second one accidentally."

Henry laughed, "Well, you ought to leave that part out when you tell the story."

Charlie was struggling. Raymond's pack was heavy, and the portmanteau was not intended to carry it down a sandy highway.

"GOT D…" Charlie pivoted, "I'm already lathered up!"

He dropped both bags, pulled out his canteen, soaked his yellow bandanna, and laid it into his straw Stetson. He slid the holster to his left hip in a cross-draw fashion. He slid both arms into the backpack. Charlie strapped his bag over his shoulder so it would ride on his hip. He then picked up a better pace.

"He should have been here by now; I bet that greedy rascal waited around the yard and ate twice before leaving. Wad was right; he'd plow a damn field for an extra biscuit. He probably hung around there sweet-talking that other girl that hangs around Melly Duncan. The chubby one, what's her name?"

Charlie heard a wagon coming up behind him, turned, and backed up, falling into a patch of Beggar's Tick. A one-ton wagon barreled his way. Charlie rolled further off the road. Junior Duncan's 14-year-old son Malachi was standing and leaning to pull his mollies back from a full gallop. The newly promoted teamster leaped from the seat and hugged Charlie.

Malachi forgot to tie off the reins and set the brake on the wagon. Charlie instinctively jumped up into the wagon as the mules started to trot off. "Ho, ho, ho, there, gals, you ain't leaving just yet! Dang, Malachi, you going to jump off the wagon without setting the brake? We'd a never caught a lathered-up team running across the county!"

Malachi was up on the seat before Charlie finished fussing.

"Oh, Sweet Jesus, I ain't never been so glad to see nobody at no time like I am to see you, Mr. Charlie! We was coming up the road, making good time. I was just about to have a biscuit my sister Melly give me out behind the Tasty Plate when we come round the bend and saw a white man, dragging what looked like a, a, scarecrow behind him on two sticks like dey be settin a scarecrow up on in the garden, and THAT WADN'T NO SCARECROW! That was a dead white man! But he ain't look dead at first till the white man draggin' him stopped and, OH MY GOD, MR.CHARLIE, the dead man, rolled his head to the side and FLIES COME FLYIN OUT HIS MOUTH!"

"Whoa, Mal, hold up a bit, where is Jasper?"

"He done give 'em both a ride and helped load the dead white man on the wagon! Like he was driving a hearst to the graveyard, Mr. Charlie! He said, 'I'm fittin' to help this man out, but you need to get Mr. Charlie up this road.' And I said, Jasper, I ain't got no idea where he is or where this road goes! I'm ol' follow you back to Fort White! And he say, 'Get yo scary ass down this road and find Charlie, like I told you, and tell him I'll be there before he gets to Alachua!' I'm sorry for cursing, Mr. Charlie, but that's what he said, with his ol mean ass; OH, I'm sorry again, Mr. Charlie."

"Mal, Jasper just turned his rig around and loaded the dead man up on his wagon?" Charlie asked.

"No, sir," Malachi answered and stopped to take a sip of water from Henry's canteen. "The man said he was glad to see us, and he started talking to Jasper about Mobile and the Army, then Jasper said, 'Your man don't look so good.' And the man said, 'Well, he has been better, but he had a rough day yesterday.' And then, he put the handles down, and the dead man's head kinda flopped over, and FLIES COME OUT THE MAN'S MOUTH!"

Henry asked, "You sure the flies came out of the man's mouth?"

"YES, to tell the troof, I wadn't studyin' no flies. I just wanted to get on up out of there." Malachi turned back to Charlie, "And Jasper did, too, 'cause he started to snap his mules and before I could, too, THAT CRAZY MOLE CRICKET done dragged that scarecrow over in front of my wagon! I ain't know what to do, Mr. Charlie! I didn't want to be running over NOBODY, live or dead, on my first day! Then, he went to talk to Jasper and next thing, they was moving ol' Scarecrow up on his wagon!"

"The crazy man didn't say anything else?"

"He did after Jasper said he wanted to see some birds first," Malachi said, "he said he had more eagles than he needed; just please help him get his friend to the next town."

Henry looked at Charlie and said, "Eagles."

"That's right, I think they was trying to be funny, 'cause them ol blue and green flies was so big, but wadn't none of it funny to me. Old Deadeye looking up at me from the back of Jasper's wagon. Just nasty."

Charlie said, "Then you did what Jasper said: find me. How far back was it?"

"A long way, I run them mules pretty hard. I'm just glad I seen you restin'. What now, Mr. Charlie?"

"We'll head toward Gainesville; that's where this meal is going, ain't it?" Charlie replied, reminding Malachi of his job.

"Yes, sir, that's a fact. Y'all need some help with them bags?" Malachi started to rise.

Charlie said, "No, we got 'em, but if you have any more biscuits, we'd take one."

"One's all I got, but y'all are welcome to it. It's from the Tasty Plate."

Henry said, "Got any of that coconut cake from up there?"

Charlie laughed and said, "Naw, he's keeping that a secret!" He then hopped in the back of the wagon next to Henry.

"No, I ain't, Mr. Charlie!" Malachi snapped the reins and started to feel more grown than he had ever felt.

Charlie positioned himself to see the road behind and before him. He estimated time and distance, but there were too many variables. He was grinding it up, pointing his finger to and fro, rolling his eyes up, and mumbling.

"An hour," Henry said, "he'll catch up, stop before you churn into butter."

"That's some mighty quick math straight off the reel, Henry. What makes you so whip-smart?"

"No more than you, but my guess is as close as whatever you get twisting a hole in that sack of meal. He'll be along when he gets here. Unless"

"Unless, what?" Charlie said, "No, I'm not worried about Jasper and all that gold. He goes at everything full chisel, but he ain't no thief." Charlie continued to stew for a while and then moved up to the box with Malachi.

Henry thought to himself, 'If he's not worried, then why did he bring it up? These are some peculiar folks.'

"I heard a rumor there was a Tasty Plate biscuit up here. Is that true, Mal?" Charlie asked.

"It was a while ago, Mr. Charlie, but all that talk about butter made me eat it. Do you believe we'll be back in time for dinner?"

"Somebody found that appetite they lost, Mr. Henry!" Charlie laughed, "Maybe in Gainesville."

Several men in High Springs tried to flag them down, asking if they could catch a ride to Gainesville. Charlie just waved and told Malachi to keep moving through town.

The ride continued with little conversation. Henry was lying between two sacks of meal and was startled by Jasper's loud whistle.

"Move that bucket over to the side! Hot freight!"

Charlie guided the reins to keep Malachi from running into the ditch. Jasper pulled his 2-ton wagon with four Jacks alongside, and they stopped.

"What y'all hauling, corn meal or ugly folk? Both! Charlie Herlong! Where is you gwine?"

"I'm fittin' to make your wagon prettier," Charlie returned. "Mr. Henry! Move up here and let Malachi teach you how to drive mules!" He stepped over to Jasper's wagon.

"That's right, nigga! Breaktime's over!" Jasper called out and snapped his team to pull ahead.

"Where the fire have you been?" Charlie hissed. "Malachi was fittin' to run back home, having a fit. He told me you drive a hearse, now!"

"Calm down, that little nigga was just scared. He ain't never seen nothing dead before but livestock and little critters. What about Jasper? Wadn't you concerned about me?" He laughed, "You ain't gon believe it when I heave it. Call me a liar, but I made more money today than I could have in two months."

"Is that a fact?" Charlie asked, "Tell it all to me. Wadn't you the one telling me you ain't doing anything slick?"

"Look here, Charlie," Jasper's tone got serious, "I did say that, and not for showing out, either. I do what we do, like Mr. Wad say, 'Do the right thing, hear the birds sing.'"

"Jas, every time he says that I wonder what the hell he's talking about. Birds singing, what's that got to do with it?" Charlie laughed, and Jasper smiled.

"Me neither, but we know. Do the right thing."

"Yeah. You're a good man; it's your face I can't stand. Get to the story." Charlie added.

"Quit smellin', I'm tellin'. Me and Lil Junior was riding through Fort White, people hollering at us to take them to Hogtown. Wadn't hearing it. Got about halfway to that little spring with the shelter, and here come this old boy, dragging a dead man on a skid. I slowed down. You don't see something like that every day."

"Ever," Charley answered, "been a lot of that lately."

"Hell, the mules turned and looked. I didn't want none, steady talking about Alabama and the army." Jasper paused, "Crazy varmint! Dragged that contraption in Lil Junior's way, and that was too much for the boy."

"I 'magine it was," Charlie said.

"His Mollies started agitatin', and I pulled this ax handle," Junior checked to make sure it was still there. "I dog-cussed you for making us leave too early to get Wad's scattergun."

"That turned out a good thing, though."

"Sho did, 'cause ol boy come up to me again and said, 'I'll give you two weeks' pay to take us back to Lake City.' I said, 'No, you ain't, cause I'll be looking for a new job tomorrow, that's 4 hours out my way," Jasper seemed to be enjoying the story.

"Four hours?" Charlie asked.

"He ain't know that! I was negotiatin'!" Jasper said. "Then he said, 'How about just to that train station, back there? I'll give you $40!' Now, I'm beginning to think a little harder, you know? I said, 'What kind of money, let me see it.' And do you know that rascal pulled a bunch of Double Eagles out his pocket? 'Now them's the kind of birds I like to hear sing!'"

Charlie said, "You do the right thing?"

"Yes sir, I did," Jasper shouted, and they both laughed.

"Then, I said, 'Give me three, and I'll take you straight to the station.' That booger didn't bat an eye and said, 'Bet.' So, now I got to get Lil Junior settled and down the road. And he wadn't having it! So, I cussed him out some."

"He'll be all right," Charlie said. "Y'all must have had a problem in Fort White."

"What problem?"

"It took too long. You went to Lake City, didn't you? I'm not trying to get into your money, but that kid is going to talk, and ALL of this is going to have to be straight." Charlie explained.

Then, it was Jasper's turn to ask some questions. "Why do YOU have to have it all straight? And who give you a gun to wear? Y'all been doing right? Who killed Walter's buddy?"

Charlie quickly said, "Who's Walter?" and looked into the woods.

Jasper said, "Charlie, you can't lie worth a damn. Did y'all kill that boy, Raymond?"

Charlie said, "How do you know their names?"

"Walter ran his mouth till I dropped him off at Demps...." Jasper abruptly stopped talking.

"OK. I'm going to tell you everything you need, but the less you know, the better. Stick to what you know. We didn't kill Raymond. He shot it out with three men, and when the smoke cleared, Walter was the only one left. We came on them as it was happening. But you do need to tell me about your time with Walter because people saw y'all in Fort White and Lake City. Why'd you take him that far?"

" 'Cause Walter was dealing gold like playing cards. The more he was showin', the more I was goin'!" Jasper sang, telling Charlie he was getting near the truth.

"The guy at the station, Mulberry? He said keep that body downwind till it gets undertook. And you know Dempsey, don't hurry for nobody ..." Jasper said, and then they both said in unison, "Cause they ain't going nowhere today!"

"I said I didn't have time to go to Lake City and then back to Gainesville, even though I probably could. Then he said, 'I'll give you three more!' and brother, I heard them 12 birds singing!"

CHAPTER 12

Jasper stopped in Alachua to water the teams. Alachua had a stalled freight train, so there were fewer travelers to avoid. It held military cargo and several livestock cars. Two cow hunters, Florida's version of cowboys, were cutting six cattle out at a time and watering them in the corral next to the station. Henry was impressed and mentioned how adept they were with whips.

Charlie said, "Crackers have been handling cattle since the Spanish first offered them land to come and settle. They rounded up wild cattle in the woods and sold them to the Spanish from Cuba. Old folks still have that Spanish gold and won't spend it, saying it holds good luck."

"The hell you say, Charlie. That they're so rich they won't spend their good luck money!" Jasper said.

"It's what I've heard," Charlie said, wondering if the doubloons in his bag brought the luck of Walter's gold.

"Well," Jasper said, "I don't know rich folks; I know broke folks. We think spending money is good luck."

"Just the same, go easy flashing that gold," Charlie said.

"I ain't fittin' to hold on to it like a damn rabbit's foot," Jasper said, "I ain't never had one gold dollar, Charlie. I bet I can figure out how to use a hunnert!"

Charlie said, "When we get there, let's get some change to make it easier to spend."

Jasper whistled and announced, "Let's get moving; else, we'll be waiting around for folks to finish dinner."

Jasper replaced his water bags on the side of his wagon and climbed into the box, "Charlie, I believe you ort to take over for Lil Junior. It'd be better if you was driving in town."

He then called to Malachi, "Lil' Duncan! Did you put that water bag back where you got it? Empty? Good man, treat other people's stuff like your own. Come ride with me, Tex! I don't trust Charlie with a pistol!"

"I don't know anyone named Tex," Henry said. "My name is P. Henry Whitfield. Let's keep it cordial and relatively respectful, if you will."

"Nigga, you best climb up here, quick, else we gon' be callin' you, Walker! Ha!" Jasper laughed, "You might better loosen up that hickory stripe shirt and quit gettin' your feelings hurt, too. This ain't no church social!"

Henry walked over to the other wagon, grabbed his pack, shouldered it, and started walking. As he passed, the mules turned their heads and watched him walk by. Jasper snapped his reins hard. Sampson turned and looked right at him.

Jasper said, "The hell you looking at Sampson, let's go!" He snapped the reins again, and the four large Jack mules eased forward, at a walk, keeping pace with Henry. Jasper snapped the reins again to no change of pace. He was astonished and turned to Charlie, who hadn't moved a foot and was still watching.

Jasper pulled the team up and said, "Mr. Whitfield, will you please accompany me up here in the box? I promise to treat you sweet."

Henry removed his hat and grinned, "Absolutely, Mr. Jasper, I would consider it an honor," and swung his pack up into the cargo bed, "I'm sorry, but I missed your last name."

"Hell, it don't matter, ain't nobody ever call me Mister no how. Mr. Gallum? That's some ol' nigga that left town a long time ago." Jasper snapped the reins, and the mules took off, glad to be moving again.

"I'll call you Mr. Gallum if you don't mind. I believe it's respect that you deserve," Henry said.

"Suit yourself, whatever makes you and Sampson happy," he cracked the reins extra hard, and the team picked up its pace.

After a half mile or so, Henry broke the monotonous sound of tack and axles, "Mr. Gallum, how long have you worked for the company?"

"18 years, I reckon. My mama used to help Ms. Evelyn up till the point she passed. Drove her wagon when she went to town, whenever they had big chores to do, my mama was there. Grinding cane, hog butchering, canning vegetables, whatever. Didn't matter. Ms. Herlong was always working. My mama was there, and so was I. They'd set me and Charlie on a rug and tell us to watch after each other. And whip us both if one of us done wrong! To tell the truth, I loved them both, but they was mean as hell. They had us do everything on that place. Workin' was like play for us. When we got old enough, we tended stock and helped the crew. After while, we went to work for the crew, Mr. Judee and them."

"So you and Charlie have grown up together, right?"

"Well, yeah, I reckon so, but when we started to school, a lot of that went away, we was just part of the crew. I ain't got no brothers, and all my sisters are grown and moved off. We never saw Charlie's brother too much; he stayed inside a lot."

"So, what do you think about Charlie going to Jacksonville?"

"Hell, I don't know, just Charlie being Charlie. It seems to me he's got it pretty good right here. He keeps talking about you can't see no elephants here, but I ain't never heard of no elephants in Jacksonville, either."

"I believe he's talking about things he's never seen before," Henry said, "like a metaphor."

"I ain't never seen a metaphor," Jasper replied, "If you see one, you let me know. I ain't never seen nobody let Charlie wear a gun, though. Who give that to him?"

"A man we met."

"He sold it to y'all?"

"Nope, gave it to Charlie and sold him some other guns."

"Sold 'em to Charlie? Charlie don't know nothing 'bout no guns."

"That's not what I saw this morning."

"What you seen?"

"I SAW him shoot a bird perched and another on the wing."

"He bought a shotgun, too?"

"No, sir, with that pistol he's wearing right now."

Jasper turned to Henry. "All right now, Mr. Whitfield. Don't get mad, 'cause I'm just asking ..."

"Go ahead," Henry answered.

"Why is you lying? Charlie ain't shot no damn bird perched, and he damn sho ain't shot one in the air neither! Man, you some kind of bullshitter!" Jasper laughed so loud and hard it startled the mules.

"Geehaw, Sam! Settle them mules down, son," Jasper cried, pulling the reins left then right in short moves. "This rascal is trying to tell me Charlie is a sharpshooter!" Then he snapped them together, and all the mules started bobbing their heads, picking up the pace.

"I saw it this morning. He says he's only shot a gun three times. No one is that lucky," Henry said.

Jasper was still laughing, "Man, he might be lucky, but here's what is. Everybody else around Charlie is UNLUCKY if that rascal is shooting. Buzzards, too! Let me tell you about Charlie, the only time he ever shot a gun."

"Please do," Henry responded.

"You need to know that Mr. Judee used to be in the Army, and he wouldn't allow no guns out when we was workin'," Jasper said, then in a raspy voice, "If they ain't nothing need to be shot, no need for guns."

"No guns. Even if we was out in the woods clearing timber, with bears and gators and snakes, we had one big ole ten gauge, and it stayed in the lockbox up under his wagon. One day, we come across about a dozen snakes, big ol rascals all balled up. Man, they was niggas running all over! Judee said they was fixin' to mate, and he told Charlie to get that shotgun. Charlie was begging Mr. Judee to let him shoot, and Judee loved him some Charlie, so he said ok. Charlie could barely lift that heavy ass gun and aim too. Charlie forgot to cock the hammers, and by the time he got right, snakes was spooked and all over! Judee hollerin' 'Shoot Charlie, Got Damn it!' by the time Charlie shot?" Jasper started laughing and coughing, then choking; he gasped, "He done shot Tommy Forrest in the foot!"

The Jacks slowed to a stop while Jasper recovered and continued, "It was only one ball of #4 buck, but it was enough for Tommy to get rode into town! Everybody was laughing except Mr. Judee, Charlie and of course Tommy. But really, all he cared about was if he was going to get paid for a whole day! Blood wastin' out his heel, and he wanted ALL his money! Ha ha! That's your sharpshooter, Charlie!" Jasper was yelling and laughing so energetically that it made Henry laugh, too.

Henry said, "Yessir! Sharpshooter Charlie never misses!"

"Liar's time is over," Charlie said, pulling alongside Jasper. "Looks like they've kissed and made up, don't it, Mal?"

"I don't know about no kissing, Mr. Charlie, but they have been telling better jokes than we have," Malachi answered.

"That is a fact, son," Charlie said and turned to Jasper. "What's the plan, Dan?"

"Up yonder is Paradise. They usually ain't nobody there. If there ain't y'all need to use the outhouse, you might not get a chance in Gainesville." Jasper said matter-of-factly and cracked his reins.

They pulled into Paradise, a station closed since the demise of a former railroad.

"Charlie, let's water 'em again, just in case." Jasper said, then to the others, "Y'all drop some weight and hurry back."

Jasper and Charlie were watering the mules, and Jasper said, "Charlie, when they come back out here, I'm going to say y'all need to hide your guns in town, and you need to back me up on that."

"They don't enforce that rule, though."

"That's true for white folks, but I want to be clean. I don't want to go in there, nekkid, either. Y'all got any more guns?"

"Yeah, three .44s with full rigs. Why?"

"Gainesville has changed a bit," Jasper said, "Peckerwoods with no job or money, always looking for trouble. Besides, I hear you've found yourself a quick trigger finger!"

With that, Jasper jogged off toward the outhouses as Henry and Malachi were coming back.

"Mr. Charlie, they even had a Wish Book in that dropper back there!" Malachi exclaimed.

Charlie moved Raymond's bag up in the box and removed his gun belt. He took out one of the rigs and handed it to Henry.

"Put that in the box under your seat over there, and Jasper is going to want you to take yours off and put it in there, too. I think that's best." Charlie said, and Henry did as he asked.

Malachi collected the waterbags, emptied them, and put them away as Jasper jogged out and got up in the box.

"What y'all waiting on?" Jasper cried.

All three said, "You!"

Chapter 13

"No, you ain't!" Jasper cried, cracked the reins, and his team broke into a pace.

Once underway, Jasper said, "I see you took off your rig. Can you get to it?"

"It's under here," Henry replied, "Is there an ordinance in Gainesville?"

"A gun law? Yeah, but that don't matter. I ain't ever seen a sheriff. It's an outlaw town, full of peckerwoods with no job and looking for trouble."

"Charlie told me to put one of the pistols under the seat, too," Henry said.

"Under here?" Jasper pulled up to reach under the seat.

"Let me get it, you have a handful of Missouri Mankillers," Henry said.

"Come on, now, they big, but they gentle like me," Jasper said.

"OH, yeah, you're a lamb; you could carry a couple of eggs around in your pocket till dinner," Henry said, chuckling and reaching under the seat.

"They from Jacksonville, bred from draft mares. Sampson came straight from wean when I was still working the barn. I'm as close to him as Charlie, but don't tell either one."

"I've seen one of them before. It looks just like the .45, 'cept that trigger guard. It got that lil' do dab that kicks out the shells?" Jasper asked.

Henry showed it to him, "Yes, sir, it does. It makes a big old bark, too."

Jasper said, "Tie the holsters up under the seat so we can get to 'em."

"If we need to be heeled, why not just wear 'em like men?" Henry asked.

"I don't know about Texas, but here in Florida," Jasper said, "they's lots of crackers think they ain't got shit 'cause niggas take all the jobs, so they see a nigga with a heavy leg, they want to bow up. Problem is if a cracker gets shot ... well, you know how it is."

Jasper pulled up at Boundary St. and waved for Charlie to come around.

"Charlie, you need to lead us into town, and when you get to Liberty Street, you'll know it. There'll be about a hundred wagons and horses going all which ways. Ain't no good way to get across but to stick your nose out there and go. Them Mollies might be timid, but snap the fire out of them, and they'll move. I'll be coming, too," Jasper said.

"If these mules are timid," Charlie asked, "How come we can't follow you?"

"Cause if they won't give us room, you'll get across first. If they run into this big ol' heavy rig, they'll bounce off. They'll stop, by God, or we all will! Charlie, just pick a hole and go! If you're scared, he'll do it, won't you, Mr. Duncan?"

Malachi's eyes got big, and he said, "Uh, they ain't no need, Jasper. Mr. Charlie can do it!"

"I ain't never been scared. Y'all can kiss my foot!" and snapped his reins.

"Hold on there, Chief! Let me give you the paperwork!" Jasper glanced over at Henry and winked, "Chewin' his bit, ain't he? At that corner, you'll see Dutton's sto' cross the street, the loading dock is in the back. Here's your bill for the meal. When we get across, turn left on Union Street and pull into the lot. Can you read, Malachi? Charlie ain't never been that good in school."

"You need to hush," Charlie laughed. You know Mal can't read either."

"Yes, I can!"

"Okay, Old Henry and I will get to the cotton exchange and unload, then we'll see if he can smell fried chicken somewhere that'll serve us." Jasper was in his element. "Ok, y'all straight? Lil Duncan, hold your water when Charlie crosses that street. If you cry, you don't get pie! Charlie, get 'em movin'!"

Charlie snapped the reins, and the mollies moved down Main Street. The traffic was much busier than in Lake City. Charlie wondered about Jacksonville, and it excited him. Liberty Street was broader and more crowded, with two lines of traffic going both ways.

"Oh lawd, Mr. Charlie, you can do it; I don't believe I want to try it today," Malachi said wide-eyed.

"Hush, son, I know what I'm doing. See if you can find the bank while I find a hole," Charlie snapped.

The traffic kept coming, and Charlie saw no hole and muttered, "Look at the dang people."

He started to crack the reins and held up as a carriage changed lanes and barreled past, close enough to make the mules raise their heads.

Jasper whistled and boomed, "Got dang it, Charlie! They ain't never going to be nobody! Go on!"

Embarrassed, he cracked the reins as hard as he could.

Malachi covered his eyes and wailed, "Not now, Mr. Charlie!"

They were off and into the street, horses and drivers pulling up and cursing. Jasper's team was so close that Sampson's head was over the back of the meal wagon. Jasper was right; they stopped, calling all four men just about every name they could be called, both in and outside of polite company.

When they got to the other side, they were whooping and having the time of their lives under an avalanche of profanity and ill will.

Charlie pulled down the block, made the turn onto Union Street, and then left into the lot behind H. F. Dutton's Mercantile. Jasper and Henry continued toward the Dutton Gin and Cotton Exchange. Charlie pulled the wagon to the right near a pump and some troughs.

"Whooooooo!" Charlie exclaimed and looked at Malachi, "How about that, Jack? I feel like trying that again!"

"Oh no, Mr. Charlie, I believe that's enough for right now," Malachi said.

"Yeah, maybe after lunch," Charlie laughed, tied off, and set the brake. I'm going inside. If somebody comes out and says move the rig, just do it. DO NOT let anyone else touch it. OK?"

Malachi answered, "This is my rig, Mr. Charlie. I only let you take it over to see how you do it."

Charlie walked to the pump, removed his hat, pulled out the yellow kerchief, and soaked it. It was cold, like spring water, and tasted sweet, unlike the shallow wells at home. "Hey, Mal, dump our canteens and fill them with this sweet water. I'll be right back."

Charlie walked across the yard and up the broad stairway in the middle of the porch. He opened the ornate doors and entered. Stepping inside caused Charlie to sigh. Cool and shaded, the room had a very high ceiling with a catwalk and doors leading to second-floor rooms around the perimeter. Each door had a transom window, some open with closed doors and vice versa. Downstairs, when his eyes adjusted, he didn't see any food. What he saw were textiles, bolts of fabric, curtains, and all sorts of linen. A large section of the room had women's clothing and accessories. There was an entire wall of notions and tools for household work.

A half dozen well-dressed ladies were browsing about, and then a tall, dark-haired woman appeared before Charlie. Her presence caught him by surprise. In her early thirties, she had deep blue eyes and was impeccably dressed.

"Were you looking for something in particular?" she asked, and Charlie stared like a stunned calf.

"Uh, ma'am?"

"May I help you find something?"

Charlie stuck out his hand, "Hey there, my name's Charlie."

"Welcome to Dutton's, Charlie. My name is Dorotha Dunwoody. What's on your mind?" She didn't extend her hand.

"Um, yes, ma'am, how do y'all keep it so cool in here?"

"We're fortunate to have a modern cooling system, fans." She replied.

"Fans?" He gave her a curious look.

Dorotha cocked her head a bit and then pointed toward the ceiling.

Charlie looked up and saw a dozen huge ceiling fans that drew air up toward the ceiling and out the transom windows.

"How about that? I 'magine some folks would come in just to cool off," Charlie looked into her eyes and got a little swimmy-headed.

"We hope making folks comfortable will help them find what they want," she kept a warm smile. "Is there something I can show you? We have a small selection of accessories for gentlemen."

"Oh, well, yes, ma'am, maybe in a bit. I have a load of corn meal outside, but I don't see many groceries here ..." Charlie was distracted again by this tall, attractive woman.

"Well, not for us; we're a dry goods store." She enjoyed seeing a man flustered for a change and blushed just a bit.

"I see some penny candy over there. I might get some for my helper outside. He's 14, and this is his first day on the job. Can you break a 20-dollar gold piece?" Charlie tried but felt he was digging a deeper hole with every word.

"It's still early. That would empty my till. Maybe you can step across the street to the bank. I'll go upstairs and see if one of our other businesses is expecting a load of meal. Excuse me." Dorotha turned, walked across the room to the stairs, and started to climb. Charlie realized he was still watching her, recovered, and headed for the front door. Dorotha watched him crossing the floor and smiled.

Charlie ran across the street to the H F Dutton Bank. He cashed in four double eagles for an assortment of gold and silver coins all the way down to Picayunes. He put the money in three small cotton pouches.

The time in the bank had settled him down. He breezed into H F Dutton as Dorotha handed a package to a well-dressed lady.

"I'm sure they will be lovely," Dorotha said, seeing Charlie and holding up a finger. She carried a small paper sack and walked over to where some men's hats and neckties were arranged. Charlie followed.

"I found out they'll take the corn meal over at the commissary. It's like a store for Mr. Dutton's employees. I took the liberty of selecting some candy for your helper. There is a good variety here," Dorotha said in a cheerful voice.

"I saw your helper taking care of the mules and the wagon, and he seemed so proud. I might suggest another gift for him if you don't mind," she said to Charlie, her hands folded at her waist.

"Oh, I don't think he would need fancy clothes, ma'am."

"I'm sure, but he's a little grown for candy. How about a Barlow knife, a popular item for boys becoming young men? Or maybe a kerchief to cool off a bit, as you do with yours," she mentioned.

Charlie looked into his hat and said, "Maybe I need another one, too. This one is getting worn."

"We have some regular cotton bandannas in red, blue, and green, and that would be a nice choice for you and him. They're a dime each. None in yellow, though. I admire your style for color," she said.

"Yeah, I like yellow," Charlie said, "Maybe you'll have yellow next time."

"Oh, we have some small yellow scarves made with Sea Island cotton; it's our specialty. Maybe for some special lady you know, so hers will match yours." Dorotha pitched.

"Oh, no, ma'am, I haven't met anyone that special yet. I have lots of friends, though," Charlie answered.

"Well, Charlie, I'm dubious. I'm sure several of your friends would like one." Dorotha offered.

"Well, then, I'm dubious, too. How much are they?" Charlie replied.

"They're $1.50 each," she said, with a slight pivot, "it's a lot, but they're special. I like them."

"They must be. I'll take two; maybe I'll find some lady to give one to. I'll also take four Barlow knives, three bandannas, one of each color, and that bag of stick candy. Is there any Horehound candy in there? I wouldn't say I like it, but I have a friend who needs something that tastes like medicine. Just put one in the same sack."

"I have some horehound candy; let me gather your things," she took long strides back across the floor. "Charlie, would you like these items individually boxed?"

"No, ma'am, just wrap the knives in the bandannas; I'll put one in my pocket. But, yes, ma'am, put one of the yellow scarves in a box and give the other one to me. Your perfume is so nice. What is that?" Butter wouldn't melt in Charlie's mouth when he wanted to be charming.

"Oh, thank you. It's Cuban Violets. We just got it in from Tampa. Would you like to sample some?" Dorotha blushed again.

Dorotha returned, arms full, "Let's put this in a nice bag. It comes to $6.43."

"Did you bring the smell good?" Charlie asked.

"I beg your pardon?" Dorotha stopped wrapping the knives in the bandannas, "Oh! The Cuban Violets! Yes, it's right here."

Charlie opened the box with the scarf and put a few drops in. Then, he put a few drops on the other and hung it around his neck, tucking the scarf into his shirt.

"Oh my," Dorotha said, "your style."

Charlie dropped three quarter-eagles on the counter and handed the box to her. "Take this, Dorotha, I believe you're pretty special," then turned and walked toward the back door.

"Oh! Why, thank you, Mister ...?" Dorotha said.

"Herlong, but call me Charlie, Dorotha!" he said, shaking the door for an extra ring of the bell.

She opened the box, smelled the cologne, and wondered if she had ever met anyone like Charlie Herlong.

CHAPTER 14

Malachi was already at the base of the stairs, and Charlie hopped into the wagon.

"You figured it out already?"

"Figured what out, Mr. Charlie?"

"That we're in the wrong place."

"No, sir, that man up there told me, said we needed to take this to the commiserary or something; I figured you'd know," Malachi answered and snapped the reins.

They passed through a gate into a working yard surrounded by multiple buildings. Malachi pulled next to Jasper's empty wagon, tied off, and set the brake.

Charlie reached into the Dutton's bag and said, "I got some candy at the store. What kind do you like?"

"The kind with sugar in it. If you don't mind, I'll wait 'til we unload at the commissionary. I want to enjoy mine." Malachi said, drinking from his canteen, "You was right, Mr. Charlie. This water is sho good." He offered it to Charlie, who took some, too.

"There are all kinds," Charlie said, handing him the bag. "Leave those brown ones for Jasper; he likes them."

"I don't know why; that's a medicine that looks like candy," Malachi said and jumped, hearing a gravelly voice.

"We've been waiting for you!"

The voice came from a short, sparsely bearded, barrel-chested man wearing a straw Stetson.

"Are you Mr. Charlie Herlong?" The man asked.

"That depends. Are you the undertaker?"

The man chuckled and said, "No, sir, I am not, and as far as I know, it's not your time yet. I'm Norwood Causeland; call me Woody. I run the yard here."

"Pleased to meet you, Woody. I'm looking for the men who drove this wagon," Charlie answered.

"The lumber has been received, and your men are having dinner in the commissary." Woody said, "Their bags and hardware are locked in my office. Would you like to stow yours in there, also?"

"Well, I'd like to offload this meal first," Charlie answered.

"Yes, sir, we'll do that at the commissary, and this gentleman can join the others. Your whole crew are guests of Mr. Dutton, who asks if you will join him for lunch upstairs." Woody politely offered.

Charlie told Malachi, "Go on over there and meet up with Jasper, and when y'all finish eating, meet me right back here."

"Yes, sir, that's a short walk for them, and we'll have your wagon here. We'll feed and water your mules," Woody said as another man appeared and stepped into the box.

"Mr. Charlie, this is my rig; I'll be driving it, right?" Malachi resisted giving up the reins.

"That's up to you, Malachi, but it's ok to let him drive it back while you have dinner," Charlie answered.

"Your other man was the same way. You must train them up well," Woody said as he reached for Charlie's bag. They resisted giving up the wagon and the gear, including their firearms."

Charlie kept his bag, "I bet Gallum and Whitfield were happy to let y'all unload that lumber. But they're probably wondering why they're being treated like hotel guests. Maybe you can tell me what's in store for us, Woody, before I go upstairs for my free lunch."

Woody opened the door to his office, "Mr. Dutton wants you to feel welcome."

"Woody, I'd feel more welcome if I knew what I'm walking into up there," Charlie said as he put his bag down next to the others.

Woody sighed and took a deep breath. "Mr. Herlong, it wouldn't be prudent of me to speak of Mr. Dutton's business. I have pressing issues here. The trains are a problem."

Woody stayed at the open door, so Charlie sat in a chair and crossed his legs.

"Yes, they are. I'm trying to get to Jacksonville. Call me Charlie."

"We are short of teamsters and wagons as all our stock is going to Chattahoochee to pick up finished goods for distribution. My biggest concern is finding four wagons to move freight over to Hawthorne. All I have are some broken wagons I might be able to cobble together. Charlie, Mr. Dutton knows much more than me."

"I see, Woody. Thanks." Charlie winked and stood. Hey, when Jasper gets back, tell him I said he knows all about busted wagons. Maybe he'll have some ideas. Is this the way, those stairs down there?"

"Yes, sir, right up those stairs. They'll lead you to the business offices," Woody said, turned to walk toward the yard, then turned back to Charlie. "You say Jasper is the one that knows freight wagons?"

"If you have something to pull it, he can make it!" Charlie called and headed to the stairs.

Charlie knocked on the door at the top of the stairs, waited, and then opened it. He stepped into a hallway leading to another door at the end. He heard voices get louder as he approached.

"Of course, it's too much! So? We need teams and drivers! If not, you'll walk that stock to Hawthorne. Hell, look out the window; there are wagons and mules all over the place! Now, get out and find us some, and leave that sandwich here. Till you do your job, you don't eat!"

The door opened, and a man came out, dressed like the men he had seen earlier.

"Yes, sir, Mr. Dutton, I'll have one within the hour." The man said and rushed past Charlie.

Charlie stepped through the doorway and saw a half-dozen similarly dressed men putting food on plates and eating, one drinking beer. One was looking out the window at two wagons and six mules being fed and watered.

"Gentlemen, I hear someone wants to buy me dinner up here," Charlie announced, already sure he didn't want to get involved with H.F. Dutton or a bunch of dudes wearing ties.

One of the men, tall and thin with a thin strip of beard from ear to chin to ear, turned to Charlie and said, "I beg your pardon, sir, I don't believe we've met; who are you, and what is your business here today?"

"I'm Charlie Herlong, and Woody Causeland tells me someone wants to see me. Are you H.F. Dutton?" This caused a nervous laugh around the room. All eyes were on the man at the window.

"Why, no, of course not," the man clucked, "don't be ridiculous." The other men chuckled.

"NO, I guess you couldn't be. That would be ridiculous." Charlie walked over to the food table and helped himself to a roll, slice of tomato, and bacon, adding a spoonful of mayonnaise. "Man, we're lucky there was bacon leftover from breakfast."

Dutton turned and faced the room, "I'm Henry Dutton, Mr. Herlong. Would you like some chicken on that roll? I love a good club sandwich. Sanford! Would you make me a club sandwich? Mr. Herlong is making me hungry. And will you draw a glass of beer? Beer, Mr. Herlong?"

"No, thank you, but that chicken sounds good." Charlie said, then to Sanford, "If you have some spring water, I'd love that."

Dutton motioned for Charlie to join him at a café table near the window. The other men in the room shrunk into little cells of conversation as Charlie sat in a cushioned café chair.

"Mr. Herlong, I like the way you handled Halford just now," Dutton said, "how did you know he was a jackass?"

"I didn't," Charlie said, "but I knew he thought he was where he belonged, and I knew I was. One look at that bonnet ribbon beard might have made me a little bold."

Dutton laughed and said, "Indeed. We have some freight that must be in Hawthorne by three o'clock, and we're short wagons and drivers. We wired G.W. Watts, thinking he could contract the freight over there, and he referred us to your father, whom we haven't heard from yet," Dutton was calm and sincere, which belied his tone when cursing out his employee earlier. "When we spoke to your man, he said we needed to speak to you, so we thought we might make this happen today."

"Well, I don't believe you'll hear from my father today, and I'm not sure that we can move the amount of freight you're talking about," Charlie explained.

Dutton countered, "Not so fast. You have four men, and I believe we can get another two wagons within an hour."

"Mr. Dutton, I'm on my way to Jacksonville and rode down with the men to find a way up there. Getting around is getting difficult. My associate, Mr. Henry Whitfield, is affiliated with the Army, 10th Cavalry, and he's going to Tampa. I think it's a matter of some military importance, judging from his efforts to get there. He is a valuable man to have around and has been a great help to us. As you know, the roads are filled with folks unable to travel by train," Charlie was spinning it. "If I may, how valuable is this cargo, and why Hawthorn?"

"You may know, Mr. Herlong, my business is mainly Sea Island cotton, and we have a mill in Georgia where we make finished textiles. Ours is the highest quality cotton, and our linens are gaining a reputation. Henry Plant is interested in using them at his hotel in Tampa. Plant has a railroad line that runs from Tampa through various points north to Hawthorne that he keeps open strictly for Plant business. I need to get as much of our stock into that hotel as I can. I believe it will be a boon for us."

"Mr. Dutton, I believe we can get some stock to Hawthorne, but doing so would have to be seen by my father as beneficial. I'm sure if you sent double the amount of money to my father that you sent to Mr. Watts, he would be satisfied." Charlie said.

"So you'll do it?" Dutton turned.

"I beg your pardon, Mr. Dutton. There are things to consider. Will you pay our teamsters for the extra time on the road? Let's say ... what do you pay your drivers per day? They must get back to Lake City before dark." Charlie was methodical.

"Hell, we pay our white drivers $4.00 a day. I'll pay them half a day's pay." Now, Dutton was bargaining.

"I'm sorry, Mr. Dutton, but I'm fresh out of white drivers." Charlie grinned.

"I'll go $3.00, and I bet they'll be happy, won't they? So, that's it? We have a deal?" Dutton stuck out his hand.

Charlie cocked his head a bit and said, "Well, ..."

"Hellfire! Oh yeah, you need to take care of the soldier and yourself, don't you?" Dutton asked.

"Whitfield is easy. He needs a ride to Tampa. Can he go along with the cargo?" Charlie asked.

"Well, I can't speak for Plant; it's his train. But I'll try to get him in there. And you?" Dutton sat down at his desk. He seemed to smell a deal finishing.

"One horse saddled, and I get to keep a wagon and team to take to Jacksonville. I believe the freight business is pretty good right now." Charlie stuck his hand out, and Dutton slowly extended his.

"Hellfire, son, I'd offer you a job, but I don't believe I could afford you!" Dutton stood and shook Charlie's hand, "Gentlemen, I need you to wire Henry Plant's offices and secure passage for a Dutton Agent to accompany the linens to Tampa from Hawthorne. Start a transfer of sale for a wagon and team, plus a horse and saddle, to Charlie Herlong of Lake City. Halford! See what the hold-up is on those wagons and tie up your bonnet strings! Ha, Ha!"

Charlie turned and went downstairs to give the news and plan the trip.

As he went through the door, he thought to himself, 'I like that H.F. Dutton.'

CHAPTER 15

In the lowland areas of central Florida, people handled livestock in many ways. During his forty years, Tiger Driggers had tried every way at least once. His family had been making their living with cattle and horses since arriving 150 years before. They came from what became Southwest Georgia to avoid Europeans doing what they've always done, acting as if they owned it. That's how Tiger would tell it; he wasn't sure.

He had been told he was a member of the Hitchiti tribe, though he didn't feel like an Indian nor knew what being an Indian felt like. He had been told that his great-grandfather was Cuban, who had come to buy cattle and stayed until he died. His grandmother, Tav Rodriguez, would spit on the ground when referred to as a Seminole. She was Hitchiti. She was still bitter and angry over her husband, the son of escaped enslaved people, taking a deal from the US government giving him land in the Arkansas Territory. Tiger's grandmother refused to accept the offer, reminding her husband that they had already been promised the land they were standing on forever. Tiger also remembered her saying, "Yaht-kitis-nognee ca-wah-yee yu si," which he was told meant, "What idiot would fall for it twice?"

The Rodriguezes were Hitchiti, 'The Mean People,' so confrontation could be met with more intensity than with others.

Tiger's mother, Lakni Rodriguez, was born soon after her father left for Arkansas in 1838. They supported and fought with Micanopi, and when Micanopi was captured, they returned to their home near the Withlacoochee River. To avoid removal to the Indian Territory, they asserted their Cuban and African heritage to remain in Florida. This was an irony not lost on them, their family, or the others in their community. Throughout the 1840s, 50s, and into the '60s, Tav and Lakni would catch hogs and cattle that grew wild in western central Florida. They were excellent equestrians, riding Marsh Tacky horses or hybrids. They would often work cattle drives to southwest Florida, even after the railroads had forced cattle barons to fence their land. They used trails through swampy land, long forgotten by Indians and white cow hunters.

Tiger was the product of a long drive to Punta Rassa, where Lakni, whom the whites called Lacey, met a cow hunter from Kissimmee. During the post-drive celebration, Tiger was conceived. Lacey and Tav recalled his being tall, white, and handsome, so Tiger assumed he looked like his father. Tsitaga Rodriguez worked livestock from a very young age and soon supported the three of them by himself. Tsitaga's name morphed into a more anglicized pronunciation. That didn't bother Tiger much. As far as he could tell, people hate poor folks, regardless of where their ancestors came from.

Tiger preferred to work alone and depend on himself because good, dependable help was hard to find. Today, he thought he might need to hire a hand or two as his string of horses and small herd of cattle were expanding. Tiger didn't know why there were so many beasts running wild these days, but he didn't want to jinx it by asking dumb questions to which he had no answer.

He was currently working with a hobbled horse, a large bay gelding reasonably easy to handle. Tiger assumed it was due to the three-inch US brand on its left shoulder and another he didn't recognize on its left hip.

He set up a makeshift stock chute between four trees, two at the front of the animal about 18 inches apart and two more offsets down the sides. He tied straight poles horizontally to keep the horse in the chute. A flour sack was placed over the horse's head to help calm him.

He retrieved a branding iron from a fire. The iron was shaped in a large C to place on the US brand to signify the horse had been condemned or removed from service. He had two more horses he had retired the previous week. Tiger was amazed he just found them in the woods, near the edge of the prairie. They were easy to catch, not requiring the services of Tiger's dogs. Moon and Shine could herd or collar any animal that happened to appear in their vicinity. They were black mouth curs, good but mean, and they seemed to fear nothing, man or beast. They had killed several black bears and provided meat for Lacy's village near the Withlacoochee. They were loyal to Tiger, following his direction to a T, which he gave through whistles, grunts, yells, and occasional profanity.

This horse had already been branded and started to fidget the moment Tiger brought out the iron.

"Hey, don't worry, I was just cooling it off," Tiger cooed.

He tightened the rope around the horse's neck and side poles. Tiger showed a short stick of wood the size of the branding iron.

"Ok, there, Sarge, here it is nice and cool," and placed it on the horse's right shoulder.

Tiger then pulled the hot iron from the fire and pressed it against the horse's flesh. The horse started bucking and pulling the ropes, gaining a few inches with each lurch. The ropes stripped the bark off the tree and became looser, bending the tree over. The horse was out of the chute, still hobbled, and careened into the string of horses and mules nearby, scattering them in every direction.

Moon and Shine, seeking to curb the disturbance, each grabbed an ear of the hobbled horse and pulled back until the large gelding calmed down.

"I don't need you collarin' THAT horse, you dumb sumbitches! Go get the others!" Tiger whistled as loud as humanly possible, causing Moon and Shine to race off to catch the fleeing horses.

Tiger sat at the edge of his prairie, watching his nine cattle grazing contently. He walked across the meadow to a stand of Bay Laurel and Palm trees that had grown since Lake Alachua drained into the Alachua sink, stranding a flat-bottomed steamboat. The stand of trees, the steamer, and Tiger had taken up residence there since. He planned to enjoy his homestead till the lake filled again or some jackass from Tallahassee made him get out. The vessel was flat-bottomed and had two levels. The lower level was designed for freight and provided a breezy platform during the hottest months. The upper level had windows and rooms that could be closed, warm shelter during the rare inclement weather of Alachua County. Tiger stayed on the lower level, which he called the porch. This dwelling was luxurious if compared with any place his family had ever lived in.

Tiger spent half the year providing service to ranchers throughout Florida. The spring still offered some actual cow hunting, finding calves and their mothers deep in the woods and swamps. Herd round-ups and drives to railheads in North Florida would happen during the autumn months. Tiger hadn't driven any cattle further than 75 or 80 miles since he was a teenager. He spent most of his time tending his large garden, which carried an assortment of vegetables, ornamental plants, and flowers that he sold to vendors in Gainesville. He often thought that some folks had way more money than sense. Plants could be reproduced or outright foraged from the woods in the immediate area.

Tiger checked his garden for water and the leaves for insects. He found a few hornworms. He filled a can and watered the ornamental plants on the porch. Sacred Heart of Jesus plants were a popular seller. Tiger found that anything related to religion, race, or bloodshed would sell. He had a dozen or so Wandering Jew plants growing in hollowed-out palm trunks: Cherokee Bean, Blood Sage, Button Snakeroot, and Bloody Cranesbill. Flowering plants that grew wild in the swamp were placed in clumps wrapped in burlap.

Tiger sat on a bent willow rocker and poured rum into a jam jar. He hoped the dogs wouldn't come back while the florist was there. They annoyed the man, who only made it worse by acting so scared. Tiger wondered how the man would react if he came upon a bear on the trail. The florist preferred to pick up the plants, and that was curious to Tiger.

Tiger saw Moon and Shine coming up the trail from the Palatka Road, each with a halter tie in his mouth, leading jack mules. He hustled out to them, pulling a picket line to tie them off. The dogs ran straight back up the trail. He could hear them barking and hoped they hadn't gotten on the scent of game, as he needed that stock and was expecting the florist. That and he wasn't in the mood to start a hunt of his own this late in the day.

The barking wasn't aggressive, almost playful, and then faded. Tiger then heard the florist urging his horse at full gallop to slow down.

Virgil Coke finally slowed the mare and came to a stop at the porch.

"Mr. Driggers, I wish you could do something about those dogs. They bother my Sophie something fierce!"

"Well, they're probably wondering why you come way the hell out here when I have offered to bring them to you," Tiger answered.

"Mr. Driggers, I prefer to come and pick them up," Coke answered.

"Well, then you spend the whole time out here crying about my dogs," Tiger said, "They live out here, they're just saying, 'Howdy.' There must be some other reason you do this to Sophie every week."

"Well, truth be told, Mr. Driggers, I would rather save the money," Coke said flatly.

"Well, truth be told, Mr. Coke, I'm having a hard time making ends meet, and I need you to pay more. I understand times are hard, but I'm spending more time with these plants, and it's cutting into my cattle work."

Tiger remained seated on the freight deck as Coke stood flatfooted on the grass. Coke looked flat, and Tiger thought he had just killed his golden goose.

Coke's face began to turn red, and he blurted out, "How much did that son-of-a-bitch offer you? The last time I came out here, I saw him trying to follow me. That's why I was so late. How much? I'll double it." Coke was livid and sure that someone was trying to steal his supplier. "That's why I don't like you delivering to my store. The horticulture business is cutthroat! Tell me! How much did Wesley offer you?"

Tiger struggled to keep a straight face. He was just curious as to why Coke would come all the way out for nothing. He hadn't even thought about raising the rates. Right now, he was more interested in how serious Coke was about doubling them.

"Mr. Coke, I'm a little insulted. I'm glad my dogs aren't here right now cause they would be, too, I think. I'd never heard anyone say horticulture until you just did, and I ain't never cut nobody's throat in my life. I wouldn't discuss business with anyone until I spoke to you first. That's just the respectful way to do business, I believe," Tiger then added, "If you still want to do business with me, I'll be happy to accept your offer of double your current rate without considering anyone else. Now, let's get your wagon loaded."

Coke wasn't sure what had just happened, but he began loading, relieved that he could continue to be the exclusive retailer of Tiger Driggers' goods.

Tiger wasn't exactly sure, either, but he was sure that he had just doubled his income on plants and flowers, and he thought it was because his dogs were a pain in the ass. He sat down again and had another dose of rum.

Chapter 16

Elbows on the back of the bench, feet on the buckboard, sticky face and hands, Malachi was on the edge of sleep. Charlie and a stable hand hoisted three bags up into the two-ton wagon.

Malachi stomped both feet, pulled imaginary reins, and said, "Whoa!"

"How was lunch?" Charlie asked, "Did you get enough to eat?"

"Mister Charley, I sho did. They had beans and rice and squash that taste almost as good as Miss Darla's," Malachi gushed, "and sausage! They give me an extra piece."

"Enjoy it while you can," Charlie said. "I believe these folks might be puttin' on the dog for us."

"I don't know ... that lady was saying to Mr. Henry he could eat like this every day if he wanted to," Malachi said.

"I bet she did," Charlie chuckled, "where is our handsome friend?"

"He in yonder trying to buy a horse and trade eagles for it," Malachi said, shaking his head, "The man done told him the horse don't belong to him."

Henry walked out of the stable, scratching his head.

"I hear that gold is burning a hole in your pocket, Henry!"

"I can't find anyone to take it off my hands," Henry said. I guess it's not as lucky as that Spanish gold."

"Well, it might be, yet." Charlie said, "Which horse were you looking to buy?"

"The only one. I offered the hand $100," Henry said, "for a nice, grey quarter horse gelding. It's just perfect for the 10th and my Uncle's Troop. That palafrenero in there wouldn't budge. Can't buy a dang horse thief around here." Henry joked.

"Well, he's bound to run back out here in a bit and try to get it from you, I bet." Charlie laughed.

A man from upstairs walked past them toward the stable. "You say the only horse in there looks good?" Charlie asked.

"Doesn't matter, he's not for sale." Henry deadpanned.

"Maybe you can borrow it," Charlie said as he moved toward the wagon barn.

Charlie poked his head into the shop where several men were working. He didn't see Jasper, but he could hear his voice.

"Hold on, Mr. Woody! There's one mo nut down here being hardheaded! S-S-S-S-S-T! That's it. OK, Mr. Woody pull it on up!" Jasper was under a wagon with two broken axles.

Another man pulled a chain hoist, and the whole freight deck rose into the air. Jasper was up and trying to drag the undercarriage off to the side.

"Got damn it, y'all goin' to watch him outwork every damn one of you?!" Woody yelled at the others standing around, watching in amazement as Jasper was slowly moving it by himself.

"Oh, hey, Charlie! We ain't fittin' to go right now, are we? We 'bout to put this box on that Concord over there. See that busted-up stagecoach? It's gonna be somethin', man, I'm talkin' 'bout fast! It's gonna get gone, ... boo-getty, boo-getty!" Jasper walked toward Charlie, who motioned him outside. Jasper looked back and said, "Hey, don't bust them suspension studs off that Concord; they'll be handy for tying down freight."

Charlie walked out into the noon hour sun and saw Henry pacing a grey quarter horse around the yard. Henry then turned the horse through the entrance onto Depot Street, which made Charlie jump.

"Hey! Henry!" Charlie whistled.

"He'll be back, Mr. Charlie," Malachi said, sitting up in his seat. All his stuff is settin' right here."

"He better; that horse ain't paid for yet." Charlie said as he turned Jasper, "We need to get these wagons loaded up and ready for the road."

"What you been up to," Jasper said, "You been wheelin', dealin' or stealin'?"

"I don't want to say too much; there are still cards to turn over." Charlie answered, "But I did get y'all a present."

"What did you get us?" Malachi asked, excited. "I like working with you, Mr. Charlie."

"Calm down, Lil' Junior," Jasper said, "Find out how much it cost."

"Not one sprig of nutgrass to you," Charlie said, "and you might make a dollar."

"What color do you like, Mal?" Charlie asked, reaching into the shopping bag Dorothy had given him. "I got red, green, and blue."

"Red"

"I'll take green, just like US money," Jasper said.

Charlie handed them the Jack knives wrapped in the bandannas and said, "I reckon Henry gets Army blue."

"Hey, thanks, Charlie," Jasper said, "I been lookin' for another knife. What we got to do for it?"

"Stop it. I might not be seeing you for a while is all. But I might have a deal for you, I hope," Charlie turned his head to an office type walking toward him. "This might be the news I'm looking for right now."

"Mr. Herlong?" The man held out a yellow envelope, "I have a wire from Lake City."

"Lake City?" Charlie wondered, "Certainly not my father..."

Western Union

Lake City, FL – Herlong Company

Gainesville Fl – Charlie Herlong private c/o HF Dutton Co

Received payment for freight moved 16 miles to Hawthorne. Carry on making company decisions provided they triple our regular rates, like this. Will notify family Duncan boy will be home tomorrow. Would this be an Elephant? Continued good luck.

DW Herlong

"Well, you just going to stand there, Mr. Fancy Dan Telegram Man?" Jasper was eager to get back to the wagon building. "Here come Cowboy Bill Pickett."

Henry rode in fast, drew up just in front of them, then backed the horse up several steps and turned it in a circle.

"How do you like my horse?" Charlie asked.

"Oh, this is your horse?" Henry dismounted, "He's pretty high-spirited. Can you ride?"

"Not like that!" Jasper shouted, "Man, you MUST BE Bill Pickett!"

"He's part of the deal I'm putting together," Charlie said, "Ok..."

"Give Mr. Henry his present, Mr. Charlie!" Malachi shouted.

"Yes, sir, Charlie, a trophy for stealing your horse!" Jasper was wound up, too.

Charlie sighed and reached into his bag, "Ok, then y'all going to let me talk?"

"We got one, too, Mr. Henry; only ours was wrapped in a different color! I ain't never got a present just for working!" Malachi said.

"Oh, a jackknife, why thank you, Charlie," Henry said, "and we all got one, like The Three Musketeers. Well, that's something. It smells good, too. Where'd you get this, Charlie?"

"That's Charlie smelling sweet. What'd you eat for dinner, Charlie?" Jasper jumped on.

"Mr. Charlie, come out that sto smellin' like that," Malachi offered, and all three leaned in and took a smell.

"Y'all need to back up off me," Charlie cautioned, "before I give you something to smell. Can I talk now? First off, Henry, you don't need that horse cause I believe you'll be riding a train down to Tampa. We have to get over to Hawthorne to catch it, and we're short on time. Your fare is us hauling freight over there."

"That puts us back at the yard mighty late," Jasper said, now serious, looking down at shadows. "It's about one o'clock now."

Charlie held up the telegram and said, "Well, evidently, Dutton has told Daddy about it 'cause this says y'all might not go back till tomorrow."

"Tomorrow?" Malachi turned his head and raised his eyebrows. "My Mama is expecting me home this evenin'."

"Don't worry, your Daddy will tell her." Charlie cautioned.

"Mr. Charlie, it don't matter what my Daddy say. My Mama said, 'You come back to me this evenin' just the way you left.' Y'all don't know my Mama, she ain't playin'," Malachi said, worried.

Charlie tried to reassure Malachi, "She just wants you to be safe and do the right thing, that's all."

Jasper laughed hard and said, "Damn, Charlie, you fittin' to get Junior, Lil' Junior, and a few more Duncan asses whipped!"

Henry put his hand on Malachi's shoulder and shook his head a bit.

"You ain't helping me here." Charlie continued, "You just tell your Mama that Jasper made you, and she'll whip him."

"Shoot, she come up on me, she gon' catch a dose…" Jasper was mumbling, and Charlie cut him off.

"Anyway, Dutton needs four wagons of freight in Hawthorne and is supposed to have two more for us. Henry, I'm assuming you can drive a wagon. We already found out you can ride. You two are getting a bonus for the extra trouble." Charlie, satisfied with his delivery, leaned back against the wagon. The others stood there quietly; then, all three started peppering Charlie with questions for a solid minute, all speaking at once. Charlie listened to them all, eyes darting from one to the other. Then they stopped.

Charlie took a deep breath, "This is what I know. We're taking as much freight as Dutton wants to Hawthorne and putting it on a train. Henry, you may not get on the train; that part is between Dutton and Henry Plant; he owns the private train we're meeting. Now, if you don't ride the train, you can take the horse and head to Tampa. Does the Army make you bring your horse? If they don't, sell the horse and saddle and wire half the money to me, Western Union, in Jacksonville. You're welcome. Malachi, didn't I tell you not to worry? Yes, we will try to eat supper and breakfast if we need to. You and Jasper will take your wagons back here, then to Lake City, empty if we don't find freight that needs to go there, but I bet something will need to be moved. And no, you can't go to Tampa. I can't blame that on Jasper, and I don't want to fight your mother; I hear she fights dirty. I'm just kidding, son. I'm sure she fights fair. Jasper? I don't know. William Plant owns the railroad, and he has a big ol' fancy hotel in Tampa, where the freight is going. I don't know how the wagons are going to get back from Hawthorne, but it ain't going to be me; I'm headed to Jacksonville. What's in it for me? One wagon will belong to Dutton, and the other one will be mine, along with the team. I hope it's decent. That's all I know and most of what could be. Anything else? Whew."

Malachi raised his hand like he was in school, which he was. "Uh, Mr. Charlie, what's a bonus?"

Jasper said, "Outstanding question, Mr. Duncan!"

"It's something extra for doing a great job, and when we get the freight on the train, you'll get three dollars," Charlie said.

"For me? In my hand, not to my Daddy, my money?" Malachi couldn't believe it.

"You're earning it, but we have to get the freight on the train," Charlie said. Are you in?"

"Yes, SIR, I am!" Malachi said.

"Can I borrow your horse? I have some business," Henry said.

"We have some here, too. Hurry back, we're on the clock."

Chapter 17

As time moved past the dinner hour, more workers appeared. Two employees fought over the use of a cotton wagon. Dutton must have dispatched every freight wagon to Chattahoochee. The railroad dysfunction was affecting all sorts of businesses.

Charlie saw the dude Dutton cursed out come through the front gate. He was driving an ancient, wobbling wagon, being pulled by an even older mule with the tell-tale slumping back of age.

Charlie told Malachi, "Get Jasper."

The driver pulled up next to Charlie, and the mule groaned and nickered. The mule then did something Charlie had never seen: He started flapping his lips. "Sounds like your mule has something to say," Charlie remarked to the driver.

"He was asking me where I'm going to be working tomorrow," the man said.

"Well?" Charlie asked, "What do you say?"

"I don't speak to jackasses," the man said, "I only work with them."

As the man walked away, Charlie said to the mule, "He said, 'Somewhere else.'"

"Charlie Herlong, where is you gwine?" Jasper sang as he walked up, saw the mule, and continued, "I hope it ain't nowhere on this shaky-assed wagon!"

"No sir, I most certainly am not," Charlie said, "I'm fittin' to go upstairs and make sure this ain't the one we're expected to haul freight on. But, just in case, see if it can be tightened up a bit."

"I'll let one of them work on it," Jasper said, "If any of us touch it, they'll say it's ours. We want the one we been making in there. The Concord Buckboard; I'd buy it myself if I thought I could afford it."

"Oooh, he stank, too," Malachi said, walking away and waving his hand in front of his face.

"This mule is sick, Charlie," Jasper laughed, "flapping them lips, saying 'Jesus, take me now!'"

"Malachi, if Mister Woody comes out here to take our wagons to be loaded," Charlie said directly to Malachi's face, "you stay with your rig and these bags. Let them drive if he says so, but you stay with the bags and the wagons. Understand?"

"Yes, sir."

Charlie turned and walked to the stairs. He looked back, grimacing, worried, as Woody arrived at the wagons. A shop hand jumped into the box of the old wagon and tried to move it toward the shop. He snapped the reins once, twice, to no movement from the mule. He then jerked the reins violently and snapped again, and the mule finally moved.

Charlie paused before entering Dutton's office.

"Get over to the dry goods warehouse and see to filling the order for the Tampa Hotel. And you stay over there until you hear from me, and Wilson, if you don't hear from me, you keep going back there every morning until someone fires you. Do you understand?" Dutton bellowed. "Go ask Causeland if he has wagons to load and get them over there."

Charlie stepped in as Wilson passed, with Dutton following.

"Oh, Mr. Herlong, just the man I was looking for." Dutton said, "Impeccable timing. I'm going to check the telegraph, stay right here. Are you still hungry? Have Sanford prepare something."

"I'm always hungry," Charlie said, "and please, call me Charlie."

"Me, too!" Dutton said, "And you can call me Mr. Dutton," and went down the hall.

"We have salami, cheese, and German mustard that just came in from Savannah, Mr. Herlong. Do you like rye bread?" Sanford asked.

"If it don't taste like whiskey," Charlie said, "I'll try it."

"We have Rye Whiskey, too," Sanford said.

"Oh, no, thank you," Charlie said, "I need to keep my wits around here."

"Yes, sir, we all do. I believe you'll like this sandwich," Sanford said.

Sanford placed the sandwich on the café table by the window. Charlie took a bite of the sandwich, which was unlike anything he had ever tasted: the spicy, fatty slices of meat with cheese and vinegary mustard. He chewed and watched Wilson speaking to Causeland, who walked into the barn. Wilson directed Malachi to step off his wagon, but Malachi resisted. Wilson tried in vain to grab him, but Malachi would scoot to the other side of the seat as Wilson tried from each side. Wilson climbed into the box, and Malachi jumped in the back. Henry rode up, grabbed one of the Mollies by her harness, and caused the wagon to lurch.

Wilson fell off the side of the wagon, and Malachi leaped into the seat, took the reins, released the brake, and drove the wagon in a semicircle.

Causeland trotted up with a second man and shouted, "Wilson! What the hell do you think you're doing?"

"He was tryin' to take my rig, Mr. Woody! Mr. Charlie say don't let nobody take it unless you say so!" Malachi said defiantly, "And for me to stay with it!"

Henry was up in the two-ton wagon, reaching into Raymond's bag and retrieving one of the Russian pistols. He put the pistol into a new saddlebag hanging on the pommel of the gelding's saddle.

"Your man seems very capable." Dutton was standing behind Charlie.

"Yes, sir, both of them," Charlie said, "Did you hear from my father?"

"As a matter of fact, I did. I'm hoping he can help us with moving freight from Chattahoochee." Dutton replied and moved to his desk, "Please, have a seat, Charlie."

"Mr. Dutton, I'm more concerned with our arrangement from this morning. I believe we are running out of time and still short two wagons."

Dutton held up a yellow telegram sheet. "Well, we have a little more time due to events in Tampa last night. There was some trouble with the colored Army down there, and it delayed the train. We now have until tomorrow at three. Plant's train leaves when he says so."

"So, they might leave tomorrow morning if Mr. Plant gets a notion to," Charlie said, "I'd like to get over there as soon as possible in daylight. So, I'd say we should leave this afternoon and spend the night in Hawthorne. I'm assuming you have an arrangement with a livery over there. That way, we can load the freight, send the Herlong wagons home, leave your wagon at the livery, have Mr. Whitfield settled on the train as a Dutton Agent, I suppose, and I can be on my way to Jacksonville with that grey gelding from your stable tied to the back of my wagon. I suppose the only issue that needs to be decided is the wagon and team I am supposed to receive." Charlie's mind was racing to keep track of everything he needed to.

Dutton laughed, "Charlie, I don't know why your father is letting you go to Jacksonville. Are you expanding the business there?"

"I'm hoping to expand MY business over there," Charlie nodded.

"What business is that?" Dutton was intrigued.

"Well, it depends on if I get stuck with that rickety wagon and that Confederate army mule down there." Charlie grinned.

Dutton laughed again, "Touché, Charlie. It seems to me that your father would want you in Lake City, helping run the company so that he could relax a bit." Dutton was buttering Charlie up, and Charlie knew it.

"Do you have any sons, Mr. Dutton?"

"Why, yes, Charlie, my son Henry will be attending Vermont University this fall," Dutton said with pride.

"When are you planning on turning the company over to him?" Charlie asked, knowing it was bold, but sometimes Charlie could not resist.

"Ah, I understand. Your father isn't quite ready for the porch, either? That's an excellent point. But that doesn't mean I'm going to give it away in the meantime. As far as I remember, our agreement was for a wagon and a team. You weren't very specific, and right now, that's the only wagon and team I have available. The rolling stock I have must stay here to operate on the premises, at least until the wagons I have sent to Chattahoochee return, and we don't have that much time." Dutton was enjoying this, and Charlie could tell, but he saw the opening he needed.

"Mr. Dutton, you don't have a team available for me, either. You have one mule that may have fought at Olustee and a wagon whose tracks look like a rat snake left them. And with all due respect, I sincerely doubt either will make it to Hawthorne, and that does neither of us any good. The point here is to get as much of your Sea Island linen to The Tampa Hotel as possible until the trains start running again. You have a wrecked Concord Coach down there; I'll take the chassis, whatever freight box is lying around, and two mules that are less than 20 years old. That way, you can keep General Lee and that wagon so your man Wilson can run errands in it."

"OK, you can have both wagons, yes, both. If Wilson's is that bad, I don't want it either. And all three mules." Dutton sounded like he was giving up.

"And?" That's all Charlie said; he could hear Jasper's voice in his head, though, 'What's in it for you?'

"Yes, there's more," Dutton said.

Charlie wondered if Dutton could hear Jasper's voice, too.

"I need you to go to Tampa." Dutton just let it lay there.

"Me? What for?" Charlie hadn't expected this, "No, sir, this is way more than our agreement. Tampa is on the other end of the state!"

Charlie was angry that he had lost his composure. Dutton just sat there, so Charlie decided to do the same thing. Wait him out.

"We do have an agreement, Charlie. One that has already been paid in full to The Herlong Company." Dutton's expression had not changed.

"That's okay with me. Let's load up the wagons and go," Charlie said. Henry can ride to Tampa."

"It's not that simple." Dutton said, "The disturbance in Tampa was a full-scale battle between white and colored soldiers, including many civilians, lots of blood, and property damage. It's not a safe place for Whitfield."

"It doesn't sound like a safe place for Charlie, either!" Charlie raised his voice.

"And it's especially not a safe place for my linens." Dutton leaned forward, "Let's understand each other, Mr. Herlong. My, no, OUR linens, and they are ours, by the way, since OUR contract has been verified by the Herlong Company's receipt of payment and your father's written confirmation. As for our agreement, your saddled horse could be the mare that foaled that old mule we were referring to earlier. And your wagon could be a cart and two goats. For the sake of both companies, we need to come to some resolution right now because I am not the kind of man to wait."

"We swimmin' in deep water, now, ain't we?" Charlie said quietly.

"Well, I'd say wading. I shouldn't have sent all of my security to Chattahoochee, or we wouldn't be having this meeting. And you would still be looking for a ride to Jacksonville." Dutton said, "This situation can be managed. I wouldn't ask you to do this if I didn't think you could handle it, and I very much need to get it done."

"Look, I ain't no tough guy, but Henry is. He has to go with me. I ain't dying for your linen, no matter how soft it is."

"Agreed, except you will protect my linen. I think you can avoid death, especially if you can keep Mr. Whitfield from throwing white men out of wagons," Dutton added.

"We both get badges and documents from you and Plant, whatever you can put together, for the trip there and back. I want to be able to buffalo any jack-leg train conductor or hotel clerk we run into. I want two NEW shotguns and two boxes of shells just in case some desperado needs pillow shams. And $150 for expenses in Tampa or to buy another horse or two mules or anything."

"Charlie, how would you like to see Tampa?" Dutton spit it out like a gift, then stuck out his hand.

"I'll take the cash or gold." Charlie did not extend his hand.

"Char – lee, don't pout. This is a good deal. I'll have Halford bring you the badges, documents, shotguns, and $150 in gold over at the dry goods store. Do we have a deal or not?" Dutton extended his hand again.

Charlie reluctantly stood up and said, "I don't know why we're shaking hands; this deal changes when the wind blows."

"Because that's the way gentlemen behave, son. I'll see you when you get back." Dutton said as Charlie turned to walk out.

"You might, but that ain't no part of our deal." Charlie walked out of the room, understanding now what Woody had said about it being a snake pit.

Charlie made his way to the shop area, looking for Woody Causeland, hoping to influence the mule selection. He looked around and saw three white men watching Jasper and two black stable hands putting the fourth small wheel on the wobbly wagon.

"What made you decide to work on that turd?" Charlie asked.

"Woody said this wasn't staying here, it's what we got, and wouldn't none of them rascals over there work on it with us." Jasper said, continuing to work, "I reckon they only work with niggas when Woody makes them. Is this ours?"

"So, it seems. Those wheels look funny, don't they?" Charlie asked, seeing Jasper give him a look. "I'm just saying, I know you're having to use what you can get."

"What you need to be looking fo is them steel hubs and skeins." Jasper scolded, "We got these wheels off a cotton wagon, so it'll be a low rider, but it'll get to where we going."

"You hear how that nigger is talking to that white man?" A white man leaning against a tool bench cracked, "I can't figure out which one is the boss and which one is the nigger."

"If I were you, I'd find something to do before I find something for you!" Charlie barked. "As a matter of fact, the first two that find me another cotton wagon get to keep their jobs, and the third one gets to mine phosphate."

"How close are we to being done?" Charlie asked, then whispered, "What are they doing now?"

"They gone! I 'magine to get a dang cotton wagon," Jasper said and started laughing, "Hell, I started to go, too. You sounded like Bob Wadby!" Which made all four of them laugh.

"We need to go, Jas," Charlie urged, "Who knows how far that old mule is going to make it before we're looking for another? Where's Woody?"

Jasper said, "Blacksmith. We done," and turned to the men helping him, "Jake, Willie, one of y'all want to help that mule over here, so's we can strap him up?"

"Jasper, we put him on some feed mixed heavy with chopped grass and peanut hay. We put a couple of bales in the back. I believe that mule's been eating potatoes. He'll perk up!" Jake said as he headed out the door.

"It don't matter to me, I ain't going to be sitting behind him, Charlie is," Jasper said.

"Well, then we'll clean him up a bit so we don't get run off, too!" Willie laughed.

Charlie headed out and looked around for the Blacksmith shop, thinking this place was like a little town.

Woody came out of the shop, driving the Concord Buckboard, and it was a sight. Huge back wheels that were as high as the sidewalls on the original Flint Wagon, so Woody had more planks added to help keep road dust and dirt out of the cargo area. He had salvaged the front boot to place under the driver's box, which was out in front of the cargo area and provided additional storage capacity. The original suspension thoroughbraces on which the previous cabin had ridden were supporting the cargo area, which Woody and Jasper agreed would not only provide a soft ride but also lessen wear and tear on the chassis.

"Charlie, I can't believe Mr. Dutton is just going to give this wagon to you," Woody said to Charlie as he rode up.

"Yes sir, I want to get it out of here before he sees it and changes his mind," Charlie said.

"Well, sir, he's standing up there in his office staring at us, so you better get going. Where's Jasper? I tell you, you were right about him and wagons. He knows a lot for a young man," Woody said.

"Yes, sir, we've been around them most of our lives, and we've had to build a bunch of them, but Jasper loves it; he loves to drive a team, too," Charlie said.

"Well, I'll be honest and tell you, I offered him a job down here if he ever left y'all. We'd be proud to have either of you work here, I believe." Woody said.

"You're awfully kind, Woody, but I'm not so sure how welcome we'd be by some of the others around here," Charlie replied.

"Well, you know how folks are when they're being outworked and outthought, Mr. Herlong," he said, sticking out his hand. It's been a pleasure. I hope to see you again soon."

Jake walked the old mule out, leading the wagon, which seemed much more solid than when it arrived, and said, "Mr. Charlie, Jasper asks if you'll look over this wagon and see if it's ok."

Charlie said, "I'm sure it's all right, but I'll take a look."

As Charlie walked around the wagon, inspecting it, Jasper snuck around and replaced Woody in the driver's seat.

Charlie saw him up in the driver's box and said, "You are an aggravating rascal, you know it?"

Jasper laughed and said, "I can't help it. I took too much whippin' as a child. Go easy on Methuselah; he's delicate!" Jasper snapped the reins, and the Concord lurched off, rocking back more than Jasper had expected. Charlie followed, eager to get to the dry goods warehouse.

CHAPTER 18

Malachi was sitting on the back porch of H. F. Dutton Mercantile, his legs dangling off the edge. Henry was sitting on the grey gelding, watching the warehouse ramp.

"What you going to name your horse, Mr. Henry?" Malachi asked.

"It's Charlie's horse," Henry replied. I think I'd like to buy him."

"He needs a name, though. All tame animals need a name." Malachi said.

"Do those mules on your wagon have names?"

"Yes, sir. Melly and Patty." Malachi was grinning.

"Malachi. I know you didn't name a mule after ...." Henry was laughing.

"My sister, I sho did. Cause they both stubborn as, as, ..." Malachi was stuck on the word.

Henry cocked his head, "Do they know why you named them?"

"They ain't that smart, they mules, Mr. Henry." Malachi dismissed the thought.

"No, I mean your sisters!" Henry exclaimed.

"Oh, I only named one after my sister; the other one is after her friend, Patty," Malachi explained.

"She kind of chubby?" Henry asked.

"YES. How'd you know? And mean, too. Sometimes, I feel bad for Patty the mule because she's sweet, but it's too late now. That's her name." Malachi jumped off the porch, a six-foot drop, and asked Henry. "You want me to fill your canteen? The water out that pump is cold and sweet."

"My canteen is in my pack," Henry answered. "I wonder what's keeping them. I hope that old mule makes it. Whom are you going to name him after?"

"I don't know," Malachi rubbed his chin in thought, "I don't believe I know anybody that old. Jasper will name him after somebody in the Bible; he always does."

"He does? Hold up. I'll come with you; take this horse." Henry stood in the saddle, stepped onto the porch, and opened his bag. He thought he smelled his blue bandana, but it was deep in his bag.

"You must work for Charlie Herlong," Dorothy Dunwoody said.

Henry saw ladies' brown buckskin shoes, brown stockings, and a hint of an off-white petticoat peeking out from a khaki, calf-length skirt. He craned his neck to see and quickly stood.

"Oh, pardon me, ma'am," Henry took off his hat, "I work WITH him; how did you know?"

"Well, I saw the young man out here earlier, and I saw how you stood up on your horse with style." Dorothy said, "Is he around?"

Henry noticed she was wearing a yellow scarf, loosely tied and hanging over a white, buttoned blouse. "He should be along any minute now, ma'am. You should see the stylish wagons he's bringing!" He then reached into Charlie's bag and brought out a canteen. "I was just getting his canteen to fill for our ride today."

Dorothy scanned the yard and sighed, "Well, if I miss him, please give him my regards."

"Yes, ma'am, I will," Henry said, backing down a few steps and skipping the rest with style.

Soon, Jasper and Charlie came around the corner, and the whole lot was abuzz seeing a wagon unlike any they had ever seen. Jasper came in fast, turned the mules, and then held them up during the turn. The wagon, light and unloaded, slid sideways into the lot. Those in attendance gave a surprised "Oooooohhhhhh!" Some cheered, having never seen a wagon like that driven like that.

Charlie was glad Jasper made the entrance he did because it pulled focus from his shabby rig. He made his way to the ramp and stepped off. Methuselah had stopped leaking, and Charlie was grateful for that. He saw Malachi and walked to the pump.

Malachi handed him a canteen, and Charlie took a long swallow. "Ain't this some good water?" he asked, "That alone is enough to make you want to do business here."

Henry said, "That and the women smell like lilacs. Like your girlfriend up there."

Charlie saw Dorothy on the porch, wearing the yellow scarf. He instinctively reached for his. "That would be Cuban Orchids. It's nice, isn't it?" Charlie rinsed his scarf, wrang it out, and started to place it in the crown of his hat. He then tied it around his neck as Dorothy had.

"Henry," Charlie asked. "You've checked in freight at y'all's store, haven't you?"

Henry chuckled, "Only about 11,000 times."

"Would you mind showing Malachi how?" Charlie said.

"No foolin', Mr. Charlie?" Malachi was eager.

"Yeah, but first, go tell Jasper when the show's over; we need to load his wagon. I'm going to check if Miz Dunwoody has any paperwork."

"Is that your gal, Mr. Charlie?" Malachi asked.

"No, she wouldn't ask me to take out the trash. But she sho is fun to talk to. Let's get moving, fellas. I'm about tired of Hogtown." Charlie turned toward the stairs, adjusting his hat and pushing his hair back.

Jasper saw Malachi coming and shouted, "Who's next, Mr. Duncan?"

Malachi looked around, and his face exploded into a wide grin, "You is, Mr. Gallum!"

To which Henry, Charlie, and Jasper said in unison, "You ARE!"

Charlie watched her as he crossed the yard and climbed the stairs. Dorothy stood tall with her hands folded at her waist. She smiled, and as she began to speak, a woman popped her head through the door and called her inside.

"I'll be right back," she turned and looked back, "Lovely scarf, Mr. Herlong."

"Likewise," Charlie replied, then put his hat back on and looked around.

A man directed a dolly cart toward him and asked, "Are you, ... Gerald Halford?"

"No, sir, I'm Charlie Herlong. That would be Mr. Halford over there, the thorny one with half a beard talking to the one looking for a new job." Charlie pointed. "But you might as well wait; he'll be coming over here in about ... now, it seems."

Halford walked over, frowning and opening his case.

The man cut him off and said, "Mr. Halford, I'm from Steenburg and Thomas. I have a delivery for you: shotguns and shells. Please sign here."

Halford signed and snapped, "Just stack them over there."

The man said, "They're a new style. Don't you want to check them over? Let me show you."

"Nope, they're for him," not even making eye contact, "Herlong, here are your documents ..."

Charlie cut him off, too, "Yes, sir, I'd like you to walk my associate and me through it, but first, what's your name?"

"Charles Thomas, sir," Thomas stuck out his hand, "my father is one of the owners."

"Me, too, I go by Charlie," Charlie said and shook his hand, "Let Mr. Halford finish up here with the unwashed, so he can return to sucking up to H.F. Dutton."

"I can't wait to hear of you getting killed by a bunch of niggers, poltroon," Halford said and handed Charlie a large envelope. He again scribbled on the hardware bill and shoved it toward Thomas.

"Is that a fact?" Charlie smiled, looking through the envelope. "Well, you'll have to wait at least a little, Gerry. But I have faith you'll be consistent in your habit of misunderstanding things. Run along now, go butter something up, or whatever it is you do."

"What'd he call you?" Charles Thomas asked, "What's a poltroon?"

"I don't know, Charles," Charlie said. Dudes like that make me itch. What have you got in those packages?"

"Call me Chick, my father's name is Charles. I have two of the 1897 Winchester shotguns, 12 gauge, pump action, and shells with smokeless powder," Chick said, "and he didn't even look at the bill he signed the second time. It included an option for leather scabbards, belts, and more shells. How many do you want?"

"All of them!" Charlie laughed and pointed. "Chick, let's get down there where my associate is so you can show us how they work. Down there at the ramp. His name is Henry. I'm going to step inside here for a minute."

"I saw them coming in," Chick said, "I'd like to get a closer look."

Dorotha came out and exclaimed, "Well! Does everyone from Lake City make a grand entrance?"

"If they don't, hide your valuables!" Charlie laughed, "I gather you met Henry."

"Yes, I did." Dorotha said, "I wasn't sure if I was going to see you again today, so I put something for you in your bag, or at least I HOPE it was your bag. The brown one that looks like a small portmanteau?"

"You're the first one who knows what a portmanteau is. I don't even know myself if I'm being sincere." Charlie added. "I'm glad we met. I'm moving to Jacksonville. If you're up that way, look me up."

"How am I going to do that, Charlie?" she asked, "Not knowing where you'll be in a vast town like that? Maybe you should write and let me know. That would be more appropriate. Or, you could just come back and have some more candy. Either way would be a thrill."

"Oh, what's in the bag?" Charlie said as he heard Jasper's whistle.

"Oh, just something to remember today," Dorothy said, "Wait until you're down the road; that will make it more likely we'll meet again."

"I hope to see you soon, Miss Dunwoody."

"Likewise, Mr. Herlong."

Charlie grabbed the bags and dragged them down the stairs. Malachi met him at the bottom and took one.

Chick was explaining the 1897 as Charlie walked up.

"This tube will hold five of these two ¾" shells. Plus, one in the chamber," Chick explained.

"Leave the chamber empty on Charlie's," Jasper laughed.

"No need to; there's a half cock on these; just ease it closed." Chick asked, "Remember, if you hold the trigger down, it will fire every time you pump it. Each belt holds two boxes of shells, that's 24."

Henry said, "Jasper, will that front boot on the Concord hold two cases of shells?"

"Dang," Jasper said, "How many did Charlie buy?"

"All of them. That's why we need to get moving," Charlie said as he swung his bag into the back of the low wagon, "Show me how to work this thing when we get out of town. Jasper, are you ready?"

"I got my britches on, don't I?" Jasper climbed into the Concord.

"Henry, can you handle a four-horse team?" Charlie said.

"I suppose we'll find out," Henry climbed up into the 2-ton wagon, snapped the reins, and followed Jasper.

Malachi was already in his rig and waiting. Charlie snapped the reins on Methuselah, and nothing. He snapped them again.

Malachi ran to the sleeping mule, slapped him in the face, and yelled, "Wake up!"

Methuselah began clapping his lips and nodding his head.

"Snap him like them Mollies today, Mr. Charlie!" Malachi ran to his wagon. Charlie did so, and Methuselah, the ancient Confederate mule, started moving.

Charlie thought to himself, 'Lord, have mercy; it's a good thing that train ain't leaving until tomorrow.'

The shadows were getting closer to the middle of the road, and it was almost three o'clock. Charlie deplored not leaving home two days earlier. He would be in Jacksonville now.

Charlie realized he wouldn't have four pistols, two shotguns, all sorts of ammunition, two peculiar wagons, a good-looking quarter horse, $400 in gold and silver, two decent mules, and another, which may or may not make it to Hawthorne.

Charlie made a turn and saw the wagons about a half mile ahead with some of the mules unharnessed. This troubled Charlie, and he snapped Methuselah with no response. Charlie wondered if mules could walk and sleep at the same time.

In a clearing near a small bridge, Jasper had set the mules out to graze along a picket line, allowing them to get to the water. On the south side of the road, Charlie kept seeing movement in the brush, but he was so glad to see the others that he dismissed it as varmints.

Charlie thought he saw two wolves come bounding out, ears back and running straight for Charlie's wagon. They both stopped just before Methuselah and were barking ferociously. Charlie pulled the new shotgun out of its scabbard and aimed it at the two animals barking and snapping. Methuselah didn't move. Only when one nipped at his heels did he get agitated. He kicked one of them, and it yelped. Charlie pointed the shotgun at one of them and pulled the trigger, but it wouldn't fire. He cocked the hammer, realized they were dogs and hesitated. He fired into the air, which caused Methuselah to rear and buck. The mule staggered to the left, stumbled, and fell into the ditch on the left side of the road.

Malachi came running, leading the two mules previously harnessed to the Concord wagon. The dogs snatched the leads from the mules' bridles, ran down a wide path, and disappeared into the woods.

Jasper was barking orders. "Get that old mule unhooked befoe he tear that piece o' shit wagon slap up! Forget about them mules! We'll catch them in a minute! Henry!"

Henry was on the quarter horse at a full gallop, disappearing into the woods. Malachi ran to the picket line, calming the other animals and tightening their leads. Charlie was off the wagon, pulling harness straps loose to ease the torque placed on the wagon rails. Methuselah was still, and Charlie could see no wounds.

"Damn, Charlie, why'd you kill the mule? Was you aimin' at the dogs?" Jasper was laughing.

"Shut up, Jasper."

CHAPTER 19

Tiger heard a horse at full gallop. He tied off the mule brought by Shine. Both mules were grazing on prairie grass behind Tiger's boat, beyond the garden.

Tiger hurried to the port side. A rider at that speed was chasing lost livestock. Moon and Shine ran back through the woods without seeking a reward, so Tiger expected more. He hoped that the rider had secured his other stock so he wouldn't feel obligated to help the owner catch it. There were advantages to dogs that would herd anything walking. Their zeal was occasionally too much.

He hastily cut an early ripened cantaloupe and peeled a few late tangerines. He soon heard hooves at a slower pace than before. The rider leaned down to find lost tracks, so Tiger knew this man was looking for stock.

Tiger whistled in a staccato, noted manner, and Henry stopped. Tiger whistled again in the way he remembered from his youth. When Henry answered, it shocked Tiger, and he ran into the meadow, waving his arms and whistling.

Henry turned his horse and cantered toward Tiger.

"Do you really understand Whistle-Talk?" Tiger said.

"No, sir, but I whistled what I thought I was supposed to," Henry said, "Did it make sense? What did I say?"

"I guess it did. It made me come out into the meadow." Tiger said, "I didn't understand it as words, but it was whistle talk I heard as a child."

"You're Indian?" Henry asked. "The only folks I ever heard using whistle talk were Indians from down in Mexico."

"I'm everything, son." Tiger thumped his chest, "My people are Cuban, Colored, White, but mostly Hitchiti."

"I've never met anyone that was everyone," Henry said.

"Me either," Tiger said, "but I like the way you put it. What brings you out here?"

"I'm looking for some mules," Henry paused, "you won't believe how I lost them."

"Yes sir, I would," Tiger laughed, "They're right over here."

Henry dismounted, and Tiger turned toward the boat, "I'm sorry. My dogs brought them here; they'll herd cattle they find in the woods or the swamp, but lately, there seems to be a lot of mules and horses around, too."

"Well, Mister," Henry paused, then said, "I believe they've graduated to stealing because they took the leads straight out of a man's hands. Right after they attacked one of our mules."

"Attacked it?" Tiger said, "They've never gone that far. Is the mule injured? Are they yours?"

"No, sir, they belong to Charlie Herlong." Henry said, "And I'm not sure if the mule is injured, but it was sick to begin with."

"Herlong? From up Lake City way?" Tiger asked, turning to face Henry.

"Yes, sir," Henry confirmed.

"Oh, boy, I better go with you," Tiger said, "Some folks react in different ways."

As they got closer to the stand of trees, "That's a ..., what in creation am I looking at?" Henry was astonished.

"I live on a boat," Tiger said.

"In the middle of the woods?" Henry asked.

"Well, it used to be a lake," Tiger said as he walked through the trees.

"Used to?"

"The lake dropped into a sink about twenty years ago." Tiger explained, "It must have been quick, too. There was still canned food and rice in the kitchen!"

"Well, if this isn't an elephant, then not even elephants are!" Henry said.

"Son, it sure ain't," Tiger said as he put a McClellan saddle on a skewbald pony.

He hopped on the horse and rode to the picket line. He hooked the leads of both mules with a short crook of switch cane. Without stopping, he had a lead in each hand. He cantered by Henry, who was absorbed in the horsemanship.

"You coming?" Tiger shouted, "Let's go see Mr. Herlong!"

Henry mounted and kicked to catch up, "Let's go, uh ..." thinking Malachi was right, animals need a name. "Go!"

Jasper had Shadrach and Meshach from the two-ton wagon to use on the Concord. "I'd rather leave Sampson and Abendigo on the big wagon 'cause they strong and know what to do."

He intended to replace Methuselah with the missing mules. Charlie was fretting, looking up the path for Henry.

Jasper called to him, "Charlie! I'm 'bout to drag this old boy to the tree line so critters will get rid of it. We gon' wait? Gettin' pretty late."

"We still have Henry's stuff, Jasper." Charlie replied, "Ain't you worried about him?"

"No, I don't worry. I plan. 'Bout getting this freight done and where we sleepin'." Jasper said, "Who gon' drive his wagon, getting back to Lake City? I ain't got time for worryin'. Why don't you take one of the dozen guns you've collected and shoot it up in the air? Bring down some supper."

Tiger rode to the downed mule. Henry rode to Charlie. Moon and Shine leaped from the brush and trotted after Tiger.

"Hey, now," Jasper yelled as he moved to the Concord. "You best control them dogs! I ain't like Charlie; they get after these mules; they gon' catch something!" He took out the Russian and buckled it around his waist. He wore it high and moved toward Methuselah.

"Mister, if they try to kill any of your stock, I'll shoot 'em myself." Tiger said, "But I'll have to borrow your pistol. What happened to your mule?"

"This ain't my mule, and them you're holding ain't neither. They belong to that man; talk to him," Jasper said, "I'm minding the rest of these, and I'll ask you to keep your dogs away from them, please."

Tiger whistled, and the dogs sat.

"Can I tie these off to your picket?" Tiger asked.

"You can tie 'em here," Jasper said. "Malachi! Hitch them Mollies up! Then I'm ol' need you over here!"

Charlie and Henry were on the other side of the road.

"He didn't offer, but I didn't ask." Henry said, "He might be your saddler's cousin. He's an Indian and he can cowboy. He's got some setup. Before you leave for Jacksonville, you need to go see it."

"What about it?" Charlie asked.

"It's an elephant," Henry laughed, "I'll put it that way."

"I ain't got time for that foolishness today," Charlie said.

"Mr. Herlong, I bet you know my cousin, Timothy Alpata." Tiger walked to Charlie with his hand extended.

"You mean Thunder?" Charlie laughed, "Yes, sir, I do. I talked to him yesterday."

"Well, in English, in Creek, it's Tomitkee," Tiger said, "I call him that, sometimes. My name is Tsitaga Driggers, but most people call me Tiger."

"I'm Charlie Herlong. I started this trip with you in mind, Mr. Driggers. I was looking for Marsh Tackies and wound up with mules, wagons, and a quarter horse."

"I ain't seen one in years; they're all bred out," Tiger answered, "Let's talk about your mule; your man says my dogs attacked him?"

"I wouldn't say attacked, more like pestered," Charlie said.

"What killed him?" Tiger asked.

"Time," Charlie said, "His name was Methuselah. He might have been on the ark."

"Maybe that heavy cotton wagon did him in." Tiger offered, "Would you say my dogs killed him?"

"No, sir," Charlie laughed, "But I'd say they stole my other mules and daylight. It's been a long day, and this freight should be on a train in Hawthorne."

"Well, you're about 8 miles from there, and I hear that train is due tonight. They won't have it turned before 10:00 in the morning, so why don't y'all stay at my place? Have supper, sleep under a roof, and let your stock graze in my meadow." Tiger offered. "It's the least I can do for the trouble, and maybe I have a mule or two we can bargain over."

"How certain are you about that train? I can't miss it." Charlie said.

"Certain. I sold four steers to a man, and he took them over there this morning. The train hadn't even left Tampa at 1:00 and still has to go through Plant City." Tiger said, "They're coming in late; they'll load in daylight, and I'll get my money."

"Well, let me think it out," Charlie said, "We have to hitch these teams up anyway."

"Well, I hope you will," Tiger said, "Y'all seem like good company. I'll help move that mule."

Charlie asked Henry, "Well, what do you think?"

"I'd like a chance to sit down and hear what we're doing," Henry said, "Am I riding a horse or a train?"

"We're supposed to be on the train guarding freight. That's why we have shotguns. Dutton wants to make sure it gets to Tampa," Charlie said, "We get there; you can find the 10th cavalry and sail to Cuba."

"What about your stock?" Henry asked, "Who is going to watch it while you're gone?"

"Hell, I don't know. This morning, all I had was heavy bags and a sore back. I reckon we should take Tiger's offer. Maybe he can watch it for a day or so." Charlie said.

"That's good," Henry said, "Besides, I'm going to get a kick out of sleeping on an elephant."

Tiger and Jasper pulled the carcass across the field. Tiger was impressed by how easily Jasper drove huge mules on foot, verbally commanding them.

"I'm Tiger Driggers, good to meet you." Tiger introduced himself.

Jasper raised his face and said, "Jasper Gallum, you kin to Alpata, the leather man?"

"Yes, sir, he's my cousin; how'd you know that?" Tiger responded.

"He say you the best cow hunter, anywhere," Jasper got right to it, "is that true?"

"I don't know, ain't been everywhere. But I've been riding and throwing that whip since weanin'." Tiger said, "But now, I've not seen anyone handle mules like you do," Tiger said.

"I started early, too," Jasper said. "Just like Charlie and Malachi."

"They sure do what you say," Tiger added.

Jasper laughed, "Today, they do! They scared Charlie gon' bust 'em with that shotgun! When you used your rope to keep his legs up, that helped him slide across that mushy ground. You been dragging stuff, too!"

"Hey, I'm going to gut him to break down and cut out a section for my dogs. Think Charlie will care?" Tiger asked.

"You sho' about that? That mule was mighty sick." Jasper said, "But, no, Charlie won't care. He quit thinkin' 'bout that mule soon's he hit the ditch."

"The dogs eat way worse than this," Tiger said, "Shoot, I've been hungry enough to do it, too. I've got some smoked beef we'll have tonight if y'all stay."

"Well, I reckon I'm working for Charlie today, so whatever he say. Smoked beef sounds good!"

Tiger went to work on the carcass when Jasper removed the gear.

"Malachi! Come get our ropes and coil up Mr. Tiger's," Jasper yelled.

Jasper hitched the team to the Concord and checked Malachi's setup. Passing Charlie, he asked, "You plan on hitching up that low boy, or you going to make someone else do it?"

"Yeah, I'm going to now. Will it take two mules?" Charlie asked. "Why do you have the chapped ass all of a sudden?"

"Because I'm ready to go and ain't got no idea where or how long it's gon' take," Jasper said, "When you get 'round to hitching them puny-assed mules, you'll know what it'll take."

"Ok, since you're ready, you can drive up that road. We're going to eat, sleep, plan, and you'll be back in the yard by dinner, where it's safe," Charlie said.

Charlie made his way over to the low boy as Malachi was coiling up rope.

"Mister Charlie, don't mind Jasper. He gets like that every afternoon about this time," Malachi said.

"Well, Charlie, am I having company tonight?" Tiger asked.

"Yes, sir, if you'll have us. I have to warn you, these boys can eat as hard as they work. This young man is Malachi Duncan." Charlie said.

"Here go your rope, sir." Malachi said, "This is the way we coil them over in Lake City."

"Hey, I like that; later on, after supper, will you teach me how to do it?" Tiger said, winking at Charlie.

"Yes, sir, I'll be happy to!"

CHAPTER 20

Charlie had gone about a quarter mile, and he noticed Malachi's red bandana tied to an overhanging branch. 'That kid's a thinker,' Charlie thought as he veered left, stood in the box, and pulled the bandana down.

The rest of the group was at Tiger's Prairie. A large pasture had two picket lines leading from a central pine tree to bordering tree lines. Two long garden plots with vegetables and decorative plants were in various states of growth. On the right, the sternwheeler William P. Tackett sat next to an artesian well, a line of trees, and another meadow.

A wisp of smoke rose, giving the impression that the Tackett could take off with a good head of steam. It came from a former boiler Tiger used to smoke beef and game to sell in Gainesville.

"Did y'all hear me?" Tiger yelled from the bow of the boat, "Secure your stock to that picket line furthest from the road; I just rotated it; there'll be plenty of grass, and there's water in that trough!"

They were sitting there, trying to fathom how in the world this medium-sized paddlewheeler made it to the middle of the woods, looking as painted and new as the day it was built.

"And bring some wood in so we can fry up some bread!" Tiger said.

The thought of eating, the smell of oak smoke, and the desire to see a boat in the middle of a prairie made them hustle. None had ever been on a floating boat, and the fact that it was navigating St Augustine grass was of little consequence.

Charlie was astounded. "It's a… how'd it … where's the… it's a damn steamboat!" he said to no one in particular. He stood to step out of the box and almost fell out. He had just that morning cussed Malachi out for forgetting to tie off and set the brake.

Jasper emerged from the palm-thatched shed where Tiger hung his tack. As he passed the woodpile, he gathered firewood. Passing Charlie, he said, "Charlie, stow your tack in that shed."

Henry was next, and he did the same, picked up firewood, and said, "Charlie, secure your tack."

Charlie continued to walk toward the freight deck where Jasper and Henry were sitting on a bench and a bent willow straight chair.

"How'd you like that tack shed? Did you hang your saddle on the rail with the rope on it? I thought that was smart," Jasper said.

"And that picket line. It had rings on the line to tie your leaders to. Let the stock walk free. I ain't never ..." Henry paused, "That's new to me."

All three heard Tiger's booming voice, sounding like it descended from the heavens. "Charlie Herlong!"

Charlie stepped back outside, turned, and saw Tiger on the top rail outside the wheelhouse.

"Charlie, are you going to let Malachi release your team?" Tiger boomed.

Charlie looked and saw that the low boy was gone and started walking, a little ashamed.

He then heard Jasper, "Charlie Herlong!"

Charlie answered, "OK, I'm going ..."

"Take care of your tack!" Henry and Jasper said it together and then laughed.

Tiger came out of the boiler room, which now served as his kitchen and smoke-house. He was holding a Demijohn rum bottle wrapped in worn, broken wicker. "You men up for a taste of rum? I get this from a man in St. Augustine; he moved here from Cuba and said the Spanish were trying to starve them all to death."

"Maybe just one," Henry answered. "I don't drink much whisky."

"Then you'll probably like this. It's genuine Cuban rum. He says he ages it in charred barrels, but I think he just puts a little molasses in there. Put one of those tangerine slices in your glass," Tiger said as he poured rum into three glasses.

"You know me," Jasper said, "If it's free, I'll take three!"

"Is your friend from Spain or Cuba?" Henry asked.

"He was born in Havana, but his people are originally from Spain, so they think of him as Spanish. White." Tiger answered.

"Why are they starving out their people?" Henry asked.

"I believe they are starving everyone, regardless, because if there is no food, the rebels don't eat." Tiger said, "They have been fighting for thirty years. It's hard to kill folks who have nothing to lose."

Tiger handed them each a glass, raised his, and said, "Here's to having something worth living for."

"It'll be harder for the Spanish to kill soldiers with equipment," Henry said. "The Buffalo Soldiers are on the way."

"Is that so?" Tiger said, "Do you think there'll be any Spanish left after Roosevelt's group gets finished? That's the only regiment I read about in the papers."

"Sir, I'll let you know when I get back. I intend to be there with the 10th Cavalry; I'm trying to get to Tampa to join my uncle." Henry said.

Tiger gave him a puzzled look.

"I started on a train in San Antonio, but in New Orleans, they made all the colored folks get off and refunded the remainder of our fares," Henry said.

"That was mighty kind of them," Tiger said.

"Yes, sir, I hoboed from there to Lake City. That's where I met up with this bunch. It's a good thing because the trains stopped running by then, " Henry said. "But I'm hoping to ride down there tomorrow. If we get there, what's the name of that town?"

"Hawthorne." Tiger said, "You have to know someone to get on that train."

"Charlie Herlong!" Jasper said, "Where is you gwine?"

"Done been where I was going," Charlie replied, "and Malachi made sure we got squared away. Mr. Tiger, this is some setup!"

"Have some rum, Charlie," Tiger said. It works for me! Let me go check on our supper."

"Maybe after I have a piece of cantaloupe," Charlie said.

Malachi was up and looking at everything. He stepped to the walkway on the edge, which led around the boiler room, and turned back toward the others.

"Can I go this way?" He asked no one in particular, and no one answered.

"Charlie, we been running all day and I'll be John Browned if I know why. I know why we're going to Hawthorne, but is that Charlie business or Herlong business? If Henry is headed to Tampa, that leaves us a driver short. And where am I going tomorrow? And the boy? And you? You going to Jacksonville, tomorrow? How're you planning on doing that? Driving two crazy behind wagons with two mules and a saddle horse. If I had that many irons in the fire, I'd be eat up with dyspepsia." Jasper said.

"I have a feeling you need another shot of that rum," Charlie said, "so you can remember that you only have two irons in the fire: you and Malachi. That's it. Relax and enjoy this little boat ride."

"He's got a point, Charlie," Henry said, "We do need to make sure everyone knows what to do. I think we're fortunate to have run into Mr. Driggers."

Jasper was pouring himself another shot of rum and said, "Good luck for Charlie! I 'magine Methuselah ain't so giddy over meeting the Drigger Dogs. But, I reckon they happy! Good luck for them, too." Jasper said.

"Jasper, I'm going with Henry to Tampa and coming back the next day. Dutton hired us to guard the freight 'cause they can't keep order down there," Charlie said.

"Can't keep order? Ain't that where the army is?" Jasper asked.

Tiger came out of the kitchen area carrying a large cast iron pot. Malachi followed him with a large basket of fried cornbread, bowls, and spoons.

"The Stew's hot and ready. I hope you like it peppery. I put some Minorcan peppers in there and green onion in the pone," Tiger said. Somebody fill that pitcher with some water from that china pot."

It got quiet as they ate the spicy stew, which included chunks of smoked beef, sweet potatoes, dried tomatoes, squash, and green onion bulbs.

"Mr. Tiger, we been eating good on this trip, but I believe this stew is the tastiest of it all," Jasper said.

"Thanks, Jasper, and you can call me Tiger if you want; I ain't so big on being proper."

Jasper nodded.

"My lunch was kind of light," Charlie said. We did more talking than eating in Dutton's office."

"Charlie, you work for Dutton?" Tiger asked.

"Today, I guess I do, Mis, um, Tiger," Charlie said, "But after this run, I'll be heading to Jacksonville. I was looking for a way up there and ended up with a little more."

"It looks like you have more wagons than mules," Tiger said, "and I hear you're losing a teamster."

"Yes, sir, Henry and I are taking this load of textiles down to The Tampa Hotel. He's going to join the 10th Cavalry. Is there a livery over there where I can leave two wagons, two mules, and a horse?" Charlie said.

"I 'spect those big mules and wagons are all going back to Lake City?" Tiger said.

"Yes, sir," Jasper said, "That's Herlong stock. I bet my boss is worried sick about it. Well, that and Malachi. You think Big Junior is worried about you, Mal?"

"No. But I am. Mama told me to be home by now." Malachi said, "I might just keep on going to Jacksonville with Mr. Charlie."

"Serious woman, I bet," Tiger chuckled, "She sounds like mi Yaya."

"Charlie, since my dogs got you here," Tiger proposed, "I'd like to help you out. I have two recently retired cavalry horses and two mules that ain't served in any wars. Let's try them out on your wagons to see how they pull. The four mules will pull that high wagon, and the horses can pull that one with the cotton cartwheels. If you need harnesses, I'll put one of mine on them. That way, Jasper's rigs can run the way they're supposed to."

"Well, how much money are we talking about?" Charlie asked.

"We'll talk when you get back," Tiger said, "I want to ride over there tomorrow, anyway. Who knows? I might buy them from you. I hear wagons and teams are going for crazy money over in Gainesville."

Tiger poured another for Jasper and offered some to the others, and Charlie accepted.

"You can give mine to Jasper," Malachi said, "That way, Mama'll be tired from whipping him and leave me alone."

Jasper drank his and said, "Your Mama don't want none of this."

"That's all for you, Jasper." Tiger said, "I want to be on her good side."

"That still doesn't count for the fourth wagon," Henry said. Are you going to trail one?"

"I'll know somebody over there that will help us out." Tiger said, "For bedclothes that special."

"It's pretty special," Charlie said, "Dutton thinks the folks will love it, and they'll want it when they go home. Sea Island cotton, he calls it. I hope he's overthinking it; I'd hate to use a shotgun over some pillowcases."

"I'd hate to see it, too!" Jasper laughed, "Right now, you've got a perfect record!"

"Methuselah don't count," Charlie said, "He was gun-shy."

Henry joined in, "Buckshot or heart shock, dead is dead, Charlie."

Charlie said, "Tiger, can we try out these new Winchester shotguns so I can hit what I'm aiming at?"

"Sure, I'd like to see them," Tiger said. " You can put your gear upstairs; there are mattresses that are good to sleep on."

"You need some help, Mr. Tiger?" Malachi asked.

"No, son, but once you get your stuff upstairs, fill the wheelbarrow with those old, dried-up pumpkins from the end of the garden and spread them out in the pasture behind the house," Tiger said.

"Yes, sir, Mr. Tiger," Malachi said, "You mean this house, right?"

"Yes, sir, my house."

After a long lesson on 1897 Winchester riot guns and .44 caliber Russian revolvers, Tiger insisted they clean and oil the weapons they shot. Tiger was impressed with Henry's discipline. They learned a bit more about his life in San Antonio. Jasper was the best shot, and Malachi declined, saying that his father planned on showing him how when he turned 16.

Charlie shot a lot of rounds from every weapon, and nothing died.

CHAPTER 21

At 6:30, a 10-foot blanket of fog covered Tiger's Prairie. The teamsters awoke to a short blast from a steam whistle. Malachi stood beside a skinned and dressed wild hog hanging on a gambrel near the artesian well.

"I'm going to need some help out here!" Tiger shouted.

Charlie, Jasper, and Henry rushed to the starboard catwalk in their drawers.

Malachi yelled, "Do it now!" and Tiger pulled the whistle again. They jumped, slipped on the wet deck, and used each other for balance.

Malachi screamed with laughter, and Tiger yelled, "Did we get 'em?"

"Yes, sir, we sho did! We scared the britches off 'em!" Malachi yelled back.

Downstairs on the freight deck, Tiger was sitting at the table, drinking coffee and smoking a cigar, when Henry and Jasper walked in. Tiger said, "I figure if y'all roll by 8, you'll be over there loading by 10. If they have fancy passengers coming in from Jacksonville, you'll have to wait on their coaches."

"There's a line to Jacksonville in Hawthorne?" Charlie asked.

"No sir, Palatka. A Flagler line, the schedules don't line up," Tiger answered, "It wasn't regular before, but now, with all this war traffic, you never know what you can do."

"Man, if I'd a known that, I'd a walked to Hawthorne," Charlie grumbled.

"Dang, Charlie," Tiger laughed, "if I had any feelings, they'd be hurt. The trains are a temporary thing."

"How come," Jasper asked, "they ain't got no cattle down there?"

"People gotta eat," Tiger said, "When my friend bought my cattle at market price, I should have realized he's making money. That's why I want to go over there. I hear there are 50,000 people in Tampa, and it ain't no bigger than Palatka. That fish camp won't ever be the same."

"And horses and mules are scarce up here," Jasper said, "Ain't that crazy? Who ever seen that, before?"

"Elephants!" Henry said.

Tiger poured them more coffee, "You said that yesterday, didn't you, Henry? What about them?"

"It's something fancy folks like to say these days about looking for adventure, that they want to see things that are rare and that they haven't ever seen before," Henry said.

"I made the mistake of saying it once to some bucket-mouth friend of mine," Charlie said, "See something I ain't never seen. Some excitement. I believe I've seen all Lake City has to offer."

"Well, I've seen two rip-roaring days since I got here," Henry said.

"Where'd the hog come from?" Jasper asked, "I ain't hear no shot this morning."

"Can I tell, Mr Tiger?" Malachi said.

"Tell them who the best shot in this county is," Tiger said.

"I got up with the sun and seen Mr. Tiger saddlin' up his pony. So I asked where is he going, and he said to kill a hawg did I want to go and I said, shoot yeah, and he gives me his pony, and then he jumped on one of them quarters and rode him on nothin' but a leader and horsehair." Malachi said so fast he forgot to breathe.

"Take a breath, boy," Jasper said, "Indian style, keep going."

"Well, we rode down yonder and they was about 20 hawgs eating on ol stank breath Methuselah." Malachi giving it hot sauce, "Mr. Tiger told me to stay there at the edge of the woods ..."

"How far off was he?" Jasper was egging him on.

"I'm getting to it; you take a breath," Malachi said as the men chuckled, "Man, Mr. Tiger said, 'Gimme that carbine and my rope,' so I did. He laid up on the back of that horse like he was fittin' to take a nap and eased over to them greedy hogs just eatin', ain't give a lick, then he said, Bye-yow! Bust a big ol' sow right behind the ear. Man, them hawgs scattered, boy! That sow was scootin' and rootin' round in a circle. Mr. Tiger rode that horse around in a circle, throwed that rope, and dragged her back here, kickin' and hollerin'. Then we skinned her. Man, alive! I ain't never seen nothing like it!" Malachi said, taking a deep breath.

"You saw an elephant, didn't you?" Henry said, grinning at Charlie.

"No, sir, just hogs," Malachi said.

"That's a fine story, son!" Tiger said, "I almost forgot it was me!"

"Not a drop of lye, all soap!" Malachi cried.

"Well," Tiger paused, "Maybe a little. There were only about six hogs."

"Charlie, Malachi says you need to name your horse," Henry said.

"Yeah, and the mules, too," Charlie said. I believe the mules are Willie and Jake. I'm still studying the Grey Quarter."

"That's Henry's horse," Jasper said.

"I'm just riding him," Henry said.

"Yeah, he might be, though I've never been on him," Charlie said. I'm leaning toward 'Sam,' after Henry's hometown."

"Haaaa! Dumbass! Henry's from SAN Antonio!" Jasper laughed.

"Yeah, but "San" don't work. I'm still working it out. That ain't no worse than you calling your mule Abendigo!" Charlie yelled, laughing, "When the preacher told you it was A-bed-ne-go."

"I named him Abendigo, so that's his name!" Jasper stood up and walked out. "Let's go; break time's over. That mule ain't been to Babylon, anyway."

Charlie laughed and said, "Did you tell the preacher to kiss your behind," as he stood.

"No sir, he said, 'Kiss my ass.'" Malachi said and walked out quickly.

"That's some crew you got," Tiger said to Henry.

"I'm just riding," Henry chuckled, "and all of y'all are from this end of the woods."

"I put our teams back the way they 'sposed to be," Jasper said, outside, "Tiger's mules on the Concord and Jake and Willie on the low boy. I know you like mules on wagons."

"They make good-looking teams," Charlie said, "you figured up a cost yet?"

"No," Tiger said, "it'll be here when you get back. Hey, before we leave, can I get y'all to help me hang that hog in my smoker? I have a man coming by tomorrow to buy vegetables, and he'll probably buy the whole thing."

They hung the pork on a sliding steel rack and slid it back into the former boiler. Tiger closed the door and loaded three green oak logs into the firebox, which was already hot and had a good bed of coals.

"That ought to be good by tomorrow morning," Tiger said.

"Son!" Jasper said, "I might not make it back to Lake City today."

"Smoked meat is what I got, Jasper," Tiger said, "I sell it in Gainesville."

"Do you sell lots of horses, Mr Tiger?" Malachi asked.

"Sometimes," Tiger said, "are you looking to buy a horse, son?"

"Yes, sir," Malachi said, "I'm 'sposed to get paid today."

"You should save your money 'till the end of the summer," Tiger advised, "Prices are kind of high right now."

"That reminds me," Charlie said, "we need to settle up. Are y'all about finished up with your rigs?"

"I am," Malachi said.

"How about finishing mine while I talk with Tiger?" Charlie said, "Then come back in with everybody else."

"Oh, Henry, let's get going," Jasper said, "Can you smell that?"

"Smell like Cuban Orchids?" Henry replied, "And wood burning?"

"Charlie's thinking again!" Jasper laughed, and they left the room.

"Should I be worried?" Tiger asked.

"No, sir," Charlie said, "but I am thinking and want to learn from you. Like these cattle you're putting on that train tomorrow, how many stock cars do they bring?"

"Well, I ain't putting any on that train, Ernie DeLuca is. He's from down Wacahootee Way; he had about a dozen and wanted more. I sold him nine, so I 'spect there'll be a stock car. Why? Do you have some to sell?" Tiger said.

"No, sir, I don't," Charlie said, "but if that stock car comes here empty, it could be full next time. Do you know somebody that could handle buying a group of horses and mules?"

"Yes, sir, I do," Tiger said, "The regular price for a good horse around here is about 50 or 60 dollars. These days, we might get over a hundred."

"So, if all the horses are in Tampa are cheap and the freight is too," Charlie said, "we could make a few dollars."

"We?" Tiger asked, "I guess it's my time to ask, 'how much?' but I ain't got much anyhow."

"300 dollars," Charlie said, "Hard money."

"Son, I make money. I ain't made of it," Tiger said.

"Yeah, me either," Charlie said, "How long have your people been in the cattle business? You can't scrape together some of that Spanish lucky gold?"

Charlie had ten pieces his father gave him, but he didn't want to spend his Spanish luck. He hoped Tiger might have $300 of any kind, which would help him buy as many horses as possible down south.

"If you spend it, it ain't lucky no more," Tiger said, "How much lucky money do you have?"

"I've got about $200 after I pay these fellas, but it ain't lucky; they're just regular old double eagles." Charlie said, "I used up all my luck meeting you."

"I don't know what Cuban Orchids smell like, but I'm smelling something," Tiger cracked. "Here's what I'll do, Charlie. I'll put up $400 in gold, and all your stock and wagons stay here as collateral. After expenses and seed money, we'll split the profit. Do we have to pay Henry?"

"No, he's going to Cuba," Charlie said.

"We have to get to Tampa first," Henry said, "it's getting hot."

"This won't take long; I want to settle up," Charlie said.

"Well, if we're talking money, I've something to propose," Henry said, sitting at the table.

"Charlie, I appreciate everything you've done for me the last few days," Henry said, "and I know that Sam is worth a lot more money, but I want to buy him for $100,"

"Henry, we don't even know if you can bring him with you," Charlie said.

"It doesn't matter," Henry said, "If I leave without him, he's yours. Please?"

"You been trying to get rid of that gold since you got it," Charlie said.

"This gold wasn't lucky for Keyes," Henry said, "and that horse is better luck." He then handed the five double eagles to Charlie.

"Ok," Charlie said and turned to Tiger, "Ok, so now, I have enough."

Tiger nodded his head.

Charlie pulled out a black badge wallet with a gold badge that said Dutton Agency. He handed it to Henry and said, "Keep this in your pocket until we get to Hawthorne, then show your badge and your gun; it'll help us get your horse on the train."

"A colored man with a badge," Jasper said, "That'll give them something to aim at."

With a look of realization, Henry put the wallet in his pocket.

"Hey, are you giving me that Smith?" Jasper said, "I kind of like the way the .44 sounds. I hope the shells ain't hard to find."

"Hold on now, you're still getting your daily from the company," Charlie said, "for yesterday and today. Plus, you been bird watching, too, ain't you?"

"That ain't got nothin' to do with Tight Assed Charlie, and you know it," Jasper said.

"Oh, all right." Charlie tossed him a cotton bank bag heavy with coins.

"I'm 'sposed to hit a bandit with a sack of nickels?" Jasper looked in the bag and saw 15 silver dollars. "OK, what about the pistol? How much?"

"Keep it and a box of shells," Charlie smiled, "I wouldn't want you crying and making it rusty."

"Bet," Jasper said.

"Well, Mal, have you decided whether or not to share your bonus with your mother?" Charlie asked.

"Well, she gets everything in my pay envelope already," Malachi said, "so I thought I would buy her something. Like some of that smell good you be wearing. I think she'd like that."

"No, we ain't stopping," Jasper said, "We already going to miss dinner."

"No, but I bet if I buy your dinner, you'll stop," Malachi said.

"Let's get moving, then," Jasper said and left.

Charlie said to Malachi, "Hey, give her this."

Charlie reached into his bag, drew out a box containing two bottles of Cuban Orchids, and handed one to Malachi. Malachi took the cap off the bottle and smelled, then doused his red bandana with it.

"Whoa! Easy, there, son, that stuff goes a long way." Charlie said. He then gave the boy another cotton sack.

Malachi looked in the bag and said, "I never knew three dollars could be so heavy."

"That's cause there's six dollars in there," Charlie said, "Put some small change in your pocket for walking around money and keep the rest in a safe place. You tell Mr. Cone at the bank you want to save up for a horse. Now, here's the last thing,"

Charlie handed Malachi a $5 gold coin. "Give this to your mama. I'm not giving it to you; I'm giving it to her. It's five dollars, it's made of gold. You call it a half Eagle."

"Eagle? An eagle is ten dollars?" Malachi asked.

"Yes, but here is the thing. Now, listen to me," Charlie got serious, "Don't tell anyone how much you have, just what you'll spend. You got that?"

"Yes, sir," Malachi said, "Mr. Tiger, how much for a horse, I'll spend six dollars."

Tiger and Henry both laughed, and Charlie smiled and shook his head.

"One hundred dollars, son," Tiger said, "You come back in September, and I might have something real good for less than $50. Go save your money, like Charlie said."

"Malachi, here's a dollar," Henry said, flipping him a silver dollar, "You and Jasper's lunch is on me."

"Thank you, Mr. Henry," Malachi said, "Do I have to pay for his lunch, though? I ain't got no need to get to the commissary, now."

"No, use it if you need to," Henry said, laughing. "I believe you are going to sell this boy a horse sooner than later, Tiger!"

Chapter 22

Benson Fleet looked east and wondered when he would see passengers from who knows where up north. Since dawn, he had loaded 21 cattle and a full car of various supplies Plant's hotel needed to operate. He had two parlor cars and a lounge to cater to guests, eager to wave their flags and cheer the US army embarking to Cuba. Fleet had worked this trip every day for twenty-two straight days. It was challenging without kowtowing to rich, entitled guests. Heat, insects, and humidity were a fact of life in Florida from March to September.

His job was to run freight, not carriage trade. He understood the importance of trying to supply a war. The hubris of the jaded gentry traveling to Tampa to sweat and prove their patriotism especially galled him.

He rechecked his watch, 8:33, then looked to the west. This special shipment of linens was annoying him as well. He wanted news he could leave and forget about Yankee tourists or bedclothes.

Shine and Moon had a cracker bull backed up against a thicket. The bull had a strange set of horns; the left one rose in a normal half-U, but the right horn turned down, preventing either dog from lunging in and grabbing the neck or jaw. Shine sat down and leaned on his elbows in a huff. Moon continued to bark, occasionally thrusting, only to be blocked again.

Tiger rode from the front and pulled up at the standoff.

"Well, what are you waiting for? Send him to the house! Get-on-outta-heah!" Tiger yelled, pulling his cow whip and kicking his horse toward the bull.

He then cracked the incredibly long whip right on the bull's nose, and the bull turned and ran up the road toward Tiger's Prairie. The four teamsters were in disbelief, speechless.

"That there wadn't no elephant!" Tiger laughed, "That was damn good cow huntin'! Let's go!"

Charlie said to Tiger, "Hey, do you know the station master up here?"

"Yeah, Pem Sardin is easy to work with. The hardhead is Fleet, the conductor." Tiger said, "We're about a mile off. Why don't I ride up there and scout it out for you?"

"Yes, sir, if you don't mind, let's see what we're looking at," Charlie said.

Four Plant System coaches were standing at the station. Teamsters and porters were unloading a massive amount of luggage.

Fleet was speaking to a group of men, women, and children who stood under the awning.

"Yes, sir, it is warm for this early in the morning, but that's not unusual here. Mr. Plant is expecting some special freight due at any moment. Thank you for your patience. We'll sort your luggage and then board the train. We have refreshments in the lounge car," Fleet said.

"I'll have Murphy bring out some spring water. It'll just be a bit longer," Fleet said and walked into the station.

"Any news? I want to get some breeze on these Yankees." Fleet snapped.

"This man passed wagons a mile back. That's your freight. He's waiting with Deluca to settle up," Sardin said. Tiger walked out silently.

"Yeah, I been waiting for about an hour. I'm surprised to see you; did you bring me more cows?" DeLuca asked Charlie.

"I could have; my dogs spooked one back yonder," Tiger said. "I'm here to ask a favor."

"I been sleeping on that bench and I need to get back," Deluca said, "What kind of favor? Is there any money in it?"

"Why, ain't $90 profit for my cows enough?" Tiger said, "Can you drive a wagon back to my place?"

Sardin walked out and handed Deluca a small pouch, which Deluca put in his pocket. Tiger turned and said, "I'll be back in a minute, and we'll settle up."

"Sign this, Ernie," Sardin said, "21 head at $30, that's $630. I put some smaller gold in there, so they weren't all doubles. When can you be back?"

"I hope tomorrow," Deluca said, "you know these cows are from trains that are backed up, right?"

"I know you found these cows in the woods," Sardin said, "and they're eating a whole lot of beef at the hotel."

Charlie rounded a turn and saw Tiger waving, "Don't slow down; they're waiting on you!"

Charlie and Henry pulled up to the platform and set their badges. Henry pulled the shotgun. Jasper and Malachi drove to the empty freight car.

"I'm looking for Pem Sardin!" Charlie called out as he stepped off.

"That'd be me," Sardin said, coming out of his office.

"Pleased to meet you," Charlie said, extending his hand. "I'm Charlie Herlong, H.F. Dutton Company. By the way, Calvin Mulberry sends his regards."

"Who? Mulberry?" Sardin said.

"He's the manager up in Fort White; I won't tell him," Charlie said, "I've got four wagons of fine linen to get to The Tampa Hotel; here's my paperwork."

"Fort White, yeah, I remember." Sardin got to business. All I need is this and this. Oh, this is a telegram from The Plant Agency in Tampa. It says you and Mr. Whitfield are staying with the freight until it gets to The Tampa Hotel."

"We have an agreement; they've set things up with the Train Master down there; what's his name?" Charlie said, snapping his fingers like he was trying to remember.

"That would be Lester Donahue, and he's over in Sanford. Strickland is the one who you want at the hotel. Let me get these bills to my clerk so he can check them in," Sardin said.

"Thank you, sir," Charlie said, taking the documents. We'll help load. We'd like to get on the way. We prefer to put our bags where they'll be safe."

"You'll have to speak with the conductor, Mr. Fleet," Sardin said, "that's his call."

Charlie moved to the freight car, which was placed behind the conductor's car, followed by the stock car. Jasper and Malachi were already helping with the freight.

Jasper had noticed the change in Charlie's demeanor and the badges on him and Henry. "Mr. Herlong, can we water our stock?" Jasper said.

"Check with Mr. Sardin first," Charlie said.

"Mr. Pem ain't gon' care about that," said one of the workers, "It's that conductor that wants to be in charge of errythang."

"Oh yeah? Head swole?" Jasper asked, "Point him out so I can avoid him."

"That's him next to the parlor car," the freight hand said, "I wish I could avoid him. He yell for me erry time his rump itch."

Charlie said, "Mal, take me and Henry's bags to the front of that car right next to the stairs."

"Just drop them there?" Malachi said.

"Yes, if anyone says anything," Charlie said, "Tell them Mr. Herlong said so. Jasper, who's your friend?"

"Thadeus Ducreaux," the man said, "I like Duke, though. Keeps it simple."

"Ok, Duke. You say the conductor, Fleet, sometimes acts like he owns the train?" Charlie said.

"All the time."

"Okay, so when he starts raising hell in a few minutes, I'm going to tell y'all to start unloading," Charlie said. "But you don't unload anything; you go inside and tell Mr. Sardin that I asked you to get him," Charlie said.

"Look here, I don't want no trouble," Duke said.

"Ain't gon' be none," Jasper said. "we'll unload all of it. Just say Charlie wants him."

Fleet was already yelling for Duke. Charlie was halfway to him, walking, smiling, and extending a hand to shake.

"Hello, friend, I'm Charlie Herlong," he said, "We just put those there 'till we figured out where you wanted them. Of course, we'd rather keep that black one next to us. We've some extra equipment we'd like to keep handy."

"Mister, I don't know you," Fleet said, "the passengers on this train are special guests of Mr. Plant."

"This freight is Mr. Plant's. We won't take up much room," Charlie said.

"Well, I don't know where you're going to ride. You ain't dressed to be in the parlor cars," Fleet said.

"We'll just ride in the way car," Charlie said. That way, we can be close to the freight."

"No, sir, only Plant System employees in my car," Fleet said.

"So that leaves the fully loaded freight car or bunking with the cattle," Charlie said, "is that where we're headed?"

Fleet was looking at his clipboard and said, "That sounds about right."

Charlie didn't respond and walked to Jasper. Jasper and Malachi started walking to the corral, and Charlie began to unload the freight. By this point, Duke had spoken to Pem, who had come out of the station.

"Mr. Sardin!" Charlie shouted, "Please send a wire to Mr. Lester Donahue in Sanford; please advise him that Mr. Plant's special-order linens will not be coming today; there's no room on the train. Could you also send a copy to Mr. Plant, the Plant Agency, Mr. Strickland, H.F. Dutton, and Mr. Fleet? What's his first name?"

Pem was writing it all down, "Benson Fleet is right there," and pointed to Fleet.

"Yes, sir. I want it waiting for him when he gets there without this freight," Charlie said, continuing to unload. " Bill the Dutton Agency."

Jasper and Malachi set the brakes on their empty wagons.

"What are we doing here, Charlie?" Jasper said.

"Henry and I are going to Tampa, and we ain't riding like tramps," Charlie said, "That son-of-a-bee ain't keeping us off that train! Just wait for me before you do anything else."

Charlie walked to the men and said, "Mr. Sardin, who do I speak to about removing that freight car?"

"That would be me," Fleet said, "You're mighty protective of bed linen, aren't you, son?"

"Son? I'm not your son," Charlie stepped closer and through gritted teeth, "I wouldn't care if it were a load of cotton burrs. I've been asked to keep it secure and get it to Tampa. Due to your incompetence, the only option I have is to set up in your car. If you prevent that, I'm taking the next viable option. Make up your mind, Fleet. Am I taking this train or waiting for another with a competent conductor?"

"I'm going to be back tomorrow, just like I have for the last three weeks," Fleet countered, "This is my train, and that NIGGER AIN'T RIDING NEXT TO ME!"

"Oh, my," Charlie said, "three weeks? That's terrible. Well, my money is on you getting some rest tomorrow. And the next day. Mr. Sardis? Please send my telegrams."

"How do you know it won't be you getting fired?" Fleet asked.

"I don't, but I was looking for a job when I got this one," Charlie said.

Charlie turned and walked to his men and asked, "What are they doing?"

"Fussing," Jasper said.

"Hand me that shotgun," Charlie said.

"Oh, shit, take cover," Jasper said.

Charlie fired a 12-gauge round into the air. Passengers, workers, and two cow hunters turned toward the freight car.

"I said, UNLOAD IT!" Charlie shouted, and they scrambled into the car.

Fleet hustled over and exclaimed, "Ok, you can ride in my car, but the nigger has to stay in the freight car."

Charlie racked the slide on the Winchester and stared.

"Okay, both of you," Fleet conceded. I'll probably have to stay in the parlor cars the whole trip anyway."

Charlie handed the shotgun to Henry and walked to their bags. Tiger rode up and said quietly, "While you were dove hunting, we put your horse in with the cows."

Soon, the linens were all loaded, and Jasper was itching to get on the road. Tiger and Deluca were in Charlie's wagons. Malachi was standing next to Charlie.

"Tiger, I'll see you tomorrow. Jasper, I'll send you a postcard from Jacksonville," Charlie said. "Malachi, don't use all that smell good," Charlie said.

Malachi hugged him tight, "No, sir, I won't."

He ran to his wagon and jumped in like Charlie. Wiping away tears, he said, "You come back to Lake City soon, just the way you left. Let's go, Mellie! Pattie!"

Malachi snapped the reins and whistled the same way Jasper did.

Chapter 23

Henry was at the back door of the conductor's car. He had explored the catwalk, extensions, and the roof of the train. The front door opened, and a black man dressed in a suit coat with an apron stepped in.

"Whooo! If we're going to have riders, we need to open some of these windows," he said, then saw Henry at the back door, "Son, are you with the man out there shooting this morning?"

"I beg your pardon?" Henry asked.

"No need to beg. I'm Murphy Bulow, the porter," Murphy said, opening the windows in the cupola. "Oh, good, fresh air."

"I'm Henry Whitfield; good to meet you."

"It's Good to meet you, too," Murphy said. I'm excited. I haven't ever seen a colored man with a badge. We sho 'nuff need one."

"Some say it makes a fine target," Henry offered, smiling.

"Maybe they're right, no matter what color sheriff you are," Murphy said.

"But not sheriffs. We're watching over this freight, making sure it gets to Henry Plant," Henry said. I suppose the badge makes us seem more authoritative."

"Lord, son," Murphy said, "are you a preacher or a teacher?"

"Neither, but I know of both," Henry wanted to change the subject, "Why do you think they need guards on this trip?"

"Well, the white folks are bollixed up over the colored army," Murphy said, "But, we stick out like weevils. Some of that buck wild nonsense was whites, too. Is that why they sent you? Make the colored men settle down?"

"Mr. Bulow, I try to avoid guessing what rich folks are thinking," Henry said, "I'm only here to get this freight to Tampa and then join up with the 10th cavalry."

"They ain't in Tampa, they're in Lakeland." Murphy said, "You need to get off in Plant City or Knight's. That's an hour before we get to Tampa."

Charlie stepped in with the other two bags.

"Good morning, sir," Murphy said. I'm Murphy, the porter. Can I take those bags?"

"Hey, Murphy, is that your first or last name?" Charlie asked

"First name, sir," Murphy said, "my last name is Bulow."

"Bulow? From .... what's that new town ... Deland?" Charlie asked.

"Originally, at the sugar mill. My people are in Ocala," Murphy said, "your bags?"

"I'd rather keep them close," Charlie said.

"As you wish, sir," Murphy said.

"What's that smell in here?" Charlie said, "Smells like fried possum and fancy cheese."

"I don't know, Charlie. Mr. Bulow was just opening some windows."

"My apologies, sir." Murphy said and whispered to Henry, "It's Fleet. That's how he smells, and he's very sensitive about it."

"There's a rumor that it's Fleet's cologne," Henry said, "We might decide to ride with the stock after all."

Murphy was in the rear alcove and held a finger to his lips. He whispered again, "Don't make my job harder, boy."

"Maybe he needs some of my Cuban Orchids," Charlie said, laughing.

"I believe the less said to Mr. Fleet, the better," Henry said and winked at Murphy.

"What do you think, Mr. Bulow?" Charlie said, bringing out the Cuban Orchids. Do you think he'd mind a few drops of smell good in here?"

"I wouldn't guess, sir," Murphy said, sweeping sand from the floor, "when he's not pleased, my job gets harder."

"Of course," Charlie said, "I'll sprinkle some on my neckrag. Do you want some?"

"No, thank you, sir." Murphy said, "I must get back to the parlor cars."

"Henry?"

"No, thank you," Henry said. I'll just stay here near the back door. Murphy tells me the 10th cavalry is in Lakeland, which is about an hour's train ride from Tampa."

"So, 2 hours by horse?" Charlie said.

"What's that map over there tell us?"

"Oh, where's Tampa? And ..." Charlie said, "Lakeland. Dang, you'd have to kill Sam to get there in two hours. Hell, Henry, this train goes right past it. I reckon we'll have to switch tracks in Plant City."

"He mentioned Plant City," Henry said, "and Night something."

"Here it is, Knight's," Charlie asked.

"Murphy said the 10th is in Lakeland," Henry said. Then you came in, scaring the man to death. His boss is a jack-donkey, Charlie. If we make his job easier, he'll want to help us."

"How can he help us?"

"I don't know," Henry said, "I figure you'd unravel it. If we stop in Knights or Plant City, I'd like to ride to Lakeland."

"Yeah, sure. I don't expect anything to happen," Charlie said, "once we're out of the woods. The biggest issue is getting Sam out of the cattle car."

Soon, they were riding through shady, cool oak hammocks, and Charlie lost himself in thought.

Just before noon, the train stopped. Henry, ever vigilant, climbed the ladder on the porch and stepped over to the freight car.

"They're switching tracks," Henry said, "Looks like we're bypassing Ocala."

"We're taking a little shortcut, sir," Murphy said, "all the tracks are filled up in town. I was hoping to speak to your man, Whitfield," Murphy said, "May I?"

"Mr. Bulow," Charlie said, "We're at your service. But he's on the roof right now. Is there something I can do? We want to make your job as easy as we can."

"Oh," Murphy said, "I just thought he should know .... when we go through this switch, the brakeman will come through here on his way back to the front."

"And I'll be glad to meet him, too," Charlie said, "What's his name?"

"Musco Cranshaw," Murphy stepped over to the door again, "How long do you expect he'll be up there?"

"Henry will be up there till we leave, I imagine. This Musco character, is he going to have a problem with a colored man wearing a gun and a badge?" Charlie asked.

Murphy looked at his shoes and then at Charlie and said, "I would say likely."

"What is he going to need or want?" Charlie asked.

"He usually gets some water," Murphy said, "but I think he just likes to snoop around."

"Murphy," Charlie said, "do you have a small bottle of liquor?"

"We have all sorts," Murphy said, "Can I get you something?"

"Not for me, no," Charlie said. I need about a half-pint bottle full, but I need it before we leave the switch."

"Oh, guests leave flasks on the train all the time," Murphy said. What kind of liquor?"

"The one that smells the most will be perfect, oh, and two glasses," Charlie said.

Murphy returned in less than a minute with an engraved, silver flask.

"This got left by a man from Scotland," Murphy said, "and it's loud as a bad wheel."

"Cranshaw won't be an issue, Murphy," Charlie said, "at least not today."

"Let me get back," Murphy said, stepping onto the landing. The engineer pulled his whistle, and the train lurched, moving slowly. Musco waved his red rag to the engineer. Musco returned the switch, then walked, peering into the stock car and fiddling with the latch on the freight car.

Charlie was sitting on a bench as Musco entered. Charlie acted startled and put his hand on his Colt.

"Whoa, hold on there, Mister, I'm the brakeman," Musco said with his hands up. "Where is this nigger with a badge I keep hearing about? I'm glad it was you; he might have shot me."

"The day ain't over, mister," Charlie said.

"I'm just coming in for a drink," Musco said.

"You're thirsty? That's good to hear. I won't drink with him." Charlie pointed his thumb toward the roof. "He'll be up there till we leave the switch."

"Then he'll be up there until I'm gone," Musco said. Train don't move without me."

"Care for a drink?" Charlie asked and put two glasses on the iron stove.

"Don't mind if I do." Musco said as Charlie poured two drinks, "Man, that's some fancy bottle you got there."

"The guy I got it from don't need it anymore," Charlie said as he raised his glass, hesitating. When Musco drank and winced, Charlie poured his drink into the stove vent. Charlie immediately poured another. Again, Charlie dumped his into the stove.

"The more I drink this whisky, the better it gets," Charlie said as Musco took his third drink. Charlie immediately poured a fourth, and the engineer blew the whistle to signal the brakeman.

"Oh, shit, I gotta go," Musco said and slammed his last shot, "it does get better." Musco staggered toward the door as Henry came in, the brakeman at eye level with Henry's badge.

"Looks good on you, boy!" Musco said and staggered down the steps.

"Is he drunk?" Henry asked.

"He might be," Charlie said and put the flask into the stove.

As the train got underway, Murphy came into the conductor's car, grinning.

"Man, that jackass was struggling to get to the tender. I thought they were going to leave him," Murphy said.

"You might want to get rid of these," Charlie handed the glasses to Murphy, "Oh, I found this in the stove. We were thinking about coffee." Charlie returned the flask to the stove.

"When we stop in Wildwood, I'll bring y'all lunch," Murphy said, "and some coffee. We ain't never had no riders like y'all!"

"Mr. Bulow, will we stop in Knight's?" Henry asked.

"We might, but it's not a scheduled stop, but we'll stop in Plant City," Murphy answered, "That's five miles from Lakeland. With good time, we'll be there at 2:00 or so."

"The unscheduled stops," Henry asked, "What usually happens there?"

"Unload cows or hogs," Murphy said, "The way it was explained to me, the hotel couldn't handle too much livestock at one time."

"Imagine that," Charlie mused, "Railroad man, the richest man in the world … can't find a carpenter to build a corral…has to store them 40 miles up the road."

"Shoot, those aren't my cows," Henry said, "I'm just riding with them."

"Mine, either," Charlie said, "but that's good information to have."

"Did I just hear Jasper's voice?" Henry said, "Something about wood smoke and Cuban Violets?"

In Wildwood, Murphy brought them a basket with sardine sandwiches, pickled onion, shortbread, and muscadine jam. He also had a pot of coffee.

Later, Henry stepped on the rear landing, which was cooler. Fleet stepped into the car, kicked their bags, and sat at the locked desk.

"Why don't you have your boy carry these to the baggage car when we bypass Owensboro?" Fleet said as he unlocked his desk.

"He'll be out back getting some air," Charlie said, "I'll take care of it."

"I can't say I blame him; it smells like a French whorehouse in here," Fleet said.

"Well, that's an improvement," Charlie said, "over whiskey and chicken shit."

"Take that gun belt off before you step through that car," Fleet said, "I already told you; those are gentle people in there."

Charlie removed his Colt rig and put it in Raymond's bag. He picked up the other two bags and left the car. In the lounge car, several men were playing cards and smoking cigars. Charlie was almost to the second parlor car when one of the women at the window cried out.

"George! There are men on horses outside with masks on their faces!"

Charlie put the two bags on an empty seat and turned to run back to the conductor's car. He saw a masked man step through the door and Charlie sat down next to the bags, laid over them, and closed his eyes. He pulled the flap on the secret compartment and placed his hand on the butt of the Remington.

"Everybody, ladies and kids, too! Get your hands out where I can see them. Start taking off your jewelry, watches, rings, whatever. Wake up, you drunk bastard," the masked man said and pushed Charlie with his boot.

Charlie moved with the kick, pulled the Remington out of the bag, and backhanded the bandit across his ear, who dropped to the floor motionless, blood pouring from his head. Charlie opened the door of the other car.

"Lock that front door, now!"

Charlie reentered the second parlor car, pulled the body of the bandit out of the aisle, took his pistol, a Colt revolver, and ordered the passengers into the next car.

"Lock that door and don't open it!" he said and ran to the other end, struggling to cock the pistol to full. He entered the lounge car, all the men peering out the window, and shouted, "Get away from the damn windows and lock this door!"

He heard Henry's 12 gauge. He opened the rear door, and a man pointed his pistol at Charlie.

"Whoop!" Charlie said, ducked his head to the side, and blindly pulled the trigger. The gunman shot, splintering a cabinet next to Charlie's head. Charlie's shot landed in the middle of the man's chest, and he dropped into the doorway. Charlie stepped into the conductor's car and saw Fleet peeking out from a closet, then slamming it shut. Charlie crossed to his shotgun, cocked the hammer, and stepped onto the rear landing. A horse's head appeared, and Charlie fired point-blank under its jaw and pumped another shell into the chamber. The horse fell and pinned the rider to the ground: the rider, screaming, dry firing at Henry up on the roof. Henry methodically fired his Colt until empty at two fleeing riders.

"Is there a sheriff?" Henry yelled to a passing wagon, "Yes, please! And a doctor if there is one."

The robber, pinned by the horse, would occasionally yell and plead for someone to get the horse off of him.

"You shut your god damned mouth, or I'll give you these boots again," Fleet said, evidently gaining some courage since his refuge in the closet.

The sheriff arrived on a full-size bay horse. He wore a floppy felt cracker-style hat and a star. His huge belly covered the horn on his saddle.

"Hey, boy," he called to Murphy, "pull that sheet back so I can see who's underneath."

"That's Jackie Mobley from up 'round Riverland. I'll bet that's his brother Riley under that horse over there. I got warrants for both. Oh my god! Who took that horse's head off?" the sheriff asked as he walked his horse over.

The sheriff glanced at the body on the front landing of the car and said, "Oh, no, Will Hormuth was running with them? That's a damn shame. He's from good people. I reckon I'm going to have to send someone up there to let them know. I hate that."

"You wait till I tell my Daddy you just rode around talkin' shit while I had a damn horse laying on me," Riley said, "Get him off me!"

"Not so fast, Riley," the sheriff said, "Who was with you?"

"None of your business!" Riley screamed, "Get him off me! Please, Ted."

"Two rode off to the north," Henry said, "a grown man and a real skinny kid, about ten or eleven."

Ted Hill, sheriff of Owensboro, held his finger to his lips and said to Riley, "What's that, Riley? You say your Father, Bird Mobley, and your cousin, Mouse Loy, were with y'all?"

"Hell, no! That nigger said it, you fat piece of shit!" Riley yelled.

Sheriff Hill walked his horse over to Riley and shot him in the chest.

"Mister Fleet, will you sign a paper saying he confessed as he expired from a gunshot wound sustained in the robbery attempt?"

"Yes, I will, Sheriff. Can I mail it from Tampa?" Fleet said.

"Well, if the tracks clear up soon, you can just bring it to me. But Sheriff Griffin in Dade City may need one, too, so that you know." Sheriff Hill said.

He turned his horse and walked it back toward town, saying, "If y'all take them horses tied to the train with you, it'll save me having to track down who owns them. But if you ain't got time, just set 'em loose. See y'all next week."

Chapter 24

Henry loaded the horses, and they bypassed Owensboro. Every passenger was nervous when they slowed to bypass Dade City. The fireman, spewing a steady stream of profanity either directed toward or describing Musco Cranshaw, turned the switch as Musco slept in the tender. Every person on the train breathed a sigh of relief when the train exited the bypass and continued toward Hillsborough County.

"I don't know how Musco keeps his job," Charlie said, "but not completely useless. He let me know that we're making an unscheduled stop at Knight's. Is that where you want to get off and head to Lakeland?"

"I'd like to confirm that's where the 10th is if I can," Henry said, "That porter may be mistaken. What about Fleet? Where's he been?"

"I think he's been trying to settle the rich folks down," Charlie said, "Convincing them he saved their lives."

"Something isn't right about him," Henry said. He seemed mighty familiar with that man he put the boots to, like he was insulted they were robbing his train."

"Well, he does think it's his."

"I mean, just the way he was fussing at him," Henry said, "like the guy was a kid or something. Unexpected. Like they stabbed him in the back."

"That fat sheriff stabbed Riley in the front," Charlie said, "Why do you think he killed him?"

"Who knows?" Henry replied, "I guess dead men don't need a trial."

"You think Fleet knew them?" Charlie asked.

"Maybe," Henry said, "He was hiding in a closet? Then, he's cussing him out and two-stepping."

The door opened, and Fleet stuck his head in. "These folks in here want to speak to you," Fleet said, "and they'd like to show their appreciation."

"Ok," Charlie said and stood, motioning to Henry, "Let's go meet some rich folks."

"Uh, they didn't ask for him," Fleet said.

Charlie sat back down. "Well, if I take credit, he's going to be standing next to me."

"That's ok, Charlie, I was protecting the freight," Henry said.

"Nope, that ain't the way this gets moved," Charlie said.

"Charlie," Henry said, "I'm just in it for the ride, remember? Go ahead, bring us back a sandwich. I'd rather stay here. Rich folks make me itch," Henry said, winking.

"Me, too!" Fleet added.

"Who is in charge?" Charlie asked Fleet. Fleet didn't answer. "Ask them to bear with me a few minutes. We're trying to get things cleaned up in here."

Fleet left the car, and Charlie looked at Henry. "Henry, I'm not so sure I want a pat on the back for killing two people."

"It takes a little getting used to," Henry replied, "but like you said, protect yourself. Those boys weren't there for a social call."

"That's the thing, Henry," Charlie said, "why'd they choose to rob this train?"

"I think Fleet has been selling cattle, and somebody got tired of paying his price," Henry said. If he's the only one who can get cattle down there, he sets whatever price he's got the nails to charge."

"So, he's been overcharging Plant and whoever is buying in Knight's," Charlie said, "Fleet's got some big old nails, don't he?"

Henry shrugged, "Those boys might have been here to rob rich folks."

"No, your first impression was right. He didn't come out of the closet till he knew it was over," Charlie said. Next thing you know, he's going to teach that rascal a lesson."

Charlie walked over to the mirror, took his old bandanna, and poured fresh water into the basin. He wiped his face and neck and brushed some stains from his hat. He hung the damp cloth on a peg.

Charlie peeked in. There were gentlemen seated in groups along the windows smoking cigars and others having a light lunch. Three women were playing Dummy Whist. Murphy was smiling and waved Charlie in. The conversation and the game stopped. All watched Charlie cross the room to Murphy. Charlie noticed that one of the ladies was a cheater, looking at another's hand.

"What would you like, Mr. Herlong?" Murphy asked.

Charlie stood with his back to the room, "What are they doing?"

"Nothing. They'll snap out of it in a bit," Murphy smiled, "Are you hungry?"

"Not at the moment; who is it that wants to see me?"

"Mr. Ward, I 'magine," Murphy said, "But he stepped out to the water closet."

Charlie turned around to face the room, and they continued to stare.

"What are they looking at?" Charlie asked, under his breath, "The men look mad."

"I believe they're sizing you up, Mr. Charlie," Murphy said, "wishing they were more like you."

"The ladies are smiling, though," Charlie said.

"They're sizing you up, too," Murphy added, "wishing their man was like you. They're all waiting to see what you do."

"They're acting like cattle," Charlie said, "curious but skittish."

"Most people do," Murphy said, stepping to the table of cured meats, cheeses, and assorted pickled vegetables. When Charlie turned, the others went back to what they were doing before.

"What about this man, Ward? What does he want?"

"I can't say," Murphy said, "but I imagine he's used to getting whatever he wants. These folks have been falling all over him, waiting to see what he does first, what he has to say. I guess that's the way it is with Captains of Industry."

"He's a captain? Which industry is that?"

"You ever bought something out of a Montgomery Ward catalog?" Murphy asked.

"Yeah, that's him? Ward? What about Montgomery? Who's running the store?" Charlie said.

"Ask him; he's coming in now," Murphy said, and the room hushed.

"Murphy," Ward said, "I wonder if I might bother you for some coffee."

"Of course, sir," Murphy said, "Shall I take a few minutes and make some fresh?"

Ward immediately turned his attention to Charlie, who stuck out his hand.

"Good afternoon, I'm Charlie Herlong, from Lake City."

"My pleasure, sir, I'm A. Montgomery Ward, of Chicago," Ward replied, "Lake City, is that near Winter Park? I'll be heading up there later this week."

"No, sir, but closer than Chicago," Charlie said, "I've been traveling for three days."

"Well, we're glad you have," Ward said. You made a quick hash of those bandits today. On behalf of my fellow passengers, we thank you."

"Just doing my job, sir," Charlie said, "My partner and I are glad it turned out safe for the passengers and the cargo."

"What were they after, Mr. Herlong," Ward asked, "Are you at liberty to disclose the cargo?"

"We were just trying to figure that out," Charlie said. "They're fine, high-quality linens from H. F. Dutton. But I wouldn't expect train robbers to be after that."

"Fine enough for your employer to send you along," Ward said, "I'd be interested to see these linens."

"I'm sure they'd be happy to show them to you at the hotel," Charlie said, "it's Sea Island cotton, soft as silk and easier to clean. I'm sure Mr. Dutton would be more than happy to send you some."

Two of the men by the windows were busy writing with fountain pens.

"He is in Lake City?" Ward asked.

"Oh, no, sir. He's in Gainesville," Charlie said, "and I believe he has a factory up in Georgia."

"Mr. Ward, if I may interrupt," one of the gentlemen said, and Ward nodded. Mr. Dutton is in Gainesville. That's in Florida?"

"Yes, sir," Charlie said, "tell them Charlie Herlong sent you. Direct that to Dorotha Dunwoody for the best service."

"And you're a detective for the Dutton Agency?" Ward asked.

"Well, I guess I am today," Charlie said, "Once we get this freight to the hotel, that will be the end of this job."

"And tomorrow?"

"I'm not quite sure, Mr. Ward." Charlie said, "I think if I can use this train and its stock car, I'm going to buy some horses and take them back to Gainesville. They're in scarce supply up there. If I can use the train, I can take advantage of that."

"Well, is there anything I can do for you? We'd all like to express our gratitude for your saving us this morning," Ward said.

"Shoot, I don't know," Charlie said and rolled his eyes slightly, "I already have one of your hats. It's a good one."

"So, you're familiar with our company," Ward said.

"Oh, yes, sir," Charlie answered, "one of my teamsters was using your Wish Book yesterday. Well, it's a pleasure, Mr. Ward; I should get ready for our next stop."

"The pleasure was all mine, sir," Ward said, shaking Charlie's hand.

Murphy handed Charlie a basket of food, and he returned to the conductor's car. Henry was cleaning the shotguns and pistols, including three they had acquired from the Mobley gang.

"Hey," Henry asked, "come look at these pistols. One's a Colt, like mine, but filthy, and another one I can't even figure out how to open. The barrel says, 'Hopkins and Allen.' There's a .44 Smith; it's double action. I think I'll take it if that's okay."

"Murphy sent food. Do you want to eat?" Charlie said, putting the basket on the stovetop. "Maybe we should open a gun shop."

"You can. I just want this one. You're going to need your wagons when you get back. All this iron is getting heavy," Henry said, racking the slide on a shotgun and placing a shell into the tube. He then hung both shotguns back on the pegs and turned his attention to the pistols.

"We'll be getting to Knight's in about an hour," Henry said, "I'll take Sam when they offload the cattle. Have mercy; this is the dirtiest gun I have ever seen! Even the shells are dirty. Mm, mm, mm."

"What's so special about the one you're keeping?"

"It's like those other .44 Smiths, but double action," Henry said, "That Colt you have is a killer."

"This .38 Colt was sitting in the office," Charlie countered, "That Colt you're cleaning is the one that did the killing. I could barely get it cocked."

"Dirty guns will get you killed," Henry said, "And guns you can't open will, too, like that fancy, shiny one. Whose gun was that?"

"The one that the dirty one killed, so much for cleanliness," Charlie said, picking up the big, nickel-plated revolver, "Is it loaded?"

"I couldn't unload it," Henry said. I couldn't even open the gate."

"Hey, it's got a half cock like the shotguns," Charlie said, "That did it. Gates open."

"Man, a week ago, you didn't know a cap gun from a shotgun," Henry chuckled.

"Any fool can learn how to use a gun," Charlie said, thinking of Judee Cupee, "and a smart man knows when to use one. And I ..."

Charlie pulled and struggled with the pistol, shaking it and looking straight down the barrel.

"This thing needs a virtuoso to open it!" He finally pulled a live round out through the loading gate and looked at it. "It takes a .44. Figure it out later," he said and tossed the pistol on the table.

Henry laughed and spun the cylinder of the newly cleaned and oiled Peacemaker. He snapped the cylinder closed and dry-fired it several times.

"There it is, ready to tame the badlands of Florida!"

CHAPTER 25

The train pulled into Knights just after 2:00. Henry took his position on the roof. Fleet stepped out and quickly walked to the northern end. He looked anxious and peered down the tracks. He then went to the south end and did the same. Charlie stepped out onto the platform and spoke to Henry.

"Hey, I'm moving over here to listen in on what our boy Fleet is looking for."

"There's not a soul riding or walking that I can see," Henry replied. It looks like he's been left in the lurch."

One of the gentleman passengers stepped out onto the platform. It was the man taking notes for Ward earlier. He pulled out his watch, glanced at it, and put it back into his vest pocket. A short, balding man with a huge handlebar mustache stepped out of the station, stretching like a cat awakened from a mid-day snooze.

"I didn't expect y'all till later," the man said, "I saw the wire about your trouble in Owensboro."

"No trouble," Fleet snapped. It was just some stray dogs, and we put them down. Where's Dew Dykstra? They're supposed to take some cattle from me."

"I don't believe you'll be seeing him today," he said, "he had a run-in with some rustlers, and they shot him in the leg. Lucky for him, it missed the bone. Lost all his cows, though."

"Unlucky for you, Fleet. Isn't that right?" Charlie said, turning to the man and extending his hand. "My name's Charlie Herlong. Are you the station manager?"

"I used to be, but the railroad pulled us off the schedule," the man explained. "I used to be the postmaster until someone decided it was cheaper to run the mail through Plant City. I managed the general store until the freeze, then my boss went bust and moved to Medulla. These days, I do what I can. Oh, my name's Jack Duffie, Jack of all trades."

"I'd say a renaissance man, Mr. Duffie," Charlie said, "that's a Jack of all trades who's mastered them all."

"Hey, that's good," Duffie said, "sure beats 'master of none.'"

Fleet had heard enough and stomped away. Charlie saw an opportunity.

"Mr. Duffie, we need to offload some cattle, about nine head. Do y'all have a corral?"

"Those posts over there used to be a corral. But there ain't nobody to look after them," Duffie said, "and before you even ask, the answer is no, I ain't getting shot for cows, mine or anybody else's."

"See what I mean? A renaissance man," Charlie laughed, clapping Duffie on the back, "master of not getting shot! Yes, sir, let's avoid that."

Charlie saw Ward's man walking toward Fleet and knew he had to move quickly.

"Henry, come on down, let's talk!" Charlie shouted and turned back to Duffie, "Tell me about these rustlers, Jack."

"Oh no," he said, "I wouldn't know anything other than talebearing."

"Jack, you hear everything that comes into this town. Surely, you heard something. Were they from around here?" Charlie pressed.

"Are you the law?" Duffie asked.

"I'm not," Charlie said. This badge says I take care of H. F. Dutton's business, so I'll be discreet."

"All I know is, they've been around, but not from around here," Duffie said, "they drove cattle from Green Swamp and sold them to Dew Dykstra. They were a rough lot, even for cow hunters."

"Any named Mobley?"

"No Mobley," he said, "like I said, just folks telling tales."

"Come on, Jack," Charlie said, "Is there any law around here?"

"The Closest law is in Lakeland, but it's Polk County. Hillsborough law is in Seffner; we don't ever see him," Duffie said. That's really all I know."

"What are we doing, Charlie?" Henry asked.

"I'm not sure yet," Charlie said, "but I might need your help a little bit longer; I'm trying to work something out."

"Well, I'm getting my gear," Henry said and turned, "I'm about sick of this train."

"That's a good idea," Charlie said, "I think we'll unload Sam, at least. Maybe Jack here will help. I'll make it worthwhile for you, Jack. Like for, say, two bucks?"

"For 2 dollars? I'll unload 2 for three!" Duffie said.

"No, one is all," Charlie said, "but I'll double it for a little more talebearing, just between us."

"Four dollars? Hard money?"

"Jack, I want it all," Charlie said, "to the bottom of the cup. Tell me about these rustlers."

"Ok, if you say I said it, I'll call you a liar," Duffie said and looked around, "Dykstra and some other farmers were selling beef to the army cause the canned meat they have ain't fit to eat. When they ran out of cows, they got more from Desoto then Sumter County. Then Fleet started bringing it and that cut the ones from Green Swamp out. One of them, Milt Loy, from Arcadia, shot Dew for nothing. He didn't do a thing. Scoundrel!"

Charlie made his way toward the north end of the platform just as Fleet walked past, red-faced and agitated. Ward's man stood there emotionless, then smiled as Charlie approached, hand extended.

"Mr. Herlong, we haven't been introduced; my name is Robert Thorne."

"Call me Charlie, Mr. Thorne," Charlie replied, "Any idea what we're doing here?"

"I was hoping you might enlighten me, Charlie," Thorne said. "You can call me Bob if you like, but Mr. Ward likes things formal when we're with him. We have a meeting in Plant City to look at a building. Do you think you can help us get moving?"

"I can try, Bob. Tell me, this building has a corral?" Charlie asked.

"I haven't seen it yet, but I hope so," Thorne said. We're hoping to distribute freight out of there and expand into the Caribbean."

"Let's hope so," Charlie said, "I believe we can get moving as soon as I unload one horse."

Charlie stepped into the conductor's car, where he found Fleet vomiting into a bucket.

"Whoa, Fleet," Charlie said, grabbing the water pitcher and pouring a cup for him, "you get hold of a bad pickle?"

"I can't show up in Tampa with more than 12 cattle," Fleet cried.

"Nine more can't make that much difference," Charlie said.

"You don't understand; they're very particular," Fleet said. It'll throw the accounting off."

"You mean it'll throw the embezzlement off, don't you?" Charlie said, "Just let them loose; I'm sure your rustler friends will appreciate it."

"No, no, you've got it all wrong," Fleet was on the verge of tears, "this could mean my job."

"Easy, Benson." Charlie's tone warmed a bit. You're not going to lose your job, but you are going to lose some cattle—nine of them."

"I can't just set them loose! From a Plant System train? Have you lost your mind?" Fleet was gaining some hope.

Henry stepped in and stood at the door.

"I need my gear," he said.

"Take a shotgun. I'll be with you in a second," Charlie said. Mr. Fleet is here and is fixing to be our partner."

"Ok," Henry said, "does he know I'm still a nigger?"

"He doesn't mind," Charlie said, "as long as he's still a conductor. Right, Benson?"

Fleet raised his head, "Right what?"

Charlie said, "Pay attention, Benson. I'm trying to help you keep your job."

Charlie opened the stove vent and removed the flask, which, to his surprise, had been refilled, and he placed it in front of Fleet. He stepped outside with Henry.

"Charlie, this isn't for me. I want to get over to where the 10th is and find my uncle."

"Yeah, yeah, I know, that's what you're fittin' to do," Charlie hissed, "and you're going to find out how hungry they are. Tell your uncle we've got some steaks for him if he can meet me in Plant City with some men that can offload nine cattle. Like in an hour. Can you do that?"

"I don't know, Charlie," Henry was hesitant, "I don't even know if he's over there."

"And if he ain't, you have to come to Plant City, anyway, right?" Charlie said, "Henry, we just became cattle barons; I bet they'll bring $100 a head. Just do the best you can. I'll hold the train until you get there."

Henry stepped back in and took a shotgun, "Don't lose my pack, Charlie. Everything I own is in there. I'll see you in Plant City; give me two hours."

Charlie closed the door and turned to Fleet, whose demeanor had changed.

"You think you figured it all out, don't you?"

"No, I do not," Charlie said, "Why don't you explain it to me? Now that you've stopped pissing down your leg?"

"Which part? The accounting?"

"That has nothing to do with me," Charlie said. All I have to do is get my freight to Tampa, which you're responsible for, too. What I don't understand is what you can do for me. Because right now, it looks like I'm doing all the favors."

"Yeah, but I don't have Bird Mobley and Milt Loy wanting to kill me," Fleet said.

"From what I hear, they don't need much reason to kill anybody," Charlie said, "Tell you what, I'll just take my horses, and you hide nine cows."

"Good point," Fleet said, "are you buying the cattle from me or stealing them?"

"Hundred bucks."

"That sounds good," Fleet smiled, "do you have $900 on you?"

"Total."

"So you are stealing them," Fleet said.

"No, sir," Charlie said, "I'm buying all nine for $90."

"You just ... they're worth $90 a piece!"

"Maybe to you, but not to Milt Loy," Charlie said, "better say yes, I could just steal them like you said, $75."

"Yes!"

"Bet. Now, let's get to Plant City. Mr. Ward has a meeting," Charlie said.

Charlie ran to the stock car and saw Henry heading east at a full gallop.

"Lord, that's a good-looking horse. Fast," Duffie said, closing the door.

"That he is," Charlie said, "I wish I hadn't given it to him so cheap."

"You ain't planning on crawfishing our deal, are you?"

"Dang, Jack, I just met you," Charlie said, "and now you're insulting me? Do you have a dollar?"

"No, sir, I don't," Duffie said, "I'm poor as a hind tit runt."

"Oh, all right," Charlie said, flipping a half eagle toward him, "Keep the change."

"Mr. Herlong, I ain't seen gold in a long time, at least not that belonged to me. I 'preciate it," he said.

"Call me Charlie," Charlie said, "come on, have a sandwich before we get going."

"Yessiree," Duffie said, "I'm so hungry I could eat a neck rag."

Charlie motioned to the basket of food, then put the silver flask back in the stove vent.

"Don't tell. I'll be back in a minute; eat all you want," Charlie said and left the room. Duffie ate voraciously. The train whistle screamed, and within seconds, Musco Cranshaw came through the back door.

"What the fuck are you doing in here?" Cranshaw said to Duffie.

Duffie said the same thing, but his mouth was so full it was unintelligible. He tried to swallow and choked. He took a sip of leftover scotch, choked again, but got it down.

"Eating a fucking sandwich," Duffie said and took another sip, "Aaah."

Cranshaw said, "Who do you think you are?"

"You know who I am," Duffie said, sitting and crossing his legs, "and I work for Charlie Herlong. All brakemen, get the fuck out. The train's leaving!"

Cranshaw took a sandwich and headed out the door.

"I bet you'll get out now," he said as he ran toward the tender car, whistling and waving his red rag.

Chapter 26

Henry let Sam run halfway to Lakeland, and then they slowed to a canter. A large group of white soldiers camped next to a lake, with lots of hanging laundry and activity. He noticed a group of soldiers, many black, coming out of a chapel wearing black mourning bands. Closer, he could make out Cavalry marks on their uniforms.

"Gentlemen, pardon me," Henry said to a group, "I'm looking for the 10th Cavalry camp."

"Just follow any nigga you see; the 10th is the only colored regiment here," a corporal said.

"Keep following this path," a sergeant said, "you must be looking for F troop."

"Why do you say that?" Henry asked.

"Riding that Steel Grey horse," he said and turned to the others, "I told you Baker would find one!"

"Sergeant E.L. Baker?" Henry was surprised, "That's the man I'm looking for."

"Quartermaster Corps and Troop tents," he said, "there'll be a crowd there; it'll look like a free-for-all broke out in a Mexican market; Troop F has banners on their tents."

Henry was trying to understand what the Sergeant meant. Off to the left, next to what had been a field or a pasture, was a small town. There were hundreds of men milling around, playing baseball, a group of tables that looked like a café, men playing cards and checkers. Henry was surprised to see whites and blacks, as he was expecting only the 10th Cavalry.

Henry dismounted and tied off to a pen next to a large tent. A huge Corporal leaned against a rifle crate, standing on end.

"I'm looking for Sergeant Baker," Henry said.

"Who ain't?" the corporal said, jabbing a thumb inside. You better grab that iron on your horse, or else it won't be there when you get back."

Henry pulled the shotgun out of its scabbard and crossed the shell belt over his shoulder. Inside, three tables were lined abreast. He heard his Uncle Eddie's booming voice.

"No, sir! Hell, no! No liquor goes to the 71st till O'Hearn says!" Baker shouted, "I had to send steaks to that Captain so he could get the Sheriff calmed down! No more, them New Yorkies are buck wild as any Chiricahua, anywhere!"

Henry entered to a hush, and anyone wearing a pistol put their hand on it. Baker looked up.

"Mister, if you're here to rob us, get to it!" Baker said as several pistols were drawn and cocked. "Hold on ... Pinky! Is that you?"

Uncle Eddie Lee came out laughing and clapping.

"Men, this is my nephew, P. Henry Whitfield!" Baker said, "Why the hell are you loaded for grizzly, son?"

"Man out there said, if I wanted to keep it, I should carry it," Henry said.

"That ain't lyin'," Baker said, turning to another, "Go tell Hatch to keep an eye on that horse. Henry, you want to put that gear back on your ride? Hatch will look after it for you. What are you doing here?"

"Where'd you get that pump gun? Do you want to sell it?" a white corporal asked.

"I'm here to join up, but first, I need to take care of an errand," Henry said, then looked at the white corporal, "No, thanks."

"Join up? Do you mean like here? The 10th? Troop F?" Uncle Eddie's voice was getting softer, "Pinky, we need to talk. Things ain't like they were. Let's get the errand done first."

"Unc, can you call me Henry? I don't know these folks," Henry said, then asked softly, "How are y'all set for beef? Like fresh beef."

"Not worth a damn, Henry, I have to get it through that bunch from Massatusetts, and I ain't got enough scratch to cover cows at a hunnert bucks a half," Baker motioned him behind the tables, and the others continued their business, "You know where some are?"

"Yes, sir," Henry said, "nine head on the hoof, but I need some men who can handle them and keep them from getting rustled. I need help to get them off the train right now."

"On a train where? How much? Can you trade? I won't have any hard money until I sell one off." Baker had a gleam in his eye, and Henry saw it.

"Plant City, and they might trade horses, but right now, I got to get help and ride back over there," Henry said.

"Well, men, I got," Baker said, "But horseflesh that ain't US property, I don't. But I might find it. I'm going to send two men, and if one of them stays, you have to feed him. The other one needs to bring me back a healthy cow with paperwork. I don't trust these crackers around here. What's the cash price for the cow?"

"I'm not sure, but we'll work it out for you," Henry said.

"Oh, I don't like that," Baker said, "someone says, 'work it out,' I get worked over."

" $100 or two good horses or three mules, and I'll stand behind that price out of my pocket," Henry said, "For the first cow, but I need to get them off the train soon."

"Ok, let's get mustered up," Baker said, "Carlton, saddle up two horses and supply them with gear for handling cattle. Get Hatch and tell him to go with Henry here and pick out another buck that can handle stock. Henry, nine is all you have?"

"For now, if we can move them by train, there'll be more. Uncle, we've run into some rough characters; can your men handle themselves?" Henry asked.

Hatch, the man who warned Henry earlier, walked in and said, "Sarge, you wanted me?"

"Yes, sir," Baker said. "I don't know, Pinky, does he look tough enough for you? Hatch, I want you to go with my nephew; he's got some stock over in Plant City that we're interested in

"Yes, sir," Hatch said, "Is Carlton going to get me a good-sized horse?"

"If he don't, you let me know," Baker said, "Henry, how's your mama and them? They build that church, yet?"

"No, sir," Henry said, "They weren't too happy about me coming here, either. Mama said joining the Army just gives people another excuse to kill me."

"Sounds like her," Baker said, "How about Cy? I bet he quoted Commandment #7!"

"No, sir, I'm not married," Henry replied, "He did mention 'Thou shalt not kill'"

"That's the one," Baker said.

Several soldiers agreed, nodding and saying, "Amen."

"That's when Mama started cursing," Henry said.

"Quit lyin'!" Baker yelped, laughing, "My sister won't even say back sass!"

That drew laughs, many thinking of their mothers.

"Close enough," Henry said, "She said, 'Mother of Pearl Handled Pistols! What about honoring your Mama and Daddy?!'"

The tent erupted in laughter. Henry looked around, embarrassed.

Someone muttered, "Y'all better leave that boy's Mama alone."

Another said, "Shut yo mother of pearl handled ass up!" More laughter.

Baker motioned for Henry to follow him into a second tent with a desk-like table and assorted supplies.

"And then, what did you say?" Uncle Eddie asked, reaching for a coffee pot sitting on a tiny, tabletop stove.

"Is that just for the coffee pot? Never seen that before," Henry said.

Sergeant Baker was waiting for an answer, "Burns alcohol. What did you tell them about honoring your parents?"

"I said that serving our country was honorable," Henry said, "That serving God was honorable."

"That's honorable," Uncle Eddie said, "Now, tell me why you think joining the Army right now is so honorable."

"The Spanish are starving their people to death," Henry said, "I have to do something. You're going to do something."

"Yes, sir," Sergeant Baker said, "I'm going to do my job, which equips every man in this regiment to destroy what and whoever they are told. Me, too. I will kill anyone that command tells me to. Without judgment or regard for how I was raised or about right or wrong. Are you willing to do that?"

"Yes, sir," Henry was getting motivated.

"Are you sure?" Baker said, "Do you want to be the new man? The one who gets put out front? Have you thought about that?"

"No, sir," Henry said, "not that in particular, but I know I can get killed. Coming over here almost got me killed, but I didn't come this far to get scared and go home. Can you help me?"

"Yes, I can." Sergeant Baker said, "We can walk across camp to the officer's tent; we can sign you up today, not as a volunteer, like those yahoos looking for adventure. That's for white men. When you sign up here, you're in the Colored Army. That's a different Army. Then you'll stay here and get trained. Doing every nasty job that no one else in Florida wants to do. Soon, they'll call some of us to go to Tampa, load up the boat, and sail to Cuba. But not everyone will go because there ain't enough room on the boats. Them that don't get to go, I'll have to tell them. Men I've worked with for years are going to want to know why. They're going to be mad and pitchin' a fit, but there won't be a damn thing they can do about it but be ready to go when the ship gets back. And even then, they might have to stay because someone thought they were needed here, more."

Henry sat on a crate of Krag-Jorgenson rifles, reality draining all of the motivation he had just felt.

"But, that won't help you," Uncle Eddie was speaking to his nephew, now. "or the Cuban people. Henry, if we get hungry down there, we'll take whatever food we want. If you want to help them, wait until the shooting stops and help them get back up. How? I don't know, but I see a man who traveled a thousand miles to find me, so I know you have the passion to do something honorable."

Sergeant Baker had neutralized all but one aspiration that had pushed him for a month.

"I don't know about that, but I need to get to Plant City right now," Henry said, standing. Which man is bringing your cows back? The big one?"

"Cows? Son, I won't have hard money till I sell one," Baker said, "You're going to trust me?"

"No, sir, I don't trust anyone," Henry said, "What do you have to trade? You said there wouldn't be room on the boat; maybe there's something I can sell that you won't need or can't use. How about a wagon and mules? Are they all branded?"

"I have some mules that we bought when we got here. They're good, but they ain't Army. Two mules and a wagon? For two cows?" Baker offered.

Henry had learned from Charlie to go big when trading.

"Oh, no," he said. "That's one cow. What can you put in that wagon?"

"One? Damn, Henry, a wagon and team for one cow?" Baker said, "Is it made of gold?"

"Beef, Uncle," Henry bargained, "This isn't Egypt; it's Lakeland, and a good steak is worth it, I believe. Think of something you don't need."

"Oh!" Baker said, "I've got shells for a dynamite gun. You can set them off by lighting the fuse. Fifty pounds each. I want them gone."

"Sounds dangerous," Henry said, "and heavy. How about Colt shells? .45 or .38."

"No, I need those," Baker said, "but I have a ton of .44 Russians. Why, I don't know, we don't even use .44 Colt, but for some reason, they sent me Smith .44 Russian."

"How many rounds will you give for a cow?" Henry asked.

"Russians? 5000 rounds," Baker said. But you know that's for Smith and Wesson, right? And I have another box with a thousand rounds of mixed ammunition—all different kinds, plus a bunch of conversion cylinders. But you have to take the dynamite gun ammo, too. Ten shells."

"Dang, can two mules pull that much? Ok, when can you get them?" Henry asked, "The wagon and team, 5000 rounds of Russians, 1000 rounds of junk, and the dynamite? I have to get over to Plant City. Can you send the cow hunter with me right now?"

"Cow hunter?" Baker said, "Who have you been traveling with? Carlton! Where's that cowpuncher?"

"He's here, boss," Carlton yelled. Alvie Collins from Abilene. He used to work in the stockyard and as a butcher!"

"Get him to help you hitch two good civilian mules to a one-ton wagon," Baker yelled, "and find Hatch a full-size horse. Get him a draft animal if you have to. Make sure they both have side arms. Let's move! Get them to Plant City!"

Sergeant Baker was moving toward the front tent as he was yelling. Before he ducked through the flap, he turned to Henry.

"What are you waiting for, Pinky? I thought you had to get to my cattle?"

CHAPTER 27

Charlie needed information about Plant City and Ward's meeting, so he went to the lounge car. The train lurched, and a woman his age stumbled into him.

"Whoa, there, ma'am!" Charlie said, recognizing her, the card player with the wandering eyes. They knelt to pick up cards from a spilled board game.

"I beg your pardon," she said, "if only my father offered grace in his Wish Book."

"Or train engineers with a steady hand. Your father named Ward?"

They stood, and the woman extended her hand, "Yes. I'm Marjorie Ward. Mr. Herlong, will you join us? We're about to play a game that tells our future."

"I appreciate the offer," Charlie said, "but my present keeps me hopping."

"I'm impatient," Marjorie said. I understand Mr. Plant's hotel is a sight to behold—unlike anything I've ever seen."

"I've heard," Charlie said, "One of those 'Seeing the Elephants' things."

"Whenever I hear that," she said, "I think of the poor sap following them with a shovel."

"Oh, Marjorie," another exclaimed, "How charming. Come on, let's play."

Charlie stooped and handed her an errant card.

"Pleasure, ma'am," and turned to find Murphy.

"Mr. Herlong," Marjorie said, looking at the card, "your future, don't you want to know?"

"Does it include the word shovel?" Charlie laughed.

"It says what you seek will find you!" She said as he walked away, "Good luck."

Murphy stepped through the door, arms full, and Charlie gave him a hand.

"Thanks, Charlie," Murphy said, "We're going to be in Plant City just as we get up to speed. I need to get this tea working before the ladies get all up in arms."

"Murphy, why are we stopping in Plant City?" Charlie asked.

"Ward and his group want to look at some buildings there," Murphy said, spooning black tea into a teapot.

"Are there corrals near the station?"

"Should be," Murphy said, "Why, Charlie, you in the cattle business, now?"

"If I can keep them in Plant City," Charlie said.

Ward or his associates weren't there, so he returned to the Conductor's car. Charlie checked the basket and found two napkins and crumbs.

"I guess ole Jack was hungry."

"Well, yes sir, I was," Jack said and stepped out of Fleet's closet, "Musco took one too."

Charlie grabbed his pistol.

"Don't shoot me yet," Duffie said. "I have a proposition for you."

"Proposition? What kind," Charlie asked.

"Well, does your man work for you, or are you partners? Right, it's none of my business, but he asked how long it would take to get to Lakeland and back to Plant City. Well, I figured, based on you asking about corrals, that you or somebody needs to put their cattle ... well, that other feller has to find somebody in Lakeland and get back to Plant City... well, ..." Duffie paused to catch his breath.

"Jack, what do you propose?"

"I want to work for you."

"Doing what?" Charlie asked, "As soon as I get this train to Tampa, I'm heading to Jacksonville."

"Wherever."

"Well, Jack," Charlie sat down, "What can you do?"

"Everything," Duffie said defiantly. I've run a train station, been a postmaster, and managed a general store. Hell, people consider me the Mayor of Knights. And yeah, I know, but I was doing a fine job. I can't control railroad tycoons, the US government, or the weather. That's what killed my last three jobs."

"Well, Jack, working for me might be your fourth calamity," Charlie said, "I can't guarantee I can pay you."

"Mr. Charlie," Duffy's face was sincere, "I just now met you, and I've already been paid and fed more than I have in the last six months. I can tell you're fair and do what you say. If Mr. Henry doesn't get back before you have to leave, which I don't think he will, no offense, I'll make sure your cattle and horses get settled, and I'll guard them till you get back or Mr. Henry tells me to do something else. I guarantee it."

"Well, let's see what happens when we get there."

"Yes, sir, you will," Duffie said, "Where's this basket go?"

"I don't know, Murphy gave it to me."

"I'll be right back," Duffie said and left the car.

Charlie sat down and considered his options. Having Jack Duffie around could help with finding horses. With little cash, could he barter enough to travel to Gainesville with stock? What about Fleet? Could he be depended on? The front door opened, and Fleet stepped in, flushed and wild-eyed.

"Just what do you think you are doing?" Fleet snapped, "Hiring new crew, getting my brakeman drunk, and feeding strays? Who do you think you are?"

"Whoa," Charlie said. You know who I am. I'm Charlie Herlong, the man who's going to babysit our cows, remember?"

"Ours?" Fleet stammered, "the ones you're stealing?"

"Have a seat, Mr. Fleet." Charlie sang, "Why don't you think about trading that freight car for another stock car? I hear they need horses up in Gainesville."

"What's in it for me?" Fleet was beginning to calm.

"At the very least, more freight business for the company," Charlie said, "Let's get people what they need. They'll pay us for it."

"What about Duffy?" Fleet said, "he's in there helping Murphy right now."

"So, is that a bad thing? Murphy might need a hand, and Duffy is looking out for me, which means he's looking out for you, too," Charlie said, "Right now, get your paperwork together; we'll be in Tampa soon, won't we?"

Charlie was off the train before it came to a complete stop. He jogged down Reynolds toward Palmer Street. He continued toward the tracks and saw no corrals, returned to Reynolds, and looked north. He was working up a sweat and walked east on Mahoney Street, south toward Reynolds.

"Hello! Mr. Thorne?" A business buggy pulled up next to Charlie.

"No sir, I'm Charlie Herlong," Charlie said, "They must be at the train if you haven't picked them up.""

"They?" the man asked, "Do you know how many are in their party?"

"Five that I know of," Charlie said. But I couldn't say who would go along; I'm just out scouting the area, looking for a corral and a well."

"Jump in," the man offered, "I'm Sam Barnes. Is Mr. Thorne looking for a barn?"

"Oh, I couldn't say," Charlie said, winking, "but I'm in the freight business; a shop and livery close to the depot always helps."

"Yes, it would," Barnes said, "and one's available just east of the depot. It has good storage and a well with good water. It's been vacant since the freeze."

"Who owns it?" Charlie asked.

"Stephane Beaudry, who moved back to Atlanta." Barnes answered, "It might take a while to contact him."

"And vice-versa!" Charlie said as he jumped out at the depot, "Hey, don't leave; I want to talk about that corral!"

He was moving toward Duffy, opening the stock car.

"Jack, what are you doing," Charlie said, "you have somewhere to put those cows?"

"No, but this train won't move with the ramp down," Duffy said. Do you want to keep running everywhere, or do you want to ride?"

"Hell of an idea, Jack!" Charlie said, "Let's saddle both of them; we may need to move the cattle ourselves, but right now, I'm going to check out a place to the east."

"Hell, I'll give it a shot," Duffy said, "I notice those saddles have ropes, pickets, and rings on them. I used to sell that stuff."

"Let's hope we don't," Charlie said, "don't use the bloody saddle."

Charlie was soon riding to a group of buildings right next to the tracks. Behind the more significant buildings sat a barn with a corral and trough. He wanted to see the buildings, but his horse kept moving toward the corral. Rather than fight, Charlie let him take the lead. The horse walked straight into the corral and to the trough. The horse drank from the green water at the bottom of the trough, and Charlie dismounted.

"Are you thirsty?" Charlie asked, and the horse nickered. Charlie saw a rain barrel at the corner of the barn, found a bucket, and primed the pump to fill the trough.

"Merci, Monsieur Beaudry, I'll take it." Charlie closed the gate and looked around the buildings. All had raised floors and loading docks, and the doors had security hardware.

The horse was eating wire grass when Charlie returned. Charlie whistled, and the horse looked up.

"Come on, Thirsty," Charlie called, who was already walking toward him, "Well, I guess you're mine, now."

Charlie thought about how strange the day was and then realized that this whole week had been strange, like nothing he had ever seen.

When Charlie got to the depot, Jack was mounted at the ramp, with a rope tied to his saddle horn and leading up. Musco Cranshaw was at the top of the ramp, looking through the slotted gate.

"Musco! Just slide through the gate and slip the loop over one's head, and we'll lead them where they need to go!"

"Then the rest of them are going to rush the gate, and I'm going to get squooshed!" Cranshaw yelled.

"Got dang it, you sorry rascal!" Duffy yelled, and Charlie rode up, "Charlie, will you take this rope, and I'll go get one?"

"No, you stay right there," Charlie said. How do you know that bull isn't going to drag you all over this street? Take them to the eastbound track, and you'll see the corral. There's water in there."

Musco opened the gate, and the cattle started coming out. Charlie kicked his horse over to the stock car. He leaped onto the edge of the gate and managed to slide it shut after five came down the ramp. Musco ran to the front of the train, and Duffy started leading the first bull toward the corral. The cows followed.

Charlie followed, and the cattle moved quickly toward the corral. He turned and rode back to the depot, hoping to find Barnes.

Charlie saw them at a corner Charlie had scouted. Ward was seated in the buggy, and Robert Thorne was speaking with Barnes.

"So, please understand, Mr. Barnes," Thorne said, "We're not here to open a retail establishment. We are looking for warehouses to store our catalog inventory. Ah! Mr. Herlong! Have you found your corral?"

"I believe I have," Charlie said, "on the track leading east behind some empty packing houses. I was hoping to speak with Mr. Barnes here if he has a moment."

"Certainly, my friend," Thorne said, "It will give us a moment to discuss our options."

Charlie dismounted and walked away from the buggy.

"Mr. Herlong, I can't just rent you that property," Barnes said.

"It's been empty for two years, and the owner is in Atlanta," Charlie replied. "By the time you get word to him, he gets back to you, and then y'all pitch horseshoes back and forth; I'm going to be gone."

"This is highly unusual," Barnes said, "I don't even know what rent Mr. Beaudry would charge."

"That's right," Charlie said, "That's why I'm going to put down a sizable deposit on the property, which no one would object to unless, of course, you have folks looking to buy it. Which you know ain't so, and more importantly, Beaudry knows it."

Barnes was beginning to think about the situation in a way that he had not done before. Charlie could almost see the wheels turning in Barnes' mind.

"When will those packing houses be used again?" Charlie asked, "Three months from now? Even if the current owners don't sell to Montgomery Ward, Ward can rent them until they build warehouses. I'm sure you know some carpenters in town. How would that pie smell, Mr. Sam Barnes? And you would drive the wagon."

Charlie let it settle on Barnes a bit and mounted his horse.

"Mr. Barnes, here's that sizable deposit," Charlie said and handed Barnes a double eagle.

"This is your idea of sizable?" Barnes said.

"My idea of sizable is our business," Charlie said, "What everyone else's idea is theirs. As long as they know, I wanted to buy it first."

"Good point!" Barnes laughed and returned to Thorne.

"Gentlemen, I need to get back to the train," Charlie said to the others, "I bet Mr. Fleet is anxious to get this trip over with."

"I bet you are too, Charlie," Ward said, "You've accomplished a lot today."

"So far!" Charlie said and kicked toward the depot.

"Mr. Barnes, what about those packing houses?" Ward asked as Charlie cantered off, smiling.

When Charlie got back, Duffy was standing next to the ramp. There was a wagonload of peanut hay with a local teen in the box.

"See, I told you he'd be back," Duffy said. Mr. Herlong, this man has hay that he'll sell us for 16 cents a bale. He says that's how much they pay him at the feed store."

"Any trouble with the last three cows?" Charlie asked.

"No sir, Michael, here helped me out."

"Well, thank you, Michael. Does your daddy have a special arrangement with the feed store for that hay?" Charlie asked.

"No, sir, nothing special," Michael said, "They buy hay whenever people have it if they need it."

"So your Daddy wouldn't be mad if I bought the whole load?"

"No, sir, it's 20 bales, and they're green." Michael said, "You only have nine head."

"Yeah, but I'm hoping to buy a bunch of horses. Is peanut hay good for horses?"

"Yes, sir," Michael said, "but you need to mix some corn or oats in with it, too. That also goes for cattle if you ain't going to graze them."

"Ok, I want all the hay. I'll pay you $4.00, but you have to unload it in the barn over there. Then take Mr. Duffy to the feed store. You understand?" Charlie shook Michael's hand and turned to Duffy.

"Let's get this horse loaded; I may need it in Tampa." Charlie saw that Michael was still standing there. Mikey! Get to it. You still need to get to the feed store, and Duffy here might buy y'all a soda pop if you hurry."

"Try to get that kid to come around and run errands for you," Charlie said, "and pay him well until we get some help; I want you here to guard the stock and set up that barn."

"Fleet seems to think it's going to get dangerous around those cows," Duffy said, "Do you think I need a gun?"

"Wouldn't be a bad idea; I have a .45 with a holster rig I'll leave with you. Maybe that kid can pick you up some dinner. I plan to be back by tomorrow morning with horses or a plan to get them," Charlie was thinking out loud, "Here's about ten bucks in change and a double eagle. Use it to set up the shop area, not for blacksmithing but to make it comfortable for you and whoever is working with us; we're going to be living there until we run out of beef. Well? You were right! Henry didn't make it back, but we didn't need him, did we? You're hired, Jack. Let's get people what they need!"

CHAPTER 28

Charlie felt good about leaving Plant City. Finding Jack was good luck. Charlie could complete the linen delivery and get to see this fancy hotel.

The train lurched, and Charlie thought of Marjorie Ward, prompting Charlie to freshen up. Four days of camping made him long for the mud stall. They had a shower stall at home, and Charlie used it every day. For now, a birdbath would have to do.

He hung his shirt and used the basin to wash. Murphy came through the front door.

"Oh, Charlie!" he said and averted his eyes.

"Murphy," Charlie said, "I'm not shy. I'm just washing off some barn."

"There's a wash house at the hotel," Murphy said, "I can put your clothes in the train wash."

"Oh, no," Charlie said, "I'll be leaving in the morning."

"Yes, sir, with us. It'll be ready."

"How's that? They're washing it with water, aren't they?"

"Charlie, they got a whole building just for laundry, big stoves that heat water and dry the clothes!" Murphy said, gathering cloth, "give it."

Charlie hesitated, and Murphy continued, "Son, trust me on this; it'll be back in the morning. Ain't you staying in the hotel?"

"I figured I'd just grab a nap in here," Charlie said and handed Murphy his shirt and some socks.

"Those pants won't do for supper," Murphy said and motioned to the portmanteau, "Put that other pair on; they're clean. I'll take the shortjohnnies, too."

"Murphy, I ain't eating pants for supper," Charlie said as he touched the basket, "Thanks for the sandwiches; they'll be plenty."

"Well, Jack suggested it," Murphy said, " He was sure happy to get a job. The pants, Mr. Charlie."

Charlie handed his duck pants to Murphy, "What's the worry about my clothes?"

"Well, this ain't my business," Murphy said, "but that Miss Marjorie was asking to have you for dinner tonight. You'll need clean pants and a jacket."

"Have me for dinner?" Charlie laughed, "At or on the table? Don't bet on it."

"Maybe will, maybe won't," Murphy said. If you get a chance to eat in the dining room, take it. It'll be like nothing you've ever tasted before."

"They serve elephant?"

"It wouldn't surprise me, with wine gravy," Murphy said. Here's a key to that other closet. You'll want to put your guns in it; there's no need at the hotel. Just don't let Fleet see that key; he thinks it's lost."

Murphy bagged the laundry, and Charlie followed him out.

Seffner and Mango were busier than Plant City. Charlie was concerned to see a clear-cut forest. Timbermen would have left smaller growth alone. Camps with rows of tents held more army than Charlie knew existed. For acres, men were doing the busy work that soldiers do. There were all types of people. Every portion of the available track was occupied by trains, and some cars were open and conducting business right on the track. The only clear track, the one Charlie was on, was evidence that these people held lofty status.

There were tents and shanties everywhere, most serving food and beverage, hot baths, or barber services. More established buildings held businesses common to small towns. Occasionally, he saw men brawling or being thrown out of saloons. In Tampa, they crossed the Hillsborough River and took a spur off to the south.

"Oh, my solemn word."

Astonishing as the week had been, he was awestruck by the site of the hotel. It was the largest manufactured object Charlie had ever seen. Built with millions of red bricks, this single building was a quarter mile long in Charlie's estimation. Four floors seemed as tall as the oldest yellow pines that Rob Wadby ever harvested. Onion-shaped minarets at each corner had crow's nests placed at the top.

Huge porches spanned the front of the building, with rocking chairs filled with Army officers or fashionably dressed sophisticates. Charlie only noticed the train when it stopped. Workers swarmed to it, ready to assist passengers and unload cargo. Seeing men open the freight car made Charlie snap out of his awe and hustle over.

"Mr. Herlong!"

A man in a lightweight, grey suit with a red tie approached, accompanied by another in sleeve garters.

"Mr. Herlong, my name is Harvey Stringer," the man said, "the hotel steward. Would you like to exchange the bills of lading?"

Charlie handed his copy to Stringer, who gave it to his assistant, who hustled over to supervise the unloading.

"Mr. Herlong, we heard of your experience in Owensboro," Stringer said, "You're the talk of the hotel."

"How? We just got here," Charlie said.

"Mr. Ward sent a wire to Mr. Plant in Washington," Stringer said, "and Mr. Plant informed us. I have several for you, a personal message from Mr. Plant, another from Mr. Thorne..."

"Thorne? He's on the train ..."

"I beg your pardon. I should have been more specific, Mr. George Thorne, managing partner of Montgomery Ward in Chicago," Stringer said, "and a third from Gainesville."

"Oh, no," Charlie said, "Dutton knows about it, too?"

"Uh, no, sir. This is from a ... Tiger?" Stringer seemed puzzled. Tiger Driggers?"

"Quit lyin'!" Charlie laughed, "Tiger didn't send no telegram."

Stringer handed the envelopes to Charlie, who ignored those from Captains of Industry to find the one from Tiger's Prairie. Stringer signed Charlie's bill of lading and held his out for him.

"Your signature, sir? Then your freight will be officially signed and delivered," Stringer said.

Charlie had the telegram open and stopped to sign the copy. He removed his Dutton badge.

Western Union

Gainesville, FL – Tiger Driggers

The Tampa Bay Hotel – Charlie Herlong, private

Have found a buyer for as many horses or mules as you can deliver.

$125 for horses and $90 for mules of good quality

Tiger Driggers

"Mr. Herlong."

"Call me Charlie, Harvey. Where can I find a horse trader?" Charlie said.

"We have some additional business if you don't mind," Stringer said, "but I can have someone here for you before sundown."

"They'll come to us?"

"If we ask them, they will," Stringer said, "Mr. Lindsay, our general manager, can explain things for you. I'll take you to him."

"Well, let me get my bag," Charlie said, then turned again. Oh, and what about my horse, Thirsty?"

"It will be in the stable, being fed and watered ..."

"No, that's his name," Charlie said.

"Oh, we'll just put it under your name," Stringer said, "and a porter will take your bag to your room."

Charlie looked over at Murphy, nodding and waving as if saying, 'Go ahead!' Charlie, used to taking care of himself, was uncomfortable.

They walked to the hotel, where those from the train were already chatting with officers and other guests.

"Oh, Mr. Herlong!" Marjorie Ward called out, "If you have a minute, please meet our friends from Baltimore!"

Stringer gave a little shrug and tapped his watch pocket.

"Miss Ward, I would be thrilled," Charlie said, giving a little wave, "Hey, y'all, welcome to Florida. But I have a meeting, and I'm a little late. Maybe later?"

"Of course," Marjorie said, returning a little wave, "Will ... 'Y'ALL' have dinner with us? Please say maybe, at least."

"Y'all!" One of the ladies said, and the group giggled.

"Maybe!" Charlie said, and they huddled close to Marjorie.

Stringer said, "It seems you fit in well with the Lace Curtain crowd. That's a good thing."

The hall was enormous, with vaulted ceilings, arches, and a catwalk around a second-floor mezzanine. Fancy folk all over. Charlie itching all over. They entered an ornate door near the desk and walked down a hallway to an executive office—like Dutton's, only larger. Mr. Lindsay was sitting at a desk and stood when Charlie walked into the room.

"Mr. Herlong! Welcome to the Tampa Bay Hotel," Lindsay said, hands behind his back, waiting for a response.

"Hey, Mr. Lindsay, call me Charlie," he said, extending his hand, which Lindsay shook formally, "I appreciate your familiarity, but Mr. Plant likes formality if you don't mind."

"Call me what you want," Charlie said, "and when you want for dinner."

"Ah, you remind me of upstate New York, my home," Lindsay said, "they say that, too. Speaking of dinner, you've been invited by A. Montgomery Ward to join them in our dining room. He'd like to thank you for your bravery."

"Oh, no need to thank me again," Charlie said, "and … I'm not dressed for dinner."

"That's not a problem, sir. We'll send a suit to your room."

"What room?"

Lindsay looked at Stringer and said, "Did Mr. Stringer give you the telegrams?"

"Yes sir, three. I nearly dropped out getting one from Tiger Driggers," Charlie said, "I guess I need to read them."

"I couldn't say what's in the wires you received," Lindsay said, "but Mr. Plant has informed Mr. Dutton of your exemplary service and intends to do more business with his company. He has also instructed me to extend every amenity, courtesy, or privilege you request and to do so at his expense."

"No charge? Why would he do that?" Charlie couldn't believe it, "I was doing my job."

"And in doing so, you protected the lives and property of Mr. Plant's important guests," Lindsay said, "all traveling on his private train to stay at his hotel to consider using Mr. Plants' shipping resources."

"Dang," Charlie said, "If I'd a known all that, I'd a pissed down my leg, too."

"Too?" Lindsay asked.

Charlie decided not to mention Fleet again.

"I have a feeling Mr. Ward feels the same way," Lindsay said, "So, let's get you into a room, Mr. Herlong. We have some very nice suites available. Will you be needing accommodations for your associate, uh, Mr. Whitaker?"

"Who, Henry? Well, he should get a reward, too," Charlie hesitated.

Stringer said, "Will he be staying with us also?"

"No, sir," Charlie said, "right now, he's over in Lakeland. I think he's trying to join the 10th cavalry."

"I see," Lindsay said, "Well, General Joe Wheeler is staying here; he commands the 10th. Would you like to meet with him?"

"I better ask Henry first," Charlie said, "I'll see him in Plant City tomorrow."

"Oh, you're leaving us so soon?" Lindsay asked, "On more Dutton business, I presume?"

"No, sir. My time with Mr. Dutton ended with the delivery of the linens," Charlie said. I have business in Plant City and Gainesville while the trains are backed up, and I'll move on to Jacksonville as soon as possible."

Stringer stood, "If I may, Mr. Lindsay, Mr. Herlong is interested in buying horses and requires a broker."

"Get word to Fermin," Lindsay looked at Charlie, "How many horses do you need?"

"As many as I can get to Gainesville," Charlie said, "At $50 a head, I can buy a dozen today, as long as I can use the same stock car we used to get cattle down here."

"That car's empty, that's fine. How about two dozen?" Lindsay said, "I'll have Stringer get them for that price. We'll extend credit for the extra dozen. Interest-free," Lindsay said, "I understand you have a corral in Plant City?" Charlie nodded.

"Excuse me, Mr. Lindsay," Charlie said, "I'm a little slow. Did you just offer to give me two dozen horses for $600 down and $600 payable ..... whenever? When I see the horses, who am I buying them from? The horse trader or you?"

"Whichever you prefer," Lindsay said, "We have a good relationship with Mr. Fermin. This isn't normally how we do business, but Mr. Plant has instructed me to offer our resources to whatever you need to take care of yours. Within certain limits, of course. Would you like to take some time to decide what you need?"

"No, sir," Charlie said, "I want to get this deal on paper before somebody figures out I was just trying to avoid getting shot!"

Lindsay and Stringer laughed, and Charlie thought, 'These two dandies think I'm kidding!'

"Tell us what you need, Mr. Herlong," Lindsay said, "The Plant System is at your service."

"24 good, saddle-broke horses at $50 a head, taken by rail to Hawthorne. $600 now and $600 due at sale in Gainesville," Charlie said, "How do I get the money to you?"

"Mr. Plant does business with every bank in Florida," Lindsay said, "I would heartily suggest Florida National. They're in most places. Just send the total of $1200 to us through them. Stringer, get someone over to Fermin and see how fast he can get those horses to us."

"Just like that?" Charlie said.

"Yes, we want to make things as easy as possible for you," Lindsay said, "Unfortunately, we can not get the horses to Hawthorne tomorrow; that will take a little longer; we can get them to Plant City if you like. That would give you some time to develop your cattle sale over there. We hope to have the track crowding straightened out soon; until then, we'll need more cattle in a week. Would you be interested?

"If I come across some cattle, I'll let you know, Mr. Lindsay," Charlie said, "but I plan to get to Jacksonville soon if I can. If the tracks get sorted out, I'd prefer to go by train."

"I'm sure that you would," Lindsay said, "I'm going to sweeten our deal by giving you credentials to ride anything in the Plant System for a year. It would be our pleasure. In the meantime, Mr. Stringer will have a porter escort you to your room. Be sure to have him bring you anything you wish. If you need to speak with me, use the telephone in your room, and the operator will put you through to me."

With that, A.E. Lindsay sat down and turned his attention to his desk. Charlie stood there for a moment or two, shrugged his shoulders, and followed Stringer.

CHAPTER 29

Charlie stepped through the huge door, and the entrance hall seemed eerily quiet. Stringer had stepped away to speak with the desk clerk.

"Where'd everyone go?" Charlie muttered.

"At five o'clock, most guests go to their rooms to rest," he said.

"They've had a long day? I bet none of them rescued any Captains of Industry," Charlie said, relaxing a bit.

"Oh, you're the one?" the porter asked, "Folks have been talking about that all afternoon."

"I had no idea," Charlie said, grinning, "a hero could be scared to the liver!"

Stringer returned and handed a key to the porter, "Avail Mr. Herlong to any amenity," then to Charlie, "Mr. Herlong, I must make them available. Sammy here will show you to your room and take care of you."

"Is that a fact?" Charlie said, sticking out his hand, "Sammy, I'm Charlie Herlong. What's your last name?"

"Uh," Sammy glanced at Stringer and shook his hand, "Bradford. Your room is on the third floor. Do you prefer the elevator or stairs?"

"I've never ridden in one," Charlie said, walking to the elevator, "But I ain't scared, being a hero and all. Which do you prefer?"

"I've ridden it once," Sammy said, "porters take the stairs."

"Yeah, well, I prefer you ride. This is my first time, and I might be a little scared," Charlie turned to the white operator, "You don't mind, though, do you."

"Third floor, please, Mr. Hankins!" Sammy said, stepping behind Charlie inside the metal-framed, ornate space.

On the third floor, Hankins opened the gate. Charlie stood still as Sammy moved closer. Charlie looked at Hankin's face, who stared ahead.

Hankins turned his head slightly, "Third floor," he said, finally.

"'Preciate it," Charlie said and stepped out.

Sammy followed, grinning, and led Charlie down the hall.

"Yes, sir, Mr. Herlong, 310," Sammy pushed the door and swept his hand. "It's a corner suite with two bedrooms and a bath. The chair by the windows should let you see all the grounds and Tampa."

Charlie stood at the threshold and eased in. Bronze and porcelain art pieces were arranged around end tables, and a round dining table held a huge floral centerpiece.

"Is everything all right, Mr. Herlong?"

"I reckon so," Charlie said and stepped in. "Y'all know it's just me, right?"

"Yes, sir, all for you," Sammy said, "Compliments of Mr. Plant."

There was a knock at the door.

"Here they come," Charlie said, "my room's out back!"

"No, sir," Sammy said, "We're in the right room."

Sammy brought two men in; one held several suits of clothes, and another carried a case.

"It's the tailor," Sammy said. You'd best do what he says. If not, he'll stick you with a pin. I'm drawing you a bath so you feel good in your new clothes."

"Ah sì, Pensavo che gli sarebbe servita una 44 normale," the tailor said, holding a measuring tape, "Signore, mi permetta di vedere le sue misure. Stia dritto, per favore."

Charlie straightened his posture and held his breath. The tailor looked at his apprentice and said, "Digli di respirare prima che lo faccia scoppiare come un palloncino!"

"You can breathe, Signore Herlong," the apprentice said, "this won't take long. You will need to remove your trousers."

"Y'all ain't going to get me some punch, at least?" Charlie said, "What's he speaking, Spanish?"

"Oh mio Dio, pensa che siamo Cubani," the tailor said, "Ma perché ho lasciato Milano?"

"Is he cussing me out?" Charlie asked, "He might get stuck."

"No, sir, that's just his way. He is from Milano, Italia, and would rather be in New Orleans," the apprentice said. "There is whiskey in the cabinet if you like."

"Well, go pour us all one, so he'll settle his neck hair down," Charlie said.

"Marco, il signore Herlong ci ha offerto da bere," the apprentice said, walking to the bar.

"Sì, ma niente gin. Brandy o amaretto," Marco said, then to Charlie, "Holda out you hands."

"Careful, son," Charlie said, "I'm ticklish."

"Questi idioti raccontano sempre la stessa barzelletta!"

"And what's your name," Charlie asked, "Are you from Milano, I-talia, too?"

"No, sir," the apprentice said, "I'm born in New York. He says he likes your joke. My folks are from Sicily, so I know Italian. My name is Pietro, but you can call me Pete."

"Sì, è un ragazzo molto intelligente, per niente stupido," the tailor said, measuring, "Non come quelle scimmie laggiù."

"I know what stupido means," Charlie said to Pietro, "who is he talking about?"

"My family's home; he just called us all monkeys," Pietro said. "But don't feel left out; he thinks everyone is stupid—except for him."

"It don't seem to bother you," Charlie said, "how come?"

"He's like a barking dog," Pietro said, "I can choose to be insulted, but why? Who can speak two languages? I do. He barely speaks English and can't keep from insulting people. Who knows the fishing business? I do. He knows how to sew and is teaching me how, along with the knowledge of how to deal with assholes."

"Ah, grande assholio! Grazie!" Marco said as he looked up from Charlie's crotch.

"I told him asshole means great philosopher," Pietro said, handing them glasses.

"Ah, il nettare dell'Eden," Marco said and took a sip, "Ah!"

"What an asshole, senor," Charlie said, raising his glass to Pete, "Call me Charlie."

"Grazie. Fate in modo che resti pieno," Marco said, taking a sip and turning to Pietro, "Pietro, penso che mi piacerebbe finire qui, nella stanza, convincerlo a prendersi un cappello, un ridicolo Derby. Oh, lasciatemi misurare."

"He wants to give you a new hat," Pietro said, "a Derby."

Marco then put the tape measure around Charlie's head, "Oh mio Dio, 200 millimetri."

"Si Signore Marco, you asshole," Charlie said, then to Pietro, "Tell him a big head for big ideas."

"Grazie, signore," Marco said, finishing the brandy, "E Pietro, chiama uno stiracalzoni, possiamo farlo stare nell'altra camera da letto, io cucirò i pantaloni a mano. E manda a prendere una scatola di lustro; le sue scarpe sono atroci."

"Mr. Herlong, Signore Veneta would like to finish the alterations here in the other bedroom if you allow," Pietro said, "He would also like to send for a shoeshine."

"I'm proud to have you," Charlie said.

"Mr. Herlong, your bath is ready," Sammy said, and to Pietro, "No Derby, get him a low crown Homburg with a curved brim."

"Very nice," Pietro said.

"And dress shoes, the best we have. I'll see to the shine," Sammy said.

"You drinking, Sammy?" Charlie asked.

"No, sir. I'm working. Shouldn't we wait to serve El Assahoolio," Sammy whispered, "until he finishes the sewing?"

"Good idea," Charlie said, "Tell him I said finish my clothes, then have all he wants. Dang, you put bubbles in the bath?"

"Yes, sir," Sammy said, closing the doors, "I'll be out here if you need me."

Charley shaved and brushed his teeth. He wondered if Dorotha Dunwoody thought his breath smelled. He put on more Arnica tooth soap and brushed his teeth again.

He eased into the tub of soapy water, expecting a scalding, but the water was warm, dense, and soapy. His feet on the smooth copper and the warmth of the whisky helped ease the fatigue and stress of an incredibly long day.

❈ ❈ ❈ ❈ ❈ ❈ ❈ ❈ ❈ ❈ ❈ ❈ ❈

"Signore! Signore Herlong!" Marco banged on the door drunkenly, yelling in Italian, waking Charlie from a deep sleep. "Quanto dura questo un bagno? Il suo abito è cucito e stirato alla perfezione! Voglio vedere come le sta!"

Charlie opened the door, and Marco stumbled into him. Charlie shoved him to the floor next to Sammy.

"Mr. Herlong, I am sorry," Sammy said, "he knocked me down."

"I thought we said to hold off on the brandy," Charlie said.

"Well, yes, sir, we did," Sammy said, "but it's been an hour."

"I guess I took a nap," Charlie said as Sammy gave him a towel, "an hour? I got to go."

"We have time," Sammy said, "Dinner's not until seven o'clock. Mr. Stringer came by and left this note."

Sammy handed Charlie an envelope.

Mr. Herlong,

I have an assurance from Mr. Fermin for 24 horses of differing colors. All are high quality, young, and healthy. He guarantees their value, as do we, The Plant System. The stock will be available on location for transport in the morning, as allowed by available train space and scheduling.

Until then, enjoy our hospitality as you see fit.

At your service,

Harvey Stringer

Charlie took a bit to reread the note, then realized he was standing naked. Charlie turned to retrieve his drawers.

"Mr. Herlong," Pete handed him some. I have several short union suits for you to try. They are cut above the knee and sleeveless to account for the heat."

"Hey, and it ain't even Christmas," Charlie said, stepping into one, "I usually cut them off in the summer. Hey, let's get Marco off the floor. Let him rest in there. That sewing will wear a man slap out."

"I'll call for some coffee," Sammy said, "Cuban, that'll wake the dead."

"Nah, he's more charming this way," Charlie said.

Soon, Charlie was in a crimson vest with a white shirt and attached collar. His green silk tie was secured with a long pin. He was seated, reading the telegrams from Henry Plant and George Thorne. Pete packed up and moved the pants press.

"Hey, Pete," Charlie said, "Where do I take these duds when I'm done with them?"

"Wear them in good health. They're yours," Pete said, "What should we do about Marco? Our time here is over."

"Ah, let him sleep," Charlie said. He'll get up and leave soon. If he starts snoring, I'll poke him with this pin. Thank you, Pete. It was nice meeting you."

"Sir, the pleasure was all mine."

"These duds will be ruined in a week," Charlie said to Sammy, "I need something to carry them in, I guess."

"I'll pack them for you," Sammy said. Gentlemen need a good suit. If we need a bigger bag, we have them, too. Would you like more whisky?"

"No," Charlie said, "help yourself. Why don't you show me how to order coffee on this telephone rig I keep hearing about?"

"Yes, sir," Sammy said; he turned the crank twice and put the piece to his ear. "The operator will talk, and you just tell her what you want. Do you want to try?"

"No, you got it," Charlie said. Ask for three cups. We may want this tailor awake if he snores."

They waited, and Charlie insisted Sammy sit, which he finally did at the round table. Charlie asked about Sammy, but Sammy wanted to know how he got there.

"Good Luck!" Charlie laughed and told him about his trip, "I just wanted to get to Jacksonville and see something different, and every day, I get further away and keep seeing elephants."

"Guests say that about this hotel," Sammy said, "an elephant."

"I sure ain't ever seen anything like it," Charlie said, "It's a surprise."

"For most folks, it is," Sammy said. "Before here, I worked for the Inn at Port Tampa. It was on stilts above the water. Folks could fish out the window! That was a sight for people, then. When I came here, this was an elephant for me."

At 6:55, Sammy helped Charlie slip into his grey frock coat. He attached the watch chain supplied by Marco and brushed lint from Charlie's Derby.

"Sammy, I don't have a watch," Charlie said, "Wearing this chain is ridiculous. What if someone asks me the time? I'll look ridiculous."

"It makes the vest handsome," Sammy said. If someone asks for time, tell them there's never enough. Don't waste it looking at your watch. How does your hat fit?"

"It feels good. I have a hard time finding hats for my big ol cow head," Charlie said. Sammy, I don't want to carry this thing around all night."

"There is a room right before the dining room; they'll keep it for you," Sammy said.

"Are you coming with me?" Charlie asked.

"No, sir," Sammy said, "I'll stay here and straighten up a bit. While you're gone, I'll go downstairs and eat. I'm going to be with you as long as you're here. That's my job."

He tilted Charlie's hat a bit and motioned to the full-length mirror.

"You look good. Straight off 5th Avenue, New York. Easter Sunday." Sammy said.

You've been there?" Charlie asked, checking out his image.

"Nope. Haven't seen that elephant yet."

Chapter 30

Charlie wondered how someone could build a room with such high ceilings. He tried to estimate the number of guests, but there were too many people. He gave up when he realized he could not see the people he was counting.

"May I take your hat and coat, sir?" A woman stood behind a half door leading to the coat room. Charlie noticed the considerable room of shelves and racks behind her.

"Did all of those people give you one?" Charlie asked, "How do you keep track of them all? There must be 400 head out there."

"Oh," she said, "everyone gets a ticket. What's hard is when people lose it."

"What happens then?" Charlie asked.

"We get fussed at. But, if you lose yours, I'll remember."

"I appreciate it," Charlie gave his cute wink.

"Your name and room number, sir?"

"Charlie Herlong, oh, Shaw, I can't remember the room number; it's on the third floor."

"It's on your key, Mr. Herlong," she said, exchanging the coat and hat for a ticket.

Charlie pinned his key and ticket to his empty watch chain.

"Oh, that's clever," the woman said.

"Mr. Herlong?" The maître d asked. "Mr. Thorne said you were coming. Would you like to be seated?"

"Yessir."

Charlie felt great. After four days, he enjoyed his bath. Shoot, he forgot all about the Cuban Orchids! Ward and the other men at the table rose as they approached and began applauding. Guests at other tables joined in, and Charlie tried to find the celebrity they were clapping for.

"Charlie! We're so glad you could make it," Montgomery Ward said, "We were just enjoying the soup course."

"Sounds good. Please, have a seat, so they will." Charlie said, motioning to the other guests, "They might want me to sing."

A waiter offered Charlie a menu, and he glanced at it and said, "I'll just wait on the salad course; if those tomatoes are ripe, I'd love some."

"And the other courses, sir?"

"Bring me what you like," Charlie said, "I bet you know this food as well as anybody."

"Charlie Herlong," Ward said, "Let me introduce Mr. C.W. Dickerson. He's from Chicago and makes Sterling Bicycles, lots of them.

"I might be having some of your beef, sir," Dickerson said, "a rib cut. Rare."

"Oh, I don't know about that," Charlie said, "I'm in the cattle business this week. Today there were a few head in Plant City, which I found a lot for. 'Bout all I know about cattle is they need to be fed."

"Just like people," Marjorie Ward said, seated by Charlie, "Thank goodness we have ten courses. And lots of fresh vegetables. I'm starved. Train travel can be torture."

Her statement made Charlie laugh. He liked the train more than running freight with mules.

"Don't laugh," she said, "we've been cooped up on a train for a week. Can I call you Charlie?"

"Marjorie!" a woman said.

"Oh, Mother! We're practically old friends."

"It's fine, Miz Ward," Charlie said, "When y'all say Mister, I think my father is here."

"Tell us about your family, Charlie," Mrs. Ward said, "is your father a rancher?"

"No, Ma'am, he's in the timber business, clearing land, making lumber, running freight, and making turpentine."

"He sounds like a man of vision," she said, "I suppose it runs in the family."

"You could say that," Charlie said, "he knows how to get along and persuade folks. My late mother had a lot to do with the company's development. She could see opportunity and knew how to make it happen."

"I'm sorry, Charlie. She sounds like a great woman."

"Hard as a pine knot, but a good mama to have."

Charlie was relieved there was little hero discussion or talk about the train robbery. The men spoke of the situation in Cuba, the impending war. Charlie was happy to let those who knew continue to show how much. Dickerson asked Charlie if they rode bicycles in Lake City.

"The roads are pretty sandy," Charlie said. There are more people now that they have bigger tires. My father's new wife likes that; it gives her a reason to buy clothes."

"Pants!" Marjorie exclaimed, "They allow us to dress as we please and leave the skirt at home!"

"Do you ride, Charlie?" Dickerson asked.

"I have, but I don't own one; I have a horse and saddle. Maybe I should buy a set for my father and his new bride," Charlie laughed.

"I can make that happen, Charlie," Dickerson said, "That's Lake City? The Herlong Company?"

"There's no need for that, Mr. Henderson," Charlie objected.

"It's good business, Charlie," Henderson said, "If folks see him riding one of ours, they'll all want one."

"Well, they might want to go to church if they do," Charlie laughed, "my father can cuss like the Devil's choir!"

Charlie's choice of dessert captivated Marjorie.

"Oh, I wish I had asked for that. What is it?" Marjorie asked.

"Cuban custard cake soaked in peach liqueur," Charlie said, "here, I'll trade. What are those, little Beignets?"

"Oh, let's share," Marjorie said, splitting the two desserts, "Pardon my hands, they're somewhat clean."

"I ain't scared," Charlie said, "Take some of this juice, it's good."

"So, you've been to New Orleans?"

"No, I haven't, but my father's new wife taught our cook to make them," he said.

"You mean your stepmother?" Marjorie asked.

"No, I don't," Charlie said, "She ain't that much older than you and I."

"How old are we?" she asked. "I may be her age."

"I'm 22; I figured you were," Charlie said.

"You know that assuming a lady's age can cause trouble," Marjorie said, "What if I told you I was 30?"

"I'd say you look good for an old woman," Charlie whispered.

"I'd say you look good, too, for a rascal," she replied, smiling.

Across the table, Mr. Ward nudged his wife, "I believe Mr. Herlong is charming your daughter," he said quietly.

"She'll chew him up," Josephine said, "just like the rest."

"Maybe," Ward said, "Is she hard as a pine knot? We know he has courage. He seems smart, personable."

"He's charming her father," Josephine said.

"Mr. Herlong, I understand you have purchased some horses," Thorne said, "Will you be taking them to Plant City tomorrow?"

"That's news to me, Mr. Thorne," Charlie said, "I hope they run as fast as news travels."

"We were lining up a trip to Winter Park and hoped to do it tomorrow," Thorne said, "If the tracks are clear, that is, we didn't want to infringe on your plans."

"Gotta have freight to have a plan." Charlie said, "I suppose we'll wait until tomorrow to know that. If I do get horses, I'll want to move them straight to Hawthorne and line up a crew to move them to Gainesville."

Charlie looked at his plate and began to think.

"Bob," Marjorie said, "all this business has taken the smile right off our friend's face. Have some pie."

After dinner, the men adjourned to the Rathskeller, a bar in the basement. The three wives were moving toward the parlor and paused, waiting for Marjorie.

"So, cigars and brandy?" Marjorie said, "Men are so predictable."

"They invited me," Charlie said, "It's late, though; I'll be yawning during the jokes. Marjorie, meeting new friends is a dream. I hope to see you again soon."

"Do you mean it, Charlie?" she said, "'Friends cherish one another's hopes and dreams.' Have you read Thoreau?"

"Under threat of a beating," Charlie said, "As I remember, he built his house by himself. Friends are scarce when you're totin' lumber."

"Self-reliance," she said, "I believe you do mean it."

Charlie watched her walk toward her mother and friends, wondering what all that meant.

"Mr. Herlong!" Sammy called as he hustled through the grand hall, "I have a message from Mr. Stringer."

"Woo!" Charlie started walking a second after he opened the note, "Be careful what you ask for. What time is it?"

"Just after 9:00, sir. Your hat and coat?"

"Oh, yeah," Charlie said and turned toward the hat check, where Marjorie had retrieved her wrap. Charlie had his watchchain out, struggling to recover his ticket from his room key.

"That's some watch, Charlie," she said, helping him release the ticket.

"I can't find a watch that has enough time in it," Charlie said.

"See you soon, Mr. Charlie Herlong," Marjorie said, and Charlie watched her walk away, "sweet dreams."

❈ ❈ ❈ ❈✦ ✦✦ ❈ ❈ ✦❈ ❈❈ ❈

Harvey Stringer's note said the horses were due at 8:00. The schedule for Mr. Plant's train had not been determined, so arrangements were still pending. Charlie wondered if Henry had ever made it to Plant City. Would he or Jack be assertive enough to sell the cattle if there was a buyer? Could that corral hold that many horses and cattle?

"Will you be retiring, sir?" Sammy asked as he hung the grey frock coat. "And what about the tailor? Is he staying?"

"He's still here?" Charlie said, releasing his watch chain from the vest. "You want to throw him out?"

"Well, he shouldn't be here," Sammy said, "no matter how fancy he thinks he is."

"Well, he ain't bothering anyone but you right now." Charlie said, "You want to sleep in there?"

"Oh, no, sir," Sammy said, "that'd be more scandalous. Here are your sleeping clothes. There are pants and a shirt, pajamas."

"Hey, is it too late to send a telegraph?" Charlie asked as he removed his collar, vest, and shirt.

"No, sir, whenever you want."

Charlie went to the desk and wrote to Tiger Driggers. Be ready with wranglers to receive 24 horses in Hawthorne by train within three days. He would send more details when they became available. Charlie gave the note to Sammy.

"Have them send it to the station where this came from and deliver it to Tiger Driggers," Charlie said, and Sammy left the room.

Charlie was getting used to having someone run errands for him. He changed into the pajama pants. He thought about how the men he knew would be teasing him mercilessly over his new clothes and being in a palace. They would never believe it. He could barely believe it himself, but he did; here it is. He awakened on a steamship in a meadow. He opened the bar cabinet and poured the smoothest spirit he had ever tasted. His eyes were heavy, and he wanted to avoid sleep, just in case it was a dream.

Anne Mary McQuagge would say it was like a dream, and she would enjoy it until she woke up. He also remembered her saying one could not find the elephants, the elephants had to find you.

Charlie awoke to knocking at the door; he was still holding the glass of brandy. He walked to the door, his sock-covered feet slipping on the polished floor. He opened it and saw Marjorie, in her full-length, scarlet wrap, looking nervously up and down the hall.

"Marjorie! Is everything all right?"

"When you let me in," Marjorie said, stepping past him. "It took you long enough."

"What's on your mind?" Charlie said, thinking there must be some problem.

"Thoreau," she said, "and friends. Are we friends?"

"I think so."

"And hopes and dreams and self-reliance and how friends should cherish each other's hopes and dreams. Well, I'm being self-reliant," she said, walking around the sofa with her back to Charlie's bedroom. I'm here to cherish your hopes and my dreams."

She then opened her wrap and was wearing a silk chemise, tied with a silk belt, which she pulled partially and stopped.

"What's on your mind, Charlie?"

"I guess I'm wondering what a thirty-year-old woman looks like … naked," Charlie said.

"I wouldn't know," Marjorie said, "but this is what a woman our age looks like."

She pulled the belt and opened the chemise.

"Oh mio dio sei una dea! Che spettacolo!"

Marco was standing at the door to the other bedroom.

"Oh, my sweet Lawd, have mercy!" Sammy was at the hallway door, "No, sir! You got to go, rat, now!"

Marjorie screamed and backed into the bedroom. Sammy rushed over to Marco and dragged him toward the door.

"No, no, va bene così. Un altro drink, solo un bicchierino! Non farò alcun rumore! Lo prometto!"

Charlie knew this was a dream now. He poured two glasses of brandy.

"I'm fittin' to enjoy this till I wake up," he said, "Hell, I might go into the elephant business, too."

Charlie could see Marjorie in the bathroom, seated at the vanity, head down, and it surprised him. She had shown confidence all day. When she saw him, she stood and began to walk toward the door.

"I had no idea it would be so crowded in here. What made me think this was a good idea?" she said, then to Charlie, "I've never done anything like this in my life."

"Well," Charlie said, "this ain't the dream I was having, either. Here, have some brandy. If you go out there now, Marco might call you a spotted crow again."

Marjorie took the glass and said, "Spettacolo. It means a spectacular show."

"Well, then, what are you crying about?" Charlie said, tapping their glasses, "It ain't like he was fighting to get out the door."

Marjorie laughed. "You slide in and out of that country boy thing, don't you? What did you think?"

"Well, the first act was purty dang spectacular, but," Charlie said, "I'm a little hurt no one noticed my new sleepin' britches."

"I think it might be this Johnnie suit," she said. She released a few buttons and pulled the top section down, showing Charlie's hard chest and arms. "Now, where's the shirt?"

She handed the shirt to Charlie and sat on the arm of an overstuffed chair as Charlie put the shirt on.

"For someone who hadn't done this before, you catch on pretty quick," Charlie said.

"I meant showing up in the middle of the night. I've played dress up," she said, "Nope, this will not work with the underwear. Strip it all off and start over."

She giggled, took a slow sip of brandy, and Charlie followed her instructions.

Chapter 31

C harlie was in his house and bed. He smelled orange blossoms and heard a faint knocking at his door. That surely isn't Sassy. She should be opening windows and fussing loudly.

"Mr. Herlong, I hate to wake you ...." Sammy!

Charlie bolted up; he was not at home. He wasn't smelling orange blossoms but the lingering effects of Marjorie Ward.

"Mr. Herlong, we never wake the guests," Sammy said, pulling drapes and opening a window, "But aren't you trading horses this morning?"

A salty breeze blew into the room. Charlie was up and scrambling around

"What time is it? My britches?"

"Just past eight," Sammy said, holding out a pair of Charlie's duck pants, freshly laundered and belted, "Check your watch the Easter Bunny left you."

Charlie snatched the pants from Sammy and hopped over to the round table, putting his legs into his pants as he went. He picked up a leftover Easter card from nine days before.

Dear Charlie:

Here is a fob for your key chain. I had it set to include as much time as you need, with a good portion for me. Thanks for the lovely time at dinner; my friends and family think you are top drawer, and I agree. Thoreau was right; cherishing hopes and dreams is the way to live.

Hoping and Dreaming, Your spotted crow,

MM Ward

"When?"

"Just after sunup," Sammy said, winking, "But I was sleep, I ain't see nothin'. Look here, now, wear some socks."

"I ain't got time for that! Damn!"

Sammy was taken aback and folded his hands.

"I'm sorry, Sammy, I can't miss out on the horses and the train."

"What can I do for you?" Sammy said.

"Help me calm down without telling me to," Charlie said.

"Oh," Sammy said, opening another window, "I never thought about it like that. I can tell you that Mr. Stringer or Mr. Lindsay have never told me to make sure a guest has everything they want or need. Or to suggest everything to make them comfortable. If you're staying in this hotel, you have nothing to worry about. I have scones and coffee that might help."

"No time for coffee," Charlie said, pulling on socks and boots, "I'd like some, though. What's a scone? Can we eat it walking? Has the train left?"

"A sweet biscuit with corners," Sammy said, "I haven't heard the first whistle, and I'll show you how to get there."

Charlie grabbed his Stetson and headed for the door. The hallway was busy with guests and staff at the elevator.

"Or, I'll meet you there," Sammy said as Charlie loped down the stairs, finishing his scone.

Thorne was there when Charlie got to the freight deck. He looked at his watch and stepped toward Charlie, a concerned look on his face.

"Charlie, I heard about your horses," Thorne said, "We have a new conductor today, and he wants to get started."

"A new conductor?" Charlie said, "What about my horses?"

"They won't be here until 10:00." Thorne said, "Can your horse deal wait a day or two?"

"I can't sell horses I don't have, but I need to check on my men in Plant City," Charlie said, "Who's this new conductor? Down there, talking to Murphy?"

Charlie walked to them, and Murphy smiled in relief. The conductor's car was not coupled, and the stock cars were missing.

"Mr. Herlong, my name is Abraham Brooks," he said, "I'll be the conductor for this train."

"Oh," Charlie said, "is Mr. Fleet all right? He is well, I hope."

"I suppose that depends on your perspective," Brooks said. "He has been relieved. Lester Donahue, the Train Master for this region, has appointed me as his replacement. We noticed some security issues because of the attempted robbery."

"Oh, well, he did seem a little high-strung," Charlie said, "wouldn't you say, Murphy?" Murphy nodded.

"Well, we'll assign Plant security to this train now," Brooks said. We'll pick them up in Sanford."

"I see," Charlie said, "So, I imagine you'd like to get up there as soon as possible."

"That would be efficient, yes, sir," Brooks said.

"And my horses are holding up the show."

"In a manner of speaking, yes, sir," Brooks said.

"Well, I don't suppose waiting until 10:00 is good," Charlie said. Can you give me a ride to Plant City? I need to check on my associates there."

Brooks smiled and said, "Of course, Mr. Donahue has directed us to see to your needs. We can be coupled and ready to leave by 9:00. Thank you, sir."

Charlie turned and walked to the edge of the platform.

"Will you be needing anything from the room?" Sammy asked.

"I didn't even ask when they're coming back. I guess tomorrow," Charlie said.

"I'll bring a small bag for you," Sammy said, running toward the hotel.

Sammy's running made Charlie wonder about the time. He reached into his pocket and pulled out the chain with the keys and a slim, gold pocket watch. It had an engraved cover of flowers around a gazebo. 8:19. The face was labeled Montgomery Ward and Company. The watch moved to 8:20, and he closed it. His watch pocket easily held Marjorie's smaller watch and the two keys.

"Charlie Herlong! So nice to see you again!"

Marjorie and her mother sat in a runabout carriage. Josephine was dressed fashionably, wearing a giant hat that made Marjorie lean outside of the small carriage.

"Hello, ladies!" Thorne called out, walking to the edge next to Charlie.

"And Bob!" Mrs. Ward said, "My, what a good choice Margie made, taking the scenic route! Two of the most eligible men in Tampa!"

"We came to see the horses and didn't," Marjorie said.

"They're not here yet," Thorne said, "Charlie is going to delay his horse trading so that we can go to Winter Park."

"How considerate, Charlie," Mrs. Ward said, "Montgomery will be so appreciative of that. Does that mean you'll be staying here today?"

"Please say yes, Charlie!" Marjorie said. "Mother is making me play tennis, and I want to take a ride to the beach."

"That sounds like fun, but I need to check on my men in Plant City. They may need something," Charlie said.

"I'm sure Bob can get anything they need, can't you, Bob?" Marjorie looked at Thorne.

"If we don't have it in Winter Park, I can have it there in a week," Thorne said.

"Charlie, take a day off," Marjorie said, "Haven't you been working since you left Lake City? Bob, whatever they need, get it for them. I'll sign the order."

"No, we're not going to do it like that," Charlie said, "Send the bill to me."

"Of course, I'm not paying for it," Marjorie said, chuckling, "I'm just ordering it. Mommie, you're playing tennis with the Jurgens. I'm taking a ride with Charlie Herlong! I'll order a box lunch, and I'll call you in your room when it's ready." With that, she snapped the reins as any teamster would, and they were off.

Charlie looked at Thorne. "Is she always like that?"

"And don't make her mad," Thorne said, "What was that you said last night? Hard as a pine knot?"

"I ain't scared," Charlie said, "Does she burn hot, too?"

"I think you already know, Charlie," Thorne said and walked away laughing. "Yeah, fella, you're in trouble now."

Charlie remembered he still had items in the conductor's car. If he was taking a carriage ride, he might need his gun.

"Pssst, Mr. Charlie!" Murphy was calling in a loud whisper from the front end of the conductor's car. He motioned his head for Charlie to step up into the car.

"Hey, Murphy," Charlie said, "Don't look like you have as big a crowd to cater to today."

"Thank the Lord, I still have a job," Murphy said. Last night, they fired Fleet and Musco Cranshaw."

"What for?"

"I don't know for sure," Murphy said, "But they were asking me about the robbery and the cows."

"Did you tell the truth?"

"As I knew it," Murphy said, "I thought we were dropping off cattle in Knights, and then we weren't. Then we left some in Plant City. They asked me how Fleet acted, and I said like he always does, mean and ornery."

"Well, that's the truth," Charlie said, "What did you tell them about me?"

"What I knew, here to guard the freight, turned to mean when the outlaws showed up."

"Murphy, I'm not going with y'all today," Charlie said, "but I'm going to ask Mr. Brooks to give that black bag in there to Jack Duffie. I'm going to give this key I found to him."

Brooks stepped in and said, "Mr. Herlong, Mr. Thorne tells me you have decided to stay here for a few days. Don't you have cattle to attend to in Plant City?"

"I hope not," Charlie said, "I hope they've been sold by now."

"Do you know who they might be selling them to?"

"Someone with hard cash, I hope," Charlie said, "I bought them from Fleet. Oh, Lord, I should have known it was too good to be true. Whose cows did I buy?"

"Well, the paperwork all checks out, but we think the attempted robbery might have been about the cattle," Brooks said. "Do you think Fleet was trying to sell cattle in Knights?"

"I know he was agitated about showing up in Tampa with more cows than he needed," Charlie said, "I cut a deal to take the cows in Plant City, get them secured, and settle up today. Who is laying claim to the nine head?"

"No one that I know of," Brooks said, "we're just tying up loose ends."

"Well, let me know," Charlie said, "Hey, can you do me a favor? I have some hardware in here that needs to be in Plant City."

Charlie opened the closet and handed the key to Brooks. He pulled Raymond's black bag out and lifted it to the bench. He opened the top flap and reached in, placing the guns they took from the robbery on the bench.

"Hey, is that a Merwin?" Brooks asked, "That's a fine weapon right there."

"The one with the fancy engraving?" Charlie said and handed it to him, "If you say so. I wouldn't know. It took me the longest time to open it."

"I'm surprised a gunhand like you isn't aware of it. Do you mind?" Brooks said, opening the pistol and dumping the shells.

"Mr. Brooks, I'm no gunhand," Charlie said. I hadn't shot a pistol before this week."

"Oh, sure," Brooks said, "that's what they all say."

"If you only knew," Charlie said, tickled at the thought, "I took it from a train robber. Do you like it?"

"If I could afford it," Brooks said, "How much do you want for it?"

"I ain't got nothing in it," Charlie said, pausing a bit. If you like it and promise never to point it at me, it's yours."

"Oh, I couldn't do that," Brooks said, "I'd want to pay you something, and never is a long time."

"Okay, let's trade," Charlie said. If you deliver this bag to Jack Duffie, it's yours."

"It's still worth thirty or forty dollars, though," Brooks said.

"Mr. Brooks, you don't bargain worth a damn," Charlie said, adding, "When you give this bag to Jack, give him $20, tell him it's from Charlie. How's that, Abe?"

"Thanks, Mr. uh, Charlie," Brooks said, "That's a deal."

"See y'all tomorrow. I'm taking the day off!" Charlie walked out, and they could hear his voice, "Sammy, turn around; there's a change in plan!"

"Right there's a different kind of bird," Brooks said.

"Like none I've ever seen," replied Murphy.

Chapter 32

Charlie loped up the stairs and heard the telephone ringing. He walked to the oak box, picked up the earpiece, and listened to a woman's voice.

"Charlie! Are you there? Charlie?" It was Marjorie.

"Yeah, where?" Charlie shouted into the earpiece, "I'll meet you there."

He heard a muffled voice. "...back...kitchen."

Charlie hung up, and Sammy came in.

"Ah, Mr. Herlong, you've mastered the telephone," he said, "Do we have time to freshen up?"

Charlie said, "Call me Charlie. I think she said to meet her back there. Why did we come here?"

"Wash up?" Sammy motioned toward the bathroom. "We left in a hurry."

"Where's the beach, Sam?" Charlie said through Arnica, "Miss Ward wants to go there."

"I would suggest going through West Tampa," Sammy said, handing him a shaving brush, "much safer and nicer."

"Safer?"

"Yes, sir, there are lots of outsiders here; some are just sorry," Sammy said, handing him the razor. Go along the tracks until you get to Grand Central Avenue, then turn right. Stay on that road till you hear water; that's it."

"Grand Central Avenue?" Charlie said.

"Yes sir, past the railroad, it's nice," Sammy said, handing him a damp cloth, "regular folks. Go through some orange groves and woods, and you'll be there. About 5 miles."

Charlie and Marjorie found Grand Central Avenue. The atmosphere was calm, and the voices they heard were Spanish and Italian.

"Charlie, it's like being in Europe!" Marjorie said, "It's so exotic hearing foreign languages. I've heard Italian in Chicago, but not this much. Charlie, if you could, would you go to Europe?"

"I've never thought about it," Charlie scoffed, "It's hard enough getting to Jacksonville."

"I mean, like with me," she wrapped her arms around his bicep, and Charlie pulled up, "Just us, traveling around, seeing the sights. Would you consider it?"

"Sure," Charlie said, kissed her, and snapped the mare back into a canter, "But let's find the beach today."

"You should have been here when these oranges were in bloom. It's the sweetest smell," Charlie said and leaned close. " Well, almost the sweetest."

"Oh, Charlie," Marjorie said, rolling her eyes, "I bet that's worked up in Lake City."

They came through the woods to a smooth sand beach on the bay. There were a few birds, fewer people, and a cooling breeze. They walked the water's edge barefoot and talked.

Charlie liked listening to her. She had definite ideas and opinions on life and people. She was tactile, not aggressive, but friendly and familiar. Charlie knew if they were alone, things would be intense.

Charlie struggled to understand her lifestyle, which seemed to consist of finding activities, traveling, and visiting friends. His life was geared toward work and being productive.

The trees kept them shaded until noon, and then the temperature rose. Marjorie tied on her hat, stood, and walked to the buggy.

A fisherman walked from the south holding a string of fish. Charlie stood and asked to see them. They engaged in fishing talk for a few minutes.

"Charlie, are you thirsty? I have some cool tea and some water," she said, "Which do you like?"

"Whichever one is the wettest," he answered, "it's getting hot. The breeze went to dinner."

"So poetic," Marjorie brought glasses, and they shared a long, passionate kiss. They lost themselves in each other until Marjorie spilled her cup of water.

"Oh my, Charlie, you're all wet," she said calmly.

"Well, it was bound to happen," Charlie said.

"I think I'd like a swim."

"That water looks a bit muddy," Charlie said, "Tide's going out."

"I was thinking of the small bathing pool on the third floor," Marjorie said.

"They have a pool on the third floor?"

"In your room, can I use yours?" She ran her finger from his ear down his neck and grabbed his yellow scarf, smelling the Cuban Orchids, "You're making me work too hard, Charlie."

"Never work harder than the mule," Charlie said, gulping down his tea, "Just point him to the barn."

Riding through the orange grove, they ate cheese and strawberries. Marjorie bit off the tops and fed Charlie. She talked about literature, poetry, and her time at Columbia College in Chicago.

"Have you considered going to school, Charlie?" She asked.

"Not too much. My family wanted me to go to the Ag College in Lake City, but I didn't see much use in it." Charlie said, "We already do a lot of the same stuff they do over there. I don't think I'd want to work all day and write a book about it at night."

"But you're leaving home, aren't you?" She said, "For Jacksonville? What do you want to do?"

"I have to get there to see. If I have horses at the hotel, I'll have more opportunity," Charlie said, leaning into her, "But right now, I want to see that pool."

Charlie saw the fisherman selling his catch at a stall near the railroad.

"That fish is making me hungry," Charlie said, "if we were camping, I'd buy us dinner."

"Pull over, then," Marjorie said, "They'll cook it for us at the hotel. I'll get enough for my parents and their guests."

She reached into her purse and produced a $10 note from the First National Bank of Tampa. Charlie picked up a fish and smelled it. The man put seven large, red drum into a basket and Charlie tried to pay him with the note. The man shook his head. Charlie pulled a single eagle out, and the man smiled. Charlie said something, and he put two more fish into the basket, two large chunks of ice, and covered it with a piece of burlap.

"Your money is no good here, Marjorie," Charlie said, laughing, handing it to her.

"No, Charlie," she said, "Let me pay. It's for my family and friends."

"No, I mean he only wanted gold," Charlie said, "the banks down here must devalue their notes."

"Well, if it's no good, don't give it to me!" Marjorie laughed and took up the reins, "Why did you make him put more fish into the basket?"

"Gold price," Charlie said as he leaned back.

"That was smart," she said, "They don't teach you that in school."

The area where the railroad turned south reminded Charlie of Liberty Street. With two track crossings, the area was still backed up.

A large man with a wooden, steel-tipped staff grabbed the mare's bridle, startling her. Charlie took the reins.

"Your horse is fidgety. You want me to lead him through this mess?"

"She wasn't fidgety 'till you grabbed her," Charlie snapped, pulling on both reins, backing the mare, and turning her slightly into the man, "back the hell off my rig before you get run over!"

"You turn that horse into my baby brother again," another growled and pointed a small caliber pistol at Charlie's face, "I'm gon' dot your eye."

"Is that a fact?" Charlie glanced at the rusty, top-break revolver and locked eyes with him. "Without even telling me what you want? You look hungry. How about a job? I need two men who can handle horses. Can you do that?"

"How much does it pay?" The other man asked, "Will you trade out mounts for the work? Nat, that's our way home."

"Shut the hell up, Bub," Nat said. "We have our ride, and there are two baskets of food. Mister, you have everything I want right here. Fill this rice sack and tell your little gal there to put her baubles and purse in there, too."

"Save your breath, Charlie," Marjorie said, "I'll do no such thing!"

Charlie turned his head away from Nat for the first time and looked at Marjorie, who flashed her eyes, and he quickly turned back to Nat.

"I don't believe this one will end up at the altar, Charlie," Nat said, cocking the pistol.

"If that tramp were going to shoot, he would have done it," Marjorie said, "Let's go!"

Bub raised his staff and pointed the sharp steel tip at Marjorie's shoulder.

"Please hush, ma'am, before you get hurt."

"Shut the hell up, Bub, you dirty, pug-faced horse apple," Marjorie said, "You don't scare me, either!"

Bub jabbed her in the right shoulder. She leaned into Charlie and pulled his pistol. Charlie cracked the reins with his right hand and grabbed Nat's pistol with his left. The mare knocked Bub down, and the buggy lurched down Grand Central Avenue. Marjorie faced the rear and fired Charlie's pistol skyward three times. People scattered as Nat and Bub lay in the dust. Charlie raised Nat's pistol and dry-fired it three times. Marjorie whooped with delight.

"Ha! You didn't know it was empty?" Marjorie squealed and kissed him. "Mister Herlong, I think I love you!"

Marjorie reached into the picnic basket for a small bottle of brandy.

"I knew it was empty," Charlie said.

"Ha!" Marjorie shoved her shoulder into his and pushed the brandy toward him, "Here, have some."

"Did he hurt you?" Charlie asked.

"No, but he killed this dress," Marjorie said, taking a drink, "and injured my camisole, which I was hoping might help me see you naked again."

"You don't need help," Charlie said, "just point me toward the barn."

"Well, point me toward the kitchens. I can drop off these fish while you find your stock. Loan me your key?"

Charlie dropped Marjorie off behind the kitchens, and she kissed Charlie hard on the mouth.

❉ ❉ ❉ ❉ ❉ ❉ ❉ ❉ ❉ ❉ ❉ ❉

Charlie's horses were as promised. He pulled up and set the brake.

"Hey, that rig don't go there!"

"Right now, I'm just giving this gal some water," Charlie said, "Who do I talk to about these horses?"

"They belong to Charlie Herlong," he said.

Charlie stuck out his hand, "I'm Charlie Herlong."

"Oh!" He removed his hat and shook, "I beg your pardon."

"No need to beg; what do I call you?"

"I'm Lonnie Prevatt. I run the stables," he said.

"Tell me about these horses," Charlie asked. "They're all healthy and pretty young?"

"Yes, sir, and most of them are saddle broke," Lonnie said, leaning his head toward Charlie. "When they said no train till the day after tomorrow, I sent a half dozen back to Fred; they were pretty long in the tooth."

"Day after tomorrow? What else did you hear? I'll keep it between me and you."

"Well," Lonnie lowered his voice, "Mr. Lindsay was pretty mad about it, wanting to get them out of here before the Army ships out."

"Yeah, I've heard that, too. Lonnie, to save lives, don't tell anyone else," Charlie said, and Lonnie nodded, "Can I keep this rig and mare here, out of sight?"

"What if that gal who rented it wants it?"

"Give it to her. It's hers," Charlie said, handed him a quarter eagle, and turned to walk toward the rear of the hotel, "I'll let her know where it is."

"Uh, Huh! Yes, SIR," Lonnie said and pretended to button his lip.

"Mister Charlie!" Sammy called, walking too fast for his short legs, "That lady has a key, and she's in your room. She said you would fire me if I didn't let her in! Then she shooed me out."

"That sounds like her, Sammy," Charlie laughed, "I think she does what she wants. Did you tell on her?"

"I told you!" Sammy said, "You want me to throw her out?"

"No! I'm 'bout to go there," Charlie said, "take the afternoon off, go see your wife. You married?"

"Yes, sir, but I ain't going home; she'll think I got fired." Sammy said, "And I like working for you; you act like you don't need anything."

"Well, I need you looking out for me," Charlie put his hand on Sammy's shoulder. "But I don't think I need any help right now."

"Mr. Charlie, I'm still going to be near, just in case."

CHAPTER 33

Charlie woke and saw a small amount of light from the edges of the drapes. He heard quiet rustling in the bathroom and rose, excited to join Marjorie for another bath and startled Sammy.

"Mr. Charlie! I'm sorry I woke you," he said, "Let me get your night clothes."

Charlie grabbed a towel and tied it around his waist, saying, "No, I need my dinner clothes."

"Are you getting up?" Sammy said, "It's not sunrise yet,"

"Like, in the morning?"

Sammy chuckled, "That's when it happens."

"Where is ...? When did ...? I've been asleep all night?"

"She's been in here a bunch," Sammy said, "She left to get ready for dinner and told me not to wake you up and came back at dinner time, saying, 'He must be exhausted' and laughed. Then the kitchen sent up dinner. Can I send it back? The suite smells like fish."

"No, I'll taste it so I can tell her it was good," Charlie said.

"She knows you didn't. She came back at midnight and got mad that you were still sleeping," Sammy said. "She usually gets what she wants, but she didn't last night."

"She did. She wanted to take care of me," Charlie said, realizing he had drunk way too much. "Maybe some coffee and one of those sweet biscuits would be better for me."

"Good," Sammy said, pushing the cart out, "I'll bring back some breakfast, too."

Charlie ate well and felt better. He lifted the telephone and replaced it.

"It's early, Mr. Charlie," Sammy cleared Charlie's breakfast, "She needs care, too."

Charlie, "How do you know who I was calling?"

"A lucky guess," Sammy said, "I set your shaving tools and some tooth soap. Will you be checking on your horses?"

"I can't move them till tomorrow. I need to get over to Plant City. How long will that take for a buggy?"

"A couple of hours," Sammy said, "but that's a rough section of road these days. Are you sure you want more adventure?"

Charlie gave Sammy a look.

"Miss Marjorie told me," Sammy said.

"What'd she say?"

"She said you stared them down, offered them a job, took the man's gun from him, and went along like it was nothing. Like a sure-enough hero," Sammy said.

"Sounds like she tells a good story," Charlie said, brushing his teeth.

"Well, it might be these Cuban Orchids," Charlie said, splashing some on his yellow scarf, "I'll ride my horse to avoid trouble. If Miss Marjorie asks, tell her I've gone to Plant City, and her buggy is at the corral."

"Oh, she's going to ask," Sammy said.

Charlie rode along the railroad tracks, feeling the eyes of transient men, hungry and looking for work. He knew their fate hinged on one or a few decisions, just as his had. He thought of Raymond, the Mobley brothers, their friend, and how a split-second decision ended their life. His decision to club the robber with Judee's Remington put all this experience with Plant and the Wards in motion. He could have been shot dead in that train car. He wondered why he had been so fortunate. Maybe Jasper was right; maybe he was just lucky. Again, better to be lucky than good.

He had been riding for two hours, letting Thirsty move at his own pace. He was happy to see a sign saying 5 miles from Plant City. There were fewer walkers, and he noticed two men walking ahead. As he passed, he moved Thirsty to the left side of the road.

"You son-of-a-bitch!"

Charlie drew his pistol and turned Thirsty toward them. It was Benson Fleet and Musco Cranshaw. Charlie holstered his gun.

"Getting me fired wasn't enough for you?" Fleet barked, "You had to buy up every horse in Tampa, so I had to walk 20 miles?"

"You ran a cattle company from Henry Plant's train!" Charlie fired back, "And they don't care! They ran you off because your train was dangerous. Not one man in that company is sad to see you go, either. And you call me an SOB? Are you stupid, too? We still have to settle up. I could pay you six bits as well as $75 and feel good in church next Sunday."

They all walked in silence. Charlie knew this was a decision day. He then heard birds singing.

"Where are y'all headed? I mean after Plant City."

"Sanford," Fleet said, "I have money in the bank up there."

"I got people in Paola in the river freight business," Musco said.

"Well, let's get to Plant City, and maybe we can figure out a way to keep you from walking there," Charlie said.

Charlie kicked to a trot and moved ahead.

In town, Sam Barnes pulled alongside Charlie and smiled.

"Mr. Herlong! I have news!"

"From Beaudry?" Charlie said, "I was hoping to wait a while longer on that."

"No sir, for the packing houses, Mr. Duffy inquired," Barnes said.

"What's the news?" Charlie said, letting Barnes tell what Charlie already knew.

"He said he would rent you all you needed as long as you were out by August 1st," Barnes said.

"To me or Mr. Ward?" Charlie said, "Did he give you a price?"

Barnes said, "I believe he would be delighted with $150 a month for the three months."

"I guess he would; it's empty until August," Charlie said. "Right now, all we have to put in there are hopes and dreams. We'll talk about it this afternoon."

What was Jack Duffy thinking? When he saw the corral held three cows and Jack's horse, he kicked Thirsty into a canter.

"Well, there's rent money," Charlie thought, and he saw Henry. It was like seeing an old friend, even though they had just met. Henry was digging post holes with a hand auger.

"Pinky Whitfield, the hardest working man in Florida," Charlie called out, "you know there ain't no coconut cake around here."

Henry pulled the auger out of the ground.

"If you have some, you can call me that," Henry wiped his brow with his blue bandana.

"Why are you doing it, though?" Charlie asked. We're selling out of cows. Let's step over here out of the sun."

Henry stepped over to the pump and drank from a brand-new dipper and a brand-new tin bucket. Charlie thought Jack had been busy.

"Where's Jack?"

"He's gone into Lakeland with a load of stuff to sell," Henry said. "That guy is a moneymaker. He bought every tin pail and dipper in town and sold them all yesterday. Today, it was a load of boots, socks, and three sacks of grits—anything he can get cheap and sell to the soldiers."

"To your Uncle?"

"No, those volunteers have money. We've only sold beef to my uncle," Henry said, "and he wants more. That's why the fence. Jack figures we could sell ten a day, more if the hotel buys them. It's hard cash, too. There is no need to trade cows for horses. Have you found horses?"

"Got 'em. What about the 10th? Are you going to Cuba?" Charlie asked.

"Well, yes and no," Henry said, "I am going to Cuba, but not with the Army."

"Who are you going with?"

"I haven't figured that out yet," Henry said, "but Jack is helping me. It's a long story, and I'll explain it all right now if you want. Duffy says you and I are partners, and he works for us. Are we partners, Charlie?"

Charlie laughed and said, "If Jack says so, I reckon we are. Partners in what, though? Right now, it looks like we have three cows, two horses, and five post holes. How's Sam?"

"He's in the barn. We also have a 2-ton wagon and two good mules. Around 8,000 rounds of ammunition," and under his breath, he said, "Plus some dynamite."

"Ammunition?" Charlie asked, "And dynamite? Who's going to buy that?"

"I'll buy that," Henry said.

"How much did it cost?" Charlie was getting excited.

"The dynamite?" Henry said, "It was part of everything I traded the first day for two cows."

"Two cows? For a wagon and two mules, plus all the explosives?" Charlie said, "I reckon we are partners!"

"I figured that's how you negotiate," Henry said, laughing, "and the mules didn't serve in the Civil War, either. We sold two more cows at $125 each. Uncle is going to sell quarters; he has a butcher. Can you get in touch with Tiger? We need more cows."

"We're sending 24 horses to Hawthorne tomorrow. Shoot, I need to send a telegraph," Charlie said, "Benson Fleet and Musco will be here soon; put them to work on those post holes."

"I'm the one telling Fleet he's digging holes?" Henry asked.

"Yeah, be gentle," Charlie said, "he'll refuse. Tell him I've gone to buy a map to Sanford since he'll be walking. Tell Musco he'll get $5 a day for building the fence. That's more money than he's ever made, and when the trains start running again, he won't have to walk. When I get back, I want to hear why you've decided to start your own war."

Charlie started walking to the station and saw Fleet and Musco. To avoid arguing with Fleet, he mounted Thirsty and rode to the station.

A man with thick glasses and sleeve garters walked a few steps out on the porch and put his hands on his hips. "We won't have any public trains coming in or out till they decide to have a war,"

"When you have a ticket to Jacksonville, I'll buy it," Charlie said, "But, right now, I have a telegram to ask about."

"Well, that hasn't slowed any. We'll check the ledger," the man waved. "Is it to you?"

"It might have been sent to The Tampa Bay Hotel," Charlie said. "I forgot to check this morning. It's coming from Tiger Driggers in Gainesville, or he might be in Hawthorne."

"Who is Mr. Driggers sending it to?"

"To me, Charlie Herlong," Charlie said, sticking out his hand, "Pleased to meet you."

"James Sandy, I'm the station manager. The telegraph operator has gone to get us some breakfast, but I can check on yours," the man said. "Jack Duffy thinks mighty high of you."

"Well, the feeling is mutual," Charlie said.

"I've known him for years. He was the Postmaster of Knights," Sandy said, "He's a good man. When would this telegram have been sent?"

"Yesterday, I just sent him one night before last."

"There's one coming in right now; maybe that's it," Sandy hustled over to the receiver and picked up the tape. "No, this is for Jack Duffy. When you see him, tell him to come over."

"Jack Duffy? Who's it from?" Charlie asked.

"Oh, I couldn't say. It's for Jack." Sandy said, "If you want, I can have you deliver it if you promise not to open it. Oh, here's another from the same station to the hotel, but not you."

Charlie tried to read the tape, his curiosity getting the best of him. Sandy held the tape to his chest and said, "Mr. Herlong, please respect the privacy of our customers. Let's check yesterday's tape so you can mind your business."

The receiver continued to spit out tape, and Sandy went to a box marked relayed. He read through a long coil of tape and returned it. He then returned to the machine and began to read the new message.

"Mr. Herlong, nothing from yesterday. Why don't you pour yourself a cup of coffee over there and let me get through these messages from Orlando? They send them in bunches. Gainesville should be coming in anytime now."

"That sounds good," Charlie said, "what can you tell me about Mr. Plant's train? I'm supposed to move some horses on it tomorrow. Have you heard anything about when it will be returning to Tampa?"

"You can ask Jack when he gets his message," Sandy said, "that is all I can say. Many of your questions will be answered soon; at least we're faster than the mail."

The telegraph machine just made Charlie more curious as to the information, so he walked outside to have his coffee. Henry gave Musco and Fleet the word. Charlie could almost hear Fleet being his normal, hateful self. Musco looked around as if to see if anyone was watching and began to use the auger. Fleet looked at Charlie on the station porch and began to walk toward him. Charlie felt in his pockets to see how much money he had on him, readying himself to offer Fleet his share right now to get rid of him or to allow him to work for a more significant share.

"Oh, no. Is that Benson Fleet coming this way?" Sandy said as he emerged on the deck. "What in the world could he want?"

"To complain about something, I 'magine," Charlie said, taking a seat on an empty keg being utilized as a rubbish container. "That rascal would complain on free apple pie day."

"Well, I don't have to hear anything he has to say," Sandy said, "I've got an all-points wire inside that he is not allowed on the premises unless he buys a full-price ticket."

"Is that a fact? I can't wait to hear you tell him that," Charlie said, "but I bet he'll talk to me first."

"Does he work for you, too? I wouldn't trust him to guard sand spurs," Sandy said, "if you don't run him off, I will."

Fleet started grousing while still out of earshot. Charlie just sat there while he continued to say what he would and would not do and what scoundrels everyone was. Eventually, he ran out of steam and put his arms out to his sides.

"Well?"

"Well, what?" Charlie replied.

"Well, what are we doing?" Fleet asked.

"We aren't doing anything," Charlie said, taking a sip of coffee. "Well, I'm waiting for a telegram. You are supposed to be helping Musco build some fencing for Mr. Whitfield. I'm enjoying a good cup of coffee. Very nice, Mr. Sandy. Thank you."

"Watch this shyster, James," Fleet said to Sandy, "He'll take over your station and get you fired."

"Are you a lawyer, Mr. Herlong?" Sandy asked.

"No, sir, I work for a living."

"We need an injunction," Sandy said, then looked at Fleet. "You, sir, cannot be on the premises without a ticket. We have no tickets to sell. You must vacate the premises. Mr. Donahue has deemed you persona non grata in the Plant System."

"Hey, that sounds like Italian, Fleet," Charlie laughed, "that means you've become an international jackass!"

"Mr. Herlong, here is Mr. Duffy's message," Sandy said, handing him two envelopes. "you have one, also. Still nothing from Gainesville, I'm afraid. If you like, I can have it delivered when it arrives. Goodbye, Mr. Fleet. The mills of God grind slowly, but it is a fine grind."

Charlie mounted Thirsty and kicked. Sandy turned and walked into the station, leaving Fleet standing there in the fine sand.

CHAPTER 34

Charlie was far enough away from Fleet to read his telegram. He laid the reins on his saddle horn and opened it with his Barlow.

Western Union

Orlando, Fl – Abraham Brooks, The Plant System

The Tampa Bay Hotel – Charlie Herlong, private

Will stop in Plant City today to unload your freight. Continue to Tampa to load your horses into two stock cars for delivery. Please advise if the horses will be delivered to Plant City or Hawthorne. Gainesville is still unavailable.

'What freight?' Charlie thought, and he kicked to see if Henry knew anything about freight. He then pulled up and turned Thirsty around to head back to the station. He needed to get a telegram to Tiger, but hell, who knows if Tiger even got the last message? He turned Thirsty again, rode a few strides, and stopped again. Charlie needed information. He pulled his watch, 8:45, and remembered that Marjorie told Thorne to give him what he needed.

"Charlie, that's a pretty good horse!" Henry called out, "You had him spinning like a cutter."

"Henry, do you know anything about freight coming in from Orlando?" Charlie asked as he dismounted, "Did Jack say when he was coming back?"

"Yesterday, he was back around 2:00," Henry said, "I suppose he'll come back when he sells out the wagon."

"And the freight?"

"From Orlando?" Henry said, "I don't know anything about freight. Hey, how'd you wrangle 24 horses? That was some trading."

"Well, this says we have freight coming," Charlie said as he thought about Henry's answer. "From wherever. Like from Montgomery Ward?"

"We ordered from the catalog," Henry said, "Mr. Thorne said whatever we needed, so Jack ordered what he thought he could sell to the Army, and I ordered what I need to take to Cuba."

"How much is it going to cost?"

"Well, that I don't know," Henry said, "but I'm going to pay for whatever is mine, and Jack says we'll make a lot on what we sell. Especially when the goods come from Chicago."

"How much did y'all order?"

Henry paused, "A good bit," he said, "the man dropped one of those big catalogs on the table and said, 'Have at it.' I was thinking about how desperate those people are down there."

"And you don't know how much you spent," Charlie said, "Did Jack get carried away, too? The bill is going to come to me, Henry."

"You can ask him, Charlie. Here he comes, now," Henry said as he walked over to help Musco turn the auger. "I'm sorry if I did the wrong thing, but I'll pay for it. I'm going to Cuba and doing God's work."

"Henry, your uncle bought everything except the smaller boots. You should take them with you; they'll fit regular folks. He's also buying more beef. He wants three this time," Jack said, then saw Charlie, "Hey, Charlie! Man, I'm glad you're here. While you have been lying up in that hotel, we've been making money. What's Musco doing here? We need cows, too. Henry says you have a man up north."

"Jack, let's talk inside. Henry, do you want to hear what we're talking about?" Charlie said.

"No, Jack brought back a load of fence posts," Henry said. "I trust whatever you all decide. I'm going to teach Musco how to put in a fence."

"How do you know I ain't going to teach you?" Musco said.

"I don't. Maybe we'll both learn something," Henry said. "Have you ever heard of a slave named Joseph? I'll tell you while we're digging."

Charlie stepped into the barn. Jack had a little office area just inside. Sam and the other horse from Owensboro were in stalls and the peanut hay was stacked neatly.

"Charlie, I figured you'd be happy that we had already sold the cattle and were making money from other ways," Jack said, "do you have bad news?"

"Do you?" Charlie said, "I have freight coming in today, and I don't know anything about it. How much freight and more importantly, how much is it going to cost? Who's going to pay for it? When does it have to be paid for?"

"I only have good news," Jack said, "The freight coming in is good news. I've sold everything I have. We have three freight cars and 60 days to pay for it. You have credit, Charlie, as much as you need. Robert Thorne said whatever we needed, and I held back. We could pay for half now, but we need the cash to buy cattle. We need to have them here before the trains start running again. That new conductor says when the trains start running again, Plant will bring in cattle on regular stock trains."

"Payable in 60 days?" Charlie asked.

"Well, due in 30, in default in 60," Jack said, "But we'll have it. I can't believe how disorganized the Army is. They need basic necessities, but who knows when their money will run out. Sergeant Baker thinks war will be declared soon. He'll turn the meat business over to someone else. There'll still be lots of Army here who'll be hungry. He says that canned meat isn't fit to eat."

"You say we can pay half of it off, now?"

"Yes, but why? We may need the cash to buy from folks we have no credit with," Jack said. "This is basic business. By the way, who are we going to bank with? We have too much on hand right now, and folks know it."

"How much do we have?"

Jack reached into a saddle bag and pulled out a stack of bank notes and a leather pouch. He dumped gold and silver coins on the table. Then, looking out the door, he brought out a wooden box with leather hinges.

"Damn, Jack," Charlie said, putting his hand on his pistol. "How much do you have here?"

"You have about $1500," Jack said. "The three freight cars will cost about $3000, and we'll sell what's in two for about $6000. Depending on what you want to pay Henry, the third car will cost us a thousand. He wants to pay for it out of his share. All of these numbers are based on Army prices right now. As long as their families keep sending money, that is. We'll never make this much again."

"I need to contact Barnes," Charlie said. "I just saw him."

"Let me handle Barnes. I believe we can rent for $50, $100 at the most," Jack said, "I need you to get us some cat ... sorry, if you can get us cattle and hogs, too, we'd be in good shape, but we need to hurry, the other ranchers in the area are already thinking about it, I bet."

"You can tell me what to do, Jack," Charlie said, "I believe you know what we need here."

Charlie reached into his pocket and said, "Oh, here's a telegram for you."

"Charlie, you could have opened this; I work for you," Jack said, "Thorne says it's coming at 2:00. I have some schoolboys coming to unload it. We need to set terms with Barnes before then. They'll take banknotes. That is unless you want to do it."

"No, what else do you need from me?" Charlie said, "I'm headed over to the telegraph office."

"Figure out a bank, I guess, and make sure your lady friend over there stays happy; her credit makes it swing. That and the cows, that is."

Charlie sent another telegram to Tiger, telling him to expect the horses in Hawthorne the following day and inquiring about cattle. He expected to ride to Hawthorne if he hadn't heard from Tiger. Sandy told him the banks in Lakeland were independent and sent their business by train to Tampa and Sanford. Duffy could send deposits directly to Tampa if they wished.

He bought lumber to be delivered right away. He stopped at the café and bought dinner for the men: fried chicken, a loaf of bread, and a pail of okra, tomatoes, and rice. The woman who packed it up said to send the containers back with her son, who was helping unload the train.

On his way back to the barn, he saw Fleet on the porch of an empty storefront. He stood when he saw Charlie, and Charlie took that as a sign that he wanted to talk.

"You got my money?" Fleet said.

"Yes, sir, I have $75 in paper money," Charlie said, "but that ain't going to get you to Sanford today. Until the trains run again, you'll have to buy a horse and tack to ride a hundred miles. Are you sure you want to do that?"

"I've got $270 tied up in those cattle that YOU'VE been selling," Fleet said, "I want my fair share of it."

"Mr. Fleet," Charlie leaned back in his saddle, "You know as well as I do, that money was Mr. Plant's money. So, your financial plans in Hawthorne changed in Owensboro, didn't they?"

Fleet said nothing.

"Let's do this," Charlie said, "come back to the barn and work with us until you can buy a ticket to Sanford. You'll be fed, and you'll sleep out of the weather. You'll be Jack Duffy's assistant, and he can fire you if he wants to. Henry, too, so you should be on your Ps and Qs. Or I can give you $75 today, and you can be persona au gratin around me, too."

"Persona what?"

"It's Italian; it means anywhere but here," Charlie said.

"How much is the pay?" Fleet said.

"$4 a day."

"What the hell? Musco is getting $5!"

"Musco is pushing an auger. You'll be pushing a pencil," Charlie said as he nudged Thirsty toward the barn. "Come on and have some dinner with us. It'll help you decide."

"Am I working for that nigger, too?"

Charlie stopped and turned toward Fleet, "You're fired. See how quickly it can happen? Yes, you work for him, too. That'll be the last hateful thing you say until you don't work for us anymore, Benson. You'd best shut your bean grinder for now. You'll learn to be decent, or you might just get shot by somebody who ain't as decent as me."

Fleet followed him, struggling to keep up in the fine sand.

Chapter 35

Eating helped Fleet make up his mind. Henry and Jack agreed on the stipulation that any one of them could fire him. Charlie said there would be no gambling on when.

Henry directed the offloading of the freight while Jack was negotiating with Sam Barnes. Fleet cataloged everything and was cordial. Charlie let Fleet and Henry lead and stayed out of the way. Charlie had a few schoolboys help Musco with the fence.

A schoolboy with a straw ascot cap jogged from the packing house. "Mr. Charlie! Mr. Fleet wants to know what to do with that cannon!"

Charlie went inside and looked at Henry, "A cannon?"

"Jack says that's how I'm supposed to get to Cuba," Henry said.

"He's planning on shooting you over there? Are we putting together a circus?" Charlie cracked.

The boy added, "It ain't big enough for all that. A baseball wouldn't fit in it."

An incomplete Hotchkiss Mountain Gun was on the floor in pieces: one wheel, a broken axle, and two cases of shells—17 empty, seven intact.

"Moses' roses," Charlie said, "I hope he didn't give much for that."

"What the hell are you up to, Charlie?" Fleet asked, then said, "Don't fire me, but I ain't getting involved in no filibustering."

"Me neither, Benson. Put it over there with Henry's supplies and cover it up. The less said about it, the better."

Brooks sent word that Thirsty was loaded on the train, which would depart soon. As Charlie was boarding, Sandy came and waved a telegram.

"Mr. Herlong! It's from Hawthorne."

Charlie opened the envelope and read.

Western Union

Hawthorne – Tiger Driggers

The Tampa Bay Hotel – Charlie Herlong, private

Will take the horses in Hawthorne tomorrow and drive them to Gainesville. Cattle are my business. How many, where, and when? What is the price in Tampa? Is the train available?

"Do you want to respond?" Sandy asked.

"Tell him .... Buy all we can afford. Plant City price $100 a head. I'll send freight details soon." Charlie said as the engineer blew his whistle.

Charlie stepped into the empty lounge car. He sat by the window and tried to think of the worst thing that could happen. If something happened to Tiger, the money, or the cattle, he had paper money to pay Lindsay. He could deposit all the paper money Jack made in a Tampa bank. There was no reason to believe that Jack couldn't continue to sell goods. He wasn't worried about the Montgomery Ward debt for the same reason. He was concerned about Henry's third car, having no interest in being a savior. For once, Fleet was right; getting involved in a war was illegal and could get you killed.

"Mr. Charlie," Murphy said, with an armload of linens, "Looks like it's just you and me today. But we'll see Mr. Brooks soon. Can I get you something?"

"No, thank you, Murphy," Charlie said, "I saw him when we unloaded the freight."

"Yes, sir. He was sure impressed with how you assembled a crew so fast and how organized they were," Murphy said, "and we were all staggered by the sight of Fleet working for you."

"He needed a job," Charlie said, "and I needed help. He organized it."

"Murphy, which bank does Plant use in Tampa?"

"All of them," Murphy said, "he's got more hay than one barn will hold. Tampa National has the prettiest building, I guess that one. We sometimes move bags from there to Sanford."

Brooks came into the car, "I've wired ahead, and a crew will load your stock," Brooks said, standing, "I understand it goes to Hawthorne?"

"Yes, sir," Charlie said, "I'll have men there to offload them."

"Oh, we have hands to do that. Who will be picking them up?" Brooks asked.

"Tiger Driggers, Mr. Sardin knows him," Charlie said, "They say he's the best cow hunter around, and I believe it."

"That's good to know," Brooks said. "The hotel is going to need more cattle soon if the tracks don't clear, and I've been asked to find some."

"Tiger is finding some cattle for me. If he does, I can give you a good price. When do you need them?"

"Soon, but Mr. Lindsay will want to speak to you about that. For the next few days, this train will be moving folks from the hotel to Sanford," Brooks said, "So, we'll be loading the stock immediately in Tampa and moving straight to Hawthorne. We'll be arriving around midnight and will be back here in the morning."

"Oh, my man won't be there tonight. Should I go?" Charlie asked.

"You're certainly welcome to," Brooks said, standing, "but there's no need. The Plant System can guarantee that it will be in good shape tomorrow morning when Mr. Driggers arrives."

They shook hands, and Charlie asked, "By the way, where is Robert Thorne?"

"I saw him this morning in Winter Park; Montgomery Ward is setting up some warehouses over there. Excuse me, I have paperwork to finish."

Charlie spent most of the trip thinking about Marjorie and wondering why people were leaving Tampa.

✻ ✻ ✻ ✻ ✻ ✻ ✻ ✻ ✻ ✻ ✻ ✻

Fleet was on the loading dock. He watched his train disappear down the track with regret. He was going to miss the pay and its effect on his plans, but he hated the pressure of pleasing passengers and managers who were pressured to please Henry Plant. He enjoyed supervising the youngsters unloading the freight. Their vigor and competitive enthusiasm were refreshing.

"Mr. Fleet, what do you know about cannons?" Jack Duffy examined a live shell in one hand and an empty one in the other, "I wonder if these can be reloaded?"

Fleet felt an urge to be sarcastic and dismissive, reminding himself he was under no pressure to know. "I know it can kill me if I fool with it. You could ask the man you got it from."

"I got it from a Yankee cook. He was tired of carrying it every time they moved. If I can get more shells, it'll be worth something. That or find a wheel and axle for it." Duffy said, "I wonder if you can mount this thing on a boat?"

"Without shells, it's an anchor," Fleet said.

"I'll take 'em a case of soap; they wanted that," Duffy said, "Henry might talk him into a case of shells."

"I gave one of those straw ascots to a kid; how much are you asking for them? I'd pay for him; he's a good kid," Fleet said.

"They're all good kids," Duffy said, "If they work for us, they get a discount, two bits. I think I'm going over there with Henry to find some of these shells. Do me a favor. Grab a case each of soap and bleaching powder and put them in the wagon. I can sweeten the deal. Can you supervise those boys on the rest of the fence posts? When they finish, please pay them a buck apiece. I'll leave you silver dollars and quarters in case they want a hat."

Fleet placed the boxes in the wagon. "You're leaving me in charge?"

"Yes, if Henry can talk his uncle into it, I can do the bargaining," Duffy said, "Who else? Musco?"

"Thank you," Fleet said quietly.

"For what?"

"For trusting me, taking a chance on me," Fleet said, "You don't have to."

"Well, Charlie took a chance on me," Duffy said, "It makes me want to do well. It's kind of like those kids today, fighting to be the best one."

❋ ❋ ❋ ❋ ❋ ❋ ❋ ❋ ❋ ❋ ❋ ❋ ❋

Musco and the boys finished the last post just as the sky dumped one of those afternoon buckets of water Florida is famous for. They all ran to the barn, laughing. Fleet paid the boys and sent them on their way. Musco saw an opportunity to take a nap. Fleet collected tools left out during the storm.

"Hey, ain't you that conductor for the railroad? You in the cattle business, now?"

Milt Loy was sitting on a full-size Dun gelding. His felt hat drooped after the rain shower. He had a lever action rifle in a scabbard, a huge bowie knife, and two single-action Colts in a double holster. He was tall and thick with a sparse beard that might have been intentional or just days since his last shave.

"No, and no," Fleet answered, confident this was the man who shot Dew Dykstra, the rancher to whom Fleet sold cattle.

"Mister, I hate a liar worse than a horse thief," the man said, arching his back to stretch.

"Just horse thieves? How about cattle?" Fleet saw the horse's poorly altered brand, picked up a second shovel, and turned toward the barn.

"Some of my best friends steal cattle, but they don't steal mine," Loy said, kicking his horse to cut Fleet off. "I'm still talking to you, boy, and you better start answering. If you ain't in the cattle business, why are you building a fence?"

"I guess I'm in the fence-building business today," Fleet said, starting to lose patience, despite Loy's reputation, "as soon as the trains run again, I'll be gone from this boil on the ass of Florida."

"Watch your mouth, boy," Loy pulled one of his pistols, cocked, and pointed it at Fleet. "Who are you working for?"

"Charlie Herlong."

"That's the son of a bitch I'm looking for! Where is he?" Loy was looking around and pulled his second pistol, "You might as well tell me, or you might get killed, too."

"You're the first person I've ever met who doesn't like him," Fleet said. "I was beginning to think it was just me."

"Never said I didn't like him," Loy said. "Just looking for him. You going to tell me or not?"

"Mister, I wish you would take off after him. My hand to God," Fleet stopped and held up the shovel, "I haven't seen him in a couple of hours.

"He'll be back. How come you ain't on the train?" Loy said, holstering his pistols.

"I quit," Fleet said. "Are you planning on killing Charlie Herlong?"

"How'd you know?" Loy said.

Fleet saw that all Loy's brains were in his holsters, so he remained quiet and stared at him.

"I asked you a question!"

"Didn't you just say that?" Fleet consciously avoided mentioning what Loy had said about killing him, too.

Loy struggled to concentrate, his face contorted. "I heard there were cattle here. What happened to 'em?"

Fleet was in agony. He wanted to say something sarcastic and demeaning, but he knew if this ox became startled, he could get shot. He wasn't frightened; he was aggravated. His intolerance of idiots made him confident enough to avoid fear. Then, he noticed Loy's eyes widening a bit.

"Oh! I guess they sold them. A big nigger corporal came and got the last three," Fleet tried to sound helpful.

"A big nigger what?" Loy said, cocking his head like a confused hound.

"Corporal, you know, like in the Army, a soldier," Fleet said, wondering, 'How did this mooncalf stay upright on a horse?'

Loy craned his neck toward Fleet and said, "I know. Quit mumblin'. They must be selling 'em to the Army. This Charlie guy, is he bringin' more cattle in?"

"He didn't share his plans with me," Fleet said, "other than 'build us a fence so that we can have more room. In this cattle pen."

"They're goin' to bring more in and put 'em in this corral. And keep sellin' 'em to the Army!" Loy said, proud satisfaction on his face.

"It looks like you've got it all covered unless you kill him first," Fleet said, pausing to let Loy catch up. "Maybe you should wait a while on that. Why'd you say you were going to kill him?"

"You need to clean your ears out. He killed my nephews up in Pasco County and my sister is all tore down over it. And blaming it on me."

"Weren't they robbing a train at the time?" Fleet asked, genuinely interested in his answer, "Were you with them?"

"I didn't put guns in their hands! No, I just told my brother-in-law about it and said I'd buy the cattle," Loy said. "Hell, I was over in Tavares, looking for more cattle... to buy."

"They were robbing a train, though. That's part of it, ain't it?" Fleet said, adding, "How do you know Charlie killed them?"

"Fat assed Ted Hill told me," Loy said, "while he was arresting a plate of hoe cakes and syrup. He didn't even stop eatin' to tell me. I'd a shot him if he wadn't wearing that badge."

"So you need to kill Charlie to get her off your back? Because it's his fault, more than yours," Fleet said, "I understand."

"You don't understand shit!" Loy said, pulling his pistol again, "I'm getting tired of your mouth. Ain't nobody on my back! You sound like my sister, but you better not call me dumbass. For the last damn time, where's Charlie Herlong?"

"I haven't seen him since the train left for Tampa," Fleet said, annoyed that this cretin was so arrogant, "but I didn't see him get on, and I don't know when he'll be back. So you can kill him. For killing your kin. While he was being paid to protect the train. From robbers. Not sent by you. So I can't tell you where he is exactly, but he might be on that train. Got damn."

"One more question. If you can't tell me, what fuckin' good are you?" He shot Fleet in the chest, who dropped to his knees, still holding both shovels.

"And I definitely can't, now, dumbass," Fleet said and fell.

Chapter 36

"When are y'all 'sposed to get some more? Nephew, I got folks in town offering me hogs for cattle, 6 for 1," Baker said.

"Corporal Hatch picked up the last three," Henry said. "That's why we're here; we need to barter."

"What do you need? Is that why you brought your boss?"

"I work for him, Sergeant," Duffy said, "We're looking for these."

Duffy held out the two shells. Baker took the empty shell and pointed it at Henry.

"Pull up, you work for him? Damn, Pinky, you're somethin'," Baker said.

"My name is Jack Duffy, Sergeant, not Pinky. Fair with red hair, I'm used to it." Jack said, "But I do move cattle and other goods, so I can help you get what you need."

"I was, uh, not you ..." Baker turned to Henry.

"Jack thinks Pinky is insulting," Henry said, "and he can sure get whatever."

"Not these, he can't, the old kind," Baker said, laying it flat on the floor. It was unstable. "This is God's work?"

"How about the new ones?" Henry asked.

"We fittin' to go to war. We might need 'em," Baker said, "the question is, why do YOU need them?"

Henry looked at Duffy.

"We're looking to trade them," Jack said calmly.

"Trade them for what?"

"Passage and freight."

"You talkin' 'bout Cuba?" Baker said, "That's ignorant. If you're slick enough to get through our blockade, the minute you land, you'll be a spy. You'll be shot. No trial, no questions, and no answers. And for what? Some folks you don't even know?"

Henry continued looking at him, undeterred.

"And where did you get a breech-loader? Nope, don't want to know," Baker slapped the desk with his hands, "Look here, things are fittin' to get rolling real fast.

I ain't putting you in a spot to get killed and risking my career because you heard God's silky voice. No, sir, it can get you killed."

He handed Henry a pouch of gold coins and hugged him.

"Here, take this; this squares our account," Baker said. "I'll buy cattle all day, but I'm not selling you shells that I'm going to need later."

"I understand," Henry said, "We'll send word when the cattle get here. You say there are new shells in town? We'll find some."

They turned, and Baker said, "If you're bound to this, remember that white corporal that wanted your shotgun? He pesters me every day about it. He's with the 71st New York Volunteers. He knows what you need. But I DON'T, you hear?"

"Yes, sir, I hear. I appreciate it, and I love you."

"I love you, too, Sarge," a man catcalled, and the outer tent roared with laughter.

"Henry, he's got a point," Duffy said outside. " Is any of this worth dying over?"

"That's the question, Jack," Henry said, "How would the women and kids in Cuba answer? They're worth taking a chance for. Let's cut deals to get there."

❊❊❊❊❊❊❊❊❊❊❊❊❊

Charlie signed for the horses and $1200. He was walking toward the telegraph office and saw Sammy trotting toward him.

"Sammy," Charlie asked, "You look like you're dodging the law."

"Mr. Charlie, did you know Miz Ward moved all her things into your suite? And her Mama is looking for her all over!"

"No, I didn't." Charlie said, "What's she doing in there?"

"Waiting on you," Sammy said, "and fussing about her mother. Mr. Charlie, she has a ... colorful way of talking."

"Well, she and her mama will work it out, I'm sure. You ain't going to run her off, are you? She's kind of fun," Charlie said, walking.

"No, sir. I'd say fun like fireworks," Sammy said, "pretty to look at, but if you get too close, you'll learn something."

"Well, I have to send a telegram; where are you going?" Charlie asked.

"I believe I'll stay with you," Sammy said, "she said she didn't want to see my face when the train got here. Do I work for you or her?"

"I believe you work for Mr. Lindsay."

"Yes, sir, and he told me to take care of you," Sammy said.

"For the time being, but her Daddy is Montgomery Ward, and he means more to Mr. Lindsay than all of us. And Mrs. Ward needs to be happy for Mr. Ward to be happy," Charlie said.

"Yes, sir, but what about Miss Marjorie?"

"Well, Sam, I like to make her happy," Charlie said and stepped into the telegraph office.

Sammy sat on a bench and said, "I reckon you do! That's why we got a dozen suitcases in our suite right now!"

❋ ❋ ❋ ❋ ✦ ❋ ✦ ❋ ❋ ❋ ✦ ❋ ❋ ❋ ❋

Musco Cranshaw was awakened by the shot that killed Benson Fleet and peeked out. He saw Fleet lying in the sand and took a step toward him. He stopped at the sound of a pistol cocking.

"What's your name, boy?" Loy said, still on his horse, which drank from the trough.

"Musco." He answered, raising his hands, "I ain't armed and I ain't got no money, 'cause I ain't been paid yet."

"Who owes you money? Musco? What kind of name is that?" Loy said.

"I don't know. I mean, I do know, but I ain't sure," Musco answered. "I mean, about my name, every time I ask my Daddy, he said 'cause he said so."

"Does Charlie Herlong owe you money?" Loy asked, already getting confused, "I hope it ain't that train conductor. He ain't paying anybody no more."

"Charlie Herlong ain't been here much, Jack Duffy?" Musco said.

"Did you build that fence? Do you know when they're getting more cattle? Are they looking for more? How much are they paying?" Loy was peppering Musco with questions faster than he could answer.

Musco was trying to remember everything.

"Well?" Loy asked, making Musco even more nervous.

"I set the fence poles. I don't know when they're getting cattle or what they pay. I just got here. Please don't kill me." Musco said and looked down at the sand.

"I ain't going to kill you, boy, as long as you ain't lying. You tell Charlie Herlong Milt Loy has cattle to sell, and I'll be back in a week. Can you remember all that?" Loy said.

"Yes, sir, I promise. I'll remember everything. Thank you," Musco said.

"Thank you? What for?" Loy asked.

Musco looked over at Fleet's corpse.

199

"Oh, he tried to hit me with a shovel. But I killed him 'cause he was being an asshole." Loy said, turning his horse, "Make sure you remember that part when anybody asks."

When Loy rode away, Musco checked to see if Fleet was indeed dead. He then reported the incident at the station. Sandy, the telegraph operator, and Musco all agreed the story was suspect but could not deny the claim that Fleet was being an asshole. They wired the undertaker in Lakeland, then wired the Sheriff of Hillsborough County in Tampa.

❆ ❆ ❆ ❆ ❆ ❆ ❆ ❆ ❆ ❆ ❆ ❆ ❆

Henry rode Sam alongside the wagon. They had sold all the supplies, and the wagon contained six army cots and an entire case of Hotchkiss shells. Duffy traded Henry's riot gun and a beef quarter to be delivered when the beef arrived. No one would take the old shells. A black, hard-covered delivery wagon was headed in the same direction.

"That's the undertaker," Duffy said and snapped his reins to pull alongside, "Hey, mister, may I ask where you're headed?"

"There's been a killing in Plant City, I need to get there before that Yankee in Valrico does. I just hope the sheriff shows up," the man replied.

Henry kicked Sam into a gallop and Duffy followed.

❆ ❆ ❆ ❆ ❆ ❆ ❆ ❆ ❆ ❆ ❆ ❆ ❆

Charlie was stepping into his short Johnnie. A breeze was coming through the windows from the west and raising the sheers. Charlie could hear the train whistle telling him it was leaving for Hawthorne.

"Charlie, are you going somewhere? We're done?" Marjorie said, lifting the sheet and sliding it over her hips and legs, "These are the linens you brought from Gainesville. I can't believe they aren't silk."

"I don't believe we'll ever be done, darlin'," Charlie said, buttoning his pants, "but I need to talk to Mr. Lindsay, try to earn my keep around here. I believe he needs a regular supply of beef."

"Can it wait another hour? At five o'clock, everyone will be in their rooms freshening up for dinner. If my mother sees you, she'll be up here and cause a

200

scene," Marjorie said, "Besides, I'll just pay your account in the morning, which is something else we should talk about."

"I won't get between anybody and their mama; I've already had enough pistols in my face!" Charlie said.

"Charlie, we're from Chicago. We don't shoot people I spend my time with. She's worried about scandal as if we haven't survived that already. In her mind, I might as well be a Chippy on the Levee," she said as she rolled on her back and sighed.

"Chippy? That's what my family calls me, like Little Charlie. What's it mean to y'all?" Charlie asked.

"A soiled dove," Marjorie said, rising again to her elbow, "A fast woman? Sporting lady, dusty butt? Boy, you are farm fresh, aren't you?"

"I've heard sporting lady, and there are women in Lake City you can get favors from, but not so many there's a name for them," Charlie said, "other than Molly or Faye, but that's their name."

"I'm sure Molly or Faye would be happy to give you a dollar to earn their keep," Marjorie said.

"I couldn't take it. I might want to go to the Olympics," Charlie said. "So, you can leave my room bill alone. I'll plow your field for free."

"Ooh. All that farm talk," Marjorie said, "take your plow suit off, and let's chat."

"So you can talk me into anything? I'll stay over here for a bit," Charlie said, unbuttoning his pants.

"A girl can hope, can't she? I think I'm heading north tomorrow. There isn't much excitement here other than you. Come with me to New York for the racing season." She patted the bed to get him to come over.

Charlie thought it looked like she was calling a housecat.

"We can stay at my friend's house. It's in Queens; I'm going up to help her get ready. They'll have several parties. They have a beautiful home, and her husband won't care which room we're in. He'll be thrilled that you can ride. You don't have to answer right now, but if you're coming, you need to let me know before I leave," Marjorie said.

Charlie sat in a chair and said, "What about your mama and daddy? That worries me a bit."

"Charlie, I'm a grown woman. I can go anywhere I please," she said as she lay back down. "And my parents were just in Kentucky for the Derby. Traveling is hard on them. They'll go back to Chicago. Just think about it, okay?"

"Tomorrow? I need time to square things up here." Charlie said, stepping out of his Johnnie and into the bed, "In the meantime, why don't you show me how dusty your butt is."

"Show me yours first, Plowboy."

CHAPTER 37

"Help me understand this," Ernie Deluca said. You want me to sell you my nine cows for the same price I'm supposed to get, but I won't get it because the man who bought them last time isn't there anymore."

"Yes, sir, but I'm going to need your boys to help me get them there tonight," Tiger said, "and then help me drive about 24 horses to Gainesville the next morning."

"Tonight? Why don't I just get my money from Pem Sardin like last time? In the morning," DeLuca asked.

"Cause the man that was paying him got run off," Tiger said, "and the new man is dropping the horses then turning right around. He ain't going to buy any cattle; I'm giving them to him."

DeLuca laughed, "Now, I know you're pullin' my leg, you skunk, you ain't fittin' to give away cows!"

"Do you want this $300 or not?" Tiger said, "The extra $30 is for your boys helping me and you taking a message to the village."

"Are you talking about your mama's village? Tonight?" Deluca said.

"Not tonight, Ernie, you won't get there till the morning," Tiger said.

"I ain't going in there at any time with a sack full of money. Can I stop by my house on the way down? And I ain't leaving until sunup, and I'm gon' need $50." DeLuca said.

"That skunk you smell ain't me," Tiger said. "And that'll be 30 now for the boys and 20 for you when I hear from Lacey."

"You don't trust me?" DeLuca asked.

"Not at 50, but I did at 30," Tiger said.

Tiger and the DeLucas drove the cattle 8 miles up Palatka Road, about an hour before sundown. They quickly moved the 15 head into the corral at the station, and Tiger went inside to speak to Pem Sardin. Having been paid for the cattle by Tiger, Deluca took his sons to the small café in Hawthorne for supper. Tiger brought smoked beef, pone, and sweet potatoes for supper, and he was glad they hadn't invited him to come along. He'd rather eat with his dogs.

Inside, he thanked Sardin for delivering the message that afternoon. Sardin said he couldn't say when the Army would be leaving Tampa.

"I wish they would, to clear some trains. Things won't be back to normal until we win the war," Sardin said, "if we win. I'm embarrassed to say it, but the way things have gone so far, I'm not very confident."

"What do you know about this new conductor?" Tiger was trying to make his conversation sound natural.

"I haven't met the man, but from what I hear, he likes all the paperwork to be complete," Sardin said. Maybe you should ask Charlie Herlong. From the wires I see, he seems to be running things down there and in Plant City."

"When I met him, he had more wagons than mules; now he's sending me a trainload of horses and asking for cows. I tell you that young man is moving," Tiger said, glad to get a conversation.

"He's ordering train cars full of goods from Montgomery Ward's, too. I guess saving the man's life will grease things up," Sardin said and turned to a filing cabinet.

"Wait, saved who's life? When did that happen?" Tiger asked.

"The other day, that day y'all were up here," Sardin said, "That train full of rich folks, Montgomery Ward's people. Some rustlers tried to rob it outside Owensboro and he killed all of them. He must be a dangerous man, took out the whole gang."

"Which one did he save?" Tiger asked, "Montgomery or Ward?"

"Both, I guess," Sardin said, "a bunch of rich folks from Chicago."

Tiger thought of Charlie and how he just learned how to shoot.

"I just hope I can get that new conductor," Tiger said, "to take these cows to Plant City. Right now, I ain't got enough help."

"I'm anxious to meet him too," Sardin said, "I hope he gets here soon; I got here before the rooster. I'm getting hungry."

"I brought some supper I'll share for a cup of coffee," Tiger said, and Sardin stepped to the coffee pot.

Plant's train pulled into the station at 9:30. Every man was armed and moved under Brooks' quiet direction. He walked to the station and raised a nod to Pem Sardin.

"Mr. Sardin, I'm presuming? I'm Abraham Brooks," he says, extending his hand. " Is your corral full of cattle? Do you have room for horses, too?"

"Good to meet you, Mr. Brooks, straight to business, I see." Sardin said, shaking his hand and motioning to Tiger, "Yes, sir, but I'll let you speak to Mr. Driggers about the cattle. I understand y'all are turning back right away. Can I make some coffee for your crew?"

"No, thank you, sir. Our porter keeps us well," Brooks said and turned to Tiger. "Mr. Driggers, are those your cattle in the corral?"

"I'm hoping they'll be yours," Tiger said, "till you get to Plant City, Charlie Herlong will settle up with you."

"Mr. Driggers, I just heard from Sanford about looking for cattle a few hours ago; how did you know about it?" Brooks said, pushing his hat back on his head.

"I didn't, just good luck. Charlie sent a telegram saying to find cattle after I sold the horses, so," Tiger held his palms up, "I had these and ... I was hoping you would take them."

"Well, lucky for you, I'm going right back to Plant City, and lucky for me, too, because my boss in Sanford told me to move cattle when I found them. How many do we have?" Brooks said and looked to the corral.

"15 strays we picked up around here," Tiger said; he felt the doubloons in his pocket in case he needed to pay the freight, "hey, in a week or so, do you think you could handle twice that many, picking up further south?"

"I'll do what Sanford says, but it'll be hard to find track space, maybe on a bypass. Some trains have been waiting for over a week. I wouldn't want to pick up anything of value, either. Mr. Herlong had to kill several men over there, and we hear folks are mad at the railroad over it."

"Mad at the railroad for killing train robbers," Tiger said. "What have you heard?"

"Sheriff in Dade City said he thought it was trash from over in Riverland, barely grown men," Brooks said.

"And Charlie killed the whole gang? What about the man that was with him, Henry Whitfield?" Tiger asked.

"I haven't met Whitfield, but what I believe is only hearsay. Charlie acted like it was nothing. He claims he's no gunhand, which isn't what I hear. What I know is Mr. Plant and Mr. Ward say give him whatever he wants." Brooks said, "Let's get these animals switched out, and maybe I can get a nap before sunup."

"When you see him, will you tell him more cattle are coming? I don't know when I'll be at a telegraph office." Tiger said.

"If I see him, but your best bet is to send him a wire, just have Mr. Sardin do it and put it on my account. I believe he's been staying at the hotel." Brooks said, turning toward the train.

"Mr. Driggers, when you need to send a wire to me, just send it to the Plant System office in Sanford, and they will relay it. Where is the best place to reach you?" Brooks said, handing Tiger a card.

"Between here and Plant City, can I get the message wherever the wire is?" Tiger said.

"Yes, sir, anywhere there's a wire," Brooks said.

When the cattle were loaded, the engineer gave his whistle a short blast of steam, and they were gone.

Sardin looked at Tiger and said, "Well, Tiger, that's that. I'm going home to get some sleep. You want me to send a message first?"

"No, the morning is fine. If I can get those boys from Wacahooty up, I'll be gone. Tell him more cattle are coming. If Brooks sends me a message, send it to Charlie in Plant City. I'll bring you some meat next time I see you," Tiger said and walked toward the corral, almost tripping on Shine.

"Shoot, dog, you trying to kill me?"

❋ ❋ ❋ ❋ ❖ ❖ ❖ ❋ ❋ ❋ ❖ ❋ ❋ ❋ ❋

The train arrived in Plant City just before sunrise, and Brooks directed his men to offload the cattle to the corral. By the time Jack and Henry got to the corral, Brooks' men were coming across the field. Jack moved to the platform, and Brooks waved him over.

"Mr. Sandy will have a receipt for you in a bit. I don't have any payment information for you. Driggers in Hawthorne said Charlie would settle up," Brooks said to Jack, "I hear there was a shooting here."

"A killing, Benson Fleet," Jack replied.

"Fleet? Do you think it was related to Owensboro?"

"It was Milt Loy from Desoto County. He shot a man over some cattle up in Knight's, so maybe. He told Musco that Fleet tried to hit him with a shovel, but that didn't sound like Fleet." Duffy said. "Somebody ought to do something, but they won't. I wish we were in Polk County."

"I'll pass that name along," Brooks said, writing the name in a small notebook from his vest pocket, "Mr. Plant will not tolerate security threats."

❋ ❋ ❋ ❋ ❖ ❖ ❖ ❋ ❋ ❋ ❖ ❋ ❋ ❋ ❋

Charlie awoke to the sound of Marjorie pulling the drain on the bathtub.

"Hey, hold that water, I'll use it," Charlie rolled out of the bed.

"Ew, no, you don't; I'll start another and put some of your "Smell Good" in it," Marjorie said, trying Charlie's accent, "I love the way you smell."

"No need to waste it," Charlie said as the tub gurgled.

"Too late," Marjorie said, "Only I get to smell like Marjorie. I need to get moving; Sammy said the train might be crowded. Oh, my."

She looked at Charlie and rushed over to him, kissing his neck and mouth, then pulled away. "Oh no, you don't; the train leaves at nine."

"Me too, if you're leaving," Charlie said, "I need to find cattle."

"And then, you're coming to New York?" Marjorie asked, "By the first week of June, the Belmont is in two weeks; that's the one that Silvie cares about."

"Marjorie, I can't just travel 1000 miles to see a horse race. I got hay to put up," Charlie said, stepping into his clothes.

Marjorie said, raking toiletries in a bag, "Are you going to be on the train?"

"I need them to load up my horse," Charlie said, opening the door, and Sammy fell into the room. "Hey, Sammy. We're catching the train. Can you get Thirsty loaded?"

"Y'all are leaving? Checking out?" Sammy was alarmed.

"Keep it quiet! I need to be on that train when it leaves." Marjorie said, still packing, "You're going to need help. Can you do it?"

"I'll try, Miss Ward, but you have lots of bags. Didn't Trousdell get them up here?" Sammy asked.

"He did, and I told him to get lost and forget he ever saw me. Here, I'll give you all this Tampa money if you can get these bags on that train," Marjorie said, reaching into her purse and dumping balled-up banknotes from local banks.

Sammy looked at the money and then at Charlie as if to say, "Help!"

Charlie stepped in, "You can do it, Sam. Those kids hanging around the back of the kitchen will carry them before you untangle that money. Give them a half dollar each, and they'll fight over it. I'll have Lonnie get my horse to the train, and I'll get Marjorie's buggy. You can use it to move the bags."

"You're a genius, Mr. Charlie!" Sammy said, and his face dropped, "What about your bags?"

"Get me on that train, Sammy," Marjorie said, "and remind Mr. Herlong that I need him back here when he finishes playing with you and those kids!"

Charlie put on his hat and said, "Come on, Sammy. I hear she always gets her way."

Sammy stuffed wads of money in his coat pockets and said, "Miss Ward? Can I call you Miss Marjorie?"

"I'd love that, Sammy."

CHAPTER 38

Sammy was at the bottom of the stairs when Charlie pulled up with Thirsty tied to the back of the buggy. Charlie heard a dozen boys carrying Marjorie's bags down the steep stairs.

"Sammie, did you clean out the schoolhouse?" Charlie asked as he tied off.

"The colored school got burned down. They were all back here, looking for odd jobs. I couldn't pick, so I'll be giving all of them 2 bits," Sammy said.

"Don't forget my bags," Charlie said, mounting Thirsty. "I'll catch you at the train and you can give me a ride back."

At the stock ramp, men were moving the last of seven cattle to the corral.

"How did you manage to find more cattle without leaving the hotel?" Lonnie asked as Charlie rode up.

"Just lucky," Charlie said, "are you sure those are mine, Lonnie?"

"Your name is on the bill," Lonnie said and whistled as he smacked a yearling bull with a short whip.

"Hey, I want to put Thirsty on the train," Charlie said.

"I can do that," Lonnie said, "Oh, Mr. Stringer was looking for you."

Charlie met with Stringer and confirmed the delivery of the seven cattle at $75 a head. He agreed to hold that price until nine more were delivered through Plant City. Stringer agreed to pay the market price through Duffy from that point on. This made Charlie happy. Nine more cows and his debt to the hotel was settled. Jack could sell cattle as he saw fit, and Charlie wouldn't be on the hook for the debt.

Charlie passed Sammy leading the buggy by the horse's bridle, followed by a gang of kids, laughing and playing.

"I have your bags, Mr. Charlie!" Sammy said.

Deep in thought, he waved and kept walking. He felt sure that Tiger's Horse Deal would come through and that the profit from that would help settle the Montgomery Ward debt. Charlie would leave further Ward ordering in Jack's hands, who could run it as he saw fit. The day before, Charlie placed $800 into the account that Lindsay had established for him at Tampa National and authorized Jack on the account. Charlie wondered if this was how business worked, everything just falling into place. He felt lucky to have met the people he had in the last week. He remembered something his mother liked to say, "Good luck is a gift from God, so put it to good use because he can take it back whenever he feels like it. Just ask Job."

He hoped he could wrap things up in Plant City within a week and meet Marjorie in New York. He stepped into the room, ready to tell her his plans.

"Lock that door. Sammy has seen enough this week," Marjorie said from the bed. Come over here. I'm going to show you why you're going to travel 1000 miles for a horse race."

❈❈❈❈❀❈❈❈❈❈❈❈❈❈❈

The lounge car was filled with VIPs, diplomats, and army officers. Marjorie wanted to tell Charlie about New York, but Charlie was more interested in the troops shipping out to Cuba.

"Charlie, did you hear me? I think you're going to like Joseph; he's always thinking about work, too," Marjorie said.

"Yes, but I heard that captain, too. They may start shipping out next week, which means I might be there sooner," Charlie said, hoping it would take the aggravation out of her voice.

"I don't know why you think about it; people do these things for you automatically; you don't have to lift a finger," she said, "you can not lift a finger in New York, just as easily."

"Marjorie, I 'magine New York is something to see. I'm itching to get there," Charlie said.

"So, you are coming?" Marjorie grabbed his hand with both of hers and turned toward him, "You promise?"

"I promise," Charlie said, "if I didn't want to, I wouldn't. I can't leave today because I keep my word and do the right thing."

"Oh, Charlie, I believe that about you. That makes it harder to leave you," Marjorie said, getting emotional. "But men lie, Charlie. They say things to get what they want, and then they ... move on. Oh!"

Marjorie let go of his hands and dabbed her eyes.

"Are you crying?"

"Will crying make you come with me?" she said.

"Don't, Marjorie, that'll make me cry, too," Charlie said, "Big old desperado gun hand hero, crying."

Marjorie let out half a giggle and said, "How can you make me laugh while I'm trying to cry?"

She cried harder and said to the other women watching, through a sob, "Mind your own business, you old crows. Haven't you ever been in love before?"

The women all looked at Charlie with expressions that 'Would give leprosy to a lesser man,' a David Herlong line. Charlie didn't understand. She asked him to go, and he said yes. She admired his honesty and then compared him to liars.

Then, he felt a sense of dread. She said she was in love. Charlie knew from experience he needed to choose his words very carefully. He thought it best to wait. Then, Marjorie began to cry hard.

"Have you ever been in love before?" Charlie whispered, slightly leaning into Marjorie.

"I don't know," Marjorie sniffed. "If I were, it wouldn't feel bad like this. Have you?"

"I thought I was," Charlie said, "at first, everybody else said so."

"What happened?"

"Just things about each other that the other one couldn't tolerate," Charlie said.

"Like what?"

"I was too loud, I cussed, and the only thing I liked about church was the singing and dinner on the grounds," Charlie said, "it was adding up, I guess. Oh, and she didn't like kissing."

"You're a great kisser," Marjorie said, blowing her nose productively.

"Looking back, I believe it was kissing in general, not how I did it."

A matron in black stood and handed Marjorie another hanky, "Don't you have a handkerchief?" She glared at Charlie and returned to her seat.

Charlie said, "You think that one's ever been in love? Or just mean."

Which caused another slight giggle. She blew her nose in hers and handed it to Charlie.

A man handed Charlie a larger handkerchief, "You may need this one, too; she's pretty upset."

"Was it the kissing you couldn't tolerate?" Marjorie asked.

"It was a bother, but I wanted to kiss right. I worked on it, but she didn't allow much practice time," Charlie said.

"So you found other lips to practice on?" Marjorie said, her voice hardening, "I guess that's why she broke up with you,"

"No, I liked her. I doubt those other girls would have gone for that," Charlie said, turning to see Seffner out the window.

"Don't be so sure, Charlie," Marjorie said, "if you were being true, that would make them willing. What was the last straw?" Marjorie sniffed.

"Watermelon," Charlie said.

Marjorie, with several others, turned and said, in unison, "Watermelon?"

"Do you mind?" Marjorie said, and they all returned to pretending not to listen.

"Yeah, I couldn't believe it. Who hates watermelon?" Charlie said, turning back to the middle of the car. The matron now glowered.

"Tell that woman I'm a nice feller."

"No use. Never been kissed right," Marjorie said.

They were both quiet for a minute or so.

"I love watermelon," Marjorie said.

"What about kissing?" Charlie asked.

"I thought I liked it a lot," Marjorie said, "now that I've been kissed right, I'll never be the same."

❉ ❉ ❉ ❉ ❉ ❉ ❉ ❉ ❉ ❉ ❉ ❉ ❉ ❉

Just after reveille, Henry told his uncle there were cattle and wanted him to take them all. Baker agreed to take three and sent an extra man for security.

"How many will he take?" Jack asked as he opened the corral gate.

"Three at a time. He says that will keep the price up in camp," Henry said as he dismounted, "and I agree. We can protect these cows. Besides, Musco said the man was looking to sell."

"I'm not looking to get shot over cows; I can make money selling beans and shoes," Jack said.

"Money will get you shot too." Henry said, "We only have five. Let's see what Charlie says."

Jack said, "That devil admitted shooting Fleet for being an asshole, which is like shooting a crow for bad singing, but still. He shot Dew Dykstra because he wouldn't tell him the name of the buyer. Somebody needs to shoot him."

"I'll do it," Hatch said.

"No need for that kind of talk," Henry said, "wishing for bad luck."

"Just the same, Corporal," Jack said, "if you see him near me, shoot him dead as J.E.B. Stuart. You'll never pay for a drink around me from then on."

"That's a good deal for you. I don't drink much. But I might need supplies. My hitch is almost up, and I'm getting out." Hatch said, "What's he look like so that I know?"

"Big, ugly, dirty, half a beard, floppy cracker hat," Jack said, "Wears two pistols."

"You're getting out just before the war?" Henry said, "You mind me asking why?"

"I needed a job and signed on six years ago." Hatch said, "I've learned a lot and believe I'm worth more than $18 a month. Lots of troopers want to go."

"What about serving your country?" Henry said.

"Who? The government? They don't care about me or you either; we're colored, nothing to them," he said, "white folks in Lakeland won't sell me lemonade. I ain't cocked and loaded about killing Spaniards for them, either."

❊ ❊ ❊ ❊ ✦ ❊ ✦ ❊ ❊ ✦ ❊ ❊ ❊ ❊

Cal and Seth DeLuca were closing the gate on a corral at Coleman's Livery. At the turn through the prairie, Ernie kept following the herd. Tiger decided he didn't need DeLuca's help.

Tiger came out of the business office with $ 3,000 in cash and gold, hoping he could buy cattle with paper money. Tiger wasn't happy about having to accept $1000 in bank notes, but he had no choice.

"What's the message for your people in the village? That you're rich, now?" DeLuca said.

"They already think I'm rich, but they're just as mistaken as you," Tiger said, "and I don't need you for that, now."

"You mean riding to the Hammock? Hey, we had a deal," DeLuca said.

"Had. Not now," Tiger said, pulling himself on Mico with an easy swing.

"What am I doing here, then?" Deluca said.

"That's a good question, Ernie," Tiger said, tying a saddle bag to rings on the pommel, "Did you think five days' pay for half a day's work was for companionship? I need cows, boy."

"We done caught everything between here and my place," Deluca said, following Tiger.

"No, Ernie, your boys did," Tiger said. "You watch and talk. I'm heading south, through the Hammock, then down the Indian trails. There'll be cows already collected, and I'll buy them on the way. It's been a while since I've driven cattle, but I know some boys in the village who want work."

The older Deluca son, Cal, caught Tiger outside Gainesville.

"Mr. Tiger, if you're looking for help, Seth and I can do it," Cal said, slowing to a canter.

"Y'all do a good job, Cal. I just don't have time for y'all to get to Wacahootee, get packed, get permission, and find your way through the hammock," Tiger said, not slowing down.

"Will y'all be crossing the river at Dunnellon? I know where cows are, and we've sold cows there before. If we have cows, will you buy them? $40 a head?"

"I'll go as high as 40," Tiger said, happy to see ambition, "But I can't tell you when we'll be there."

"Thank you, Mr. Tiger. I hope to see you there," Cal said, turning south toward Sweetwater while Tiger continued toward his prairie.

Chapter 39

"Get them beeves moving, private," Hatch said. "Make sure you cut them off before that strawberry field. I'll be right along."

"Corporal! Hold up, a second!" Henry jogged along the packing house platform and jumped to the ground. " Try these shoes on!"

"I told you, they don't come in my size," Hatch said.

"These are tens, " Henry said, "Try this one just to see."

"Thanks just the same, Henry, but I have size ten already; look," Hatch said and placed his brogan on the edge of the sideboard. "I split and then restitch them."

"We'll order you some; they'll be here on the next delivery," Henry said.

"How much? These will work, and they're cheap. I just go through socks fast," Hatch said, snapping the reins and lurching off.

"You just think about what I said," Henry said, "We'll make them affordable."

"Did they fit?" Jack said, standing on the platform.

"No, that rascal's got some big old feet," Henry said, "along with everything else he's wearing. We need to order a whole set of clothes that fit. We need that man working with us."

"I hope to see Thorne when the train comes in, find out when the goods get here from Louisville, and make another order," Jack said. "Pretty soon, all the trains will be running; more and more are leaving Tampa."

✹✹✹✹✹✦✹✹✹✹✦✹✹✹✹✹

"Miss Ward, we must leave to stay on schedule," Brooks said, "Your fellow passengers must be in Sanford in time to depart for Washington and New York. We can leave you here and send your luggage back on tomorrow's train," Brooks said.

Charlie pulled away from Marjorie, who was standing on the first step, her teary face on the same level as Charlie's. Charlie backed up to his bags. He turned, picked up the new bag holding his new wardrobe, and placed it on the step.

"Here, take my new clothes, make sure they look good when I get there," Charlie said.

"OK, you're coming. You promise?" Marjorie said as the whistle to depart was blowing again.

"Yes, I'll be there!" Charlie waved, and the train started rolling away. Henry and Jack walked up behind him.

"Dang, Charlie, why'd you make her cry?" Henry said.

"Good lovin'," Charlie said, "and getting in debt. I want to take care of that as soon as we can so I can hear her laugh again."

"Charlie, are you in love?" Henry asked.

"I'll let you know when I know," Charlie said. "Jack, how fast can we get nine more head of cattle to the hotel? That will settle our debt on the horses."

"That's a good question, we have five now. The only lead we have on cattle is dangerous," Jack said, "not someone I want to do business with."

"How dangerous could four cows be?" Charlie said, "What about Fleet? Maybe he knows other cow hunters along the route from Hawthorne."

"He did. The guy killed him yesterday," Jack said, "then told Musco he had cattle to sell you."

"Killed him? What for?"

"He said because Fleet tried to hit him with a shovel," Jack said.

"That don't sound like Fleet," Charlie interrupted.

"Well, that and he said Fleet was being an asshole," Jack said.

"That, I believe," Charlie said, "but this guy sounds like the King of Assholia."

"What bothers me is he asked for you by name," Henry said, "do you know him, Milt Loy?"

"By name only, Fleet said he and a guy named Bird wanted to kill me," Charlie said.

"Bird Mobley, that fat sheriff talked about him. That kid under the horse was his son. He kept saying, 'Wait till my Daddy hears this and that.'" Henry said, "The little kid that rode off with the older man had a crazy name, too... Mouse Loy!"

"Man, I should have stayed on the train," Charlie said, "you think if I told him you were shooting at his boy, it might make him quit thinking about me for a while?"

"No, sir, just make his list longer," Henry chuckled.

"Well, I'll keep it under my hat," Charlie said, "What did the sheriff say?"

"I haven't seen him," Jack said. There's supposed to be one in Seffner, but we haven't seen a soul yet. Jim Sandy sent a wire to the sheriff in Tampa."

"You think we're on our own, then? That can be good and bad. Was anyone riding with him?" Charlie asked.

"Musco didn't say," Jack said.

"Is he still around? I want to know what was said," Charlie said, walking toward his bag.

❋ ❧ ❋ ❊ ❦ ❧ ❦ ❋ ❋ ❧ ❋ ❧ ❋

Tiger was driving the low boy behind Willie and Jake, the mules Charlie received from H.F. Dutton. He packed for a small cattle drive, estimating he could find 30 head if he were lucky. Mico was on a lead tied to the back of the wagon along with Sarge and Briar, the recently decommissioned Cavalry horses.

Their saddles and tack were in the wagon along with rope, the oiled canvas tarps from Dutton, camp supplies, food, and a smoked hog. Shine was in the cargo box, waiting for another drop of fat to leak out of the burlap. The low wheels were causing a clearance issue now that Tiger had entered the swampy hammock. Tiger heard Shine growl, then Moon's quick, high yelp and Shine was gone.

Tiger stopped to survey some standing water on the trail and wondered if he might need to use the horses to pull the wagon through. He walked the wagon through the mudhole, leading Willie by her bridle.

Tiger heard two horses moving through the scrub on either side of the trail and quickly moved to his pistol and whip in the box. He heard the lever of a rifle and knew he was too late.

"Are you slow or can't hear anymore, Tsitaga?" A voice called from behind a tree.

Across the wagon, Tiger could see through the leaves an outline of a man on a horse. With no hesitation, he reached his hand into the box and on his pistol.

"You should know that I can hear your voice and know you're from Lacey's village," Tiger said, taking his hand off the pistol and climbing into the buckboard. "Where is your brother, Snapper?"

"I'm over here," Snapper said behind Tiger, "I knew this was a bad idea for a joke. Taga, please call your dogs; they look hungry."

Tiger whistled twice, and both dogs jumped up into the wagon.

"That kind of joke can get you killed, Opal," Tiger said. "I was surprised by the sound of your rifle. It's a good thing your voice gave you away."

"We smelled your food. Can we ride with you?" Opal said, "Maybe we can kill a bear."

"I have a better idea. How many cattle can y'all drive?" Tiger asked.

"As many as you can find," Snapper said, "When can we start?"

"Let's get to the village first. I may need you to help me get this low wagon through the bottoms, and I want to give Lacey this hog," Tiger said and snapped the reins, causing Moon and Shine to run ahead.

"Look, fellas, I didn't leave Lake City to get into the cattle business," Charlie said to Henry and Jack on the platform, "or to run a general store. I was on my way to Jacksonville, and the only thing that's changed is now I'm going to visit New York and see some horse races."

"Charlie, didn't you say that rich folks make you itch?" Henry said, "Hey, it's your business, but we need a little more time to get where we want to be."

"No, it's our business. I'm just making sure my loose ends are tightened up," Charlie said, looking at Jack. "And that includes you, too, Jack. You've done it; I just met the right people to make it happen."

"Well, it's a little more than that," Jack said. "We need you involved to keep the Ward's merchandise coming and the beef business with the hotel going. Who knows what's going to happen when the army ships out? That could happen at any time."

"Next week, or when the trains start running again, it'll be time for me to go," Charlie said, "I can set it all up for you to have authority to take care of business, but as soon as someone calls me about money owed, we'll close up shop. I've put your name on the bank account, by the way."

"So, as long as the bills are paid, we can keep the store business going? What about the cattle?" Jack asked.

"After we get nine more head to the hotel, do what you want," Charlie said. "They'll pay market price for them."

"Charlie, that sounds like I have control of the whole thing; what do you want out of it? We're going to make money, regardless," Jack said, "as long as we have credit. Where are you going to be? How am I going to get word to you?"

"I don't know," Charlie said. "I kind of like the telegram deal."

"How much is my salary? And yours, for that matter, and what about Henry?"

"Shoot, I don't know that either; ask Henry," Charlie said, "all I know is the way my mother did it. She kept a third of the profit for her and Daddy; any other profit went straight back into the business. Can you live on 10% as your salary? How about you, Henry? You can hold mine, and I'll take it as I need it; as soon as I hear from Tiger, I'll take my share of the horse deal and head to New York."

Henry nodded his head, "That sounds good to me. Just take my cut and apply it to what I'm taking to Cuba. God willing, maybe I can make orders from there to you, here, Jack, that's another market we can sell in. Will you stay a little while and help me get to Cuba, Charlie?"

"I have been living on nothing for over a year; I'll manage. Charlie, you're putting a lot of trust in me; I've only known you for a few days," Jack said, his eyes welling up a bit.

"Then make it work, Jack. You've already made better decisions than I would have," Charlie said. "I'm way ahead of where I was last week, remember, Henry?"

"Yes, sir," Henry said, "how'd you put it? 'A heavy pack and a sore back!' But now, you have a fancy girlfriend and a business manager! Both of them crying, you big timer, you!"

"If I've learned anything, a lot can happen in a short time, good and bad," Charlie said, "let's figure out how to get Henry to Cuba and keep making money off the Army. I hear they're moving out real soon."

"I wish you'd come with me," Henry said.

"I wish you'd stay here," Jack said.

"No, sir. There's been too much shooting here and in Cuba," Charlie said, "and I still haven't seen the first elephant."

CHAPTER 40

T he sun had been up for two hours, and dew was heavy coming out of Gulf Hammock. Lacy had invited everyone in the area to share the hog and welcome her boy home. There had been some celebrating and Tiger was already sweating in the humidity. Tiger rode Mico along a narrow road heading east toward Romeo. Opal and Snapper both rode the cavalry mounts and herded four steers Tiger had purchased in the village. Their cousin Neha was driving the wagon, happy to be leaving the swampy hammock for higher ground. He convinced Tiger to let him come along, drive the wagon, and cook for free. Tiger figured that was a good deal, not even asking if he could cook, assuming that he had to be able to, being overweight, and named the Seminole word for fat. Tiger stopped at a fork he didn't remember and whistled to Opal.

"Where's this fork lead to?" Tiger said as Opal rode to him.

"Morganville, they got a Post Office and a store; we've sold cattle down this road; there might be some to buy," Opal said, "this is a good horse, Taga; I wonder why they got rid of him?"

"Might have kept running off, better keep a rope on him," Tiger said.

"Hey, look at these dogs; they have rabbits in their mouths!" Neha said. Moon and Shine jumped up into the wagon, dropped the rabbits on a sack of meal, and laid down on the oil skin.

"I wish they had a cow, but at least we'll have some supper tonight," Tiger said. "Can you clean rabbits? Just field-dress them right now. I want to keep going. Opal, is there good water on this road?"

Snapper had already begun pushing the cattle toward Morganville, and Opal kicked after them. Tiger said, "I reckon there is," and turned to Neha, who was gutting the rabbits.

"I hope they find some more," Neha said, "Half a rabbit is just going to make me mad."

By noon, Tiger had bought six more head of cattle from farmers in and around Morganville and felt he was making good time. Snapper shot a shoat feeding on acorns. Tiger had him field dress it and hang it from the back of the wagon to bleed out. He planned to find a butcher to trade it for salt pork and bacon. He wanted to cross the Withlacoochee on the ferry and follow the old railroad through Citrus and Hernando Counties. In Dunnellon, he was able to put his cattle in a holding pen while they waited for the ferry to return. Tiger made his way around town and was able to buy three more head, at a higher price than before. The cost would go up as they traveled south.

***

The DeLuca brothers pushed four steers, a cow, and a calf into the same corral Tiger had used the day before. Cal walked to the barn to ask about Tiger.

A voice came from the back of the barn. "Hey Calvin, where's your Daddy?"

"He ain't with us today, Mr. Blackburn," Cal said, "Me and Seth caught some cattle and were looking to sell them. Do you know Tiger Driggers? We were trying to catch him before he crossed the river."

"Son, he was here yesterday, trying to buy every cow in town," Blackburn said, "for good money. And they were moving, too, and had some Indians that could handle cattle. How much are you looking to get for yours? Of course, I can't pay what he was paying."

"We have a deal with him already," Cal said, "when did he leave?"

"About noon. No offense, son, but I don't think y'all are going to catch them boys, especially with that calf and cow. I'll give you $30 for that cow and calf if that will help you. That's what he was paying yesterday for steers."

"Yes, sir, I'll sell her to you. That will help us move faster. How much will you give for the steers?" Cal said.

"Not what he was giving, 'cause I don't want to feed them, and anyone else in town isn't going to want to buy them for as much as he was paying," Blackburn said. "Cal, I think your best bet is to take the steers over to Wildwood. You might get what you're looking for over there. Or, take them to Tampa. That's where Tiger was headed, I think."

"I believe I'll take you up on $30 for the cow and calf if you're still willing," Cal said, extending his hand to Blackburn.

They shook hands, and Blackburn said, "Let me walk over to the bank and get your money. If I see someone looking to buy, what's the lowest you'll take for them?"

Cal turned to find Seth and said over his shoulder, "$30 today. I believe we'll get more in Wildwood."

Cal found his brother outside the general store, talking to a young girl whose mother snatched her by the hand and pulled her inside.

"Well, did we beat him here?" Seth said, laughing, "I may need to leave town."

"Then, let's go. He left yesterday," Cal said, "and we're going to Wildwood."

"Wildwoods? Where's that?" Seth cried, "Hell if I'm going on a damn cattle drive, what'd Mama say? Two days. I'm getting hungry, too."

"Well, I ain't taking these steers back to Wacahootee," Cal said, "and I told you about that cussing; just 'cause Mama and Daddy ain't around don't mean I'm going to stand for it."

"Then, let's sell them here," Seth said, "you don't know if you'll get more in Wildwoods or any dang where else."

"I ain't selling them here for half of what we can get for them further south," Cal said. "There's a café over there. We'll get supper. Let's go; it's a four-hour ride."

"How much can we sell them for here? I'll take $20 a head, same as back home," Seth said as he walked with Cal toward the livery.

"You want to hear Daddy say he told us so?"

"I don't give a 'coon's dick what Daddy says," Seth said, and Cal elbowed him hard in the upper arm.

"Well, I care what both of y'all say around me," Cal said, continuing as Seth rubbed his shoulder.

✖✖✖✖✚✚✖✖✖✚✖✖✖✖

Milt Loy was seated against a Live Oak tree in a low meadow where six steers were grazing. Bird Mobley was standing on the road to Royal with a worried look.

"Got damn, calm down, Birdy. Ain't nobody expecting that nigger back till tomorrow," Loy said, sitting up and motioning for Mobley. "Come get the bottle out of my saddlebag and have a drink. When it clouds up, later, we'll head toward Sumterville and find a pen for these cattle."

"I ain't like you, Milt; I can't just kill a man and take a nap. It upsets me," Mobley said.

"I told Amelly at y'all's wedding she had to be the one with sand in her neck," Loy said. "Besides, you dumb bastard, ain't nobody been kilt. Get it straight: he got scared when he heard thunder, so we paid him what we had, $40, and he went home."

"You give him $40?"

"Got damn, you're stupid," Loy said, "That's why I put an IOU in his pocket for the other $40, so our story would hold up. What happened to him after we left ain't none of my business."

"That's what I don't get," Mobley said, "all we had was $40. And putting your name in his pocket was crazy, as far as I'm concerned."

"No, Bird. He had four steers. I told him I'd give him 20 a piece for them, that's $80. We're going to say we gave him $40 and owed him the other money... get it?" Loy stood after he said it, getting agitated.

"I don't remember that ever being said. You just shot him and stuck your name in his pocket," Mobley said, his voice trailing off as he saw Loy stepping toward him.

Loy pulled his right pistol, cocked it, and grabbed Bird by the collar of his tattered shirt, which ripped. Loy then knocked Bird's hat off and grabbed what hair he still had around his right ear.

"Listen to me, you stupid motherfucker, and pay attention. 'Cause if I have to say it again, I'll be telling Amelly how you let a nigger kill you over four steers," Loy said and stuck the barrel of his pistol in Bird's left nostril. "The nigger was riding with us to help get ours and his steers over to Wildwood. He heard thunder and got scared 'cause you know how scarish they are. So, we offered him $40 cash and give him an IOU for the rest. You know what, don't say a goddamn thing about any kind of money, just act stupid, that ort to be easy. You got it?"

"Yeah, I like that plan," Mobley said as Loy holstered his pistol, walked to his horse, and took a bottle from his bag.

"All you need to think is he was a nice nigger and trusted us to bring him back the rest of his money," Loy took a drink from the bottle, "anything else you just tell them to ask me."

"Who?" Bird asked.

"Who what? Me. Them. Jesus, shut the hell up; you're giving me a headache," Loy said and took another pull.

"Oh Lordy, look yonder, Milt, a cow is coming up the damn road!" Bird said.

Loy stood and saw the Deluca brothers guiding the four steers. He decided that those steers would soon be his.

"Calm down, Bird. Those cattle will come right over here if those boys let them," Loy said and leaned against the tree trunk, "and they will because they're hot and want some of this shade."

The cattle veered toward the cool grass, and Cal rode over to head them off. The steers quickened their pace, and he let them move.

"Might as well fatten them up a bit, they look like they been pushed kind of hard," Loy said. "Why don't y'all come over and cool off a bit?"

Seth needed no more invitation than that and dismounted, tying his reins to a low-hanging branch. Cal saw the whiskey bottle and hesitated, but when he saw Loy place the bottle back into his saddlebag, he relented. The sun was pretty hot on his shoulders, too.

"Y'all got water? It's hot today, ain't it?" Loy said.

Bird felt uneasy. Hearing Milt's cheerful voice was like a rattler, and someone was soon to be bitten.

"Where y'all from?" Loy asked.

"Wacahootee! And I'd just soon be back," Seth said,

"What kinda Hootie? I ain't never heard of nowhere like that, up Gainesville way?" Loy said and drank from his canteen. "Y'all headed down to Lakeland?"

"No, sir," Cal said, "over to Wildwood to sell these steers. Do you know how much further that is?"

"Five more miles, but the price is low. They're paying close to a hundred dollars in Lakeland," Loy said. "Hey, are you interested in selling yours to me?"

"How much are they paying in Wildwood?" Cal asked.

"$25 that's hardly worth the trip," Loy said, "That's why I'm heading south; the price will be higher. Hey, sell yours to me. I can give $80 right now."

"Thank you for the offer, but we need more than $80," Cal said, "we'll just see in Wildwood."

"Boy, you ain't going to get more than $80 in Wildwood," Loy said, the tone in his voice hardening.

"Well, we'll get over there and see," Cal said. "Seth, let's get moving. We'll try to find someone with money."

"What'd I just tell you?" Loy said.

"Yes, sir, I heard you, but we're going to see if we can do better," Cal said and mounted his horse.

"I said you ain't getting no better than $80. Right here. Right now," Loy said, walking out of the shade and in front of Cal's horse.

"I'd still like to go see, Mister," Cal said, "Let me pass, please."

"You'll pass when I'm good and goddamned ready, you little piss ant," Loy grabbed the bridle of Cal's horse, and Seth rode over.

"Hey, mister, get your shitty mitts off his horse!" Seth yelled the last words he ever would.

Loy shot Seth under the ridge of his left eye, the .45 slug knocking his hat and the top of his skull off. Loy grabbed his horse by the bridle as Seth fell off the back. He then turned and shot Cal in the back, trying to ride away. Cal fell; his horse trotted a few more yards and stopped to munch on the sweet grass.

Bird looked at Milt Loy with amazement, not surprised but shocked at how quickly he killed his second and third victims of the day.

"The fuck you lookin' at? Gather up that other horse and string them together. If we can get to Sumterville, we'll find someone to help us push these cattle to Lakeland," Loy said to Bird.

"What are you doing?" Bird said with disgust, "We're supposed to be finding the guy who killed my boys, and you're killing somebody else's unarmed kids."

"I'm makin' a thousand dollars, what the fuck have you done other than whine like a little gal?" Loy said, going through Cal's pockets. "You better get your mind right if you're ridin' with me. I ain't doing it for free, and you're broke as a wagon spoke. Do you want me to kill Charlie Herlong? Then do what the fuck I tell you to."

Loy dragged the brothers by their feet across the meadow and into the woods. He then whistled up the cattle and pushed them toward Sumterville.

CHAPTER 41

The Army was preparing for their move in Port Tampa. Plant's train continued to bring items from Montgomery Ward for C.H. Duke Company, the name given to the account and business in Plant City. Charlie wanted it to reflect their partnership, and Jack insisted they use Duke, a nickname he had as a child.

"C. H. Duke," Charlie said with a flourish, "That has a nice ring to it."

The soldiers in Lakeland wanted the goods they supplied. Charlie sent deposits to the bank and had Thorne invoice Jack. Charlie was comfortable and felt he could leave it with Jack and move on to New York.

Charlie set about trying to make Henry's mission happen. Moving two train cars of goods was a monumental task. The Tampa Hotel brought fish from the south, Punta Gorda. Charlotte Harbor Division of Florida Southern Railroad was technically part of the Plant System, but legal disputes created a loose style of management. Jack knew of a ship captain in Punta Gorda who might consider a trip to Cuba. James Sandy said he would speak to the conductor about securing cars to send freight down.

"The train from DeSoto County will come through here today. Do you want to speak directly with the conductor?" Sandy said.

"Yes, sir. I want to go down there. Does my pass work on that train?" Charlie asked.

"Yes, sir, it's a Plant System train; it just has the old company's name on the side," Sandy said. "Are you all planning to open a store down south?"

Charlie hesitated to say much, replying, "Right now, we're just going to see what's down there."

"Well, there's a store in Bartow that has trouble getting goods. Maybe you should go see him," Sandy said. "More freight on that Charlotte Harbor line helps make you friends."

"Hell, yeah, Charlie, once the Army starts moving out, we'll want another place to sell to," Jack jumped in, "we can sell stuff and never touch it!"

"Well, go armed; I hear it's rough country past Polk County," Sandy said, "but it's nice down at the gulf."

Charlie asked Sandy for wire news.

"It's only been eight days; she's probably almost there," Sandy said as he left, "and nothing from Hawthorne."

"That ain't good," Jack said, "Baker tells me every day he needs beef."

"I've been trying to find shoes for Hatch," Henry said.

"They don't make them," Jack said, "and the only clothes I can find are overalls and underwear." Jack said, "Do you know a tailor? Or a shoemaker?"

"Custom-made boots? How much?" Charlie stopped his sorting of the bullets and gun parts and cocked his head at Jack.

"I don't know yet; the shoe man's sewing machine is busted. Thorne said they don't sell parts; they sell whole sewing machines. Shoot, Henry's got one in his stuff, but who can sew?"

"We don't even know if Hatch wants to work for us," Charlie asked, "You gon' trade a sewing machine for boots?"

"Well, I thought I'd let him make payments if you say it's all right," Jack said, "He's good for it."

"What if he ain't? Are we bankers, now?" Charlie asked.

"We got money, Charlie, but C.H. Duke's got credit," Jack said, crossing his arms and sitting on the edge of his makeshift desk.

"We don't even have a building," Charlie said.

"It don't matter. If you ask Thorne and the bank to endorse us, others will, too. We can sell anything we feel like selling. All these folks coming here are going to need stuff, and like you say, 'Give them what they need.' Can you go to the bank and get them to write a few letters for us?"

"Just walk in there and ask them for ..." Charlie stopped, "what?"

"A letter of endorsement, here, I'll write it down," Jack began writing notes. Take a deposit, and I'll bag up a big one. That'll help. The shoe guy's in Tampa. Can we offer him a new machine and give him a year to pay for it? While you're gone, I'll see if we can find someone who can sew?"

Charlie started to protest but stopped: "A Hungry dog can bark, I guess. Don't send all the money; I need some to travel to New York. How about clothes? Are we getting Hatch new duds, too?"

"Buy the biggest you can find, I guess," Jack said, "If they don't fit, we'll find someone to sell them to."

Charlie caught the Desoto train, pulled by a Grant locomotive marked #700, Florida Southern. Soon, Hatch rode up on a big flea-bitten grey from Troop F.

"Hello, Corporal; good to see you!" Henry said, "Where's your wagon?"

"It's getting loaded up to move to Cuba," Hatch said, "Pretty soon, you're going to see lots of movement that way."

"What about you? Will you be going?" Henry asked.

"No, sir, tomorrow's my last day," he said, "and I'm glad. It's miserable over there. The ones going that want to are working their asses off, the ones that ain't are mad and looking to fight, and the rest are trying to get out of it. Baker sent me over to tell you he can't take any cattle, but in a few days y'all can keep the same deal going with his assistant, Sergeant Carlton Ray, he's staying."

"What about soon-to-be Mr. Hatch?" Henry asked, "You going back to New Mexico?"

"Not tomorrow," Hatch said, "To tell you the truth, Mr. Whitfield, all I know is I don't want to go to Cuba, and I don't want to stay in Lakeland."

"Call me Henry. What's your real name? I bet it's not Hatch,"

"It might as well be, been that for six years," Hatch said, "I'm from Hatch Valley; I guess folks didn't like Doris Miller, my real name."

"Why don't you visit with us for a while? There's always something to do around here," Henry said. "Say, do you know anything about cannons?"

"I know if one needs to be moved, I'm the first they volunteer to do it," Hatch said, "that Two Pounder? Does it need a wheel?"

"Yes, and the axel is broken off," Henry replied, "You know it?"

"Not particularly, but that's what usually breaks cause men are lazy and won't pack or use them the way they are supposed to. You got it cheap, didn't you?" Hatch said.

"Jack got it, so I'm sure he did," Henry said, turning toward the storage room. "You mind looking at it? Please tell us what we have. We have shells."

Hatch chuckled and followed him. "Yeah, those are important. Y'all have saddles?"

"You mean like for horses?" Henry said.

"No, for cannon, they ride side saddle. Unless you're going to tote it," Hatch stopped. "Uh, where are y'all going?"

"Right now, south. Place called Punta Gorda. I hope on a train," Henry said as he entered the room with his relief supplies. "Then we hope to catch a ride on a boat."

"Sarge was right; y'all crazy," Hatch said, looking around. "Why y'all going to Cuba?"

"To save lives," Henry said. And it's just me," Henry said as he lifted the broken axle, "right now."

"With light artillery. Man, you full of ... something," Hatch laughed.

"No, no. I'm looking to sell or trade this to pay for all this other stuff," Henry said. "If it's useful, it'll buy lots of stuff people need."

"What people?" Hatch asked.

"The people the Army say they are saving," Henry said, "but they're not going down there to save colored folks and Indians."

"They got them down there too?"

"Just like here," Henry answered.

"Why are they going, then? What are they going after?" Hatched asked.

"Sugar, tobacco, dirt," Henry said, "and money. Tell me what this rig needs to be useful."

Henry spent the next few hours learning about Hotchkiss Mountain guns and the Army's way of moving them and firing them. Henry told Hatch about recent Cuban history, from the abolition of slavery to the rebellion against Spain.

❃ ❃ ❃ ❃ ❃ ❃ ❃ ❃ ❃ ❃ ❃

Charlie walked out of the Exchange National Bank of Tampa with an endorsement and an offer of a business loan. They were delighted to meet Charlie, his reputation having grown since his "rescue" of A. Montgomery Ward. Each time he was reminded, Charlie was amazed at how his valor had grown. His cheeks flushed as his recollection of the event was more flight than fight.

He found Armando Reina's shoe shop on Twiggs Street. Reina was repairing a shoe by hand and kept working.

"I cannot give you a time en que puedo comenzar. Mi máquina needs reparación, and I must todo a mano. I cannot give you a time," Reina said from a shoe anvil, holding a needle and thread.

"Yes sir, you seem a little backed up," Charlie said.

"Dios mío, estos gringos, con su dinero," he said, continuing to sew. "No, no voy a poner your shoes ahead of otros clientes!"

"I heard your machine is busted. I think I can help you with that."

Reina stopped sewing, "E tu have las partes, the parts, para-Singer?"

"No, sir, I want to sell you a new one, uh, mucho bueno," Charlie said, holding up his right boot. "So you can make me a pair of boots."

Reina went back to work. "Quien tiene ciento veinticinco dólares? If you have shoes to fix, muéstramelos. Puedes comprar boots en cualquier store."

"I need big boots, size 14," Charlie said, holding his hands apart. "And ... I'll let you make payments on a new machine."

"Usurero! Vete!" Reina yelled, "Llamaré a la cops! Policia!"

"The policia? What for? I only need a pair of boots for a big-footed rascal! They ain't made that against the law yet."

"Me prestas el dinero e intentas hacerte cargo de mi negocio!"

Reina was still yelling.

The bell over the door tinkled, and Pete Falcone, the Italian tailor's apprentice, walked through the door.

"Mr. Charlie! I heard you went to New York! I was so jealous, but now I'm sad for you," Pete's demeanor turned to concern. "Did things fall apart with la ricca signorina?"

"She's up there waiting for me! Right now, I'm trying to convince this guy I can help him," Charlie said. "How's your Spanish? Mine is as bad as my eye-talian."

"Maybe just enough. I want to open up a shop next door. I've had enough Marco," Pete said. "Signor Reina, si ricorda di me? Sono Pete y trabajo con Marco."

Soon, they were finishing details on a 10-month installment loan for the price of a new, top-of-the-line, leather sewing machine by Singer for Reina at $15 a month, payable to C.H. Duke. When Reina understood that all Charlie needed was a pair of boots, he gave him a pair he had repaired, but the customer did not pick it up. He told Charlie he would make the new boots when the machine arrived, free of charge.

Charlie cut a deal with Pietro to outfit Hatch in exchange for a new sewing machine. They stopped in a dry goods store to pick up enormous socks, underwear, and material for work clothes.

Charlie and Pietro caught the #700 train back to Plant City just in time.

Chapter 42

Bird Mobley just wanted to go back home to Riverland. Just tell Amelly they couldn't find the man with the yellow neck rag. He was sick of his brother-in-law, getting meaner and drunker by the day since they sold 15 steers to a Yankee soldier from New York. Milt was freely spending the $1200 in gold and cash he received on food and whisky, but he wasn't sharing any with Bird, just saying, "Order whatever you want. This job ain't over till Charlie Herlong is dead," whenever Bird asked for his share.

Milt became indignant when a café owner said they had only chicken and pork. He broke dinnerware with his pistol and then gave the man $20 for damages and fried chicken. He almost got arrested for drunken fighting, but he paid the sheriff $10 to let him leave town. They made the short ride to Bartow, and Milt continued celebrating. Neither of them had seen a hundred dollars, and Milt was living "like a white man for the first time in my life."

They were in the Tip Top Saloon, Bird drinking coffee and trying to convince Milt they should be in Plant City looking for Charlie.

"Calm down, Birdie. That dandy ain't going nowhere. He's selling beef to the same people we are. He can't keep avoiding us forever," Milt slurred. "Have a drink; later on, we'll go over to that dry goods store and buy some things for my sister."

"If you'd give me my share, I can buy her stuff myself," Bird said. "Milton, I need to get home and comfort her; we've lost two of our sons, remember? Your nephews!"

Milton was the name Amelly used, Bird hoping that would spur him to some feeling of kindness.

"You best remember who you're talking to, boy," Loy said. "I'll make her a widow and buy her a husband with guts. Hey! We need another bottle!"

Bird decided to wait until Milt drank himself to sleep and collect his money. He took the bottle from the bartender to move the process along. He hoped to get at least enough to buy a new shirt and a pair of trousers.

Fairfax Brosnan, conductor for The Florida Southern Railroad, Charlotte Harbor division, knew where he stood in the pecking order of The Plant System. He stood alone as his train alone traveled south of Lakeland. The day Henry Plant removed the rails from the Long Dock at Punta Gorda, practically eliminating access to deep water, he made the Charlotte Harbor Division irrelevant. The Plant System kept the line open to service The Punta Gorda Hotel, and that was pretty much the extent of its usefulness to Henry Plant. Occasionally, freight and passengers would need service to Bartow, Arcadia, and further south. Since no one paid attention, Brosnan knew of ways to move in and out without drawing attention. Brosnan knew of a steamer, the Resolute, sitting idle in Punta Gorda, unable to participate in the Army's invasion of Cuba.

"I can't speak for The Resolute, that'll be up to her captain, Jumping Dick Hamner." Brosnan said, "But I can take as much freight as you can muster for $100 a car."

"$100 a car? That's five times the price from Winter Park." Charlie said.

"Then, take it to Winter Park, son," Brosnan said, "There's a pile of paperwork that goes with Plant System freight. Folks may think you're filibustering, no matter what sweetheart deal you're getting. Yes, sir, I know about that and the money y'all are making off the Army."

"What we're doing in Lakeland ain't illegal," Charlie said.

"Son, I know all about it," Brosnan said, "people need beef in Desoto County, too, but not at $100 a head."

"I have cattle coming, Mr. Brosnan; how about a trade?" Charlie said.

"I'm not in the cattle business and won't gouge my neighbors," Brosnan said. "I'll leave that to you and Dick Hamner. I bet Plant or Ward wouldn't like to hear y'all are planning a trip to Cuba, either."

"Mister Brosnan, we're not criminals," Charlie said, "my partner's going down there to save people's lives."

"Saving lives? In a war? What is he? Some kind of religious fanatic? Does he plan on persuading slaves and Indians to serve God?" Brosnan said.

"No, sir," Charlie said, "as he tells it, God has persuaded him to serve the sick and hungry."

"Men say a lot till other men start shooting," Brosnan said. "What's in it for you, Charlie Herlong?"

When Brosnan said it, it sounded like Jasper's voice. Charlie had to think about it. It was giving him a headache.

Brosnan pressed, "Why are you going down there?"

"I'm not. No, sir, as soon as that boat leaves, I'm headed north," Charlie said, "I'm just setting it up."

"So," Brosnan said, "Whose money is it?"

"Yours," Charlie said, "$200 for two freight cars. Maybe three. Can you do that?"

"Sure, we'll be heading back with fish in two days," Brosnan said. "Is that soon enough for you?"

"We'll see what old Hammer Dick has to say first," Charlie said with a laugh.

Brosnan laughed, then stopped, "I bet you won't say that to his face."

❄ ❧ ❅ ❄❀ ❧❀ ❄ ❄ ❄❀❄❀❄ ❄

The low boy was mired in a low, marshy spot on the edge of a cypress dome. Snapper and Opal had ropes tied to their saddles to help. Neha snapped the reins and cursed the struggling mules.

"Stop beating them," Opal said, "before you make them quit!"

"How about you get your fat ass out if you want to help them," Snapper added as his horse stumbled.

The cattle were up the grade and heading south on the road. Tiger gave a three-note whistle, and the dogs returned. The dogs rushed the mules and nipped at their heels. The mules lurched out of the hole and pulled the wagon up the grade.

"Dang, Mr. Tiger, those dogs run cattle better than most men!" Neha said as Tiger rode toward the cattle.

"We need to tighten up," Opal said, coiling his rope, "They just outworked all of us."

After 50 miles through forested floodplains, they were happy to be on high ground. Taking this route, "the route rustlers are too lazy to take," they found more cattle than they bought.

"Opal!" Tiger called, "Move ahead; there should be a road that leads southwest!"

"What am I looking for?" Opal asked.

"A sign that says Knight's, Plant City, or any other town. If there ain't no sign, ride up it a mile or so; if it gets smaller, it ain't where we go. We want Plant City."

In twenty minutes, they came upon Opal under a live oak at a fork in the road. On the right, the sign read Abbot, Knight's, and Plant City.

"Look what you found!" Snapper said, "Trailblazer!"

The #700 train pulled into Bartow, and Brosnan said to Charlie, "We're getting fuel. We'll leave in half an hour, with you or without. Hey, if you can get it, Hamner will want coal; maybe you could trade."

Charlie's meeting with William Burdine was quick. Burdine was sick of Bartow and depended on Plant trains for his livelihood. He planned to move to the east coast.

"Thank you for your offer, Mr. Herlong," Burdine said at the door, "I'll send you a wire when we get to Miami."

Bird jumped at the sound of Charlie's name and said to Burdine, "Who was that? Did you say, Herlong? Charlie Herlong? How much do I owe you?"

"With the underwear, that's close to $16, let me write it up," Burdine's son said.

"There's money in my britches. I'll come back for the other stuff," he said, grabbed his pistol, and ran out the door in new pants, shirt, and hat.

"Charlie Herlong!" Bird yelled, "Turn around! Have you been to Owensboro?"

Charlie sighed, thinking another person wanted to hear the story. He turned around, and his smile disappeared when he saw the gun. He put his hand on his pistol and turned sideways, reducing his profile, something he had read in a dime novel.

"Mister, you need to lower that pistol before somebody gets hurt," Charlie said.

Bird pointed his weapon, shaking, "You shot and killed my sons," and his eyes started tearing up.

"Wait a minute, now, is your name Hormuth? That's the only man I shot; he had just tried to shoot me!" Charlie said.

"You're a liar. Ted Hill told me you killed all three of them," Bird said.

"Then Ted Hill's the one's a liar," Charlie said, "was your boy Riley the one under the horse? Now, I did kill the horse accidentally. That sheriff killed Riley; I think because he called him a fat piece of shit."

"Shut your mouth, you're coming with me," Bird said, waving the pistol toward the saloon.

"No sir, I ain't," Charlie said, drawing his pistol out. Bird turned his gun back to Charlie, and Charlie shot just before Bird pulled his trigger. Bird's shot missed, and Charlie's put a hole through the crown of Bird's new hat. Bird dropped his pistol while picking up his hat and left it, running toward the Tip Top Saloon to get Milt Loy.

"Time to go," Charlie said.

He picked up Bird's pistol and dropped it into a watering trough. They hadn't finished loading the coal. Charlie was hungry and stepped into the Azalea Café. Charlie bought cornbread, two sausages, and a piece of pie.

"Milt, get up! Charlie Herlong is here! In Bartow!" Bird shook Milt for a full minute before Milt became reasonably coherent. Milt pulled himself up and staggered toward the door.

"If you seen him, why didn't you kill him?" Milt asked as he knocked over a chair, "where'd you get that hat?"

"I just bought it with the money you gave me," Bird said.

"Why'd you buy a hat with a hole in it ?" Milt asked.

"He shot it off my head; he's a killer!" Bird said, "He's wearing a yeller neck rag, just like I said."

Loy was still drunk and struggling. His horse spun three times before he pulled himself into the saddle.

A sober man could have walked faster than Loy rode.

"Milt! Hurry!" Bird pleaded, walking next to Milt's horse.

"Who you talking to?" Milt said and weakly kicked the horse.

Charlie was coming out of the Azalea and saw Milt. He put his hand on his pistol.

"Hey, you the one that killed my nephews?" Milt yelled, wobbling.

"Not me; you got the wrong man," Charlie said, walking toward the station, one hand on his pistol. "You're looking for Sheriff Hill. I killed your nephew's horse. Hill shot him in the chest."

"Riley, what about Jackie? Who busted him in the head?" Loy said, seeming to be more lucid.

"Somebody in that car he was trying to rob. I was running to the cargo I was paid to guard," Charlie said, "You need to go have another drink before somebody gets killed."

"Shut your hole, boy," Loy said. He pulled his right pistol halfway out and lost his grip. He left it dangling on the holster, drew the left pistol, and dropped it before he could point it at Charlie.

"Mister, if you manage to point a gun at me, I'm going to kill you. Please don't make me do it. Haven't enough of your family been killed?" Charlie pulled his pistol and pointed it squarely at Milt Loy's heart, his left hand still holding his bindle of lunch.

"Do your best," Loy pulled his rifle halfway and fired it, shooting into the sandy street. His horse reared and bolted down the street. Milt fell off, reaching for the Tip Top, and he again lost consciousness.

Charlie dropped Milt's pistols into the same watering trough as the engineer blew his whistle to leave.

Chapter 43

The #700 train had stopped in Plant City long enough for an introduction. Charlie got back on the train bound for Bartow and Punta Gorda.

Pete met the giant, a quiet and thoughtful man. The boots were snug but much better than the poorly cobbled shoes. Hatch was not a giant, but he was closer to it than any man Pete had measured or seen.

"These are the biggest uniforms the Army has," Hatch said. I've been wearing them for six years; I wore homemade before."

"How about the boots?" Pete said.

"I got my feet in; they're fine," Hatch said, "How much do they cost?"

"I'm doing a favor for Mr. Charlie." Pete said, turning to Jack, "He said there was a sewing machine? Do you have thread?"

"Gentlemen!" Hatch said, "I'm getting out of the Army tomorrow, and my discharge pay will not cover a whole new set of clothes. What is it this Mr. Charlie wants? Henry?"

"Nothing, Hatch. It's a favor. We'd like you to work with us, but if you don't want to, you can keep the clothes and the boots," Henry said. "We believe you can help us. Do you need a job?"

"I do, and I need clothes that fit," Hatch said. "What else do you need? I should get back to camp."

They looked to Pete, who said, "A shirt and trousers I can use as a pattern. Can you bring it back?"

Hatch tossed the shirt to Pete, removed his trousers, and put his boots back on. "I won't be back until tomorrow."

"Are you going to ride back to camp in your drawers?" Jack said, "What'll folks say?"

"Nothing. Folks see a man my size naked; they don't strike up a conversation," Hatch said and walked out of the warehouse.

❋❋❋❋❋❋❋❋❋❋❋❋❋

Charlie walked quickly and leaped onto the steps of the conductor's car and stepped in.

"Was that gunfire?" Brosnan asked.

"Two rascals arguing over a hat," Charlie said, "care for a biscuit?"

"No, thank you. They roll their biscuits till they're hard as walnuts," Brosnan said. "I'll wait until Arcadia."

"Tell me about Dick Hammer," Charlie said, "How come he's not in Tampa helping the Navy?"

"I can't tell you, I've never met the man." Brosnan said, "I've made trips to his boat, though. I hear he's sensitive about his name. You should stick to Captain Hamner."

"He wasn't there when they loaded the boat?" Charlie asked.

"I wasn't there; the tracks end about a half mile from where the boat docks," Brosnan said, "They had a colored church help move their freight to the boat. I've just heard stories about him."

"A half mile? You're picking up fish there," Charlie said, "How does that work?"

"Carts filled with fish and ice, but they won't help you. They're in the fish business, not the filibustering business," Brosnan said.

"Stop calling it that," Charlie said, "Henry ain't filling nothing but hearts and bellies."

"Life-saving business," Brosnan said with a smirk, "There's a telegram for you."

Western Union

The Bronx, NYC- Marjorie Ward

Plant System Station, Plant City, Fl – Charlie Herlong private

I arrived on Saturday, and Silvie took me shopping in town. I found cute cycling trousers that look like skirts. I bought you some things I believe you will love. Charlie. My sweetest love, you must

leave Florida by next Monday to arrive in time for The Belmont. Please say you will, without fail. My heart has ached since I've seen you and will continue until I do. Eternally, Marjorie.

Brosnan held out a Western Union sheet.

"We'll send it in Arcadia," Brosnan said, "Does this affect our run?"

"Not as much as Captain Hamner does. Are you sure he's there? Can I get coal in Lakeland?"

"I don't know, can you? The Army's got more coal than anyone else, but they don't share. And Jumping Dick? He'll be there; he can't leave empty. If he has black coal and gold money, he'll go wherever you want."

"Then I'm going to need another form; I got folks to talk to," Charlie said. "How many cars of freight and coal can you carry?"

"I've got cars, just say what you need," Brosnan said.

During the ride to Arcadia, Charlie thought more than he wrote. He left for Jacksonville out of boredom, and the past two weeks had been anything but. He had more money available to him than ever in his life. He could ride the train there easily. He could stand on the ground long enough to accomplish what he left home to do. Then, keep moving to Marjorie and New York to see elephants. Why was he helping Henry to this extent?

His mind returned to the spring in Alachua. Had Henry not shot Keyes' son, he might be dead. If Henry hadn't been on the roof of the freight car, how would that have turned out? Henry's connection to his uncle was vital in the forming of C. H. Duke. Henry was as responsible for their situation as Charlie.

If Henry was inspired by God, the least Charlie could do was make his best effort to help him. Marjorie would have to wait; he would get to New York after this task.

✳ ✳ ✳ ✳ ✢ ✢ ✳ ✳ ✳ ✳ ✢ ✳ ✳ ✳ ✳

Tiger and the Hodgeses moved quickly on a good, dry road. By late afternoon, Plant City had seen their first cattle drive. The dogs raced around either side, cutting in smaller arcs, causing the cattle to tighten their group to a column. Tiger cracked his whip, whistled, and directed the cattle through town and into the corral, just like in the old days.

"Henry! We've got cattle!" Jack called, picked up a shotgun, and hustled out to the corral, "Mr. Driggers?"

Tiger tied off Mico next to the gate. Moon ran to his side, facing Jack, the hair on his neck standing. Shine was in a half crouch off to Jack's left.

"That's me. I'm looking for Charlie Herlong," Tiger said, "Is this the right place?"

"Yes, sir!" Jack said, stepping to Tiger, "We're glad to see you!"

Moon and Shine charged a few steps to spots between the two men, startling Jack so that he almost dropped his shotgun.

"Yip!" Tiger called, and the dogs backed up behind Tiger and lay on the sand, "Sorry about that; I think the shotgun got 'em excited."

"They got us excited, too. This is Jack Duffie; he's our partner; he put all this together," Henry said, taking the shotgun and hanging it on a hook. "It's good to see you, Tiger. We worried when we didn't hear from you."

"Western Union don't go the way we came," Tiger said, "I thought it was safer. I figured you'd be in the Army by now. Where's Charlie?"

"Charlie's gone down south to Punta something," Henry said.

"Punta Gorda, in Desoto County," Jack said, "I'll have Musco take feed out to the corral."

"Dang, y'all have payroll already?" Tiger said, "Well, are you going to Cuba?"

"Well, one thing led to another," Henry turned and said, "It'll be easier to show you."

❋ ❋ ❋ ❋ ❋ ❋ ❋ ❋ ❋ ❋ ❋ ❋ ❋

Charlie tried to compose an answer to Marjorie, but the things he thought to write were ridiculous. He read Marjorie's message, and it made his heart ache, too. He had never experienced anyone like her, let alone the passion of their short time together.

He was distracted by his options in bargaining for the boat. He composed a wire to Jack, asking about Tiger, funds to buy coal, and his plans. He worried about how to get the freight to the boat and the cost. All in six days? Charlie's headache returned.

In Arcadia, Charlie sent a telegram to Jack. The clerk, a heavy, effeminate man, smiled and asked, "Will that be all, sir?"

"No," Charlie said, "but I don't know what to say on this one."

"Well, let's start with where you are sending it," the clerk said, "Oh, New York, how exciting. I've never sent one that far. Did you say The Bronx? Is this a business message? To whom are you sending it?" The clerk leaned forward.

"Marjorie Ward."

"May I see it?" the clerk asked, and Charlie handed him the telegram; he looked it over and almost squealed, "Oh my, a sweetheart? Do you mind?"

Charlie reached out, and the clerk pulled it back, "Oh my sacred word, this is the most romantic thing I have ever read," the clerk said, clutching it to his chest, "Do you love and miss her, too?"

Charlie's face flashed red and hot; he said, "Well, yeah, I guess she's pretty special."

"You guess? You don't know?" The clerk held up the telegram and said, "Her heart is aching! You should be on your way to her right now! There's nothing in this county more important than this!"

Charlie reached, and the clerk held it against his chest. He sighed and said, "Are you going to marry her?"

"Marry her? I just met her a couple of weeks ago," Charlie said again, reaching for her telegram.

"A couple of weeks? Oh, you must have made quite an impression," he said, reading and giving Charlie a sly look. "Oh, yes, I'm sure you did. Her sweetest love."

"Look, Mister, I'm in kind of a hurry," Charlie was getting impatient.

"Forgive me; love like this burns hot and fast," the clerk said. Only a cad would trifle with a lady's heart. Will you do the honorable thing?"

"Yes!" Charlie said, "I'm short of time, and I've got more hands to play."

"I see why you're having a hard time," the clerk said, "I write romantic poetry; I just haven't found the right person to share it with yet."

Charlie heard the whistle of the train and knew he needed to go.

"Send this. 'I am trying my best to finish up here by next week but cannot be certain right now. I love you and miss you more than anything. The only race I care about is the race back to you.'" Charlie said and leaned back, crossing his arms with a satisfied look.

"That's it? Are you trying to break her aching heart into utter despair?" the clerk said, "I won't. It's cruel!"

"I thought it was pretty good; what does it need?" Charlie asked, "I have to catch that train."

"It certainly is not sweet. Let me brush it up for you," the clerk said, licking the point of his pencil. Trust me, she'll think only of your return, and this Belmont affair will become secondary."

"Could you? Here's two bucks," Charlie turned and backpedaled to the door, "Not too mushy, now, she'll know I didn't write it." He got to the train and stepped onto the conductor's car just as it jerked to leave.

Western Union

Plant System Station, Arcadia, Fl – Charlie Herlong

The Bronx, NYC- Marjorie Ward - private

My exquisite Marjorie. Two days seem like two years since I gazed into your beautiful eyes and brushed my hand on the smooth porcelain of your cheek. I will leave in time for the race, as God is my witness.

Being without you is misery anywhere and this place makes it seem like Gehenna. Nay, Arcadia may be worse, with ugly people possessing coarse demeanor. How I long to be with genteel people in a fabulous place like The Bronx. I shall be miserable until I reach you and drink from your loving cup. Your sweetest love, Charlie.

Chapter 44

Arriving in Punta Gorda, Charlie saw several small hotels, but none on the scale of The Tampa Bay.

"Seems to be a lot of hotels for not many folks," Charlie said.

"It's summertime," Brosnan replied. "In cooler weather, these hotels will be filled, as will Plant's. He has 150 rooms. Every extra room on the east side, too, is filled with people to tote, carry, and parry the rich Yankee sporting folks. All down here trying to catch fish that aren't worth eating."

The train rounded a bend to Henry Plant's Hotel Punta Gorda. It reminded Charlie of the Tampa Bay Hotel—not as large but every bit luxurious.

"That's where you're staying?"

"I'm not sure," Charlie said, "they might not know me here. If you'll let me, I'll sleep on one of these benches."

"They'll know you if you tell them," Brosnan said. "Everybody in the company knows about Charlie Herlong; they just don't know he's planning a trip to Cuba."

"Well," Charlie said, "folks love a good tale."

"You need a good tale because they'll be happy to write one for you," Brosnan said. "However, you might not like what they come up with.

"OK, where am I going?" Charlie asked. "Aren't all the boats in Tampa? Where do they normally go?"

"Key West, I expect," Brosnan said, "let me go into the hotel first and see if they're expecting you. You being a guest will make folks want to help you."

"What, just wait here? No, sir, I've got lots to do; I'll take care of it," Charlie said.

"Son, this is going to be good for me and you. I want it to happen," Brosnan said, "Why don't you do the things I don't know about? Like the help you're going to need and Captain Hamner. The preacher's name is Caldwell. When you get back, I'll know what things are like in the hotel. It's a Plant business, there aren't any secrets."

Charlie left to find the church. Charlie asked two women with a pushcart full of laundry bags, who told him Jud Caldwell wasn't the preacher anymore. He was starting a new church.

"Who's the new preacher?" Charlie asked, "I was hoping to find folks to load a boat for me."

"Ain't got one yet," one woman replied, "and boat loadin' is what got Jud run off, so looking for free help ain't going to help you over at Bethel."

"That ain't good," Charlie said, "I was hoping to find folks to help me. Y'all know anybody looking for work?"

"Mister, errybody looking for work that pays," the second woman said. "The last time they come around here looking for workers, all folks got was a sore back, and Reverend Caldwell lost his job."

"Why'd he lose his job?" Charlie asked.

"Why don't you ask him? He down yonder, trying to turn that mule shed and brush house into a church. He'll tell you the same thing six times with seven different scriptures," the first woman said, "we got laundry to do."

Charlie walked down Cochran Street and saw a man in a black suit tying palm fronds on the roof of an open, four-post structure.

"Reverend Caldwell? My name's Charlie Herlong," Charlie said, picking up a frond, "need another palm leaf?"

"I was just now praying for a little help," the man said, "and God done sent me a white man. Ain't he good?"

"The righteous will flourish like a palm tree," Charlie handed him two fronds.

"And they will grow like a cedar of Lebanon!" The man shouted.

Charlie then asked, "I'm looking for Reverend Caldwell."

"Lots of folks do. What's your business?"

"I'm trying to move some freight to Key West," Charlie said, "I just now found out I have to tote it a long way to the boat if I can find one."

"There is only one boat in town; all the rest are gone to Tampa," the man said. "That captain, though, you better make sure everything is squared away. Once it's loaded, he may just take off."

"How much freight are we talking about?" the man asked, holding out his hand for more fronds.

"Are you Caldwell of Bethel Church?" Charlie held a couple just out of reach.

"Yes sir, that'd be me," Caldwell said, " 'cept for the Bethel church, part. I'm starting a new church, St. Luke's."

"Yeah, about that—might it have been about loading a boat—that's what I need," Charlie said, recognizing Reverend Caldwell's harsh stare.

"You think a church gets formed just from the snap of a finger? I have six members right now, and four of them owe ME money. Them Cuban boys? We'd load all day, and each man got a buck, and the church got a buck for each man. The first two times, it was fine; the third time, they left us standing there, holding our di

... devotionals. The deacons blamed me." Caldwell came down the ladder and took the fronds. "If you're looking for labor, you need to go talk to them."

"They fired you because y'all got fleeced?" Charlie asked, with a cock of his head.

"The flock and the shepherd, but not the dogs. The deacons needed a reason they could talk about." Caldwell said, "God had another plan for me and Bethel. How much freight do you need to be moved?"

"At least two cars, maybe three," Charlie said, "a lot of that depends on this Jumping Captain character. You know him?"

"Yeah, the devil does, too," Caldwell said, climbing the ladder.

"The devil knows everybody but can't hurt them that know his face," Charlie said.

"Son, I like that," Caldwell said, securing another frond on the roof, "there's a sermon in that."

"How many men does it take? How much do you think would make them happy?" Charlie asked.

"Seventeen men worked that day," Caldwell said, "Seventeen dollars to them; I don't know how you're going to get them back."

"Well, I do, Reverend Jud," Charlie said, reaching into his vest pocket and pulling out a wallet, "I've got $20 here. If you use it to pay your debt to the men and get them to work for me, you can keep the extra three bucks. It'll be almost the same deal as before. I'll pay them two dollars. One dollar in advance and the second dollar, they can choose which church they give it to. If you can get me two wagons to use that day, I'll pay you $5 for each one."

"This sounds too good to be true," Reverend Caldwell said and smelled the air with a great sniff, "but I don't smell any sulfur."

"All you smell is Charlie Herlong, Rev." Charlie laughed. "He smells like Cuban Orchids! You know what the devil looks like, and he's never been this handsome. Aren't two sparrows sold for a penny? Will you at least try?"

"What if I can't get them to do it?"

"Then keep all of the money and buy yourself some nails for this roof instead of using twine," Charlie said, handing him banknotes. "But I ain't worried. Put that dollar in their hand, and they'll be here on moving day. I tell you what, I'll throw in some beans and cornmeal. If you can find a cook, we'll feed them and anyone else that might be looking for a church."

Charlie saw the wheels turning in his head and turned to walk toward the waterfront. He smelled his yellow scarf, smiled, and picked up his pace.

Charlie was amazed when he saw the long dock pushing out into the gulf, thinking a city limit sign at the end would double the size of Punta Gorda. Closer to the shore were small sailing vessels fitted to fish. On the other side of the dock, there were several fish houses. Carnes and Monk had a group of men seated, passing around a demijohn and taking drinks.

"Looking for fish? Right here," a man called, sticking a thumb toward the door.

"If you want trash fish," another said, "you want high-quality fish, go to Sullivan's; that's where mine are!"

They all shouted and laughed, offering the location of their catch. He assumed they were all fishermen, finished with their day and having a few after work.

Someone offered a tin cup to Charlie and said, "I doubt you'll be able to get any of today's catch; as soon as it's sorted and iced up, they'll be on that train. It'll be in Tampa in the morning. Have some rum?"

"No, thank you. I've got work to do. Are they leaving tonight?" Charlie looked down the dock. "Is that the only freighter in town? I'm looking to move some."

"I don't believe he can help you. He doesn't have enough coal to get to Key West. All the available boats are in Tampa, gearing up for the Army going to Cuba," the man said.

"How come he's not in Tampa?" Charlie asked, already knowing the answer.

Another fisherman answered, "Because they got federal law up there, with a jail!"

Again, the rest of the men burst into laughter, and the man said, "I never have asked, and he didn't offer an answer. But without coal, he can't help you. Where are you going?"

"I was hoping to get some goods to Key West; they're getting low on supplies down there," Charlie said.

"We're low here, too," the man said. If you can't get to Key West, there are people here who will buy it. My name's Bill Lewis," he said and extended his hand. "Can you get freight here, too? We don't get much since the trains got jammed up north of Lakeland."

"Mr. Lewis, I'm Charlie Herlong. Contact the C.H. Duke Company in Plant City, and they'll figure out how to get it here. But right now, I need to meet that captain."

"You'd be better off without me," Lewis said. He doesn't like me too much. He's down there right now, but I'll warn you: He'll just as soon take a shot at you as take a liking."

"Well, he sounds like a lot of folks on this end of the woods," Charlie said as he headed down the dock.

CHAPTER 45

Charlie walked down the dock and wondered if being armed was the right approach to his visit. Judee's rule was, 'Carry a gun when something needs to be shot.' Two men stepped off the gangway of the Resolute and walked toward Charlie.

"I'm looking for Captain ..." Charlie said, and they passed him. He turned, surprised.

"What's your business?" a voice from the boat said. Charlie turned again and saw a man standing at the top of the gangway.

"I'm looking for Captain Hamner," Charlie said.

"Ain't no money in looking; what's your business?" the man called back.

Charlie saw a rifle barrel just above the gunnel. He felt a forearm in the crook of his right elbow and something metallic against his throat.

"Calma, cordeirinho, me deixa segurar sua pistola," a voice said. Charlie guessed it was one of the men who were not ignoring him.

"Raise your hands, boyo," the man from the boat said, "so he can check your pockets." Then, in Portuguese, "Simon! Olha no bolso dele, procura a documentação, e deixa o dinheiro dele em paz!"

The man started down the gangway. He was followed by the rifleman, who was carrying a rocking chair. The second sailor on the dock rolled a hogshead over and placed it near the rocker. Simon placed Charlie's wallet, coin purse, Barlow knife, and pistol on the cask top. Charlie unbuckled his gun belt, and the sailors readied their weapons.

"Would you mind holstering my pistol? I ain't planning on shooting anyone," Charlie said as he held it out.

"Then, why are you wearing it?" Hamner asked, "Are you going to state your business, or do you want me to tell you?"

"I'd like to move some freight," Charlie said, "but I ain't never had my fortune told, so tell me. Will I be sitting in a chair?"

Hamner laughed and said, "That's a good answer! Go get this man a chair!" The third sailor turned and hustled up the ramp.

"I'm Charlie Herlong, you must be Captain Dick Hamner."

"Richard," Hamner replied, opening the wallet and examining the contents, "but you call me Captain. Here's what I'm told. You want to take a load of household goods to Key West, which is bullshit, but let's go with it for now. You're going to get some coal cause what I have might get us to Punta Rassa. Then, you're going to find some stevedores to load it. How am I doing?"

"Captain, most of that is about you. How do you know about my freight and Key West and cow patties?" The third sailor returned, and Charlie sat.

"News travels fast from the hotel. Why Key West? Ships still sail from New Orleans. East Coast tracks are clear through Miami. Key West doesn't need your freight. Why now?" Hamner said.

"I want to take a train to New York to see a horse race, but I'd like to get my partner and his load squared away first.," Charlie said.

"Why don't you get your good friend Mr. Plant to do it?" Hamner said, holding up the Plant System pass Charlie had been given. "Why right now?"

"To save lives," Charlie said, "My partner is on a mission from God."

"God? Now I feel better," Hamner cocked his head, raised his palms upward, and looked around for some help, "Who's manning your rudder, boy? The freight, son, your partner, my boat, where does it need to go?"

Charlie paused and weighed his words. "How much coal do you need to get to Cuba?"

Everyone stopped and stared at Charlie. Everything else stopped, too. The seagulls got quiet, and then they all broke into laughter.

"Ele não tem leme, capitão!" Simon said, laughing.

"All of it! To Cuba? Ok, it's only 300 miles. I'll need all the coal in West Virginia and half of Kentucky. You should be in a traveling show," Hamner said, looking at Simon and then at Charlie, "He must be drunk! You want to sneak by TWO navies in a war. One's not dangerous enough! Son, I'm talking about gunships, not patrol boats. At God's request? Was he drunk, too?"

"The Americans haven't left Tampa yet," Charlie said, "Wouldn't the Spanish be waiting for them near Havana? Is that on the West end? Will a train car of coal get you to the other side?"

"The American Navy is already there, blocking the Spanish. Are we going to throw coal at them? Patrol boats have Gatling Guns!" Hamner waved his hand and said, "Quit wasting my time."

"Captain, all you have is time; what are you going to do? Wait here till someone sells you coal or serves the warrant they have in Tampa?" Charlie said, showing his cards.

"Better than sitting at the bottom of the Strait." The captain replied.

Simon stepped to Hamner and said, "Capitão, e se fôssemos por meio do Cayo Pino Grande?"

"Big Pine Key? Onde as restingas mudam com a lua? Você é bêbado, também? Cadê a minha taça?" Hamner said to him, "Na última vez cê 'tava mijando pela perna."

The sailor rubbed two fingers together.

Hamner sat back in his rocker and seemed to be thinking about it. "It'd have to be a one-way trip for only three men, tops. IF, if we get there, everyone gets off with the freight," Hamner said.

Charlie gave Hamner time to think and start a ridiculous price.

"$5000. In gold," Hamner said, "in advance."

"Now, you're wasting time," Charlie saw a starting point, "Capitao, you need that coal; how about I give you two train cars full?"

"Then where do we keep your freight? We need to be light. If I'm running from gunboats, I need to go fast."

"I'm sure we can find someone around here to store some coal. What if I get you something to slow the Navy down?" Charlie said.

"What, like a Gatling Gun? They shoot 2000 yards," Hamner said, "Do you have a life-saving Gatling gun, Charles?"

"Even better, Richard. How about a cannon with two-pound shells?" Charlie countered, "I bet it shoots far. And it's for sale, too."

"Hotchkiss? How much?"

Charlie cocked his head as if he were thinking, "I wanted $3000, but that's negotiable, and I'll sell you the coal for $200 a carload. Let's agree in principle and see if the other pieces fall together."

"As long as you show up here with $3000 in gold principle," the captain said, leaning forward in his rocker. Otherwise, that freight can sit here until after the war."

Charlie stood up and gestured to his gun, putting his hand on the hogshead, "Do you mind? Henry might as well wait in Tampa, then. Nice meeting you, Captain." Charlie started picking up his belongings.

"What about hands to bring it up the dock?" Hamner said, "Those darkies at the church won't work with me. That'll be on you, and I have to have gold for my men, or both of us will end up in the water."

"By the way, I paid the Reverend what you owed him," Charlie said. "But coal, a cannon mounted to your boat, and three thousand in gold is too high. We'll just have to wait."

"Not me! He made that deal with the Cubans, and they were ready to go! OK, 2,000, and that's fair, considering we could all die."

"For paper money, almost fair. I'll bring double eagles. Fifty of them," Charlie said, hoping the math didn't queer the deal, "If that ain't good enough, we'll just have to wait. In Tampa,"

Charlie swung his rig around his waist, holding the holster.

"Devil's pay! Ok, I'll do it," sticking out his hand, "I don't know where I'm going to store that coal. When do we load?"

I'm still working that out, but I need it to be done before next week. I believe I can work the coal out with Reverend Caldwell," Charlie said, "Maybe if you stopped calling them darkies and make sure they got paid, y'all could get along."

Charlie started up the dock and saw the train coming from the hotel. The sun was setting behind him. He had never seen his shadow so long and drawn out. The thought of elephants crossed his mind.

Workers were bringing carts of ice into the fish houses, so Charlie knew he had to hustle to get to the Reverend and back. Brosnan swung out of the conductor's car and walked toward him.

"How much time do I have?" Charlie said, "I need to get to the east side and then back to the hotel to send a wire."

"As long as I say," Brosnan said, "but we'll leave in an hour. How's our deal coming?"

"I never had so many irons to get hot. I need to find two cars of coal, a dozen workers and wagons to move freight up this dock, a yard to store 30 tons of coal, a cannon mechanic, and a little over three pounds of gold," Charlie stopped and turned back toward the setting sun, "Other than that? Perfect."

"Well, take a breath," Brosnan said, "I bet you don't see the sky catch fire very often."

"It'll be dark soon," Charlie said, "and where is the Western Union? What fire?"

A runabout carriage pulled up, and Brosnan said, "This boy will take you there and back. For right now, slow down; you don't want to miss it."

Brosnan pulled a flask out of his pocket, took a drink, and handed it to Charlie. The sun seemed more significant now, and Charlie was amazed at how quickly it had fallen into the sea. The sky exploded in color.

"Oh, my sacred word," Charlie said quietly.

Brosnan reached for the flask, and Charlie took a quick drink before giving it back. Charlie then noticed all the fishermen, ice workers, and anyone in the area had stopped to watch. After sharing that moment, they all went back to exactly what they were doing.

"Thanks, Lem. I'll take this inside," Brosnan said, lifting a basket out of the buggy. If you will, take Mr. Herlong to the east side and then to the hotel. When he finishes there, bring him back here. Let's go, Charlie. All the daylight is burned up. We'll be in Tampa before we see any more."

It was pitch dark when they pulled out of Punta Gorda, and Charlie was finishing dinner with some crew and Brosnan. Charlie was exhausted but confident in his plan to get Henry on his mission trip and himself on a train by Monday.

When the crew left, Brosnan asked Charlie, "Well? Would the preacher let you put an iron in his fire?"

Charlie was puzzled and then saw he meant Reverend Caldwell. "Oh, yeah, he has people and says we can put a pile of coal on his lot. It turns out when you pay folks, they want to work."

"And the hotel?" Brosnan added.

"I only needed to send a wire. The manager just wanted to talk about linens," Charlie said, "I didn't hear from Plant City, so I won't know about coal until the morning. Can you get me the cars I need to get it all down here by Sunday morning?"

"If you're ready to load by Saturday," Brosnan replied, "I'll have whatever you need. I'm assuming you're getting Army coal; I can put cars there. Are you going to have what I need? I want to work, too."

"At $100 a car, that'll be $500," Charlie said, "If you take Tampa Bank notes, we're all set."

"No, sir. I'll need gold."

Chapter 46

"Charlie! Wake up!" Brosnan said, banging his large key ring next to the bench Charlie slept on. "We need to plan."

"How long till we get to Lakeland?" Charlie asked, rubbing his face and stretching.

"You'll be back tomorrow, the way Duffy works," Brosnan said, "we just jockeyed two cars in there. You sleep hard. Duffy's already lined up the coal. Those boys are all fired up about the steak dinners they're going to be eating."

"Steak dinners?" Charlie was still groggy, "Duffy's got cattle? How many did he give them?"

"I didn't get into all that, but I'm impressed," Brosnan said, "They also said they're expecting them when we pick up the coal. You'll need a stock car. Charlie, I think you do more sleeping than you do awake. How do you manage that?"

"Good luck," Charlie said, "who's paying for the extra car?"

"It's on them; they filled my bin and said they'll fill it twice more if I make it happen," Brosnan said, "Those boys are going to be good to know, Charlie. And I have your good luck to thank for it."

"Does that mean you'll take banknotes for payment?" Charlie said.

"Oh, no. You must need coffee," Brosnan said, pouring a cup, "A deal's a deal."

"None of it matters if I can't come up with 75 Double Eagles, Mr. Brosnan," Charlie said, "and Hamner has less need for paper money than you do."

"Not when the bank is paying over $30.00 an ounce for it," Brosnan said.

"Thirty dollars?" Charlie asked, "For a twenty-dollar gold piece? That's crazy."

"Ain't it, though? Those Army boys said it was $25.00 yesterday morning," Brosnan said. "I don't understand it, but one of them offered me $32 for a double eagle not thirty minutes ago."

"So, the bank and soldiers are paying more for gold than it says on the coin? Henry might need to wait a while before he takes off for Cuba," Charlie said.

"Hold on a minute, Charlie, we've got a deal," Brosnan said.

"If I can't pay the freight to Hamner, there is no deal," Charlie said, "You may have to work with me on this before it's all over. Just think about it."

The #700 train pulled into Plant City at 6:40, nearly an hour after sunrise. The warehouse was busy, with Musco, Opal, and Snapper all working on Henry's freight at the direction of Hatch, who was dressed head to toe in new, tailored work clothes.

"Sir? Are you Mr. Herlong?" Hatch said, walking toward Charlie with long strides.

"Naw, that's my Daddy, call me Charlie!" Charlie said and stuck out his hand, "Corporal Hatch! Dang, you are big. I bet you can eat more taters than I can carry!"

"No, sir, I just put them to good use. I want to thank you for these clothes. Mr. Falcone said you were responsible for my good fortune," Hatch said.

"Falcone? Oh! Pete! The tailor. Well, I'm not the only one; it was Jack and Henry, too," Charlie said as Hatch took his bag, "y'all are up early, aren't you?"

"I'm used to it, the bugler for our troop bunks in my tent," Hatch said, "or used to; my time as a soldier is up."

"Does that mean you're going to be working with us now?" Charlie asked, stopping.

"For a little bit, I guess, I can't say for how long, though," Hatch said.

"That goes for us all if you think about it," Charlie said, "me, too. I'm just glad we're both here today." Charlie stuck out his hand, and Hatch's huge hand engulfed it.

"Charlie!" Musco waved, "Jack is going to be happy to see you! He's right in here."

"There's our good luck charm!" Jack said, walking over and hugging Charlie, "You won't believe how much money we're making."

Tiger shook Charlie's hand.

"Hey Tiger, did you bring us lots of beef?" Charlie said, "Is the Army buying cattle to take with them?"

"Turns out they want gold more than beef," Tiger said, "but Jack says they'll start buying again."

"Charlie, it's the damnedest thing; they have been buying every head of cattle we can find, paying as much gold as we ask for it, and now they want to buy the gold back for twice its value," Duffy boasted, "and we were happy to oblige them."

"How much did you pay for the coal?" Charlie asked.

"$100 in gold and two cows," Jack said. "Was that too much?"

"No, that's less than what I'm charging the captain. How much gold do we have left?" Charlie asked.

"We've still got some, and Henry has some for when he gets to Cuba," Jack said, "there's around four hundred in the box."

The color went out of Charlie's face, and he sat in a chair.

"Charlie, what's the matter? We turned 2500 in gold into $5000 in treasury notes," Duffy said, "it was a good deal. The gold price will come back to normal once the convoy leaves and the bank ships more gold in."

"Well, it's just gold and paper to me, but it affects Henry more," Charlie said, "I'm going to New York on Monday or Tuesday, regardless. The deal we have, the coal, the train, the church folk loading the freight down there, the freight leaving from Punta Gorda before the convoy leaves, is all based on gold and trade—five hundred for the train and $1000 for the boat. The conductor, Brosnan, may take paper money at double the price. Unless Henry can wait until after the war, Henry?"

"When the Army gets there, it'll be worse," Henry said, "I've got three hundred in gold; we can use that for the boat. The food and supplies are more important to the folks down there. We need to go now."

"What do you think Tiger?" Charlie said, "Did you settle up with Jack?"

"Sure, we settled up, and I sold my gold to him, so I'm good," Tiger said. "As far as I know, the boys and I are heading back to the hammock."

"What about this? Should we wait?" Charlie asked.

"Oh, I don't know about any of that; the whole thing is hadcho to me. No offense, Henry," Tiger looked at Henry, who held up his hands, then back to Charlie, "but I know Indian and Colored folks that are hungry right here in Florida. Do you have a deal with people on your word? That's important to me. Do you have a deal with Henry? What's important to you, Charlie?"

"Wouldn't none of us be here without Henry, or you, for that matter. Or Jack Duffy," Charlie said.

"Or Benson Fleet or Marjorie Ward," Jack said.

"God is the reason all of us are here," Henry said, "and he wants me to save as many lives in Cuba as possible. He'll give us what we need to get to Cuba before the Army. Because once the Army gets there, they'll be just as dangerous as the Spanish."

"If you'll bet your life on it, that's good enough for me. Jack, find out exactly how much gold we have. If we don't have at least a thousand, then let's find some to buy," Charlie said. Can we be ready to leave on the train by this afternoon? I'll talk Brosnan into taking paper money."

"The bank likes those big silver bills better than the ones with their name on them. Tell him that. Charlie, you said something about trade." Jack said, "Who are we trading with, and what?"

"That's almost as important as gold. He wants that cannon or a lot more. I told him it would shoot farther than a Gatling gun. Will it?" Charlie asked.

Jack looked at Hatch and said, "Hatch knows better than me."

"How far depends on how high you point it up," Hatch said, "what do you want to shoot it at?"

"I reckon whatever is chasing him." Charlie said, "This captain says y'all have to sneak past two navies, both trying to kill you. He wanted $5000, but I worked him down with coal and that gun on the floor. Busted all to hell. Damn. Will that thing shoot, or is it junk?"

"Y'all?" Hatch said, "Like 'Me All'? You mean, 'Them All.' I just got out of the 'folks shooting at me' business."

"I get it, but the cannon. If it don't work, the whole deal's off. Can you make it shoot from the back of a boat?" Charlie asked.

"Mr. Charlie, I don't know. You need to be able to move it around to aim it, and it's got a busted axle," Hatch explained, "we thought one off a fruit cart, but it won't hold the weight. I haven't seen the boat, so I can't say."

"I sure wish Jasper was here," Charlie said.

"We got that low boy he made." Tiger said, "Do you think the front assembly will work?"

Hatch was already walking toward the back door, and Tiger followed.

"Henry?" Charlie said, "Are you going to unload your freight by yourself when you get to Cuba?"

"Nope," Henry said, "I'll have God's help. This is the first consideration I've given it."

"Henry, I've been working my ass off, and I don't mind speaking for God when I say you need to tighten yours up and consider it," Charlie said.

"Didn't you say a church was going to help us?" Henry asked.

"I did, but they ain't doing it for grace; they're all getting paid," Charlie said, "upfront. The last time they did this, God didn't keep them from getting stiffed. This deal gets you on the boat; once you set sail, it's 'Vaya con Dios.'"

"And where is it he's taking us?" Henry asked.

"Somewhere the US Navy ain't," Charlie said, "and far away from the Spanish. God knows where."

"Well, I've been talking to God a lot. I'll ask him," Henry said, smiling. "He's been looking after us since that first day at the hobo camp."

"Well, you best ask him for two strong backs to go with you to Cuba," Charlie said.

Milt Loy and Bird Mobley were on their way to Arcadia by noon. Milt was in no mood to answer questions. It was a day's journey on horseback, and Bird was more miserable and homesick than the day before.

"Milt, we don't even know where he's going. It might be Arcadia or even be as far as Punta Gorda." Bird said, "Shouldn't we at least find someone who saw the train come through?"

"Did you see anybody in Fort Meade? That station was locked up tighter'n a tick," Milt said, "When we get to Arcadia, somebody will know somethin'. About the train or Charlie Yeller Neck Rag. Besides, I need to find some help that can do what you can't."

"I didn't run; I was gone to get you," Bird said, "I don't even know if I care anymore, Milt. I just want to get my share of the money and head back to the river. I miss my wife. And she's broke, too, you know. She's your sister."

"Your share? You ain't done shit," Milt said, "You ort to be happy with the new clothes I bought you. I need to find some help. And their pay will come out of yours. The more you talk, the less you'll get."

Bird rode along without answering, losing hope. Maybe Charlie will kill Milt, then what? He regretted not shooting Charlie when he had the chance and wondered if Charlie felt the same way about not killing Milt.

'He should,' Bird thought, 'because Milt won't waste a second thinking about it.'

CHAPTER 47

The #700 train returned from unloading fish at The Tampa Bay Hotel. Brosnan released three freights and an open stock car at the packing house. He found Charlie and said he wanted to inspect the cargo.

"This is a lot of freight. I'm not sure it will fit in three cars, Charlie," Brosnan said. "You need another car, or you have to decide what to leave. One might be in Lakeland. I'm going over there now, delivering gold for some Army big shot."

"This gold thing is complicated," Charlie said.

"Yeah, that Captain in the coal station has a dollar and a half for every gold dollar I can bring him," Brosnan said.

"How much do you have?" Charlie asked.

"In gold, $60," Brosnan said, "How would you feel about paying me some of mine so that I could make that happen?"

"A deal's a deal, ain't that what you said?" Charlie said, "We need to get to the boat first."

"Well, I've already delivered on the coal cars and these," Brosnan said, "that ought to be at least a dozen birds."

Charlie thought that Brosnan might have heard something picking up the gold he was delivering to Lakeland.

"What's the hurry?" Charlie said, "You'll get at least $500 when we get it offloaded."

"Well, I hear that people are running out of the good paper, the US money," Brosnan said, "and I don't want Tampa Bank money."

"Let's think about that a little bit," Charlie said, "I'll be back in two minutes."

Charlie ran to the barn area and told the men to stop taking the low boy apart and start loading the three cars. He then pulled Jack aside and asked him to bring out $1000 in silver certificates and ten double eagles. He walked briskly back to Brosnan.

"Charlie, we're still at steam out there; I need to go," Brosnan said, "can you help me out?"

"I'm always there for a friend. Do your friends call you Fairfax?" Charlie said.

"Not since school; my friends call me Fox," Brosnan said, "Are we friends?"

"We will be when this is all over," Charlie said. "You want a couple hundred in gold to sell. I need what we agreed on, plus that stock car and one more. Can you get a flat car?"

"I won't know until I get over there, and we need to go now," Brosnan said. "Can I have the advance or not?"

"Hear me out, Fox," Charlie said, extending his hand to Jack, who handed him a pouch and a large billfold. "Here's a sack full of gold. Can you get a flat car, then come back over here and take all of us to Punta Gorda?"

"Wait, what do you need the stock car for?" Brosnan asked.

"Stock. And if you need to know, I might need a wagon to get down that long dock," Charlie said, "What do you care? Your train can pull it, can't it?"

"If you can get it loaded, I can pull it," Brosnan said. "But that's a long setup, and you might look curious. What's that come to? Three boxes, two coals, stock, and a flatbed? All for $500? That doesn't sound too friendly, friend."

"By the time we get loaded and near Bartow, it'll be dark," Charlie said. Brosnan nodded. "So, I count six cars. Your Army buddy paid for the stock car. That's $600 in gold. Instead of selling $600 in gold to him for $900 in paper money ... how about we do what I need for a thousand? Hell, you'll be the richest man in Desoto County!"

Brosnan looked confused, "For that Uncle Sam kind."

Charlie opened the leather billfold, pulled out a $100 silver certificate, and handed it to him. Brosnan looked at it closely, turning it over, and thumped it with his finger. "It's big, ain't it?"

"Big and pretty, just like the US of A. When the price of gold comes back down, you can trade ten of these for 50 of those birds if you want to. Do we have a deal?" Charlie said.

"Yeah," Brosnan said, "Load up the cattle. I'll get to Lakeland and be back here around two. Can y'all be ready to go?"

Brosnan turned to walk to the train, and Charlie said, "Hey, I'm going to need that bill; you'll get that when we offload, remember?"

Brosnan looked disappointed and said, "Oh, yeah. I kinda wanted to look at it for a bit."

"Hey, do you have that $60 in gold? Let's trade. That's the friend's rate, but I'll take all you can find," Charlie said as Brosnan handed him three double eagles. "You're a banker, Fox. You just made 40 bucks with a handshake!"

The loading went smoothly, and Brosnan's estimate was accurate. They put the mountain gun in first and packed the wagon with household goods and tack.

Charlie hoped he could sell cattle for gold when he got to Punta Gorda. Tiger and the Hodgeses would go along to work the livestock for trade and cash. The

Hodgeses were thrilled to ride a train, which was a first for them, and Tiger said he couldn't miss an adventure like this.

Charlie returned at 1:00. Jack dozed at his desk. The room was quiet despite Neha snoring on coffee sacks. The brothers and Hatch sorted the box of ammunition and gun parts. Hatch taught the brothers differences in shells. Henry said he would give them some shells that fit their rifles. Hatch was working on a handgun and trying assorted parts for fit.

"Hey, Charlie," Henry said, "We're all packed up except that box of lead. I'd just as soon leave it; each shell looks like a life to me."

"That's money," Charlie said, "it may be the most valuable thing you're taking down there, especially if I have to use your gold for the boat."

"Anything in town?" Jack asked.

"None," Charlie said, "I've never seen any ... if you say 'elephants,' I'll rassle you to the floor."

Henry chuckled, saying, "Ask, and it will be given to you."

"The lord must take Saturday off," Charlie said, "I've been asking, seeking, and knocking all over town."

"God never takes a day off," Henry said.

"Henry," Hatch said, "Here's something that might work."

"Hatch, we're going to need you down south," Charlie said, "Will you help us?"

"Yes, sir, Mr. Charlie, I'm looking forward to it."

"I appreciate it." Charlie said, "Please call me Charlie. Is that Judee's pistol?"

"Told you," Henry said, "Charlie, I hope you don't mind."

"This is a conversion cylinder," Hatch said, "not from a factory, though, it won't take a .46 or a .45 shell."

"Will it take a .44?" Henry asked.

"We have all kinds of .44s," Snapper said.

"They might all fit," Hatch said, "They might all blow up in your hand, too."

"Well, it's been good luck so far," Charlie said, "I'll put in what fits for an emergency."

Charlie removed the cylinder and tried different shells, leaving any that fit. He left one cylinder empty for safety.

"Jack, can you spare Hatch? I don't want to get down there with no idea how to mount that cannon," Charlie said, "I want to get down there and get out."

Jack stood and said, "Sure, I have Musco. How many cows are you taking?"

"Ten. I'm going to need $500 in gold, and the hotel might be the only place down there that can give it to me," Charlie said.

"But $50 a head?" Jack said, "They need beef down there, for sure. Getting $500 in gold is the thing. Word spreads fast."

"That boat captain won't go once the Army leaves, and I don't blame him," Charlie said, trying to spin the cylinder, but it clicked twice and stopped.

"Take US money, and you have Henry's $300," Duffy said, leaning away. "Charlie put that away. We have pistols that work."

"Henry's going to need that gold worse than the Army in Cuba," Charlie said, walking across the room and aiming out the door. This thing saved my life; I'm going to hold on to it."

Charlie pulled the hammer back to full cock, and the men in the room scattered. He eased the hammer back and walked to his portmanteau. He placed it into the bottom compartment.

"This rascal will clear a room, though, won't it?"

A local boy brought a telegram envelope for Charlie. Inside were open-date tickets for passage to The Bronx.

Western Union

The Bronx, NYC- Marjorie Ward

Plant System Station, Plant City, Fl – Charlie Herlong– private

Oh, my Charlie. My sweetest love. So romantic it brought tears. Silvie's rabbi says Gehenna is no place for a good man. So, get out now. I can think of nothing else. I have arranged for open passage on all lines between there and here. My cup won't be filled until you come back to me. Your yearning love Marjorie.

"Boys, get anything and everything we need. I aim to be on my way to New York by Tuesday!" Charlie yelled.

Opal came in and said, "Mr. Charlie, our horses are ready to load. Tiger wants to know if we should load yours and Mr. Henry's."

"Yeah, if there's room," Charlie said and looked around, "Henry! Let's talk about Sam Antonio."

"Do you think we can take him to Cuba?" Henry asked, seeing Charlie's face. "I guess not; I'd like to ask Tiger to sell him to Malachi for whatever money he comes up with."

"That's a lot of horse for a kid, we can sell him," Charlie said, "if we need to."

"Do you want him?" Henry said.

"I want to get this thing done," Charlie said, "two weeks ago, I would have wanted him. Things change quickly, don't they?"

"If you're lucky, they do," Henry said. "I've been blessed since then. Charlie, I appreciate everything you've done for me. I know I'm going to save a lot of lives in Cuba."

"You did as much as I did. We've done it together," Charlie said, "And we had help."

"Yes, and we still do," Henry said and knelt to pray, "I sure wish you were going with me."

Charlie said, "I'm going to check on the cattle and ... give y'all some privacy."

As Charlie walked away, shaking his head, he looked up and said a little prayer of his own, "Lord, show him the way, 'cause WE BOTH KNOW he don't know what he's getting into."

❈ ❈ ❈ ❈ ❈ ❈ ❈ ❈ ❈ ❈ ❈ ❈ ❈ ❈

Milt Loy and Bird Mobley found no one to help them kill Charlie. They found out a man with a yellow scarf sent a telegram to New York.

"I don't know why you had to slap that clerk around, Milt," Bird said, "he would have told you if you had just been nice to him."

"That sissy looked like he wanted a dance partner," Milt said, "so I slapped the perfume off him. I ain't got time to waste. He said Yeller Charlie was fixing to leave for New York. We'll miss our chance if that train heads north. We have to go all the way to Pine Level to find men with some sand. Arcadia used to be a man's town. Not a damn saloon in it, not even a back room to get a shot of shine."

Bird couldn't forget the image of the clerk crying on the floor. "Nothing makes any sense anymore," he said.

"Sure don't," Milt said and kicked his horse into a canter.

Chapter 48

The cattle awakened Charlie. He stepped over several men and opened the door to the landing of the conductor's car. Brosnan's crew had separated it and maneuvered the remaining six cars onto a loop. Brosnan walked toward him, and he stepped off the platform.

"Charlie, as soon as they pull those pins, I'm moving up to the hotel," Brosnan said, "You need to figure out where you're putting those animals."

"I'm hoping to put the cattle up at the hotel," Charlie said, "Do they have a corral up there?"

"Not much of one," Brosnan said, "how many?"

"I don't know yet; I need to cut the deal," Charlie said. "Is there a butcher in town? Someone who can buy cattle with gold? I'd hate to take all this back to Plant City."

"Me too. It's been good so far. Get your crew up. I don't know how long we can layover here," Brosnan said.

Henry directed the men to remove their gear from the conductor's car and move it to the flat car.

"Charlie, have you arranged a place for this stock?" Tiger asked, "There's a livery on the other side of the tracks."

"No, sir. We need to find something quick, though. Bring out the horses, and we'll look around," Charlie said, "Henry needs to meet the preacher helping us out."

Charlie was trying to explain the deal he had set up when they turned into Cochran Street.

"You met him and gave him twenty bucks, just like that?" Henry asked, "Did you speak to anyone at the big church?"

"No," Charlie said, "there wasn't much time. I found a man who said he could make it happen, and I trusted him. He's a preacher, Henry."

"How many pastors have you known in your life?" Henry asked. "Church politics can be rough, but a flock turning out a pastor takes some doing."

As they approached the mule shed, Charlie saw that the Reverend had finished putting palm leaves on the brush house. It was still early, but he could smell breakfast and faint sounds coming from the houses.

"I hope he's up," Charlie said, "but as far as I know, he may not even be here yet. I see he finished the roof on his little church back there. What do you think?"

"Behold. Stand at that door," Henry said, smiling slightly and waving his hand. "Maybe we'll get breakfast."

Charlie knocked politely. After half a minute, he knocked with more force, and the door eased open. Caldwell was lying half off a bunk in the corner of what did indeed look like a mule shed. On the table in the middle of the room stood a whisky bottle, not quite empty. Charlie was angry, and it surprised Henry, as he hadn't seen this side of him.

"Hey! Caldwell! Get up!" Charlie said, stepping toward the bunk, "You drunk? I reckon the devil knows more than just Captain Dick Jumper."

Caldwell sat up, pointed a pistol at Charlie, and said, "What in God's word told you you could walk in my house?"

"Whoa! Whoa! Reverend, don't shoot him; the door was open," Henry said, "Charlie, didn't you say you needed to talk to the man at the hotel? Why don't you do that, and I'll talk to the Reverend?"

"And who in God's world told you I wouldn't shoot you?" Caldwell said, turning the gun on Henry, "Who said I needed to hear you?"

"God said, just now," Henry said, "When he saw you about to kill due to a hangover. He sent me here; I heard him clear as day. You didn't?"

Charlie backed out the door as Caldwell lowered his pistol. He was comfortable leaving this conversation with two armed men of God. He mounted Thirsty and kicked him into a quick canter toward the hotel.

The sun was up and burning by now, and Charlie was hoping the hotel manager was, too. He was sure the manager could handle five hundred dollars for beef. The question was, could he trade gold for it?

Charlie met with the manager, James Upton, who was very interested in the beef but could only pay with banknotes. Plant management had called in any gold to Tampa.

"Are you sending anything by train today?" Charlie asked, hoping the train would not have to leave town right away.

"Not really; we have a handful of guests, this being summer. But I haven't talked to Brosnan," Upton said, "Sometimes he gets news before I do. Please reconsider your terms for the beef, Mr. Herlong."

"Do you have a butcher, Mr. Upton? I may consider trading a side for his services as soon as this afternoon," Charlie said, "but I need the gold as much as you need the beef."

"I do, and we'll be ready. It would be best if you spoke to Mr. McAdow. He made his fortune in the gold fields of Montana, and he may trade with you," the manager said. He directed Charlie down Marion Avenue.

Charlie figured he needed to get his gold today if he wanted to leave for New York tomorrow. He nudged Thirsty and turned to the manager, "Which house is it?"

"It's the biggest one in town; you'll see it!" he said, pointing down the street.

❋ ❋ ❋ ❋ ❋ ❋ ❋ ❋ ❋ ❋ ❋ ❋ ❋

Tiger had quickly arranged for the cattle to be contained in the corral at the livery. The Hodges brothers offloaded the cattle while Hatch and Neha began unloading the freight.

"Mr. Tiger, Neha has been telling me about your dogs," Hatch said, taking the reins of Mico as Tiger dismounted. "He says they handle cattle as well as any cowboy in the state, that they could burn on a brand if they had someone to start the fire!"

"I ain't said nothing 'bout no fire, just wouldn't be surprised if they could read a brand," Neha cut in.

"Sometimes I wonder if I work for them," Tiger said, "They generally do what they please. As soon as they pushed the cattle toward the pen over there, they took off. They're good dogs; I just hope they don't cause trouble here in town."

"Trouble? Like cowboys come to town?" Hatch laughed, "Chugging whisky and shooting up the saloon? Fighting over sporting ladies?"

"Well, yeah, I suppose," Tiger said with a chuckle, "'cept for the drinking and gunplay. They do love the ladies. And cats."

"See, Mr. Hatch? I ain't ever seen dogs sidling up to cats," Neha said, "Mr. Tiger, they love cats?"

"They love to eat them, son," Tiger said, "I imagine they'll be over at that fish house raising Cain soon enough."

"What about this breech gun?" Hatch asked, "Any idea where we're supposed to set it up?"

"I imagine on that steamer down the dock," Tiger said. "And your guess is as good as mine till Charlie and Henry get back."

"We need to release that axle or find a wheelset around here somewhere," Hatch said.

"Mr. Tiger, can I talk to you for a minute?" Neha asked, and Hatch turned to step away, "You, too, Mr. Hatch, if you don't mind."

"Has Mr. Henry asked either of y'all to go to Cuba with him?" Neha said, "he's asked us a few times. Opal and Snapper told me, 'No way in Hell. Snapper can't swim, anyway.'"

"Are you going back to the village?" Tiger asked, "Your cousins probably are, to take care of their Mama and them. Is somebody back in the village depending on you?"

"My granny acts like I'm a bigger burden than I'm worth," Neha asked, "so, no, there ain't."

"I have a pretty good deal going on in Gainesville." Tiger said, "So, I'm heading back there. If you're looking to leave with him, it's alright with me."

"I'm not looking to quit; I just need to figure out what to do," Neha said. "Mr. Henry is the first person to offer me a job. Did he ask you, Mr. Hatch?"

"Yes, he did, but I told him I wouldn't go," Hatch said. "The Army would have given me a raise in pay, a third stripe, and a free ride down there. I've had enough shootin' and scootin' to last me. Going down there to rescue a bunch of folks I never met ain't for me. Besides, I can't swim either. How much is he paying?"

"Three dollars a day," Neha looked sideways at Tiger and said, "Don't get me wrong; I was okay with our deal. I wouldn't have seen anything like this in the village, or ridden on a train, or seen that boat as big as a house yonder. Shoot, I only saw salty water once."

"The question is, what do you want, Neha?" Tiger said, "What's good for us might not be good for you."

Hatch said, "I have a question. Why would you go?"

"Why? I don't know," Neha said, "I ain't never been to Cuba. Shoot, I ain't never been here, wherever here is. I know I ain't had three dollars at once, let alone twenty-one for a week's work. Mr. Henry says we can keep selling to the Army like they've been doing. He also said people's lives depend on it, Colored people, and Indians, like me. He called it seeing elephants."

"Sounds to me like you've already made up your mind," Hatch said, his demeanor seeming to darken. "Henry is doing it because he says God told him to. You should know that seeing elephants might just kill you." Hatch then turned and walked toward the long dock and stopped, his hands on his hips.

"Is he mad, Mr. Tiger?" Neha asked, "I'm just trying to figure out what to do."

"Not at you, son," Tiger said, "he might be doing the same thing, choosing which path to take."

"I'm not even sure what an elephant is," Neha said, "ain't it like a real big ox with a long nose? Do they have them in Cuba?"

"That I don't know, I haven't been to Cuba. We're not talking about real elephants, either. Hatch is talking about things you see in a war. The horrible part that no one wants to see, but you're forced to if you're in a war." Tiger paused for a minute, then added, "Henry may be talking about seeing things that you haven't ever seen before, the wondrous part of life. Like what you were just talking about. Maybe you've been seeing elephants all along on this trip."

"I think I'm more interested in seeing that three dollars a day," Neha said.

"If three dollars is worth the risk of dying, I guess that's as good a reason as any," Tiger said.

Neha turned and looked out toward the gulf. After a moment, he turned back to Tiger.

"Mr. Tiger, we've been moving cattle through the swamp to avoid cattle rustlers, and I did that for free. Shoot, I hear just being Indian and working cattle can get you killed around here," Neha said, "I ain't going to Cuba to die; I'm going to live."

CHAPTER 49

Charlie walked up to a grand white house with balustrades and gingerbread trim on the porch. The rocking chairs reminded Charlie of the Tampa Bay Hotel, motivating him with thoughts of Marjorie. An older man, sweating in a vest and tie, was struggling to use thin rope as bracing for a young tree to the right of the porch. Charlie noticed his coat hanging on the railing of the porch.

"Good morning! I'm hoping to find Mr. McAdow. Is this his place?" Charlie asked, pausing at the gate, "Has that tree been trying to run off?"

"I wish it would," the man said. "It's about to make me cuss on a Sunday morning. I'm McAdow; come on in."

He began reaching into his pockets, and Charlie assumed he was looking for a handkerchief. Charlie came through the gate, pulled out his yellow scarf, and handed it to him.

"I'm Charlie Herlong. Are you looking for something like this?" Charlie asked.

"Thank you, son; what can I do for you?" McAdow said.

"Well, sir, I'm trying to ship some freight out, and the shipper I have will only take gold," Charlie said. "I'd like to get it loaded today. I'd rather not wait for the bank to open tomorrow. I hope it won't be too audacious of me to ask if you might know where I could buy some."

"What kind of freight? Is it legal? If you're dealing with the Resolute down there, I'm not so sure I want to get involved," McAdow said, "Besides, I'm sure the bank has sent all their gold to Tampa, but you know all that, don't you?"

"Yes, sir, I do. I was in Plant City last night, and my partner is willing to pay the price they're getting in Tampa," Charlie said as he tied the braces for the sapling loosely, just tight enough. "My partner is taking food and medical supplies for the people in Cuba. I hope that will still be legal when the US takes over. My business with you concerns the gold. We also have beef to trade."

"Beef? We haven't had beef down here in a month. Have you tried the hotel?" McAdow asked.

Charlie was getting impatient, "He has no gold, sir, but is willing to pay $100 a head for beef. I have ten head of cattle and Silver Certificates from Washington. Do you have any gold?"

"How much gold do you need? I have some five-ounce bars; I've been holding onto them for sentimental reasons. I'll trade four bars for all the cattle," he said.

"Four bars? Twenty doubles." Charlie thought that was a lot of sentiment, and twenty ounces of gold was still $400 to Captain Hamner. "Well, some of those cows are like family to me, so I'm sentimental, too. How about eight head?"

"Four bars for eight cows and ... a $100 silver certificate. That's a little better than today's rate, but this gold is pure from my first mine back in Montana. So, it's worth a little more than US coinage." McAdow said.

"Lucky gold? I've heard of that," Charlie said, "I'll do it. Maybe it'll be lucky for me."

"It's all lucky if you can find it, Charlie," McAdow said, "When you spend it, it becomes lucky for someone else. Why are you doing this?"

"My partner is doing it for God, and I'm doing it for my partner, a good man," Charlie said, shaking McAdow's hand.

"Charlie, if that's true, you're doing it for God also," McAdow said and turned to walk inside. "Let's get this done. My wife is almost ready to go to church. Would you like to come with us?"

"I'd love to," Charlie lied, "but I need to load a boat. Maybe next time."

❋ ❋ ❋ ❋ ❋ ❋ ❋ ❋ ❋ ❋ ❋ ❋ ❋ ❋

Henry and Jud Caldwell walked the four blocks down Cochran Street to Bethel Baptist. Henry was leading Sam as they walked.

"Slow down, boy. I ain't looking to be lathered up when we get there," Caldwell said. "Besides, the service has already started."

"I was just thinking that's a good thing," Henry answered. "We can ease in the back during the sermon. Then, we can be there for the altar call. Y'all pass the baskets after the sermon?"

"We did when I was running the service; I don't know what they doing now. I always wanted to take collection after dosing them with some fire," Caldwell said, "Dang, why are you in such a hurry?"

"I'm not, but I'm not hungover, either. I am excited about going to church. It's been a few months. I like church, and I need to go."

"I don't see why you need me there, anyway."

"I don't. But I believe they need you there, and you do, too," Henry said. "God needs you there."

"He's sho got your ear," Caldwell said, stopping, "You can't shit a shitter, son, you need that boat loaded. Just like those Cubans the last time. They might toss us out."

"And they might not. I'm praying that he'll guide my words and their ears," Henry said. "Rev, I can hear that choir now. They're letting it loose! Let's go!"

Charlie returned to the hotel and traded the two remaining cows for $100 in banknotes, a dressed side of beef, and ten cases of pineapple. On his ride back to the dock, he felt relief in getting the payment needed for Henry's passage to Cuba.

Charlie tallied in his head the gold he now had: twenty Double Eagles from Jack, 20 ounces in bars from McAdow, and ten Spanish doubloons. He could cover the $1000 in gold if he used every ounce he had. He hadn't wanted to use the Spanish doubloons still resting in the secret compartment of his portmanteau. Charlie had never considered himself superstitious, but he could not deny his run of luck since his father had given him the ten Spanish coins. He remembered what McAdow said regarding all gold being lucky if one can find it. He resolved to buy more to keep when he got further north, where the price of gold had not spiked. Better safe than sorry, he thought.

He was glad Henry would still have gold to use when he got there, but US coins might be dangerous for him. He decided to trade the Spanish gold he had to Henry. If there were any luck to it, better Henry have it than Captain Jumping Dick Hamner.

Charlie returned to the dock and asked if anyone from the boat had come.

"One was watching Hatch," Tiger said, "he just left."

Hatch had loosely mounted the cannon on the lowboy axle. It was smaller and required a means of securing it.

"Henry?" Charlie asked.

"He's still trying to get help," Hatch said, "and we need a blacksmith, too. I can't do anything else without a way to secure it."

"Ok, take my horse and find him," Charlie said, "He's at Bethel Baptist Church. Tell him we have a side of beef and cash to close the deal. We have half a day."

The choir at Bethel Baptist was in full voice, and the congregation was in full spirit. The song leader called phrases to the response of "God Will Take Care of You." Henry knew this was a point where an altar call should be made.

Henry turned to Jud and said, "It's time to call it."

"For an Altar Call?" Jud asked, "Who's going to make it? They fired me."

"God is making it," Henry said, trotted to the altar and kneeled in prayer.

The pianist was startled but slowed to a quiet chord progression. A member came, then another.

"God is calling you," they sang, "God Will Take Care of You."

Reverend Caldwell appeared at the altar and kneeled, followed by others, some in tears, who put their arms around him. The choir transitioned into "Come, Let Us Go Back to God" and continued until Caldwell stood, surrounded by everyone in the room.

"Will you be our preacher, again?" a voice called, and others shouted yesses and amens.

Caldwell raised a hand and said, "That's not why I'm here, but we can discuss it as a church family if you would consider it. Right now, may I lead you in prayer again in this precious moment?"

"Father God, thank you so much for this church, its family in Christ, for our lives, and for Taking Care of Us, always, no matter how large our mistakes or how far we stray. Thank you for allowing your servant, Henry Whitfield, to take time from his holy mission for you and give us the chance to heal the wounds we have inflicted upon this, your holy house of worship. In Jesus' name, I humbly and gratefully pray, Amen."

The pianist started the refrain from "God Will Take Care of You," and Caldwell raised his hand again.

"I have a gift to repay the church," he said, "and those who helped load the boat on that unfortunate day last year."

He placed coins in the offering basket and handed dollars to some of the men gathered.

"Please allow me to introduce my guest, Henry Whitfield," he said, "in the middle of a journey to serve God."

"Reverend Jud is right," Henry paused, surprised to be speaking, "I'm on a mission for God. When I left Texas, my goal was to join the Army. I thought I was going to kill people, not save them. God let me know that feeding, dressing, and healing were acts of love, doing his will. That is what brought me here, to Reverend Judd and you. I'm trying to get to Cuba before the war starts."

"Liar! You just need hands to load that smuggler's boat at the dock! And he owes the church $17 from last time." a balding man with a white beard said, "Shame on you for using God's house of worship to filibuster a war. And shame on you, Caldwell! To use it to weasel your way back in!"

"You must be a deacon," Henry said, placing a $20 banknote in the basket, "called to protect the church. Are you Ananias? Which one? I urged him to come here, and God led him to the altar; you don't get to judge. He just told us if you want him back, he will discuss it as a family. Know this about me: I'm never ashamed to do God's will in his house or anywhere else. Feeding hungry people is not filibustering. You are right about one thing. I do need help, but I'm not here to ask your permission. I'm offering them a job."

He turned to the others, "If you help me today, I'll pay you a dollar to start and another when you finish. You can decide to keep both or offer one to your choice of church. I have rice, beans, and cornmeal to feed us all if someone will cook it."

Hatch had entered the sanctuary and said, "And beef to feed our friends! Mr. Henry, Mr. Charlie says we're all set to load, and we need a blacksmith!"

CHAPTER 50

Charlie rode Thirsty down the dock to the Resolute and tied off at the gang-plank.

"Move that animal to the other side of the dock; that's our front door!" Hamner's voice said, "You're wasting time; you should be loading."

"Making sure we have hands to do so, Captain," Charlie said, "Show me how we're doing it."

"When they load the coal, you'll see," Hamner said, "Do you have my gold? How is your man coming on my cannon?"

"I've got my end covered; where are we putting the freight?" Charlie said, "We'll do that and the cannon first."

"Don't forget the gold; we're not leaving without that," Hamner said.

"Or the coal," Charlie said, irritated, "the freight and Henry Whitfield. When we get loaded, you'll get paid."

"The Hotchkiss. Simon tells me it's in pieces," Hamner said, moving to the stern, "have you secured it to the axle?"

"We're looking for shackles," Charlie said to Simon.

"A gente têm." Simon said in Portuguese, "Capitão, a gente deve carregar aquilo primeiro. Podemos configurá-lo assim como queremos."

"There's some more help," Hamner pointed to the loop, "bring the cannon first so we can get it set up."

Henry arrived at the loop with a wagon and three men. Tiger directed them toward the freight cars. Charlie was whistling, coming down the ramp and running to Thirsty.

"What's he saying, Tiger?" Henry said, "In whistle talk."

"'Hey, look at me?'" Tiger said, "What do you think, Snapper?"

"It sounded like ... 'Neha is still fat.'"

Neha came back with, "Liar, he said you're almost as ugly as your girlfriend."

"We're almost rolling!" Charlie said, dismounting and handing the reins to Neha, "They want to get the cannon up there first. They have hardware; do we have a blacksmith?"

"Charlie, this is Solomon Roberts," Henry said.

"Everybody calls me Stony," he said, "Henry says y'all need hardware?"

"I keep hearing that, Stony," Charlie said, "what we need is to make that cannon solid and mount it on that boat."

"I might have to make something in my shop," he said, "it's up the street."

"Whatever Hatch or Simon needs," Charlie said, "they need to leave by sundown. Use the box from the lowboy to load the boat."

Reverend Caldwell brought more help. They set up an area to cook and another to clean, like dinner on the grounds. Caldwell approached Charlie and took off his hat.

"Charlie, I want to apologize for this morning," he said. "I believe now that God sent you to me, and I want to thank you."

"Rev, since I left Lake City, I've seen gun barrels a couple or three times a week," Charlie smiled and shook his hand, "I've learned not to take it personally. You should thank Henry. Your church is growing!"

"God is showing us the path. We'll figure out the Church later," he said, putting on his hat. "I'm at your service."

"Can you put that load of coal somewhere and look after it for Captain Hamner? He's coming back for it," Charlie said. "By the way, he says the Cubans told him y'all were square before. Take that as you wish."

"I'll take care of it for you," he said and returned to the cooking tents.

The #700 train backed down the track with Brosnan on the platform, waving Charlie over. Charlie jogged over, and Brosnan said, "How did you get this set up so fast?"

"Good luck," Charlie said, "But I can't leave, yet. I'm hoping they'll set sail by sunset. Are you going to be here?"

"Yes, but you don't have forever," Brosnan said, "Today, I have a load of pineapples going to Bartow. Mr. Plant has called us to Tampa by tomorrow to move passengers. The Army must be moving soon. Who's coming with us? What about livestock?"

"Horses and mules. At least three men," Charlie said, "to Plant City. Can you do that?"

"I'll be here tonight," Brosnan said, "You must be loaded and ready to go, or you may have to wait a few days. One more thing, Charlie. The $500?"

"Oh! OK," Charlie said, reaching for his wallet. " I need my bags!"

"Your bags are with the others, thanks," Brosnan said, putting the bills in his wallet, "I'll be back tonight, but be ready."

"Charlie, do you want me here or on the boat?" Henry said, "We're ready to load the first wagon; Tiger hitched the low boy to it."

"I need something in my bag," Charlie said, moving toward the flatcar, "where do you think you need to be? It's your freight."

"Up top, then, how's the captain?" Henry followed, "has he been paid?"

"No, not yet," Charlie said, "Freight first, the coal last."

"Do you need gold from me?" Henry asked.

"Yes, I want to trade this Spanish gold for your double eagles," Charlie said, reaching into his portmanteau. "I think it'd be better in Cuba."

"Your lucky gold?" Henry asked, handing him the coins.

"If it's lucky, better you have it than Captain Hammer Dick," Charlie said, "when you go to the boat, take your gear and stay on it till you get to Cuba. Have you found anyone to go with you?"

"So far, I'm the only one, but I have faith."

"Henry, you need help unloading," Charlie said. "Faith in God is one thing; faith in smugglers and armies is another. Once you're on that boat, God knows what can happen."

"And only He knows it." Henry said, "My faith in smugglers and armies is laced with hope and doubt, but my faith in God is not. And my faith in you is certain. Thank you for this, Charlie."

"Maybe God is telling you this isn't such a good idea," Charlie said.

"Look around, Charlie," Henry said with a sweep of his hand, "I'm seeing the opposite."

Neha approached and said, "Mr. Hatch said to ask y'all if someone is going with him. The cannon is ready."

"You are," Charlie said, "drive the wagon."

"I need to talk to Mr. Henry," Neha said, "for a minute."

"Do it walking; he's going with us," Charlie said halfway to Thirsty.

"Can you hear him, Charlie?" Henry asked.

"Yeah, the cannon is ready," Charlie said, bounding into a stirrup, "breaktime's over."

"If that job is still available, I think I'll take it," Neha said.

"I'm blessed to hear it," Henry said, sticking out his hand, "Three dollars a day. Now, let's get our freight loaded."

The freight loading settled into a steady pace, and by mid-afternoon, all three freight cars were empty. The smell of food and laughter eventually drew more church members and other residents of the east side. It had a festive atmosphere, and soon, people were singing and dancing.

Reverend Caldwell directed the unloading of the coal—half to the far end of the lot and the rest to the Resolute.

The installation of the Mountain Gun was not as easy; Simon wanted to secure it to the boat's decking and allow movement to aim it. Stony Roberts returned with steel salvaged from the construction of the hotel.

"I never throw anything away," Stony said. "The spikes came from the track that used to be right there, and the plates were for the boilers. They have been in those crates for ten years."

Caldwell came to the boat with food for the crew and men installing the cannon. Caldwell and Hamner discussed a plan to sell the coal and if a buyer would meet the price. Neha brought his bedroll and Henry's bag.

"Charlie, are we close?" Henry asked, "Tiger is asking about the train so he can load the stock."

"Rev, can you tell Tiger the train is due at sunset?" Charlie said, "I think we're very close."

"We still have business," Hamner said.

"I've got you covered," Charlie said, "$800 in US coin and 20 ounces of pure gold bars."

"Let's see it," Hamner said, "before that train gets here."

"You will," Charlie said, "before I leave on that train. Do you know how to shoot this gun?"

"Your man dry fired it; I'd like to hear it pop," Hamner said, "I'd hate to get out there, and it is an anchor."

"That joke's getting old," Charlie said, "Hatch? Can we fire off a live round?"

"Yes, sir, if you don't mind being the man that attacked Florida," Hatch said, "Y'all need to get out there in the harbor, at least."

"Y'all? As in 'Me all?'" Charlie said, repeating what Hatch had said in Plant City: "Y'all don't need me out there. I'll pay you when the gun's ready to test. If it doesn't work, come back in, and we'll fix it."

***

The night before, Milt Loy, using whisky and promises of cash and cattle, convinced five men to ride with him to Punta Gorda. By Sunday afternoon, three were making the ride: Oscar Altree, his cousin Phil, and a third man who refused to give his name. Milt named him Nunya. They crossed the Peace River at Nocatee and followed the railroad to Punta Gorda.

"Just remember, you're here to help me kill Charlie Yeller Neck Rag," Milt said, "We'll take the cattle when he's bled out."

"If he's yeller, why do we need five men to kill him?" Oscar asked.

"Because I have $20 for you to help," Milt said, "if you're scared, tell me now. With you or not, I'm going to kill him."

"He just showed you he's scared," Nunya said, "They're both more interested in getting paid than doing the job."

"You don't know me," Oscar said, "you son of a ..."

Nunya had a pistol cocked and pointed at Oscar before he finished the sentence. When Phil started to pull, Milt had his pistols out and pointed at them both.

"Hey, there'll be plenty of opportunities for y'all to kill each other tomorrow," Milt said. "Let's do the work first. It sure is nice to be around men for a change."

Bird was ahead of them, but not so far that he didn't hear what Milt said. He wished all of them had started shooting and kicked his horse into a canter.

❄❉❄❉❄❉❄❉❄❉❄❉❄❉❄

By late afternoon, the Resolute was loaded with freight and coal. The church members were packing up their cooking gear, distributing leftovers, and relaxing, waiting for sunset. Tiger set a picket line for the stock in the long shadow of the freight car where the bags and supplies were stowed. Three horses remained saddled to use when loading the stock. The Hotchkiss was installed.

"This screw on the bottom moves it up and down; that's mostly for distance; the higher you shoot it, the further it goes," Hatch said, "This slide opens to load a shell. If it doesn't slide closed, the shell ain't in there far enough. When you push the slide in, lock it with this handle here. Now, you can attach the lanyard. Check your aim. Pull the trigger. Detach the lanyard and put it in your pocket. Open the slide, the shell will eject, and it'll be too hot to touch. That's it." He removed the shell and put it in the box.

"Charlie, time to pay up," Hamner said, "we'll be at pressure in a few minutes."

"Oh, shoot," Charlie said, "Neha, go get my bag and bring it to me."

"Tell anybody leaving on this vessel to get on board or get left here," Hamner yelled, "Pull all the lines except the bow and stern and be prepared to pull the brow. Simon, go through the steps. Keep doing it till we fire a round."

Milt Loy followed the tracks past the hotel and to the dock.

"If that train ain't back yet, he's here," Milt said. "I wonder why all these folks are down here on a Sunday night?"

"I see cattle and a picket line of horses and mules," Oscar said, "and a bunch of niggers laying around in the shade. I bet there ain't no law around this late in the day."

"We're looking for Charlie Herlong; he wears a yeller neck rag," Milt said, "Bird, ask that Indian on the horse."

Neha had Charlie's portmanteau, Raymond's oilskin pack, and two Army-issue bags hanging on either side of Thirsty.

"That's Jackie's horse," Bird said, kicking his horse. "He's here!"

"Don't spook him! Tell him we want to buy cattle!" Milt yelled.

"What do you do if the slide won't close?" Hamner asked, "And why do you put the lanyard in your pocket?"

"You push the shell in," Hatch said, "for safety, attach the lanyard only when you're ready to fire."

"Put a live shell in it," Hamner said, "see how that fits."

"The rule is, only when ready to fire," Hatch said, "only when the commander says to load."

"Last time I checked," Hamner said, "I'm in command of my fucking vessel, load a live shell!"

"And put that rope on the trigger!" Hamner said, "Because I said so."

Hatch stepped back, mimicked wiping his hands and showing his palms, and handed the lanyard to Simon.

Charlie looked for Neha, wanting to be done with Hamner, Punta Gorda, and the State of Florida, for that matter. Neha was coming up the gangway, carrying four bags.

"Thanks, Neha," Charlie said, "Oh, you didn't have to bring the black one, and those two aren't mine."

"I brought everything I didn't recognize to make sure. Mr. Charlie, there's a guy down there who says Thirsty is his horse," Neha said. "He just rode in with some rough-looking white men."

"Charlie Herlong!" Bird called from the dock, "Milt wants to talk to you!"

Charlie reached into the pack and took out his rig. Hatch walked over and removed a sidearm rig from one of the two extra bags. Charlie pulled out a cotton bank sack and handed it to Hamner.

"Captain, you can count it if you want, but I've already done it a dozen times," Charlie said, then stepped to the gunwale, "Bird! Is Milt drunk again? Remember, last time, he was trying to kill his horse!"

Bird said nothing, holding Thirsty's reins.

"Neha here tells me that's your horse," Charlie said to Bird, "Is it Jackies? I just borrowed it that day when you and that little kid were running away from the train. I'd keep him away from Milt if he were mine."

"Yeah, well, I'm taking him back," Bird said, "Come on over by the train. Milt wants to buy cattle!"

"Tell him I'm getting out of the cattle business; too dangerous," Charlie said, stepping to the stern to see Milt and three cow hunters mounted and waiting. He didn't see Tiger or the Hodgeses.

"You know why we're here. You're a murderer and a horse thief," Bird said, "Milt hates to wait. You're not fixing to leave, are you?"

"No, but I'm taking the train later," Charlie said, looking at Hamner, "tell him I'm coming down just as soon as I finish this deal."

"Where's that shooter that aimed a rifle at me the other day?" Charlie said, "These rogues are more dangerous than I am."

"This has nothing to do with me. We're leaving. This harbor is hard to get out of in daylight, and it's about to be dark. If we get out there and this gun doesn't shoot, we'll be right back," Hamner said, "then you'll have us mad at you, too."

Hamner ordered his crew to pull lines. Charlie checked his pistol and placed a sixth shell in the chamber, "I reckon I got nothing to worry about, do I?"

Nunya and the Altrees were already stirring up trouble, walking their horses into the tents and throwing cow whips at people.

Henry was buckling his rig, getting ready for a fight, and Charlie stopped him.

"No, sir. We didn't put all this work in to stop now." Charlie said, "You heard the captain, you're leaving. Me and Hatch got this, they're murderous morons. And I have Tiger down there, too."

"Then, we need to get down there," Hatch said, "and walking up that dock with no cover ain't good. Those boys are rotten onions."

Charlie stepped to the stern to see Bird riding to Milt, still astride his horse in front of the fish company. When Phil Altree rode near the picket line, Moon and Shine pestered his horse, nipping at his fetlocks. Phil emptied his pistol and missed them six times as his horse kicked and bucked. Phil tried to reload, and Shine dragged him to the sand, ripping his clothes and flesh. Moon chased his horse out of the yard and returned to help.

Oscar rode toward Phil, firing his pistol. When he passed, Tiger threw his whip, which wrapped around Oscar's neck, snapping it and pulling him to the ground. Tiger dismounted to retrieve his whip, and Nunya rode up, aiming a carbine at Tiger.

"Motherfuckers!" Charlie said and turned toward the gangway. His foot caught the steel ring of the trigger lanyard, and Charlie fired the Hotchkiss Mountain Gun. The two-pound lead projectile hit Milt Loy in his chest, disintegrated him, and continued to the fish house, taking a corner from it.

"Acho que funciona!" Simon said, "Aquele vaqueiro desapareçeu. Capitao, devemos sair!"

"Sim, caramba, devemos ir!" Hamner yelled, running to the wheelhouse, "Esse idiota! He just attacked the United States!"

The crew hadn't waited for orders. The final lines had been untied, and the gangplank was clear of the dock. The deckhand who untied the lines climbed up the rope, dragging it in the water. The crew knew how serious this was. So did Charlie.

"Wait! Wait!" Hatch pleaded, "I'm not going with y'all. Stop! How deep is that water? Oh, my God ..."

"Snapper can't swim, either," Neha said.

Opal shot and killed Nunya just before the cannon shot. The Altree cousins were dead. Milt Loy's lower torso was still intact, and Bird was emptying the pockets of its bloody trousers. Everyone else stopped to watch the Resolute go west into Charlotte Harbor as the sun dropped into the Gulf of Mexico.

Henry was seated on a barrel of salt pork, and Charlie sat on another barrel next to him.

"Well, I reckon it was a dream," Charlie said. "It looks like my good luck finally ran out."

"Mine just got better," Henry said, watching the train get smaller and the shadows disappear.

Charlie thought of his mother. "Good luck is a gift from God; he can take it back whenever he feels like it. Just ask Job."